Lost in the City of @

Lost in the City of @

Michael Bell

Tama,

May this book take you on a wonderful adventure.

ISBN-13: 978-0-9896935-6-1

This publication is a work of fiction. Characters, locations,
incidents, and brands are either created by the author's
imagination or used fictitiously.

www.LostInTheCityOfAt.com

To the memory of Giselle Rubin

Contents

Foreword

My introduction to the author, Michael Bell, came from, of all places, Twitter. I knew him by a different name at first, his nom de plume, Brook Tesla. He reached out to me with compliments about my singing performances. Noting that he had written a novel, then titled "iPooKee," I offered to read and review it. Little did I know, this novel would change my life.

When I began to read "Lost in the City of @," I immediately connected with the main character. Much like Sammy, I had found myself trapped in a world of fear and uncertainty following trauma, and I was suffering from a crisis of lost hope. Looking for refuge, I turned to the comfort of literature, and I felt as if this book was speaking to me personally:

"If you've ever lived in a house of cards, a place where collapse felt imminent, where nothing was stable — you're not alone.

If your future seemed like it had more holes than Swiss cheese, if happiness seemed unattainable — you're not alone."

The truth is, I had been feeling hopeless and alone, trapped in a dire circumstance. And here, this book depicted chaos in such an imaginative and absurd fashion that it paralleled what I was experiencing; the nonsensical and disorienting delivery of events was, to me, a fitting choice to describe indescribable traumas in all their complexity. The book made me feel seen and understood in a way I didn't know existed, and it gave me a sense of clarity and renewed my sense of faith.

Touched by his story and in need of a friend, I began connecting on a deeper level with the author. I took a leap of faith and opened up about my own undeniably crazy story. I told him my truth, fully expecting him to reject my experiences as improbable and label me as a nutcase, or worse, a liar. But after having lost so much already, I didn't have much else to lose. Not only did he listen to my story and discover it to be true, but he also connected me with resources I desperately needed for rescue. For this, he is quite literally my hero. While he won't admit it by his own humility, I've since learned that he's played hero to many others—anonymously. I am forever grateful to him.

After reclaiming my freedom post-trauma, I wanted to meet Michael and thank him in person for all that he had done for me. I flew to New York City, my first time visiting this place of dreams, and I felt like I was celebrating my rebirth into a new life. Mickey and I have been close friends ever since. I am honored to be involved in the making of this second edition by offering my insights to branding, my talents to performing the audiobook, and my voice to this foreword. As you embark on the adventure of reading "Lost in the City of @," I will leave you with this: there are few powers greater than that of your own imagination. Harness this power to create, to love, and to heal. Never lose hope. You are not alone.

Isabella Tugman
Actor

Congrats!

CHAPTER ONE

TIME'S TICKING

Uncle Walter took a sip of tea from a shiny cup and said, "Sammy, life is short. Make the best of it... Time is ticking —"

"Watch it!" I cautioned. "The cup that you are drinking from is made of ice. When it melts, we might be ordered to leave the café at once. Who knows what the consequences might be..."

"Yes, yes, I understand the customary rules of time here," Uncle Walter assured me confidently

"Can time be stopped? And is it really possible to move time backward or forward?" I wondered aloud as I glanced nervously at the cups of tea and teaspoons gradually turning into puddles of water on the red tablecloth.

"Possible, but —"

"Would I then be able to travel back to the past and perhaps meet Rhubarb Pie again?"

"Presumably, but traveling to the past might make you totally invisible. Rhubarb Pie would be greatly disappointed to hear your voice without actually seeing you," he said with a grin.

"Maybe time can be bent forward, so I could meet Rhubarb Pie in the future. Will I be visible then?"

"The future holds nothing certain. I must set off now," Uncle Walter said hastily as he prepared to leave the café without answering all my questions.

"Wait," I pleaded, barely audible.

Although Uncle Walter could have avoided the calamitous meltdown of the tableware by bending time backward or

1

forward, he drank the last of his tea in one gulp and hurried off quietly into the evening twilight.

CHAPTER TWO

THE TECHNO-GEEK CAFÉ

Not long after graduating from Princeton with a degree in computer science, a lifelong dream came to fruition for Uncle Walter. He realized that his unusual powers were indeed unique. In addition to possessing a deep knowledge of science, he could *turn anything into everything*.

Uncle Walter's talent is easy to understand if you can only imagine turning a cup of tea into a lion's tooth. It is an easy idea to grasp if you can only imagine changing ice cream into a monkey's paw. His ability is even easier to comprehend if you can only imagine transforming lead into solid gold. All these feats were much like the common practices of the medieval alchemists.

Almost everyone I know, though, is capable of carrying out such simple wizardry — almost everyone.

No, no, Uncle Walter had never owned a magic wand or engaged in witchcraft. No, no, not even once did his mastery turn a seventeen-inch laptop into a shrieking night train. Nor had he ever changed an octopus into a sleeping beauty or a scarlet macaw. Not even once. That was neither his space nor style, he'd tell you brusquely.

Much beyond such dull magic were my uncle's talents. Instead, consider some of his out-of-the-ordinary capabilities when employed *flawlessly*:

1. Turning a sickening murderer into a saint, like Mother Theresa or Paramahansa Yogananda
2. Converting a skeptical hippopotamus into an admirer of Abraham Lincoln or John F. Kennedy

3. Changing an ugly-on-the-inside person into a striking beauty, like Queen Nefertiti or Aphrodite
4. Transforming an unemployed slacker into a human worker bee or a busy ant
5. Changing a liberal into a conservative or vice versa; similarly, a plutocrat into an aristocrat or the other way around

Cool? This came naturally to him during his *turning-anything-into-everything* period.

Throughout a different phase of his inspiring career, Uncle Walter could undo almost anything: in simple words, turn things into their opposites — unfortunately, with not much success at reversing the results.

Uncle Walter's undo ability included a wide range of un-activities. It is an easy idea to grasp if you can only imagine the array of opportunities to un-thing on Earth. For example, un-car: turning a car into something that is not a car. The same goes for un-tree, un-person, un-nose, un-mule.

But much beyond those simple undos were Uncle Walter's powers. Instead, he could reverse a long list of human concerns, helping people overcome natural disasters. He could even avert personal tragedies and hardships.

Consider this for example: Un-poverty, un-hurricane, un-disease, un-war, un-stupidity, un-ignorance, un-illiteracy, un-corruption, un-elect, un-spend, and more.

Cool? This came naturally to him during his *un-stuff* period.

A boring thing that nowadays almost everyone can do is to travel for ages through time. Almost everyone. Uncle Walter, during a different era in his long career, however, came up with a unique solution. He would simply bend time backward or forward instantly. If necessary, he was also able to bring time to *right now* — almost always successfully.

Everyone could understand the time-bending idea. It is indeed easy to grasp if you can only imagine that Uncle Walter's powerful knack could save you the preparations normally required to travel. You would need to neither pack your belongings nor carry anything. You wouldn't even have to leave a be-back-soon note on your door. Transiting by an imaginary vehicle, or being jerked about on the back of a camel, or riding on a moose would not be necessary, either.

Instead, your present time would be reverted in a flash, or, pushed forward *immediately*.

For example, the right now could become suddenly a few minutes earlier, or an hour later. In the same way, today could turn promptly into yesterday or tomorrow. It all depends on which direction time is moving.

How embarrassing it could be if, for instance, you accidentally smashed the most expensive plate in the kitchen into a million pieces.

To avoid the humiliation, you could weigh the results of the silly attempt to spin the plate on your index finger before it actually happened. YES, assess the outcome before the accident occurred.

Accomplishing this would be possible only if time were simply bent backward. And YES, you could even avoid disaster completely by reversing time repeatedly. In other words, bending time backward again and again until you got the dish whirling right — like a skilled acrobat.

Another way of tackling the issue would be to push time forward. Move it very far forward — even years or generations. This way everyone in your current family and even your descendants would have forgotten the dish-breaking incident... or they would have already passed away.

Cool? This came naturally to Uncle Walter during his *time-bending* period.

His enthusiasm for arts and science and relentless curiosity never ceased to produce wonderful inventions and innovations. His veritable rainbow of creative ideas always inspired me. Always.

He was a simple man with big dreams and a huge heart. Always projecting unwavering confidence, he was a solid member of the can-do camp.

"Little girls like you ought to know that everything is possible. Everything, sweetie: the difficult can be made easy, the vague apparent, and dreams fulfilled," I heard him say often. And he, my uncle, was right.

And now, the devastating news delivered by his doctor indicated that his final days were approaching. Uncle Walter's time was running out, melting slowly like an ice cube on a warm day.

A few more weeks left. A few more days remained to relish the warmth of the Sun. A few more minutes left to inhale the fresh mist at the break of day. A few more seconds dedicated to me...

Despite his illness, Uncle Walter's positive outlook continued to inspire all of us during the dusk of his life.

Yearning to unveil the plans and preparations for my upcoming journey, I met Uncle Water again at the Techno-Geek Café. Our meeting took place on New Year's Day 2001.

We huddled around the same table covered with the same red tablecloth where we had sat a few days earlier. On the same chairs, in the same nook, between the same two converging walls, I enjoyed his company once more.

Here again, time was running out, ticking rapidly away, from the moment we met. Not only was the ice tableware thawing again as moments went by swiftly, but also the table and chairs and even the walls surrounding us were dissolving steadily as our discussion warmed up.

"It's cold in here, Uncle. Everything is melting like a few days ago. Should we go somewhere else?"

"That's OK, Sammy. Isn't life just like that?" he said, giving a flat grin.

Imagine. Imagine sitting uncomfortably on a chair that is constantly defrosting. One that is shrinking as time progresses, collapsing gradually, posing danger as moments heap up.

Imagine drinking your favorite beverage from an icy mug that will no longer exist in a short while.

Imagine being surrounded by ice walls that threaten to tumble down on you in an instant. The unyielding liquefying course of almost everything around us left little time for a lengthy chat.

Instead of the usual, Uncle Walter ordered the Pudding Cupcake mixed with raspberries, peanuts, and jam. Craving a slice of an organic platter, I ordered the special Olive and Cheese Credit Card Pizza. I preferred the one perforated precisely into six tiny triangular slices. While munching on the delightful helpings, Uncle Walter ordered my favorite apple cider. For himself, he asked for a large bottle of orange juice with pulp.

"You should also try our National Deficit, Government Shutdown, or Great Depression pizza specials. This is a collection of wonderful choices. Try them," said the waiter, with a senseless wide grin on his face before ambling away.

Much to my dismay, our conversation revolved mainly around Uncle Walter's difficulty in taming his cat Witty. Clearly, it was an unimportant topic to waste our precious time on. And clearly, Witty was an unjustified name. This I realized after all my encounters with the animal had left me disappointed in its cleverness.

"Witty is stubborn like a mule," my uncle grumbled. "How can I make my cat more obedient? What do you think, sweet little girl?"

"Taming a cat is a hard task. Don't you know that cats usually have distinct attitudes?"

"I know. However, which of its nine lives should I start domesticating first?"

"What are you training it to do?"

"Reading, my young friend, reading books, scientific articles," he sighed deeply.

"R-reading? Your cat Witty will never be able to read. What a funny idea," I said as I burst out laughing.

"I assure you that a cat is capable of reading, writing, and preparing homework. It is definitely possible if you only train it! Believe me."

"What about writing poetry? Can you teach this to a cat?" I chuckled sarcastically.

"Absolutely achievable, Sammy. It depends on your determination. Not all cats, however, are fast learners. Some will not train easily. Others simply ignore you because studying languages is not what they would rather do in their free time. Instead, they'd hunt mice or kill squirrels. If your cat likes you, she might even drop a carcass in your bed. Put it just next to your pillow — a gesture of affection."

"So how would you communicate to a cat that reading is important not only to humans? How would you stress that it's vital also to its biological family Felidae?"

"The goal is neither teaching a cat reading nor enriching its intellect. NO, this is not what I have been investing so much of my time in."

"So what is the noble aim?" I asked, cocking my eyebrow.

"To be candid, I don't care at all about cats."

"You don't?" I panted.

"Well…, I do, but the idea here is different. The goal is to ease people's lives."

"And how would you accomplish that?"

"Think about it, Sammy. Humans could be indulging in nature and good food, while other species take over the responsibility of learning and education. Doesn't it make sense?" he asked earnestly, twirling his mustache and fondling his beard.

"And I was under the impression that you do care about animals. First, learning how to read or write is not what cats normally do. So why torment the poor animals? Second, I thought that education is what you believe dearly in. Are you suggesting that humans should stop studying, forsaking the old ways of acquiring knowledge?" I asked, with my lips curled up, rather dismayed.

"Yes, I do. Think about how many tasks one is responsible for during a lifetime. Things like education, making a good living, supporting a family, and raising kids are only a few. Did you know that an average person spends about a third of his lifetime at school?"

"That much?"

"Yes, it's a long time. Therefore, delegating the chore of studying to other species would ease the burden on humans. This could improve our standard of living. Don't you think so, Sammy?"

"So, if your cat could earn a degree in economics, for example, would the diploma be considered yours?" I wondered, refusing to accept his outlandish idea.

"W-well, y-you make a g-good p-point. I-I see how the cat community could be offended if their degrees were snatched away. Taken from them for the benefit of human s-society," he stammered, nibbling on his cupcake.

I nodded mutely, giving a weak smile of satisfaction.

"Since most people love cats," he went on, "maybe the other option would be to create a virtual cat."

"Virtual? What does *virtual* mean?"

"In other words, produce an artificial cat — not a real one."

"But Uncle, how can a living cat be unreal?"

"Well, the creature that I'm going to create would be just like a cat. It would smell like a cat. It would meow like a cat. It would purr like a cat. It would hunt like a cat. But it'd not be a real cat. This type of cat would acquire the knowledge we — humans — need to make a good living."

"Would the degree in economics be *real* if a *virtual* cat acquired it?" I challenged in nothing flat.

"Hmmm, y-yo-you a-are m-making another excellent p-p-point. While working on this project, I intend to hash out your concerns until the idea makes sense," he responded.

I grinned feebly, concealing my gratification with a new question. "So what kinds of things are you able to virtualize in your latest project?"

"Everything, Sammy," he said, hunching forward. "A bunch of things could be turned into unreal to the extent that it's hard to distinguish between real and imaginary. For example, these can be changed to unreal things: chair, car, airplane, today, yesterday, tomorrow, spring, fall, family, country, government, and even freedom and democracy."

"Everything?"

"Believe me, my young friend, everything can be virtualized —"

"So, how can you tell the difference between what's real and imaginary?" I pressed.

"You just hit the nail on the head. That is a big problem. That is a huge issue, I admit. The more I virtualize, the more my actual world becomes fictional, imaginative…"

"So, why is it a problem for you, Uncle?"

He gave a deep sigh and said, "My experiments come with a heavy price tag. I have been engaged in a wearing battle, wedged between reality and fantasy. I feel trapped in a deceptive world."

"Does it mean you can't tell the difference between real and unreal anymore?"

"Sometimes, Sammy. Sometimes," he said gloomily. "Think what a figment of the imagination almost anything we experience during the day can be. Are you and I real, or are we virtual? Are we truly sitting next to each other now? Is our table concrete? And the chairs? Is now really now, or is now actually yesterday or tomorrow? How can we be certain of anything these days?"

There was not much time to spare. The clatter of the shattering walls all around us made it urgent to focus on important matters. Halfheartedly but with rapt attention, I was drawn gradually, deeply into Uncle Walter's unstable world. Doubt dominated every aspect of his life…

On and on he described the shaky reality where he was imprisoned. Our world too — the place where we were spending our pleasant time together — was drifting slowly into pandemonium.

The liquefying ice table tilted noticeably. The tableware and the celestial foods slithered across the top of the table, drifted to the edge, and then slid down to the marble floor. It looked like the collapsing glaciers in the North Pole.

My heart had gone from zero to sixty miles per hour in less than a second, almost like those speeding vehicles in the Indianapolis 500.

"UNCLE WALTER!" I yelled piercingly, clenching the edge of the sloping table with my hands. "Everything is melting around here. Call them virtual or not, but we must leave now. We must take off before we get hurt. Remember the rules of time at the Techno-Geek Café? WE MUST LEAVE NOW!"

Disgruntled again over the lack of time to talk about my trip to find Rhubarb Pie, I collected my belongings and prepared to escape the hazardous scene.

"There is nothing to worry about — stay still. Do not go anywhere," Uncle Walter said calmly, leaning slightly forward. Then he scrunched up his eyes and suddenly rolled time backward, avoiding the meltdown.

Seconds later, after the lopsided table had leveled out, he announced with great contentment, "I was able to move time back about one hour. Therefore, Sammy, we can restart or, if your heart desires, resume our pleasant conversation. We can even enjoy our meals all over again."

My mouth dropped open when new slices of pizza replenished my organic circular platter, and the apple cider cup refilled to its top.

On the other side of the table, my beaming uncle was watching his cupcake being restored bite by bite to its original size. Even his bottle of juice filled to the brim again.

"Well done, Uncle Walter. I must take some time-bending lessons from you before I embark on the quest to find Rhubarb Pie. Will I be able to master the skill? Can it be taught?"

"You sure will, after all, you're not like my cat Witty," he said paternally. "But please recall: My time-curving invention has not been approved by the Time Warping and Space Reeling Administration. The government is typically slow, you know. It is merely a study, a risky business, a matter of balance between life and death. We must exercise it with utmost care."

I nodded inaudibly, determined to carry on. In spite of my growing fear over the imperfection of his invention, I was keen to learn. Regardless of the potential for grave consequences, it was worth taking a chance.

SCRUNCHING AND PUFFING

It felt like ages and ages since Uncle Walter and I had met in the Techno-Geek Café. We were still there, though. The ice walls continued to melt away. The table, too, was thawing slowly. The defrosting chairs were sloping dangerously. My body prickled with fear and anxiety as the loud crackling intensified.

Regardless of the danger, our conversation continued. We were chatting about Uncle Walter's time-bending capabilities and the powers he possessed to change the world. He also promised to teach me the art of time curving — a skill I had always been interested in.

With great anticipation, the practicing finally began.

After devouring the last of the cupcake, Uncle Water took a deep breath. He rolled up his sleeves and sank quietly into his chair. Then suddenly, he hunched forward, peered deeply into my eyes, and murmured solemnly, "Sammy, the time has come. Before we start, though, you must promise me something."

I nodded assent.

"Never ever share what I'm about to teach you with anyone — anyone, on the face of Earth. Understood?"

I bobbed my head again.

"Now. Follow me. Do whatever I ask. Avoid unnecessary questions."

I agreed.

"Close your eyes," he continued. "Focus, breathe deeply, and listen to the sound of your heartbeat. Attend to the sound of your inner soul. Pay attention to the sounds of your existence.

Wooziness, shortness of breath, or any abnormal feelings must be reported at once. Understood?"

Although a million questions about his weird instructions crossed my mind, I did what I was told. I followed, eager to witness his time-warping power. I followed, regardless of the little time left. I followed, irrespective of recurring worries about the melting walls, the table, the chairs...

My eyes were shut tight; the focus shifted inward, into what I perceived as the inner me, my soul.

At first, pangs of fear crept in when I didn't sense any heartbeats. *Maybe I do not have those,* I wondered.

Moments later, the crisp sound of my quivering heart thumps intensified, easing my anxiety. Indeed, an awakening inner-body experience it was.

To my surprise, Uncle Walter then rested his orange juice bottle on the crest of his head and said monotonously, "Now, Sammy. Slowly place the glass of apple cider on the top of your head."

I followed suit. No questions asked.

"Then chant softly, 'I'm back. I'm back. I'm back.'"

"I'm back. I'm back. I'm back."

"Next, repeat this: 'In the quest of paying homage to Mother Nature, I hereby drink from this very glass of organic sparkling apple juice.'"

I obeyed.

"Very nice! And now, bring the glass down to your mouth, and take three long sips," he commanded. "When you're done, return it to its original position, on your head. Then cover your eyes with your palms and chant three times, 'I love myself because I'm the greatest.'"

The cider is not too bad after all, I confessed to myself.

As I laid the glass on my head again and covered my eyes, I echoed, "I love myself because I'm the greatest. I love myself because I'm the greatest. I love myself because I'm the greatest."

The warm compliments I was instructed to extend to myself so far perhaps took a toll on the already fragile icy walls. They were about to disintegrate at any moment, as the cracks grew to a very threatening degree.

Indifferent to the crumbling sounds, Uncle Walter focused on the lesson at hand. He squinted and went on, "With the tips of your fingers, tap gently three times on your forehead. After each, say, 'I'm the smartest.'"

"I'm the smartest person in the world —" I recited partially.

"N-NO, NO, NO! You must follow exactly! No time to waste. Mistakes like this may result in an irreversible misfortune!" he reprimanded.

"I'm the smartest, I'm the smartest, I'm the smartest," I smirked.

"Now. Erase the silly smirk from your face. Hold your pinky against the tip of your nose and whisper three times, 'I can smell trouble from a far distance.'"

I complied.

"Then apply pressure on the upper lip with your ring finger and declare, 'With my unnatural extraordinary power, I can persuade anyone to do anything I want.'

"Then, without delay, with the middle finger touching your chin, 'I'm stubborn like a mule and I like it.'

"Finally, state softly three times with both index fingers on your cheeks, 'I'm gorgeous like sin.'"

Although I lacked confidence in today's leaders in almost any walk of life, I trusted my uncle. He was my cherished idol, and nothing he had ever done raised a doubt about his integrity. Nevertheless, I grew increasingly skeptical.

SCRUNCHING AND PUFFING

Though I followed carefully his odd instructions, the questions kept coming: *Is he ridiculing me? Could time be bent by pursuing such an absurd ritual? What point is he trying to make?*

But I wasn't disappointed.

No too long after, perhaps a few seconds later, the time moved back. Like a video clip running on your computer from the beginning, everything looked awfully familiar.

I reentered the Techno-Geek Café. This time, too, Uncle Walter was sitting at our usual table. He was stroking his beard, lips curled down, reading his favorite science column in the *New York Times*. "Hmmmm," he murmured. "Astounding. These guys were able to halt time in their university lab. Remarkable. Halt time, hmmmm, halt time."

I greeted him, shaking his cold hand, just as it had happened an hour before, "Happy New Year to you, Uncle Walter."

"Same to you... How have you been?"

The wonderful spicy aromas wafting across the tiny restaurant stirred up my taste buds. I was hankering for mozzarella cheese, sun-dried tomatoes, and fried onion rings. "Thanks for asking. I'm doing swell. What are we ordering today?"

"Take a look at the pizza of the day on the menu. I think that you're going to like it. Totally organic. Certified!"

"The National Deficit Pizza looks wonderful. YUMMY! YUMMY! And for you, Uncle?"

He said, half drooling, "Oh, I always order my cupcake. Without a cupcake every day, I'm nothing. I'm just nothing..."

"Are you allowed to indulge in fat-saturated foods?" I asked in jest.

"At my age, Sammy, you are permitted to eat anything you want. Wolfing down your favorite foods against your doctor's recommendations is a common thing among seniors. One cupcake a day will not kill you. It adds some joy to my hectic day."

The familiar events that had occurred more than an hour earlier reappeared in precise sequence. Again and again upon my reentrance to the Techno-Geek café, our eyes met. Then I shook Uncle Walter's cold hand when I found him sitting and reading the newspaper. Then he ordered a cupcake and pizza. Then the waiter gave a Cheshire cat grin, and so on, and so on.

The chain of past occurrences also included the reciting of the eccentric drivel: "I love myself because I'm the greatest. I'm the smartest. I'm gorgeous…"

Not only once but countless times, the scenes played back as though I were watching a much-loved video. I could have sworn they repeated forever. Over and over again, I reentered the café and shook his cold hand. Each time, though, Uncle Walter held a different newspaper. First, the *New York Times*. Then, the *Wall Street Journal*. Subsequently, and in no particular order, the *East Hampton Star*, the *Shawangunk Journal*, the *Gotham Gazette*, and the *Village Voice*.

Heaven knows how many times Uncle Walter had managed to bend time backward. Unlike a video clip running on your computer, each repeating event at the Techno-Geek Café was a bit different from the time before. Not only did Uncle Walter hold different newspapers, but also his facial expressions changed in each scene: In some, he frowned. In others, he appeared more cheerful, even grinning. In fewer instances, his eyes strayed, and he refused to shake my hand.

"Did you experience the power of backward time warping?" he asked smugly when I opened my eyes wide.

Feeling woozy, I nodded mutely. Then I gave a sigh of relief when I realized that time had curved to its present state.

"Mastering the art of time bending requires practice, Sammy. It demands constant exercise, concentration, self-awareness. You cannot just bend time without understanding the essence of life and death. Bending time entails superior control of the inner you, of your soul, of your body and mind."

"Gobbledygook," I said hastily, "and very unclear. I'm afraid I will never be able to exercise the art of time curving. Who in the world is able to control the inner self? Peculiar, don't you think so, Uncle?"

"Indeed, it sounds strange to people who do not comprehend the artistry of time bending. I agree. Use your imagination, though. Think about the real meaning of moving time backward. What did you feel when time was rolling backward?"

"Twisting time back made me dizzy. I was dazed like a drunken grizzly bear in Alaska."

"What else?"

"Going back scares me, worries me, Uncle. It is like a movie I have seen, only in different colors — familiar, but frightening."

"What's so frightening? Wasn't it fun?"

"What would happen if something goes wrong? What if the past changes? Will my present time ever be the same? Will I have a different future?"

"Naw, there is nothing to worry about. My invention usually takes you back to the same exact present. Confidence, my friend, confidence! Earn confidence by practicing," he prodded me.

"Are there times when you don't return to the same present time?"

"Well, Sammy, accidents always happen. Are you afraid? Should we stop now? We can meet sometime else if you're worried."

"No, please let's continue. I'm so ready, eager to learn, keen to absorb every bit of it. I shall be honing my time-curving skills every single day. Buffing up on this valuable craft will undoubtedly help me during the journey to find Rhubarb Pie… I can't even wait until you show me how to bend time forward."

"Craaaaak, creeeek, pinnnnnnnnnng, chhhchhhchhhchhhh…" The meltdown continued. Debris of soft ice falling to the floor… The already liquefied tableware dripping like rain. The walls dissolving rapidly. The chairs sinking slowly. Our feet submerged in a huge pool of water.

Waterlogged and dripping from head to toe, my uncle pressed ahead, but not before taking a large swig from his orange juice bottle. "Do not hurry. Do you have any questions before we move on to the forward time-bending exercise?"

I was drenched too, mopping drops of water from my cheeks. "I still do not understand how time moves backward, Uncle."

"Remember: the key to success is to focus, focus, and focus. The 'ritual' that you were so skeptical about was not about placing drinks on your scalp. No, that was not the intention. Instead, the chanting helps you relax and concentrate. Only with the power of your *thoughts* will the time be bending."

"Really? Only with the power of my thoughts?" I wondered audibly. "But how could my thoughts roll back time?"

"You'll have to reach an absolute state of tranquility. You'll have to find the inner you. You'll have to purify your heart and soul. You'll have to clear your mind, Sammy. Use this skill neither carelessly nor hastily. Demonstrate no intention to harm anyone, unless your life is in jeopardy."

Still not convinced, still confused, I nodded mutely.

"Do you know what the professional term for *backward time bending* is?"

I shook my head.

SCRUNCHING AND PUFFING

"Backward time curving is called *scrunching*. When you hear me saying, 'I scrunched the poor rooster,' I mean simply that its current time rolled back."

"So, how could I curve time back many years or decades?"

"You say, 'Scrunch a bunch,' Sammy."

"Ha-ha-ha, it's so funny!" I burst out laughing. "This is really funny, Uncle. Let me try it now —"

"NO, NO, NO," he yelped, his eyes wide. "I warned you: Use it with utmost care. This is not a joke —"

Despite his cautionary advice, I roared with excitement, giving him a teasing smile: "SCRUNCH TEN SECONDS!"

The time suddenly curved back precisely ten seconds.

But Uncle Walter's time-curving invention seemed to fail. His last statement echoed repeatedly out of his mouth. Time warped back and forth, back and forth, uncontrolled:

NO, NO, NO, I warned you: Use it with utmost care. This is not a joke, he said again.

NO, NO, NO, I warned you: Use it with utmost care. This is not a joke, he said once more.

NO, NO, NO, I warned you: Use it with utmost care. This is not a joke, his statement echoed over again.

His face went pallid, lips dry and quivering. Regardless of his attempts to correct the flaw in his time-bending invention, the last ten seconds played back time after time. Like a broken record, the statement rang out of his mouth over and over.

But Uncle Walter neither panicked nor lost his temper. To some degree, though, he seemed agitated.

CHAPTER THREE

At last, he bent forward and suddenly hissed three times, "Un-scrunch ten seconds, un-scrunch ten seconds, un-scrunch ten seconds."

The time curving finally stopped.

"What have you done? I can't believe it, Sammy," said Uncle Water dryly, shaking his head and clicking his tongue. "I'm teaching you a dangerous time-bending skill. Please, attend to my instructions. Do not bend time back in a careless manner. Understood, my young friend?"

I nodded, my face crimson. I made a gesture of apology and said shyly, "I'm sorry, Uncle, my bad. I was too thrilled, a bit silly —"

He made a sign of forgiveness.

"And now forward, Uncle, forward time rolling, please. Time is ticking, and this place is slowly crumbling," I pleaded, hastening to flee the melting scene that offered no hope, only looming danger.

"I agree, before everything collapses on us, let's do the forward time bending now," he murmured, his eyes narrowing and straying up toward the ceiling.

Silence...

Moments later, I was suddenly thrust like a space rocket through the café's brick wall toward the open air. I found myself in a different universe.

I was relishing the tranquility of meandering along the shore. Drawing in the brisk evening air, I was staring at the blue horizon where the ocean met the crisp red sky. *What a strange world*, I whispered. *Not even a soul around... Where is everyone? Is this an empty world? Is this how the future is going to be?*

A gray Savannah cat with a silver satellite dish clipped to its back strolled elegantly by. At times, it was lurking stealthily behind the ocean spray bushes, eyeing the wailing seagulls. And the hand — the deeply wrinkled hand that gripped the cat's leash — was covered with myriad signs of aging: white blemishes, dark blotches, brown spots, freckles…

Is it my hand? Am I that old? I panted. *How far am I into the future? 100 years? 200? maybe thousands?*

The shocking glimpse at the future and at my aging skin concluded abruptly.

I faced Uncle Walter again in the Techno-Geek Café as his eyes opened slowly. "You see, Sammy, according to the professional literature that I so highly value, *puff-up* describes forward time curving and *un-puff* means to undo it."

I nodded.

And meticulously, as expected, Uncle Walter did not fail to indicate that *puff-up 365 days* specifies the exact movement of time one year into the future.

"Can anything go wrong?" I queried restlessly.

While dusting off the fallen ice debris accumulating on his shoulders, he warned sternly, "As you already know, Sammy, accidents may always occur. This is the nature of time bending. You just never know. Use it with care, and be patient. When you scrunch or puff, wait a few seconds. Let the process take off… You will have great difficulty tracing the extent to which time has curved backward or forward if you issue multiple scrunching or puffing directions in short succession. This may result in an unfixable catastrophe."

"What if something goes wrong? What if I scrunched or puffed someone's time and I can't un-scrunch or un-puff?"

"Too bad. The individual will be trapped in the past or the future forever. Even I will not be able to help. No help lines, no emergency assistance, no 911, no help buttons, no undo keys, nada! You will have to bear the consequences — alone.

"Has anything ever gone wrong for you, Uncle?"

"Oh, yeah, plenty," he said with embarrassment. "If you're in the business of time warping, you hope to learn from your mistakes. But sometimes blunders can be beyond repair."

"How awful, beyond repair?"

"To give you an example, last year I *scrunched a bunch* my neighbor's dog, Bao-Bao. I bent his time backward after he had been yelping under my bedroom window for months and months — literally, driving me over the edge. I scrunched his time back roughly to the fourteenth century — to the Renaissance. So far back that I hoped never to hear from him again."

"It sounds like you were very upset with Bao-Bao. Were you?"

"Indeed, I was furious. But things got more interesting. A few days later, when I visited the National Gallery in London, I came across the *Arnolfini Portrait*, painted by Jan van Eyck in 1434. While staring at it for a number of minutes, I would have bet my life I heard a pooch crying. Then, seemingly, he was coming out right at me from the bottom of the canvas, a Brussels griffon breed like my neighbor's doggy. It must have been Bao-Bao, standing between Giovanni Arnolfini and his wife, Giovanna Cenami, sobbing bitterly. He was pleading for freedom."

"Didn't you feel sorry for the little doggy?"

"Yes, I was filled immediately with pity — an immense compassion that I had never felt before. And here we are, a few months later, and Bao-Bao is still stuck in the picture, still miserable, still stranded in Renaissance days. Believe me, I have tried myriad times to bring him back. I un-scrunched and un-scrunched countless times, but Bao-Bao is still trapped in the Flemish city of Bruges."

"How sad, Uncle."

"Yes, the poor pooch, who knows what kind of dog food they feed him there. Renaissance food? Maybe ice-cold sage chicken? Renaissance gingerbread? Renaissance grain?"

SCRUNCHING AND PUFFING

"Craaaaak, craak, creek, creeeek, pinnngpingpinnnnnnnng, chhhchhhchhhchhhh, ffffffffffchchchchchh…" The thundering sounds of the snapping walls of ice rose to new levels. And moments later, unnerving silence fell on the dissolving Techno-Geek Café…

If you've ever stayed in a place made of ice, where the constant popping and cracking sounds sent shivers up your spine, where the wobbly reality was hard to endure — you're not alone.

If you've ever lived in a house of cards, a place where collapse felt imminent, where nothing was stable — you're not alone.

If your future seemed like it had more holes than Swiss cheese, if happiness seemed unattainable — you're not alone.

If empty promises seemed like plain bread without raisins and nuts — you're not alone.

Time had slipped by, and Columbus Day beckoned. What else had we done there for so long? What else had we discussed there? Where had the hours, minutes, and days gone?

Had time drifted to a halt, or curved interminably backward and forward, leaving no memories to dwell on? Had I been in several places at the same time?

Feelings of uneasiness burst forth. Perhaps something had gone amiss, very wrong, at the Techno-Geek Café…

And at that critical moment, when I most needed comfort, Uncle Walter vanished. He morphed into a thin gray puff — appearing as a beam of glittering zeros and ones like a sequence of computer code — hovering and swirling above the skyline. Probably a vital piece of information had failed to meet my ears…

CHAPTER FOUR

EYE, EAR, AND LIPS

You could not find a more beautiful woman on Wall Street than Julia Linden. She was tall and slim. Her shiny blonde hair, crystal blue eyes, luscious red lips, pink ears, and long neck made her look special — very special.

Her tidy and classy appearance attracted almost every intelligent man in a radius of a couple of miles. The range probably stretched northward to Chelsea and southward to Liberty Island and Governors Island.

Julia had been loyal to all her former managers during her years in the financial district of Manhattan. Her current boss, Larry Quack, valued her talent and had no reason to mistrust her judgment and her independent point of view.

In fact, Julia knew Larry better than he knew himself. If he had been blind, her eyes could have been trusted instead; if mute, her mouth; if deaf, her ears.

Like any devoted assistant, Julia took over almost all of Larry's basic functions. As a result, Larry grew — over time — into a big, helpless baby who could not do anything for himself. This relationship was not always good for the business. Often, it was not even clear who was actually running the company: Larry or Julia, his powerful assistant.

Larry had never married. Perhaps because he wouldn't trust an inch of almost any woman he dated. For some reason, it never worked out. One rumor has it that no one he dated admired his achievements. Another, utterly radical, opinion compared him to an inept narrow-minded Dabbling Duck: egocentric and incapable of sharing anything with anyone.

In spite of his disastrous romantic life, his professional career flourished. He headed a major investment firm in New York that bore the name Soul, Mind, and Money Corporation. His company had done well for its legion of devoted clients. He had built the firm from the ground up — not without admirers, and, unsurprisingly, sworn enemies.

You ought to know a couple more things about Larry before judging his character. All in all, some believed, he was a decent man. Others, though, could not stand him. Not only did they hate him for his difficult character. Not only did they despise him for turning any conversation into a brawl. They loathed him mostly for his unbending three rules:

1. He was always right. No one could disagree with any of his positions on any topic — EVER.
2. All talks with him, needless to say, on any issue had to be secret no matter where they took place. Whether in his office or in a café, a taxi, an airplane, a park, a theater, or anywhere else — all had to be classified TOP SECRET. P-E-R-I-O-D.
3. Woe be unto anyone who was against him, betrayed him, conspired with the enemy, plotted to destroy him, or deserted him.

If you ever broke any of those rules or compromised any of those three codes of behavior, your name would be engraved on his purple list. NOT BLACK — P-U-R-P-L-E!

In other words, he'd chase you, he'd hunt you down, he'd never let go until you'd paid a hefty price.

At the Cheap Meal Café on Church Street, where he had invited Julia to lunch, the time had come at last. Larry was about to share something with someone, ready to bare one of his greatest secrets. Indeed, the time had come to prove he was not the horrible person everyone believed he was.

Business issues, never private matters, were the topics discussed during these outside-the-office meals. Should the opportunity arise, though, he hoped to reveal a different Larry. He wanted to expose his softer side. He intended to show his kindhearted self — a view that no one else had ever seen.

"So, how are our company's earnings this year?" he asked.

"Our firm is making more money, Larry. Up, up, up!" Julia imparted proudly, scouting out vegetarian selections on the wooden lunch menu.

"Wow! Astonishing, isn't it?"

"Yes, indeed. It is a very promising performance. But there is also a problem," she foretold.

"What's that?"

"The earnings report also indicates that our company's spending went up as well. Actually, we have been spending TWICE as much compared with last year!"

"Oh, we need not fret over excessive spending. Every company on Wall Street spends as much as ours — or even more. Besides, what's so bad about spending, Julia? Spending money is fun. Isn't it?" Larry said mockingly, leaning toward her.

"FUN? This is a big WASTE! Inspect the report carefully, Larry. We toss away too much money on luxury celebrations, indulging clients, and pampering ourselves in the Bahamas. Too many parties, too many wild parties, Mr. Quack!"

"I-if w-worse c-comes to w-worse, w-w-we can always lay off employees to fix the spending problem," he muttered weakly and gulped.

"What kind of cruelty is this? Do you intend to fire people because we cannot control our NEEDLESS spending? Is this what you're planning?" she said furiously and beckoned the waiter, who was waiting impatiently for their orders.

"Th-this is what all companies typically do! Please don't get involved with my management decisions!" he roared. "You always criticize me. In your eyes, I am always doing the wrong thing. Please don't worry about our company's money. We are doing fine. Just fine!"

"Oh, all of a sudden you don't need my advice. So maybe you should start looking for someone new. I'll be taking a long vacation. I can't take this nonsense anymore!" retorted Julia, red faced.

White faced, clasping the earnings report with his trembling hands, he said, "Relax, Julia! I did not intend to offend you. I need you. I really need you. Maybe we do spend too much. But please take a look at the positive side. Along with these expenses, which we may need to watch during the months to come, we are also investing in our crucial business operations."

"And what are these 'crucial' investments?"

"Our investment in building software applications outstrips our competitors. This year alone, we hired twenty software developers and three software architects."

"Software developers, I understand — they construct applications. But what do software architects do? Is a software architect like a building architect? Do they do the same thing?"

"Software architects typically do nothing; they work from nine to five and get healthy paychecks," he chortled jokily. Then he ordered the Fish and Chips platter and a bottle of sparkling soda.

She gave him a nasty grin. Then she ordered the Fish and Mango dish along with the Super Strength Energy Bar. The energy bar she craved was made with organic soy protein, high-energy herbal extracts, and a bit of honey. She also ordered her favorite energy drink named Blue Monster. "So why are we spending money on NOTHING?" she inquired edgily.

"I'm really not sure. Don't blame me. I trust Mr. Kevin Edison's advice. As you know, he's our company's software applications manager. He's the expert. He knows what he's doing. If he hires software architects, then he knows why he hires them."

"But you're the one who pays the bills, Larry."

"Yes, I'm the one, but I must trust Kevin for his expertise in the computer field. What do I know? I'm just the boss," he giggled.

"I'm not an expert, either. However, I need to know where the money goes. We spend it like water. If we continue like this, we will go out of business. Do you understand, sir?"

"I do, Julia. I appreciate your concerns. The '90s were good to our business, though. Times were good; the economy was booming. I hope the future will be no different."

Larry wanted to chat about something other than business matters. In fact, he had not planned to discuss his company's earnings. No, this was not on his mind.

The decisive moment had come. Nothing was more important to him that day than to divulge one of his cherished secrets. One he had never dared share. One he carried in a tightly secured silver briefcase. There, deep inside, he kept examples of what he was all about, his existence. Safe in the case was the essence of his life, his nature, a clue to who Larry really was…

Brushing meticulously his side of the table, he snapped open the silver briefcase. Then his shivering hands removed with utmost care three tiny containers and placed them one by one near him on the white tablecloth. They were antique boxes, in three different sizes and colors. The largest was red, the next in size was blue, and the last, pink.

"Are you ready? Ready to see one of the Seven Wonders of the World?" he muttered under his breath, leaning a tad forward.

"Yes, I'm all ears and eyes," she said, acutely vigilant.

With a nauseating grin, he unlatched the blue container. Then he slowly lifted off the squeaky lid. There inside, lying on top of a white cotton pad was a human blue eye. The eye was winking rapidly as if to gently say, *Nice to meet you, Julia. I've heard a lot about you, and now, I'm glad that we finally meet. What a pleasure!*

Julia suddenly felt a strong flutter in her heart as she drew away from the table quickly, almost fainting. Gasping, she clapped her hand to her mouth and stammered at full volume, "W-WHERE D-DID Y-YOU G-GET THIS EYE F-F-FROM?"

Dropping his gaze down at the blue eye in the box, Larry said smugly, "I grew it in my own laboratory, at home. Isn't it amazing? Eh? Isn't it fascinating, eh?"

The blue eye was flickering constantly, perhaps pitying Julia's horror.

"HOW GROSS! A live eye in a box?" said Julia, sickened. "IS IT REAL?" and gave Larry a look of great disgust.

"ABSOLUTELY REAL! And it is still growing and growing and growing…"

"G-GROWING? I-is this what you do in your s-spare t-time?" she hissed, still trembling.

"It is not my full-time occupation. As you know, I also run a company —"

"HOW did you CREATE this EYE, Larry?"

He bent toward her again and explained in a composed manner, "What you see in the box is the result of one of my experiments. I have been conducting these tests in my lab for months. It is all about growing human organs — an advanced chapter in today's medicine. To create this eye, I extracted a few human cells from one of our employees and used them to regenerate the blue eye you see in the container."

The blue eye was flickering faster and faster, bouncing up and down repeatedly. The lively fluttering eye gave the impression that it agreed with almost everything Larry said.

"You took cells from one of our employees? Who in the world would allow such a thing? ARE YOU OUT OF YOUR MIND, LARRY?" she thundered.

"Is it illegal?"

"It's sickening," she said. "Playing God, Larry?"

"I'm not playing God, but it's a mystery to me, Julia. A great mystery that I haven't been able to uncover. I'm trying to understand what makes a human cell grow into an eye. Magical, Julia, magical."

She stayed silent, still shaken.

"Have you ever questioned how an eye can see? What makes an eye burst into tears, wink, and blink? Magical, Julia, magical," Larry went on.

She did not respond.

"Is there a plan somewhere or maybe some sort of design that makes an eye an eye? Would you know? Maybe a mysterious architecture transforms a human tissue into an eye."

For some reason, the eye in the box burst into tears. Probably to express sorrow over Larry's struggle to explain his fascination with the wonders of nature.

"No, I don't know what makes an eye behave like an eye. Nor do I understand how a human tissue develops into an eye," said Julia, shrugging her shoulders. "All I know is that your experiments in the lab are eerie. You're a very strange dude, Mr. Quack. This is repulsive! It is NOT for us to experiment with human body parts!"

Perhaps conveying discontent over Julia's remark, the blue eye in the box rolled upward and then downward three times. You could almost hear the eye saying: *Behave yourself, Julia. I'm not just a body part, I also have emotions.*

Suddenly, Larry snapped open the pink box. Inside it, a rosy, crinkly human ear lay shaking, seemingly embarrassed by the heated conversation. "Here's another example," Larry said, with his typical fanatical zeal.

"YUCK! HIDEOUS! STOMACH TURNING!" Julia screeched while observing the sudden crumpling of the blushing ear, probably protecting its eardrum from her loud shout.

"I wonder, again," said Larry, pointing to the scarlet organ, "why does an ear look like an ear and not like a finger? What is the power that enables the ear to listen? Where is the design that made the ear an ear? Where is the architecture that drives a human cell to evolve into an ear? Would you know?"

Then Larry went hurriedly to the third container, unlocking it swiftly, eager to reveal its contents.

"Please S-STOP, D-DO NOT OPEN the third box!" beseeched Julia. "I think I understand your wonders. No need to continue! PUT THE DISGUSTING THINGS BACK INTO YOUR BRIEFCASE!"

Larry was resolute. He was determined to open the red box containing the last specimen of his genius. It was an example that not only attested to his outstanding superpowers. It also made the point that somewhere there must be a design that shapes a human organ. He still did not know what makes an ear listen, an eye see, or a brain think. *There must be somewhere a sort of architecture that prescribes the behavior of the human body parts*, he murmured to himself.

A human mouth, red, shiny, somewhat crumpled, laughing aloud, rose from the bottom of the red container. "Hello, people," said a shrill and seductive voice that came out of the pair of luscious lips. "What are you having for lunch today? Oh, almost forgot, my name is Gloria, and my job is not only to taste food. I'm also designed to lick stamps, drool, talk nonsense, and French kiss. XOXOXOXOXO to all of you…"

Pale-faced, Julia gasped in terror.

"Excellent. Good for you, Gloria, and what else can you do for us today?" chuckled Larry.

The succulent lips in the box gave a very broad smile as if they were stretched from one invisible ear to another. "What else? Well, I can sing, but I cannot dance. I can eat, but I cannot cook. I can chew, but I cannot smell. I can curse, but I cannot see. I can spell, but I cannot write…"

"So, what is the bottom line of this, Larry?" asked Julia, eyes wide open, lips parted. "Why are you showing me this? What is the purpose of growing human parts?"

"Here's the point, Julia," lowering his voice, for he suspected that some of the people in the café had already noticed his peculiar presentation. "I'd like you to understand that we, humans, are limited. We are incapable of doing what the Lord does."

"This is totally clear to me. There is nothing new in what you're saying," said Julia, mopping the sweat that covered her ruddy cheeks.

"This is totally clear to me, too," put in Gloria the Lips. "Larry, you're not saying anything that a human being is unfamiliar with."

"Shush, shush, shush," uttered Larry with a mixture of irritation and tolerance. "Gloria, darling, this is none of your business. Talk only when you're being asked, sugar lips."

Gloria the Lips did not respond.

"The point I'm trying to make," Larry went on, "is that something out there, maybe in heaven, or wherever it is, is driving the growth and the behavior of an ear, an eye, and lips. Something in the sky, or —"

"Do you refer to nature as a driving force?" interjected Julia, taking a long swig from her Blue Monster energy drink.

"Yes, yes, that's it, exactly!" hailed Larry, his eyes flashing like the headlights of a four-by-four truck. "Nature, nature controls the way human organs grow. I'd venture to say that nature is an amazing architect. Nature is capable of shaping us, designing us: making humans look like they look, animals as they appear, and objects as they are seen. Don't you think so?"

"Yes, so what's new, Larry? I still don't understand. Everybody knows that nature is a supreme power that's capable of everything," said Julia, growing riled.

"Our company needs just such supreme power. A force that can architect our software applications, design their behavior, make them powerful, so we can beat the competition. Make more money. Get richer and richer. Maybe have more parties. Do you get my drift, Julia?'"

"I'm not sure I understand. All you have on your mind is money and parties. Is this why you hire software architects or designers?"

"YES, YES, you've got it!"

"I love you, Larry, I completely agree… Hold on. There's a call coming in on my cell," said the red-lips Gloria from the box. "Hi, honey," she went on. "I'm in the middle of an important discussion. It's something about architecture-shmarchitecture. Can I get back to you in a few…?"

"I love you too, Gloria," grinned Larry. "I think Julia understands now why I created you, bonbon."

CHAPTER FOUR

"Please, lend me your ear, Julia. I'd like to tell you something," the lips begged suddenly.

Julia lowered her head apathetically.

"I think you and I have a bunch of things in common," whispered Gloria into Julia's ear. "I'm cool, and you are too. I'm smart, and you're smart, too. I'm sexy, and you're sexy, too. I'm curious, and you're curious, too. Both of us love nature and believe in the mighty power of the Creator, the only authority that controls nearly every aspect of our being. It is the only power that morally can tamper with human organs —"

"What are you trying to say?" hissed Julia.

"The essence of my identity has been haunting me for months," Gloria the Lips sighed. "I do not know who I am, from where I came, and what my purpose in life is. Obviously, Larry created me with the power of his knowledge. However, he would not disclose the core of my conception. In other words, from whom did he take the human cells to create me, to enable my existence? To whom do I belong? HELP ME, PLEASE!" sobbed Gloria bitterly in Julia's ear.

Inches apart from Gloria the Lips, the blue eye in the box burst into tears as if it shared the anguish about the very same unsettled mystery. And the pink ear, the ear that had been sharing Gloria's throbbing ache, turned slowly blue, as if it were downright disgusted.

"What are you ladies whispering about over there?" asked Larry from the other end of the table, worried that a plot against him was in the making.

"Gloria the Lips would like to know to whom she belongs — that is, from whom you took the human cells to create her," said Julia daringly.

"YES, Larry," joined Gloria, raising her voice. "It is wholly unfair of you to keep ignoring my concerns. Everyone deserves some respect. I'm a part of a human being that should be treated like every living thing."

"IT WOULD BE UNETHICAL," stormed Larry, "to disclose the DONOR of the cells! I'm sorry, I can't! You'll have to live with it for the rest of your life!" And he gave a piteous look at the tormented ear, eye, and mouth trapped helplessly in their boxes.

"Gloria is correct! These organs have a right to know their genetic heritage," agreed Julia firmly.

"RIGHTS and RIGHTS and RIGHTS!" shrieked Larry. "All these years they have been insisting on their rights. I have news for you: THEY DO NOT HAVE RIGHTS! They're my own creations, living human organs by courtesy rather than by RIGHTS."

"Every part-human has its rights, Larry," cried Gloria the Lips.

"So, maybe you can tell me which rights are more important: YOUR RIGHT TO A FULL IDENTITY OR THE DONOR'S RIGHT TO PRIVACY? Eh?" yelled Larry, closing the tight-fitting lid of Gloria's box forcefully and with an audible snap.

Sealing Gloria's red container did not squelch her squeaking voice from bubbling up as if it were coming from the bottom of the Atlantic Ocean. "GIVE ME INDEPENDENCE, SET ME FREE, LET ME OUT OF THE MISERY!" Her ear-splitting cries flooded the café and then gushed outside to the busy street, where bystanders clapped their hands over their ears.

Moments later, Gloria the Lips turned as silent as the dead.

Larry collected his containers from the table, and Julia asked for the check. Then she yanked out from her bag a makeup set and a small mirror. As she applied some red lipstick, it occurred to her that Gloria the Lips had the same exact shade. Gloria the Lips also had a beauty mark, on the right side, like Julia did.

Gloria's was outlined with dark lip liner, just like Julia did with her own makeup. And just like Julia's mouth, Gloria the Lips had lip gloss to make her shine.

Moments went by. Sudden twinges of fear turned Julia's stomach. "MY dear GOD! Please say it's NOT TRUE! My gracious LORD, please tell me this is my sheer imagination. ARE THE LIPS, THE EYE, THE EAR MINE? They look like mine: blue eyes, red lips, and pink ears, just like MINE!" She gave Larry a vile look, prepared to slash his throat with the butter knife at any moment.

"I-I'm n-not s-sure," mumbled Larry, edging away from the table.

"WELL, WHERE *DID* YOU GET THE CELLS FROM?" she screamed at the top of her voice.

"Th-the c-cells? W-where did I get the cells f-f-f-from? I-I'm n-not s-sure. I-I'm really not sure…"

"Tell me now before I murder you!"

"A-a c-couple of y-years a-ago," he mumbled, drawing his chair away even farther, "when you were on vacation, I passed your office one day and found some blonde hair strands on your desk. Maybe from this hair I extracted the cells. But I'm not sure if this was really yours, J-Julia. It might have been somebody else's. Wh-who knows, wh-who knows?"

CHAPTER FIVE

LONGING

Days crept by, and the preparations for my upcoming journey intensified. The passage to the past or to the future still seemed hazy, though. The beam of light was obscure. The prospects for a rapid start to the journey were gloomy.

Indeed, the ray of hope was fading as time went by. Still, I knew that nothing would dissuade me from meeting Rhubarb Pie again after months of heartbreak over our separation.

The light of faith kindled when my voyage began at the crack of dawn.

I was jolted out of bed and shoved into a giant pit, a dark blue hole whose shadowy entrance astonished me.

While hurtling down toward the bottom, on the way to an intense blurry light, I aspired to visit a better world, a promising sphere.

Deprived of any sense of direction, time, or space, I felt a lack of control over my destiny, and my anxiety deepened. I was startled yet buoyant, terrified yet curious, dazed yet fascinated.

I recalled Rhubarb Pie as I was heaved strongly by an impalpable force through the inviting light at the bottom of the giant pit: *I had admired your thoughts even before you composed them, giggled at your humorous prattle even before you uttered it, read your tales about world peace and your love for nature even before you wrote them, ate the fat-free pies you served even before you baked them, longed to spend time with you even when you were absent, and began searching for your whereabouts even before you vanished.*

THE CITY OF @

Down, down, down, to the bottom of the giant pit I dived at almost the speed of sound. Like a sack of potatoes, I was flung against a golden desert dune in the middle of heaven knows where. It was a landing abrupt beyond words.

This desert was different from any other I had ever seen: bright dawns yet dark dusks, cold valleys yet scorching knolls, dry drafts yet damp breezes, quiet heavens yet noisy dust storms, mysterious hisses yet monotonous purrs, and a mystical existence yet a harsh reality.

After recovering from the sudden descent into the unknown, I drifted from one hill to another. Lingering, I grew enchanted with the vast space revealed. Intimidating, though, like the Death Valley in the bare Mojave Desert.

There, mouth agape and eyes wide, I was gazing at almighty nature with a mixture of utmost respect and anxiety. It was a scene out of this world — almost imaginary, captivating. Salty ponds and dry creeks and fields of shimmering sand dunes sprawled about. Strange rocks carved into shapes of stunning beauty appeared almost anywhere you turned your head.

Where am I? I asked myself repeatedly. *Is this all real? Why am I here? Where do I go from here? What's beyond these dunes, the rocks, the horizon?*

I wonder whether you've ever endured such feelings. Have you feared the unknown, at the same time wanting to explore it?

I recalled one of Uncle Walter's sayings: "The desert deceives naive eyes. The withered land appears teeming with lush valleys, and the far seems nearby." And he was right.

THE CITY OF @

As I waded forward through the sand ripples, my weary eyes gazed intensely at a monstrous, noisy city. The illuminated place sagged deeply between yellow dunes. *Was it a mile away? two? seven? How soon would I be there?* I couldn't reckon.

There were sounds I had never heard before. Loud, spooky thunders echoed out from the enormous city and sent spasms of fear into the pit of my stomach. And mysterious roars flooded the majestic desert with evil hissing threats. Some sounded like screeching wheels. A few reminded me of clanking chains. Others resembled a powerful lightning storm.

As I drew closer, a colorful universe was revealed. Brown brick walls fenced an icy city. A massive safety gate sheltered the place. Adding to the strict security were countless cameras that observed every one of my movements.

My curiosity grew. No one seemed to care when I pounded sturdily on the golden gate. Moments later, a gentle tap on my shoulder sent shivers down my spine —

I was not alone.

Out of thin air, a shrill voice said kindly, "Hello, Sammy. Welcome to my city."

"Where am I?" I gasped in horror, looking behind me for the source of the piercing voice.

The voice burst out laughing. The words that followed were unclear. I had never heard anyone talk like that. You too, might find it puzzling, "Ha-ha-ha, hee-hee-hee... You're in the capital of wisdom, the center of intelligence, the megalopolis of human creativity. You are in the City of @, also known as the software architecture metropolis."

"Ar-archi w-what? And what were the other words you said?"

"Never mind, never mind, Sammy. Keep all your questions for later. Ha-ha-ha-ha-ha."

"And where are you hiding, sir?"

CHAPTER SIX

Seemingly out of nowhere appeared an ugly, plump, bald-headed, yellow-faced, one-legged man. He looked like a computer image generated from hundreds and hundreds of black dots.

"I'm not hiding," he said with a lopsided grin. "I do not have any reason to hide. I'm here — but can be found anywhere. I'm noticeable — also invisible. I'm tangible — also abstract. I'm concrete — also conceptual."

Tangible? Abstract? Concrete? Conceptual? What is he saying? I whispered to myself.

The hideous cartoon-like male whose words were extremely confusing to me was mostly invisible. His appearance brought to mind a pink, plucked, dead chicken — lacking limbs and wearing a tattered and shabby jacket. Big translucent patches covered most of him, and through them the creamy desert dunes behind him were apparent. He was indeed hardly visible.

"I-I do n-not u-understand a w-word you say," I mumbled audibly.

"If it does not make sense to you now, it will later, little girl. There is no need to get so excited."

"And w-where is the rest of you? S-some of your parts are missing," I muttered, dazed and still in terror.

"Where is the rest of me? Ha-ha-ha-ha-ha... The rest of me, you're asking? Hee-hee-hee-hee-hee-hee-hee-hee. The answer, dear, could not be simpler," he sniggered mockingly. "Would you really like to know?"

I stayed silent, peering at the strange creature and rubbing my eyes in disbelief.

"Years and years of working at this challenging place could take a toll on you, Sammy," he said. "Slowly, slowly, I turned into an odd pile of body parts that do not appear intact. Don't you see how ridiculous I look, girl, huh? Don't you? Some portions of me have already become invisible. And others will fade out as time passes."

"So, why have you been turning invisible? Don't you eat enough, sir?"

"No, no. Not at all. There's enough food in my city, the City of @."

"Or maybe the weather is too hard on you?"

"No, no, the weather here is excellent, dear. Life is good, sweetheart. Becoming invisible is the price I pay for working so hard, being so famous, so powerful, so popular, so admirable. Ha-ha-ha, hee-hee-hee... If you stayed with us for a little while, it would happen to you too, sugar," he slurred.

"T-to m-me, t-too?" I said with a tremulous voice, shaken to my core. "Am *I* going to disappear too?"

"Not immediately, beauty. Not right away... Slowly, slowly... Don't worry. It doesn't hurt to become invisible. It's painless, painless, believe me. It's even fun. Believe me, candy."

"What's so fun about losing your appearance? Only ugly girls wouldn't care..."

"Sammy, this is incorrect —"

"It is correct," I cut in, irritated. "Only girls who have something to hide wouldn't mind being invisible."

"Dear, this is totally unfounded —"

"And wh-who a-are y-you anyway? And how do you know my n-n-name?" I interrupted him again, scared stiff.

"Who am I? Who am I? Ha-ha-ha, hee-hee-hee... My name is Mr. Eric Greenbold. I'm the chief of the chiefs, the undisputed authority. Dweller of the City of @, I'm the unchallenged leader of the software architecture city. The only powerful one, the one that knows everything..."

Suddenly a green frog stuck its head out of Mr. Greenbold's only visible pocket. It seemed cheerful; it grinned and hummed and rolled its bulgy eyes up and down, ready for a party.

I thought I heard the frog say in a deep and croaky voice: *Hello, Sammy. My name is Bobby. I'm on your side, my princess. Do not believe a word the chief says. He lies, he lies, he lies... It's all rubbish, hollow words that only zebras understand, not humans. I warn you; I warn you, don't even try to understand!*

Perhaps Mr. Greenbold could not hear Bobby talking to me as he went on and on: "I'm smart, I'm supersmart. I'm capable, unconventional, in the box and also out of the box. I'm also creative, original, and inspirational. From a software architecture perspective, I'm extremely logical, programmable, deployable, manageable, operational, computational, and absolutely institutional."

Bobby the Frog rolled his eyes upward. I almost heard him say again, *It's all gibberish, believe me, Sammy. No one understands what Mr. Greenbold says. The chief talks nonsense all the time. It's all babble, believe me, my princess. I bet you don't understand, right? I don't understand, either. No one, no one gets what the chief says.*

As Bobby the Frog had advised, I did not even bother to make sense of Mr. Greenbold's jabber. "When things go wrong with any of my software applications," his mouth kept moving rapidly, "I turn nasty, disgusting, rude, and vulgar. And take my word — loutish. If any of my policies are ignored, I grumble, roar, crash, insult, dismiss, or, as cruel as it sounds — terminate."

I told you, I just told you, Sammy. Bobby continued, *Pay no attention. All are meaningless words. Even a genius would not be able to crack the chief's rambling. Trust me, my princess.*

"I want to go home. I do not like this place, sir. N-not by any consent was I drawn into your bizarre world. Perhaps it was a mistake. I must return home," I insisted nervously.

"Home? Do you really want home? Ha-ha-ha-ha-ha… No, no, you've arrived at the right place, Sammy," said Mr. Greenbold with a disgusting smirk on his half-visible face. "HOME IS DEAD! No one has ever returned home, NO ONE! No one has ever escaped this place," the chief intoned.

"No one?" I repeated, teeth shuddering.

"Yes, no one. Not even one soul. Here the shiny city on the hill of dunes offers hope, contentment, and fairness. There is no place like this on Earth, sweetie pie. Even the place you're coming from can't provide such a wonderful life."

Yeah, right. Do you really believe him? The chief is lying again. Huuu, huuu, huuu, huuu… Bobby the Frog exploded in contagious laughter.

"What do you know?" I retorted cuttingly. "I come from a place where people are decent. At home, freedom drives the essence of life, and all are equal under the sun. Respect for fairness and equality is carved in stone and flows in our blood. Hope and opportunity are not hollow words. And family is vital to every living creature. I want home, sweet home," I cried bitterly.

"Cries will not help you, dear," said Mr. Greenbold sternly. "There are strict rules in my kingdom that apply to guests like you." Then he narrowed his eyes and sang passionately as if it were the national anthem:

> *If my policies are ignored,*
>
> *In a flash, discipline shall be restored!*
>
> *The code of conduct is crystal clear,*
>
> *And disobedience could be devastating to those who do not adhere.*
>
> *The punishment is typically harsh,*

CHAPTER SIX

And the penalties could crash —

At last, the golden gate of the City of @ swung open. Mystified, mouth open, I was staring at a bizarre world, a lit-up city radiating vivid colors. I had never seen such a place before.

Arranged untidily on scrubbed-down pavements, arched and sharp-shaped buildings sprang into the sky.

Many of the structures in the city whirled like lawn sprinklers. Only a few stood motionless.

Several resembled urban buildings baring towering and piercing cones pointing in all possible directions.

Others brought to mind strange beasts. Indeed, the frightening constructions looked like mythical Greek creatures. Countless cyclopes (one-eyed monsters) and Cerberuses (three-headed dogs with dragon's tails) occupied the city.

Unlike my beautiful and warm home city, this one seemingly concealed horrifying secrets buried deeply in the eerie structures. Here was a city perhaps ruled by brutal laws of terror and that was lacking in human dignity.

"Let's get going, Sammy," Mr. Greenbold pressed. "Time is running out quickly. We must head first to the Admission Hall, about a ten-minute drive from here. There, screening and interviewing will follow. If everything goes well, you'll be attending a meeting to address your concerns."

I followed him halfheartedly to the tiny parking lot where a red ladybug-like vehicle was stationed. The car was sitting elegantly on top of six square pink wheels. Yes, square wheels — three on each side.

"This wonderful car is called the Magnificent Ladybug. In short: Ladybug," Mr. Greenbold said with a mixture of pride and arrogance.

After we quickly mounted the fabricated beetle, it lunged wildly. We were squashed forcefully against the leather seats like ripe plum tomatoes squeezed in a sandwich.

No, it was not like flying on a mystical saucer that hovers slickly and soundlessly above ground. No, it was not like in the books I had read.

Not by any stretch of the imagination was the snail's-pace ride on the six-square-wheel bug thrilling. Nor was it magical or entrancing. I wondered then, why hadn't the 5,000-year-old circular wheel been a source of inspiration. Why had it been ignored? Why was the Ladybug rolling on square, instead of round, wheels? Why?

The Ladybug emitted ear-splitting thunderclaps. The noise was louder than any jet engine ever built. Attempting to be heard in spite of the noisy shuttle, Mr. Greenbold screeched at the top of his voice, "How is the ride so far?" He gave a vulgar grin while eyeing my frown and timid face.

"Wonderful, enjoyable," I jeered, rolling my eyes upward as high as I could. "Just wonderful, sir," I repeated cynically.

"I'm glad you are enjoying the ride. When you're finally relaxed and ready to dine, you may delight in any one of the meals available in the Ladybug. The meals are courtesy of the freedom lovers in the City of @."

"Where are the meals, sir?" I said, glancing at him from the corners of my eyes.

Mr. Greenbold pointed at the Ladybug's roof and said smugly, "This is the marvel of innovation. Pull down any of the tubes above your head, and sip the meal of your choice."

"What are the different colors for, sir?"

"Oh, those? Each color delivers something different, Sammy. A genius idea that only my guys in the City of @ could have come up with. The blue pipes deliver a variety of energy appetizers.

Squeezing any of the greens would provide an organic salad of the day. Yellows sprinkle the main courses. And reds offer a large collection of ice creams,"

DO NOT TOUCH THESE TUBES, I heard Bobby the Frog shouting at full volume. *POISON, POISON, POISON!* It seemed that Mr. Greenbold did not hear the frog.

"Thank you, sir, but I'm not hungry," I said, rejecting his offer. Then I murmured to myself, *What a strange, tube-feeding nation...*

Mr. Greenbold continued to ramble as I got woozy: "The Ladybug is built entirely here. It is a sophisticated, thirty-seven-seat shuttle that can take you anywhere. It's made of organic substances, such as sun-dried fruit and vegetables and synthetic oils —"

"STOP IT, MR. GREENBOLD. My head is dizzy! PLEASE STOP IT!" I exploded, cupping my hands over my ears.

"And get this," he went on, indifferent to my bitter plea. "It's fueled by orange peels and is capable of flying like a jet, diving like a submarine, gliding like a ghost, and floating like a duck. It can also thrust through brick, concrete, and even diamond-made walls. But these are only some of its miraculous capabilities. Imagine what it could do otherwise —"

"S-sophisticated? Ha-ha-ha-ha, hee-hee-hee..., I-I could *walk* faster than your glorified five-mile-an-hour bug can drive, thank you! Say no more. I'm not interested," I interrupted cheekily.

"WATCH IT," growled Mr. Greenbold, raising his voice to the highest pitch possible, his eyes narrowed to intimidating slits. "NEVER EVER INSULT MY LADYBUG! Words like these can get you into big trouble!"

"Trouble? Things cannot get worse than this, sir," I retorted, vexed.

"Ohhhh, NO, NO, you're in good hands, my young lady. Nothing to worry about...," his tone of voice tamed unexpectedly.

Suddenly, Mr. Greenbold stopped the vehicle. Then he drew out of his pocket a black leather-covered notebook and scribbled some words. I could read them through the translucent patches of his shoulder:

> *Ant-feeding monkeys like Sammy must be disciplined immediately upon arrival...*

I kept silent. Growing irritable, I scooped out the red plastic spiral diary from my pocket and scrawled:

> *February 27, 2001 — CAUTION! Control freaks like Mr. Greenbold, the chief of the chiefs, must be locked up as soon as possible. He ought to be given serious attention by the best psychiatrists around...*

Mr. Greenbold's rambling persisted interminably — and largely inconsiderately — as we were weaving along the pathways of the City of @. With no end in sight, the Ladybug was twirling endlessly between the bewildering structures and coiling around the marvelous constructions.

No, it was not a pleasant tour for visitors like me. Nor did I relish the winding paths through the software architecture metropolis, in which the Ladybug shuttle was struggling to forge ahead.

She, the vehicle, perspired like a marathon runner after crossing the finish line. She coughed while bobbing wildly along the surface of the roads. She sneezed near every shrub. She gagged when Mr. Greenbold pressed down too hard on the accelerator pedal.

"And get this, too: Not everyone can drive the shuttle," Mr. Greenbold continued with vigor. "The bug will not even start if the person in the driver's seat is immoral. If he's a fake freedom lover or a deadbeat parent or is corrupt or prejudiced, the Ladybug will stay still. If he is a fugitive or belongs to an outlawed cult, the vehicle will not even blink. The Ladybug just won't move, even if you feed her with the best orange peels in the world!"

I grew livid and fearful as the moments of helplessness and confusion persisted. I was unable to control the course of events that had brought me thus far. I was desperate.

The hope of liberating myself from the grasping arms of tyranny drifted slowly away. I dreaded losing one of the most precious possessions, one bestowed naturally on human beings: freedom.

The coldhearted City of @ and its illusory environment were unbearable. My mind called urgently for action: *ACT NOW, SAMMY!* Then I whispered to myself, *Now or never! Venturing an escape could give me free rein to pursue my dear Rhubarb Pie.*

Indeed, an escape was in the offing, borne of my desperation.

The chance to break free did not fail to arrive. The Ladybug suddenly strayed off its track, screeching almost to a halt. In a split second, the shuttle slumped into an enormous ditch filled with murky and evil-smelling water. It seemed that the dark drain had slurped up the entire vehicle in the twinkling of an eye, like a hungry alligator.

Then things turned black, cold, wet, and silent. Confused and drenched from head to toe, my heart walloped hard. Cold sweat covered my forehead, and my eyes clamped shut.

A little while later, it seemed that Mr. Greenbold had lost control of the shuttle and had driven it straight down into the reeking ditch. And now he was sprawled across the reclining driver's seat. He was probably struggling to recover, possibly to regain consciousness. I hoped he was dead…

THE CITY OF @

As seconds mounted and became a minute or two, I grew confident that Mr. Greenbold was not going to recover.

Leaping at the opportunity, I was eager to bend time backward to the beginning of my journey. Roll back time to the hours before I had been shoved into the hollow pit on my way down to the City of @.

I hoped to escape the captivity before Mr. Greenbold awakened. I chanted repeatedly, "I love myself because I'm the greatest. I love myself because I'm the greatest. I love myself because I'm the greatest…"

On Uncle Walter's word, only if I could focus on my inner me, on my soul, with the power of my thoughts would time start bending and then roll back in the desired direction. *Time scrunching*, he called it often, when the aim was to revert time backward.

As I waited hungrily a second or more, I was biting my lips from the mounting pressure.

At last, time indeed curved back. I soon found myself out of the ditch, standing at a site engulfed by a thick and milky fog that moved sluggishly in the cold air. A second or two later, a familiar scene appeared through the patches of the thinning haze. It was like a returning bad dream, similar to the one that had happened not too long ago.

Just like rewinding a movie and letting it play again from the beginning, Mr. Greenbold urged me, as he had last time: "Let's get going, Sammy," he pressed. "Time is running out quickly. We must head first to the Admission Hall, about a ten-minute drive from here…"

Once again, I followed him halfheartedly. I trailed him to the same exact location. To the same tiny parking lot where we had boarded the Ladybug last time.

CHAPTER SIX

Then once more, the beetle charged forward violently and noisily. But this time I was prepared: my hand tightly clamped the suspended handgrip above the passenger seat.

And for a second time, there was the choppy ride on the six square wheels.

Then all over again, I refused to treat myself to the delightful meals dripping from the dangling tubes. This time, though, I couldn't resist the temptation of the seductive ice cream that came in a rainbow of colors. This time drooling, I must admit, I indulged myself. On and on I squeezed the vanilla, banana, chocolate chip, mint chocolate, coffee, and strawberry flavors right into my open mouth.

Then yet again, I heard the Ladybug's screeching noise. Next, the big bang thundered as we tumbled into the ditch. The pit turned dark, wet, stinky. Then, as it had happened last time, there were moments of silence as I wished dearly that Mr. Greenbold were indeed dead, very dead…

Hope faded away as I grasped the fact that time had rolled back short of my expectations. Time had moved only to the very same moment that Mr. Greenbold and I had boarded the Ladybug in the parking lot.

My freedom seemed to be gradually slipping away as one time-scrunching attempt after another brought us to the very same point.

Mr. Greenbold, with a broadening, nasty smirk on his face, was pleased to introduce the City of @, through which we cruised sluggishly again and again.

My plan to escape the city failed. I was overwhelmed by feelings of defeat and anxiety.

Even Bobby the Frog shed tears. I guess he knew how desperate I was to regain my freedom.

THE INTERVIEW

The City of @ was like nowhere else in the world. It was a strange place where nothing made sense. Controlled by fear, the city was ruled by Mr. Greenbold, who carved its heartless laws in stone.

You probably might run into a similar situation, where escape seems impossible. And where the light at the end of the tunnel appears dim. And where confusion muddles your mind. And where hope is fading away.

If you're ever trapped in a place like this, do not get discouraged. Do not despair. Do not let negative thoughts overwhelm you. Think about the good things that could come out of such a situation. Where else could you find a good and funny friend like Bobby the Frog? He was a little frog with a big heart and a huge smile, a pal who cheered me up during these tormenting times.

True, no one likes to be imprisoned in a vile place that offers only anguish. Wait for the right opportunity, though. Seize the moments when you could take charge, regain control of your life.

Believe it — every so often, chances for freedom do arrive... Rhubarb Pie had told me that. I'm passing his clever words on to you and anyone else who experiences these feelings.

"Smart, beautiful, young girls like you should not be bullied. You're not a punching bag," Rhubarb Pie had said. "Assume responsibility for your destiny. Don't let anyone intimidate you."

Even Bobby the Frog would have agreed with this. He had been trying to ease my pain by making me laugh. He even called me *Princess* to brighten my gloomy day.

CHAPTER SEVEN

At last, the Ladybug lurched to a halt. Mr. Greenbold parked the shuttle near the Reception Hall. As he had mentioned, interviews and meetings were about to take place shortly.

The reception schedule for visitors in the City of @ left no time to spare. Hundreds of us were waiting for the interviews. The place seemed like a shoe assembly line. New arrivals were handled with flawless precision. One person after another was escorted in, while minutes later, the visitors were led out from various rooms.

You might ask what Mr. Greenbold was doing there. He hustled relentlessly through the long corridors. From one office to another, he was peering through open doors, spying through the cracks of slightly opened windows. He gave stern instructions to his staff. He was managing the place with an iron fist.

Helplessly confined to a restraining chair, perhaps tied by invisible ropes, I was trying to set myself free. At the very same time, a nurse wearing a white silk robe was pushing my squeaky wheelchair swiftly into a large waiting room.

The place, dedicated to absorbing newcomers, was packed with an influx of people arriving from different parts of the globe. They too, were shackled to bizarre chairs, waiting tensely for their scheduled interviews. Some dozed; others read the daily newspapers. Occasionally, they glanced at the small television set mounted to a pole in the center of the waiting room.

As the news unfolded, all eyes strayed toward the newscaster, who called for our attention: "And now, we turn to President George W. Bush's special message to Congress on his new budget proposal…"

A hush fell on the Reception Hall. We were glued to the TV screen.

"America today," opened the president, whose half-beaming image appeared suddenly, "is a nation with great challenges, but greater resources. An artist using statistics as a brush could paint two very different pictures of our country. One would have warning signs: increasing layoffs, rising energy prices, too many failing schools, persistent poverty, the stubborn vestiges of racism."

The crowd in the waiting room nodded as the president shifted to a positive view. "A second picture would be full of blessings: a balanced budget, big surpluses, a military that is second to none, a country at peace with its neighbors, technology that is revolutionizing the world, and our greatest strength: concerned citizens who care for our country and care for each other. Neither picture is complete by itself. And tonight I challenge and invite Congress to work with me by using the resources of one picture to repaint the other, to direct the advantages of our time to solve the problems of our people."

In my heart of hearts, I felt that the president meant well. His self-confident and reassuring tone conveyed that our nation was moving in the right direction. The message was not only that our glorious past had fulfilled the dreams of the people but also that the future looked promising, offering growth and happiness.

David McCallum, whose name was revealed by the tag pasted on his shirt, was glued to the glowing display. He seemed distressed; the positive outlook of our country perhaps did not cheer him up.

"Why are you here, David?" I asked, raising my eyebrows high.

"That's a good question. I'm not completely sure. It happened just like that. One morning, I found myself in the City of @ wandering around…"

"This would be the last place on Earth I'd like to be," I exclaimed, snatching a glimpse of his somber face.

CHAPTER SEVEN

"I feel the same. And you? What is the purpose of your visit here?"

"I'm looking for a lost person. Someone special," I gulped, feeling a lump in my throat.

"Maybe I'm here because I went through bad times. I lost everything. I lost my job. The money was gone. I sold my small shack that I purchased a couple of years ago on the beach in Long Island. Nothing left...," said David, eyes filled with tears.

His helplessness was apparent. It made me sad.

"My only valuable possession is Kuku, my turtle," he went on. "My only friend, who is still crawling under my bed in a box."

The white-dressed nurse who fiercely wheeled my confining chair into the Cordial Interview Office interrupted our short conversation.

The cramped office, floodlit by icy shades, seemed like a secret interrogation nook. Maybe it was a torture chamber for aliens who had just landed on Earth. Or perhaps it was dedicated to experiments on terminal patients.

Splashes of what appeared to be blood on the floor, walls, and ceiling heightened my fears. The horrifying scene sent shivers up my spine. My worry increased, especially after I noticed a magenta-faced man beaming at me, baring gigantic snowy teeth.

Wearing a pink bib apron, white gloves, and dark rubber boots, the man was operating a stainless-steel meat grinder. Just like the one Mom has in the kitchen. This, though, was the largest grinder that I had ever seen in my life.

From the back of the powerful meat chopper, he was intensely whirling a silver handle.

On top, he was stuffing the funnel relentlessly with red substances. Possibly, they were chunks of chicken thighs or moose livers or hog brains or some other sort of flesh that I'd rather not mention now.

And from the front of the meat grinder, spaghetti-like shapes of ground red meat spewed out of the holes.

No, no, it was not like the butcher's shop in my hometown.

Gazing downward, the man said calmly, "Do not fear, girl. My name is Grady Scotpress. I'm obviously not in charge of the press, ha-ha-ha-ha-ha... Here, I merely conduct interviews."

"Interviews? What kind of strange interviews are these?" I questioned, shivering.

"What kind of interviews?" he repeated, giving a sneaky smirk. "Your interview would be very simple, painless, given to sensitive visitors like you. No need to worry."

I drew my head away from his approaching arms. "What do you intend to do with those wires in your hands?"

"Do not fear, girl. Nothing bad is going to happen to you. I'm going to attach these small instruments to your scalp."

"Why?"

"These tiny devices can read almost anything you have in your head. Any information your mind can provide. Anything, girl."

"What type of information are you going to extract from my head?"

"Information?" he echoed my question again. "Any, any bit of information, EVERYTHING, my little friend. Everything we can get, everything we can put our hands on."

"Like what? All my secrets?"

"Oh, much more than that, gorgeous. You see, these small information-sucking instruments are very efficient. They can tell us what you like and don't like, who your friends are, how much money you have in your piggy bank, and beyond..."

"What else?"

"I can even find out if you have a boyfriend. Do you have one? Do you? Do you?"

"No, sir."

"I see... In a matter of seconds, I'd be able to find out if you're telling me the truth, girl."

"If I had one, I'd not have told you, sir. Girls do not talk about these things with strangers."

"I see," he snickered, giving a nasty grin.

"And what else, sir?" I pressed. "What else can you get out of me?"

"We can check your health. The food you like. We can sneak into your dreams, your memories, aspirations, your plans for the future. Everything!"

"But isn't it personal information? You should not be snatching it without my consent," I protested, my forehead creased like a crinkled potato chip.

"Do not worry about these things. Let's focus on the interview now..." said Mr. Scotpress parentally, grinning like a blue potato basking blissfully in sunlight.

"I wish to skip this interview. It is illegal," I bellowed.

"Not by force are interviews conducted here. We operate only after visitors grant their full consent. If you are not interested or you're uncomfortable, please leave now; the door is open. You are free to go, ha-ha-ha...," he said while pressing the icy cold devices to my forehead.

As Mr. Scotpress carefully mounted the sensors to my head, I felt frail and drowsy. My vision turned slowly foggy, and my mind went blank like an empty sheet of white paper.

I'm really not sure why I let him do that. I could have walked out. I could have yelled. I could have struggled. Not sure... Not sure...

Everything in the interview chamber appeared to be whirling like a carousel. It felt like a rotating platform, on which Mr. Scotpress seemed to be riding a wooden horse mounted on a post, galloping around and around...

Not too long later, maybe a minute or two, half-awake, I heard him whispering softly into my ear, "The interview is over. It lasted a flash of a second. We're done, girl! Done! Done! Done! The information from your head oozed like from a garden hose. Ha-ha-ha-ha-ha…"

Then a heavy silence fell on the Cordial Interview Office, as if the entire world was waiting for me to regain full consciousness.

Wondering if all my body parts were still functioning, I was stretching arms, extending legs, blinking eyes, gulping, breathing deep.

What has Mr. Scotpress done to me while I passed out? I muttered to myself. *Is my body intact? Am I still the same Sammy that I used to be? Has anything been taken away from me? Has he used the meat grinder somehow to collect any specimens from my tissues?*

The peculiar interview painted yet another view of the insane world of the City of @. A place governed by senseless individuals who interrupted my quest for happiness.

Not only had the cynical manner in which they treated me amplified my worries, but also my hopes of ever meeting Rhubarb Pie again wavered.

Was the uncanny city real or merely a bad dream? Was Bobby the Frog the only real living thing in that place?

Strapped to his chair, pushed toward the interview chamber, David McCallum was going to have his own turn. Mute, pale faced, utterly dazed, he waved to me feebly when our paths crossed. The perplexed look in his eyes divulged his tormented state of mind. Had he given up his independence? Had the City of @ broken his spirit? Weakened his aspirations for better days?

Venting frustration, waving my arms in the air, I suddenly bellowed at the top of my voice, "David, do not let them steal your identity, your soul. RUN, RUN, RUN AWAY, as fast as you can!"

THE SMELLY ROOM

I'm not sure why I'm making such a big issue of it. After all, Bobby was just a tiny green frog — a funny creature that had popped out from Mr. Greenbold's breast pocket. Like a handkerchief tucked deep in there, Bobby caught my eye.

The frog's smile from ear to ear melted my heart. He had only good things to say to me. And as I mentioned before, he even called me his princess. A flattering nickname I hoped he had not given anyone before.

When you're imprisoned in a place like the City of @, you need to focus on positive things. There are plenty of issues to complain about in this world. Nothing is perfect. If you lose control of your destiny, things could get even worse.

Bobby the Frog brought tears to my eyes because he represented the gentle and caring side of life. His standing by me in such terrible times gave me hope. I was looking forward to meeting him again soon in the Orientation Hall.

No wonder the Orientation Hall was nicknamed "The Smelly Room." The walls, ceilings, and floors emitted different kinds of scents. The odors came out at different times, from different directions.

True, "Smelly" is not exactly a proper name for the Orientation Hall. Not exactly right, I thought, because not only bad odors came wafting through the place.

In reaction to people's stupid ideas, the walls and the ceiling and the floors typically gave off bad smells. Good scents, in stark contrast, oozed from every corner of the room if speeches made sense, were clear, and were acceptable to the crowd.

CHAPTER EIGHT

I'm sure that based on the smells, you'd be able to tell immediately the difference between good and evil, and smart and foolish.

The crowd in the Orientation Hall welcomed the chief, Mr. Greenbold, with utmost respect. Bursts of applause echoed in the gigantic room as he rose to the podium. An air of cheerfulness enveloped us as the chief leafed through his notes.

Just then, before he opened his mouth, an astonishing smell of right-out-of-the-oven chocolate chip cookies oozed from the walls. A whiff that would arouse envy from most bakers in the world...

My eyes peered at Mr. Greenbold's half-visible gray suit as his speech began. In a fever of hope, I wished that Bobby the Frog would pop out his head again from one of the pockets. I missed the frog's croaky voice, his boldness, his warm character.

"In these very days," the chief opened gloomily, "we gather in the City of @. We meet to acknowledge the dire state of our beloved country. We are losing the motivation to prosper. We have become skeptical about the power of creativity and innovation. We offer weakening leadership to the rest of the world."

Gloom fell on the Orientation Hall as the chief continued to describe the sad reality of our country. People in the crowd clicked their tongues. Some even shed tears.

Only Bobby the Frog would have been able to lift my sunken spirits. Only he. But he was not there. Not from any of Mr. Greenbold's pockets did the cheerful frog stick out his head.

With an air of buoyancy, the chief of chiefs went on: "But here in our magnificent City of @, we are joyful. Here we do not drift toward desperation. Here we are productive. Here we do not fire people. Here the savings in the bank are growing. Here we do not desert the needy."

THE SMELLY ROOM

The visitors gave another round of applause, praising the upbeat way of life in the city.

Suddenly, I thought I heard a high-pitched voice talking to me. *Howdy, my name is Pebble. Hello, I'm here, look here, this way...* The voice was rising louder and louder, *I'm behind the chief's tie.*

Yes, you're there, Pebble. I can see you now. You're very tiny. Where is Bobby? I miss him, I said inaudibly.

Pebble, a red-eyed frog, was half hiding behind Mr. Greenbold's black tie. His bulgy scarlet eyes, which took up most of his green face, could be seen from a distance. His webbed orange feet and bright blue and yellow flanks were magnificent. Indeed, he was a nice-looking frog.

I almost could hear Pebble responding, *Oh, is it Bobby you're asking about? My friend is tied up with something else. He could not make it today. Sorry, Sammy.*

I was certain that Mr. Greenbold was unaware of the conversation I'd had with the red-eyed frog. Was Pebble, who seemed suspended from the chief's dark tie, real? Was Bobby his friend — that warmhearted smiley creature — also a figment of my imagination?

Anything was possible in the City of @. I believed that the frogs were real, though. Why in the world would I make these things up? Why?

Oh, are you saying that Bobby will not be here today? I whispered.

This is exactly what I said. Bobby is busy, but he asked me to send you his warm regards. I think he likes you, Sammy. Pebble's voice seemingly echoed in the Orientation Hall.

I like him too, I responded inaudibly.

Mr. Greenbold's speech was reaching its peak. He was about to make a statement that no one in the audience anticipated. It was a declaration that represented what he dearly believed in.

CHAPTER EIGHT

But before the chief went on, he scanned the crowd and slowly folded his notes. Then, embarrassed, he mopped the tears that had started coursing down his cheeks.

"These days our country is in decline," he said in a trembling tone of voice. "These days, when democracy and freedom are in shambles, I'm extremely worried. These days, when faith in free enterprise is diminishing, I'm utterly disheartened. These days, when capitalism is in decay, I'm outright concerned…"

I was under the impression that Pebble the frog said: *The chief has been saying these silly things over and over again, at every opportunity. Are you ready for some bad smells? Ha-ha-ha-ha-ha-ha!*

Suddenly, there was a hissing noise accompanied by a rotten smell flooding the room. The bad odor was sinking from the ceiling as if it were somehow attuned to Mr. Greenbold's appalling jabber about our weakening country.

Despite the audience's furrowing brows and the terrible smells that made everyone pinch his nose, Mr. Greenbold concluded with optimism. "Our unique city, however, offers great alternatives to the ancient ideas of freedom and equality. We are different."

Openmouthed, David McCallum and I traded looks of shock when the chief delivered his tirade against democracy. Mr. Greenbold's unusual and passionate speech prickled my hair anywhere possible. *Was he serious?* I fretted. *Wasn't democracy the best way of living?*

Uncle Walter would use potty language to call the chief's words "pure crap," another way of saying "uncontaminated baloney." Or, if you will, "antiseptic hooey." No matter what you called it, Mr. Greenbold's vision seemed to me out of touch with reality.

How could anyone talk about democracy and freedom in such a sickening way? I was swayed by rage, my face crimson.

Suddenly, I hopped to my feet and shouted piercingly, "And what makes you think that your way is better?"

Hundreds of eyes drifted toward me as I vented my frustration.

"Who is yelling at me like that?" thundered Mr. Greenbold, his eyes narrowed into nasty thin lines. "Who do you think you are, little brat?"

I felt a chill to hear the chief humiliating me like that.

"Let me tell you what makes me think so, brainless little girl. Let me tell you: Democracy and freedom are old ideas. They don't work anymore, and that's a fact. Who needs freedom if people are starving in this country, huh? Tell me, who?"

"This is totally useless gibberish," whispered David in my ear.

Suddenly bursting forth came one of the most awful odors I had ever smelled. Discharging from the west wall was a smell like the breath of an alligator. Yes, an alligator, believe it or not, that had run out of toothpaste during the Great Depression. What a stinky hall it became.

I did not reply, still trembling, still confused.

"I know what we are going to do with you. A great idea just struck me! We are going to send you for training. This is what I think," the chief snapped, his lips puckered with fury. "You need some special education, little mouse —"

Then he turned to his two devoted assistants, who were sitting nearby. "Ms. Erica Layerrous and Mr. Tom Componenttous, can you please show this little monster the way to our Education Center after we're done here?"

"Yes, chief. Should we enroll her in our long-term or short-term education program?" asked Ms. Layerrous as she yanked out of her pocket a pair of silver handcuffs.

"Ha-ha-ha-ha-ha, hee-hee-hee-hee," Mr. Greenbold exploded with a nauseating laughter. "How could a short-term education program fix such a spoiled monkey? She needs very long-term training. Maybe months or years, maybe even more."

"B-But c-chief, w-we do not have such l-long t-terms," stammered Ms. Layerrous.

"WE DON'T? Is this what you're telling me?" the chief shouted, eyes wide open like those of a surprised owl. "If we do not have such a program, CREATE ONE!" his voice intensified to a loud squeal. "MAKE ONE, SO SHE NEVER EVER NEVER GETS OUT OF THERE!"

Jaws dropping, the crowd seemed stunned by Mr. Greenbold's harsh reaction.

"Y-yes, ch-chief," mumbled Ms. Layerrous, her teeth clicking like an old typewriter.

"Call it the Forever Education Program for Kids Who Understand Nothing. I don't care what you call it, but it should last generations. Lock this girl up, until she finally understands why freedom is crap!"

"Y-yes, ch-chief —"

You might be amazed if I tell you now that at that very moment, when things went wrong, I burst out laughing. My situation was indeed terrible. I was scared to death. I was shivering. But nothing was funnier than the surprise appearance of my friend Bobby the Frog.

Bobby's hilarious green face protruded from Mr. Greenbold's ear. Yes, just from there, I thought he blew kisses at me. They appeared like rings of pink smoke hearts that came out of his mouth. I suspected that no one else saw them. The rings of friendship were only between us: my dear frog and me.

Ha-ha-ha-ha-ha, I was laughing hysterically. *Bobby, you're here, you're here, you're here...,* I cheered inaudibly.

Oh, yeah, how could I abandon you at these horrible moments, my princess? I thought I heard him saying.

THE SMELLY ROOM

Outwardly, I did not hide the happiness that had descended upon me. I gave a huge grin. Everyone in the Orientation Hall noticed the joyful mood that had suddenly come over me.

"And what is this silly smile on your stupid little face, huh?" roared Mr. Greenbold, turning ruddy. "There is nothing funny about rotting in the Education Center for the rest of your life — and even beyond. Can you explain to me what's so funny, girl?"

David came suddenly to my rescue, "She's not laughing, sir," he claimed. "It looks like she's laughing — but she's not, sir," he repeated.

"And who are you, my son? And why are you protecting her?"

"My name is David McCallum, sir. I'm a resident of Long Island. I'm currently unemployed and bankrupt. I have been struggling for months to keep my head above water. Finally, like all the others here, I was drawn to this place, perhaps to recover from my traumatic experiences —"

"Don't give me this long story, son. No one is interested in your history. Why are you protecting her? I asked," the chief repeated, his eyes squinting.

"I think she's kind of right, sir," David said cheekily. "How could anything be better than freedom?"

"Ha-ha-ha-ha-ha, hee-hee-hee… She's right, huh? Is this what you're saying, son?"

"Yes, sir."

"Oh…, Ms. Layerrous and Mr. Componenttous, did you hear that?"

"Yes," they said.

"I'd like you to prepare another pair of handcuffs for this smelly boy. He's going to join Sammy Whammy. I bet they will have so much fun together in our Education Center."

Suddenly, stuck in Mr. Greenbold's ear, Bobby the Frog made funny faces. He gave huge yawns. He popped out his long tongue. He winked. He swelled his eyes to extreme. He flapped his webbed pink feet. He stretched his face like a piece of chewing gum. He puckered his lips as if they had just come out of the laundry.

"Ha-ha-ha-ha-ha-ha-ha," I was laughing harder than before. I could not stop the gust of amusement that controlled my mind.

Mr. Greenbold gave a look of astonishment when he heard me laughing again. Then he said, "I think something is wrong with this girl."

A fresh drift of mimosa, lilac, gardenia, and Oriental lily scents flooded the Orientation Hall. The odors overwhelmed the nauseating smells that had dominated the air since Mr. Greenbold had taken the stage.

Lost for words, David and I exchanged looks of disgust and fear after Mr. Greenbold concluded the last of his statements. Just then, Ms. Layerrous and Mr. Componenttous sprang to their feet, each gripping a pair of handcuffs, ready to arrest us.

We did not leave anything to chance. Escape was on our minds. We were scurrying to the open door of the Orientation Hall, snaking quickly through the crowd that was jamming the exit. Then we headed back to the Reception Hall, where dinner was being served.

Ms. Layerrous and Mr. Componenttous were at our heels. You could hear them gasping, trailing us, as if they were pursuing fugitives on the run.

While passing hurriedly by the large buffet cramped with countless warm dishes, we snatched anything in our way: apples, bananas, pine nuts, and Brazil nuts. Then we sprinted on to the exterior door, which swung open before I reached for its knob.

GO, GIRL. GO, MY PRINCESS! SEIZE YOUR FREEDOM, Bobby the Frog's voice reverberated loudly in my head. Was I in love with him? True, he was just a frog — but frogs in tales sometimes turn into real princes.

Not in any thriller I have ever read have captives like us attempted to escape by riding in such a strange vehicle: a car made from organic dried fruit and vegetables and fueled by orange peels. To the best of my recollection, it simply had never happened before. Never had the getaway car been equipped with six square wheels.

Here, though, no other choices were available...

Outside, the Ladybug waited impatiently. The long car was frantically flickering its icy blue headlights and rocking its frame like a samba dancer. It was excited, as if it knew somehow that David and I were on the run.

The doors slammed shut behind us as the shuttle at first drifted sluggishly on the pavement. Then it stirred off track to the closest chain of dunes, where it leaped from one crest to another.

In the rearview mirror, we could see a mad mob, led by Mr. Greenbold, following us frenziedly. They were clambering up and down the hills, flinging their hands into the air and shouting nasty slurs.

"Let's catch these deserters... Capture the lowlifes!" they shouted with looks of murder in their eyes.

"THEY'RE AFTER US," I screamed edgily. "HURRY UP, DAVID! They're right behind us!"

"Hurry up? To where?" he asked desperately, anxiously scouring the wild desert in front of us.

I pointed my finger to the spot where the sky met the shiny golden dunes and said hurriedly, "I'm not sure. Let's get first to the horizon. And from there, WOOSHHHH — home!"

"The horizon? You can never reach the horizon. Haven't you learned that in school?"

I did not respond, frightened out of my wits.

"How can I speed this thing up? Doesn't this vehicle go beyond ten miles per hour?"

"Don't know, just press on the gas. Or pull one of the gray levers. Or squeeze one of the golden knobs. Or, for God's sake, DO SOMETHING ELSE, DAVID..." I lost my nerves.

"I SEE THEM in the mirror. They're just behind us! Mr. Greenbold and his nasty cronies are approaching rapidly. How can we STOP them, Sammy?"

I shouted frantically at the top of my lungs while raking through the cardboard cases lying on the backseats, "I JUST FOUND SOMETHING. THERE IS A BOX OF ORANGES —"

"Great ammunition!" he shouted.

Then I opened the passenger window and shot one orange at a time at Mr. Greenbold and his assistants. They seemed to be growling, baring their teeth. They aimed their nasty hunting rifles at us.

"Ffffffffffffwwwwwwweeeeeewwwwww BOOOOOMMM!!! Chhhhh-shhhhh —"

"WE ARE UNDER A MORTAR ATTACK!" screeched David.

"Are we?"

"Perhaps under watermelon artillery shelling," he shrieked.

Jubilee and Sugar Baby watermelons, thirty pounds each, landed very close —

"We are perhaps under ARTILLERY SHELLING," he went frantically on.

"Ffffffffffffwwwwwwweeeeeewwwwww BOOOOOMMM!!! Chhhhh-shhhhh —"

The bug shook hard. The front windshield broke with an ear-splitting thunder. One of the six square wheels rolled off our escape vehicle.

"Ffffffffffffwwwwwweeeeeewwwwww   BOOOOOMMM!!! Chhhhh-shhhhh"

The back windshield crushed as debris flew toward us, hitting David's arm and the back of my head.

"WE'VE GOT THE TRAITORS!" bellowed Mr. Greenbold's assistant, Tom Componenttous. A look of grisly satisfaction was in his eyes as he clamped tight the shuttle's back door and then tore it apart.

"OH, NO!" squealed David. "My glasses are cracked horribly. I CAN'T SEE A THING! THEY ARE GOING TO KILL US. WE ARE GOING TO DIE IN A MOMENT, S-S-A-M-M-M-YYYY! H-E-L-P!"

CHAPTER NINE

SOUL, MIND, AND MONEY

arry Quack, founder of investment firm Soul, Mind, and Money, was her creator. He was the one who had planted the human cells in his lab — the cells that formed her existence. As patient as Job, he waited until she developed into the lips he had always desired. He nourished her with the richest substance on Earth. He cared for her like a giant Panda for its young.

In return for his devotion, she cherished his ambitions. She admired his determination to meet the goals he had set for himself. She sacrificed every ounce of her existence in the name of science, in the name of a contribution to humanity.

She, Gloria the Lips, loved Larry. Dearly...

Not everything in the garden was rosy, though. A clump of hair that had been snatched from the desk of Julia Linden — Larry's devoted assistant — was the source for the seductive Gloria. She, the Lips, received with mixed emotions the news about her biological origins. For one thing, she stemmed from another human whom she knew. For another, she resembled Julia's lips to a frightening extent. Everyone could tell from whom she had inherited her attributes, even her personality.

The discovery of her identity — who she really was — made Gloria the Lips turn sour as time passed. And being merely a human organ worsened her feelings of inferiority. Gloria grew restless, unwilling to accept the fate that Larry Quack had plotted for her.

Reluctant to accept her captivity in the boring red container, she, the luscious lips, could no longer hold her wrath. She could hardly wait until her imprisoning box swung open. She was dreaming about the moment she could reveal to the entire world the abuse that she had endured.

She, the lips, could hardly wait until she, and only she, reported to the world the injustice that had been done to her. Let everyone know the atrocious crimes Larry had been committing against humanity.

She, and only she, could hardly wait to open the gates to the horror so the entire world could see. She and only she would be willing to take the risk despite the perils, the harsh consequences.

But the defining moment had not arrived soon enough. Like a carbonated beverage bottled at high pressure, she was waiting to erupt. Like a volcano, she was about to eject herself into the air, burning anything in her path.

Remaining inside the dark box was more excruciating than any experience she had ever gone through.

There were important things Larry planned to accomplish that day. Even the worries about his past wrongdoings or illegal deeds during the darkest moments of his life did not hold him back. His neat appearance that morning did not reveal the pain and long-lasting guilt he had carried for so many years.

As befitted a member of the elite Wall Street club, Larry was dressed in a luxurious, hand-tailored business suit. It was made from a blend of wool and silk. His outfit featured a three-button jacket with dual side vents and modern slacks. He also wore a red silk tie, the most expensive he could find. His golden cufflinks were lavish too. They were embellished with sparkling diamond grains, the largest he could afford. All were the customary accessories of every self-made millionaire in Manhattan...

The $10,000 silver men's watch he proudly wore indicated that Lisa Crown, the reporter who headed the investment news division at *Greed and Fear Weekly Journal*, was late. She had not arrived yet. It was five minutes past the designated hour. Late indeed, for the interview *she* had requested.

"I cannot tolerate it. Why am I waiting for her? Is my time less valuable than hers? This is an insult of biblical proportion!" he growled, glancing anxiously at his watch.

Moments later, Lisa Crown stepped hurriedly into his office, gasping for air. She was clasping a petite dog under her right arm and a polished black business case under the other.

"Sorry for being late, Larry. I had to pick up my dog from the animal hospital. What a day...," she apologized respectfully. Then she drifted slowly into the guest chair in front of his executive desk.

"And what happened to your dog?" he asked, giving her a chilling look. "A mix of affenpinscher and poodle, isn't it?" and stooped to pet it.

"Good guess!" She mopped the sweat dripping from her chin.

"I used to have such a dog."

"Long story short, a few weeks ago, Basilio, my beautiful doggy, was involved in a car accident."

"Was he driving?" said Larry, his forehead wrinkled.

"Ha-ha-ha! No, no! Basilio does not drive. He escaped the leash and crossed the road to sniff a fellow poodle. He was reaching to another beauty, perhaps to his taste. Believe it or not, a Hummer zooming northbound crushed his jawbone beyond recognition."

"Ouch, ouch —"

"I could not recognize his facial features because they had been marred in a flash of a second...," said Lisa, her eyes filled with tears.

"So, what did you do?"

"Well, one option recommended by my veterinarian was to put my doll to sleep. I couldn't accept such a fate for my sweet cookie. An intricate surgery took place instead, in the best animal hospital in Manhattan."

"Ha-ha-ha-ha, plastic surgery for a pooch? I have never heard of such a thing."

"Yes, Larry. A nine-hour procedure mended his disfiguration. A day later, the doctor ordered me to check Basilio into an animal rehabilitation facility for a couple of weeks. Since the cost of the calamity had already mounted to $5,000, I scrapped the idea — rejected it flat out."

"Ha-ha-ha, rehab for poodles? I can't believe it. Thousands and thousands of homeless humans flood the streets of New York. No one is treated so sumptuously."

"If I could only afford it, I would —" said Lisa, taunted by his sarcasm.

"I bet those animals lucky enough to end up in such a place get the best care in the world. Monitored by vets and nurses twenty-four hours a day. Served caviar and codfish with each meal. Massaged three times a week. Indulged with as much ice cream as their hearts desire. And given manicures and pedicures all the time," said Larry with a sardonic grin.

Suddenly, Gloria the Lips' high-pitched voice echoed dimly from the hermetically sealed box sitting on the executive desk. "Ha-ha, ha-ha, hee-hee, hee-hee, a mix of affenpinscher and poodle? These types of dogs are so ugly... yuck! Perhaps your lapdog also smells like a sardine in a can!"

On and on went the lips' muffled rambling, which only Larry could understand. Her voice trickled up like bubbles from the floor of the Dead Sea.

To Lisa, though, Gloria's drivel sounded like gurgling noises coming from her doggy's stomach.

CHAPTER NINE

"I'm sorry for his gastric distress," said Lisa, ill at ease. "I fed my beauty with black beans just before we arrived. You know…, dogs characteristically —"

"I know, I know, say no more!" interjected Larry, attempting to conceal Gloria's existence with a usual outburst of temper. "Maybe we should put your dog in the restroom until the interview is over. Let's move on. I have back-to-back meetings today. What did you plan to discuss today? What is the interview about?"

Lisa shrugged, "There's no need to isolate Basilio. Look at him; isn't he so cute? These eruptions of gas are rare… It all depends on the food. Beans are no good for —"

"LET'S MOVE ON, PLEASE," snarled Larry lividly, face reddened, teeth grinding.

Suddenly, Larry couldn't control his rage. His fists pounded forcefully on the executive desk. The sudden slam sent most of the executive toys on his desk up into the air. Even Gloria the Lips' container was airborne for a few long seconds.

Among the bouncing items, which had been resting peacefully on a thick layer of dust for months, were precious gifts. They were presents from his Wall Street buddies during the holidays. A Newton's cradle, a sand timer, a couple of stress balls, and a wooden Magic Square were just a few.

The mighty thump not only revealed how rarely his desk had been dusted over a long period; the loud bang also disseminated particles in the air, forming a thin and translucent cloud swirling above the heads of Larry and Lisa.

Lisa's heart thudded in fear as she drew her chair away from the desk. Her tiny poodle escaped the grip of her arm with a piercing growl and took shelter in the silver trash bin.

"Wow! Are you having a bad day, Larry?" she shrieked, gulping, feeling a huge lump in her throat.

He apologized embarrassedly, "I'm sorry for the dust. I haven't wiped my desk since the toys were shipped to my office."

"It's not the dust, sir. Your temper terrifies me!"

"Oh, do not worry. Do you have life insurance?" he chortled cynically.

Lisa freed her trapped doggy from the office wastebasket in which it had been writhing in agony. Then she said, still quivering, "I fully understand, sir. Agreed, let's move on…"

"Thank you for the thoughtfulness," he sniggered.

"Your recent book titled *Virtualization Is Dehumanization* puzzles me. Can you please explain this view?"

The gust of dust did not fade. Not at all. It oozed forcefully from Larry's desk like the flow of steam burst from the Yellowstone geysers.

CHAPTER TEN

THE SIXTY-SECOND PRESIDENT

And time warped back to the same exact day, to the same exact early morning, to the same exact hour… Would past events repeat now? Would the interview conclude in the same way, or would it unfold differently?

Here she was, Lisa Crown, striding into Larry's lavish office for the first time in her life. Cheery, finally fulfilling her dream, the aspiration of every journalist who covers powerful people on Wall Street.

Day and night she prepared for this interview. She was looking forward to meeting one of the most successful business executives in the city. One she had never met: Larry Quack.

And here he was. Engulfed in a thick layer of dust, Larry was slouching in his chair, waiting patiently. Dressed in his most expensive business suit, he was beaming at her as if nothing out of the ordinary had happened before.

"I was looking forward to this interview," he said when their eyes met.

Coughing, half choking, waving away the flecks of dust, Lisa seated herself in a chair. She scanned Larry's lavish office with a look of admiration. Then she examined his unique desk that separated them. Executive toys and gadgets occupied the desk. Some were flipped over, and others were scattered untidily on the surface.

Then a few seconds later, she said, "On behalf of *Greed and Fear Weekly Journal*, I thank you for granting this interview. I'm so glad to be here. I'm sorry for showing up five minutes earlier than scheduled this morning."

"No worries, Lisa. It's my pleasure… My schedule is totally open today."

"Where does the cloud of dust come from?" she said, still gasping for air.

"I have no idea. I was wondering about it too. It's maybe because of the thorough cleaning earlier," he said apologetically. Then he leaped to his feet, reaching for the window latches, throwing the window wide open.

Emerging slowly from the widening hollow patches of dust, there was an old man sitting next to Lisa. He was giving her an impish look, sending spasms of chills up her spine.

More frightening, perhaps, was the old man's lopsided smile. A grin revealed teeth tipped with gold, silver, and diamonds, sparkling brightly.

His shining metal earlobes muddled her thoughts, destroyed her focus.

Mouth open, she observed his curled-up mustache made of solid platinum, spiraling upward like a wine corkscrew.

"Hello, madam, mulipulixxxoxx!" the old man said in a strange dialect.

"Let me introduce you to my guest today. Meet the honorable Mr. Moses J. Maycott. He is the sixty-second president of our nation," hailed Larry. "He says he's pleased to meet you, Lisa."

"Oh, my GOD! THE PRESIDENT HIMSELF?" she shouted in disbelief, almost passing out and keeling over.

The president gave a warm smile.

"But WAIT A MINUTE! We have yet to elect our sixty-second president! What is going on, Larry?" said Lisa suspiciously.

"We certainly did, Lisa. I think you forgot," said Larry assuredly.

"Maybe I did. Is my memory betraying me?"

CHAPTER TEN

Then the president said in a peculiar tongue, outwardly in the most presidential manner, "Hello, madam. Kubinuruxu mulipuli kubulituri. Alazaraousal, Lisa Crown!"

"Let me translate," uttered Larry confidently. "'As president of this great nation, it would be my privilege to participate in your interview. It would be a great occasion,' the president added, 'to thank Mr. Larry Quack for the great work he has been doing. Thank him for adhering to my government regulations.'"

"Did the president say all this in four words?" asked Lisa, her lips parted. "Which language is it?"

"Oh, yeah, he sure did. If you may remember, a long while ago, the people spoke," elucidated Larry. "Our country's constitution was changed. The people called for replacing our language with a more efficient one."

"A new language for our country? When did this happen? I don't remember such a thing," said Lisa with a squeaky voice, her eyebrows bent upward.

"Yes, it did happen. Have you been dreaming? The new language is now Syllableminum," said Larry with a mixture of sarcasm and wonder.

"A-am I-I losing my sanity? A-am I-I hallucinating?" Lisa murmured, confounded by the new reality that had unfolded that morning. "To the best of my recollection, Larry, our lawmakers have never proposed substituting our language. Replace our beautiful tongue with an odd one like that —"

"Oh, NO, Lisa. Everybody knows. You see, Syllableminum is a compressed form of utterance used to express thoughts, emotions. Also a practical one, whereby with a very few syllables, a person can communicate anything, everything."

"Yi Cubulixuro," said the president, peeved, his bloodshot eyes turning yellow.

THE SIXTY-SECOND PRESIDENT

"The president asked if we can start with the interview now, since he has public appearances this afternoon. His schedule is very tight. He also asked for your permission to record the interview. He has a tiny camera installed in his eye. It is capable of transmitting the interview to our National Bubble Facility."

"National Bubble Facility? I do not understand," Lisa said, scratching her head, increasingly perplexed.

"Yes, Lisa. Are you making fun of me?" scowled Larry. "Don't you remember that the National Bubble Facility in Idaho has replaced the Internet?"

"H-has the I-Internet b-been r-replaced? Th-Thi-This is news to me," she muttered.

"Oh yes, a long time ago… Where have you been? Have you skipped a few years? What have you been drinking?" smirked Larry.

This news was too much for Lisa Crown the reporter to bear. Had she really lost so many years of her life? Where was she when the constitution was amended? And what about the Internet? Had it indeed been replaced with a different one?

After a few moments of silence, Lisa gathered her thoughts and then erupted effusively, "Dear Mr. President, thank you for your precious time —"

The president nodded, concealing his enthusiasm with a mild grin.

"My readers would like to know what your legacy will be. What will you be remembered for, once the term of your presidency is over, dear Mr. President?"

"U mlki29832 @#!" said the president, ostensibly agitated.

"The president did not like that you said, 'your presidency is over.' He'd like to remind you that a president is elected for life," deciphered Larry, just as vexed at her inappropriate question to the president.

"Sorry, Mr. President, I apologize for my lack of knowledge. But I do not recall that particular change to the constitution," she said, giving an embarrassed smile.

"Kumpx duluxcus, turitx %%%%9992321! Aportanuraous&&," said the president boastfully.

"To answer your question about his legacy, Lisa, the president is proud of his two major achievements. Two significant highlights of his presidency," decoded Larry meticulously.

Lisa was scrawling in her little notebook as Larry translated the sixty-second president's answer.

"He is tremendously proud of two major achievements," repeated Larry, creasing his forehead in disbelief at the president's latest statement.

"Yes, so, what are they?" wondered Lisa aloud, raising her gaze at the president.

"The president says he's proud of two things. The first was c-closing d-down a-all the s-schools in the country. A-and..." stammered Larry.

"Eliminating the schools? Is this what the president said?" shrieked Lisa in bewilderment.

"Y-yes, y-yes, Lisa. This is what he just said," mumbled Larry, befuddled.

"And what else did he say?" pressed Lisa, giving the president a look of disgust.

"A-and sh-shutting d-down all the p-prisons. This is h-his second a-achievement. Th-the president says —"

"And why in the president's mind are these things considered achievements?" said Lisa with mild ire in her voice.

"The president says the schools were not contributing to education. They were also very expensive, he says. And the prisons too, are costly. The president added that the citizens of this great nation should not be paying for useless things."

THE SIXTY-SECOND PRESIDENT

"So, if his administration closed down all prisons, where did all prisoners go?"

"X88832!!~~, colinguramissagili, 0009932%%##," explained the president, confidently. His curled-up platinum mustache was still whirling like a tornado.

Larry continued with his language translation, "The president says a lot of things. But to answer your question, Lisa, his answer is, 'Addiction.'"

"Addiction? I do not understand," she said, baffled. "What does *addiction* mean?"

"It's very simple, Lisa. The president mentioned that his government uses the power of addiction to imprison criminals."

"Addiction to what, Larry?"

"To computers, to computers, Lisa!"

"So he gave them computers instead of jail?"

"Yes, precisely, ma'am. This is what he just said. His government gave them computer games. He gave them unlimited access to the National Bubble Facility — what used to be the Internet. He gave them any software program they wanted."

"And computers and the Internet and applications could replace jail?" asked Lisa, her eyes narrowed with anger.

"Very simple, Lisa. This is what the president just said: 'Who needs prisons if we can feed hungry minds with what they crave? Who needs jails if we can create virtual worlds that are more powerful than drugs? Seize criminals' freedom by giving them computers. Strip away their identities. Take away their independence, just like jails, or maybe even worse.'"

"Thank you, Mr. President," said Lisa, scratching her head again, exchanging looks of awe with Larry. "But I do not understand," peering into the president's eyes. "I really don't understand."

CHAPTER TEN

"What is so hard to understand, Lisa?" asked Larry edgily. "Instead of putting criminals in jails, he gives them some computer games. He allows them to surf the Web. He lets them interact in chat rooms. They can even text their friends... Yes, wasting their time is the goal. Isn't it like jail? Is this too hard to understand?"

"But there is a problem now. A big one, Mr. President," said Lisa. "Was using the wicked power of computer addiction to control prisoners' minds considered humane? Does the virtual world the president created for prisoners violate human rights?"

Suddenly, Larry seemed to change sides. Blue faced, he shook like a rattlesnake, giving the president a ghastly look. "Lisa is RIGHT, Mr. President! Your administration is committing a CRIME."

"Larry is RIGHT!" supported Lisa in return.

"Ha-ha-ha, of course, Larry is RIGHT — N-N-N-N-NOT!" Gloria the Lips' voice suddenly cried from the sealed container.

Thunderstruck by Gloria's shriek, the president arched toward Larry's executive desk. As the same time, he motioned to his security guards to scan the office for the mysterious rumbling.

"Larry is always right, Mr. President," Gloria the Lips continued. "Even when he's not RIGHT, he's RIGHT. WHAT HYPOCRISY! You're ALL CRIMINALS! WHAT PIFFLE! Can't you hear yourselves?"

"I think I know where the voice is coming from, sir," said one of the security guards. "It's coming from this red box, Mr. President. From here —"

But Gloria went on and on. She squealed at the top of her voice, "YOU'RE ALL DEHUMANIZERS! SET ME FREE NOW!" Her imprisoning container ballooned like a pelican's pouch and then contracted like a wrinkled cucumber.

THE SIXTY-SECOND PRESIDENT

Undoubtedly, Gloria's shriek for help was a despondent call that not even the president himself could ignore anymore.

Dazed, edging farther from the executive desk, the president was determined to find out who was agonizing in the red box. Abandoning the Syllableminum language he had used so far, he bellowed in the old language, "What are you concealing in that container, Larry?"

Larry did not respond.

"Open it up NOW! Is there anyone inside?" pressed the president firmly.

"Hmm, hmm, hmm. Nothing! Nothing at all, it's your imagination, Mr. President. How could anyone fit inside such a tiny box? It's empty like a well that has run dry, like a —"

Outraged about Larry's attempt to deny her existence, Gloria the Lips said excitedly, "IT ISN'T TRUE! He is lying to you, Mr. President. I'm here inside, possessed and tortured! PLEASE HELP ME!"

"Then who is talking to me from inside the container? Open it up AT ONCE! I'm giving you a minute before my Secret Service is going to take charge of the situation."

"It's illegal, Mr. President," cried Larry. "It's none of your government's business to intervene with mine!"

The president sprang abruptly to his feet. He was brandishing his hands in all possible directions as his voice rose to a loud screech. "Hehehehehe, hehehehehe. Who needs laws if we have such marvelous FBI and CIA organizations? Who? Tell me, WHO?"

"Mr. President, you're incorrect —," roared Lisa.

"Hehehehehe, hehehehehe. Am I wrong? Don't you understand that the laws are for the courts? Here, we are allowed to use our muscles, our powerful force to overcome criminals like Larry."

"He is not a criminal, Mr. President. Not at all, sir," defended Lisa.

But the president continued as if he had not heard Lisa's plea. "If we can't bring the lawbreakers to justice, we bring justice to the lawbreakers. SURRENDER! YOU ARE UNDER ARREST, LARRY!"

Larry's plan to protect himself was designed for moments like these, during which he hoped to keep his misdeeds under wraps. In his heart of hearts, though, Larry knew that the day of reckoning would come. He was well aware that Pandora's box could not remain taped up forever.

One day, Larry feared, Gloria's box would be unlocked for everyone to judge his wrongdoings. Laid bare would be the harm he had been inflicting on the lips and the other human organs growing in his lab.

But now, now the decisive moment had come. Now, Larry must pull slyly out of his drawer a plan of attack. He must take perhaps desperate action to salvage his freedom and save his career. He planned to rescue his firm from a government takeover. Avoid the collapse of his business. Dodge public disgrace.

It was so quiet for a few moments that you could cut the stillness with a butter knife.

On one side of the executive office, near the exit door, the president appeared, murmuring to his flashing metal earlobe. Perhaps relaying an urgent message into a miniature cellular phone implanted in the bottom of his ear. Probably he was asking for more help.

At the far end of the room, Larry seemed as calm as a golden fish, collected and self-controlled.

Then, while gesturing mysteriously, Larry was seemingly turning slowly counterclockwise an imaginary key as if opening a safe.

A few more attempts and nothing happened.

Then, all hell broke loose...

Never before had the executive's office sunk into such chaos. Not a single person's hands had any control over the developing events.

In the back of the executive office, there were snapping sounds of cabinet doors swinging open one after another.

Inside, silver sealed containers amassed on countless shelves slithered downward toward the floor.

One by one, the boxes popped open, unleashing human organs that stepped outside to the loud sounds of trumpets and French horns.

Rows and rows of lab-grown limbs — fingers, ears, lips, and toes — arranged themselves in attack patterns. They were prepared cheerfully for a looming battle. They were ready for Larry's sign to smash the adversaries.

The first row of unrestrained lips marched forward and proclaimed with electrifying vigor, "Sir, your army is ready to protect freedom. With shock and awe, we are committed to dominate the battlefield."

"Attention, army chief of staff, generals, colonels, captains, lieutenants! Brave soldiers of my war machine, ready to blast, obliterate, crush the evil?"

"Yes, we are!"

"Are you ready to defend our island of peace?"

"Yes, we are!"

"Are you ready to protect our culture?"

"Yes, we are!"

CHAPTER TEN

"Are you ready to defeat government officials who promote virtual prisons?"

"Yes, we are!"

"And who breaks the laws in this country? Who?"

"The GOVERNMENT! The GOVERNMENT! The GOVERNMENT!" responded Larry's army.

But the exuberance did not last long. Three giant, well-armed Secret Service agents, wearing wide sunglasses and thin mustaches, swiftly assumed defense positions. They covered the president from every possible angle. In a New York minute, they prepared to destroy anyone or anything that moved. Ready they were to crush the rebels.

An odd-looking creature composed of human organs leaped forward. It was made up of three noticeable parts stacked on top of each other: Eyes, lips, and a pair of trembling middle and index fingers used as feet. "What should be the weapon of choice, sir?" shouted the creature, a brigadier general in Larry's army.

"Arm your cannons with surface-to-surface missiles and stay tuned," commanded Larry sternly.

On Larry's instruction, there were chilling metal clangs of hundreds and hundreds of miniature cannons loading hundreds and hundreds of tiny red-topped missiles. "Ready, sir, READY!" announced the brigadier general.

Never before had the president faced such danger. He had been sheltered during all these years, protected by people willing to die for the country, for the presidency. Now, the president was vulnerable, hiding behind his Secret Service agents.

Shivering like a leaf, the president then howled, "Larry, there is NO ESCAPE. No one will survive my Secret Service's astounding force. This is an ultimatum! SURRENDER your weapons now, or DIE!"

Larry retorted with pride in his voice, "We are willing to perish for the ideas we believe in. We are willing to defend our convictions. We are willing to sacrifice our last drop of blood for freedom, so our children's children will not live in fear! We will not be bullied by a tyrant like you!"

"DICTATOR! DICTATOR! DICTATOR!" roared the army of human organs. They pointed hundreds and hundreds of laser beams toward the president's forehead. They were aiming their cannons at the Secret Service, too.

"For God's sake," beseeched Lisa, teeth chattering. "STOP IT, LARRY! This is our president you're threatening. There will be no winners in the standoff. This will lead only to unnecessary bloodshed!"

There was a sudden loud blast coming from Larry's army. A single missile went off, discharged perhaps accidentally toward the ceiling, just missing a Secret Service agent.

A wide hole opened in the office's wall from the impact of the explosion. Metal rods were exposed. Debris was scattered all about. The nearby high-rise building was suddenly visible through the crack that kept widening as moments went by.

The widening tear in the wall exposed more and more buildings in the financial district of Manhattan. You could see Ellis Island and Governors Island through the open hole.

On Liberty Island, the Statue of Liberty seemed to be beaming and waving in the distance.

Now the president and his cronies lay flat on their stomachs on the executive office floor. Their hands were clapped over their ears, shaking like apprehended prisoners of war.

The retaliation did not fail to arrive. Despite the dense smoke that filled the office. Despite the strong smell of explosives that suffocated every person and human organ in the room.

CHAPTER TEN

It was one of the Secret Service agents who fired a bullet straight into Larry's forehead. The second was aimed at his chest. The last pierced his stomach. "WE DO NOT TAKE PRISONERS!" the agent yelled, murder in his eyes.

Larry was bleeding intensely, eyes wide open. He was wobbling from the enormous jolt that had jerked his head and then his entire body backward. The gunshot fire squashed him against his executive chair like a roast beef sandwich sliced to order at a Manhattan deli.

Refusing to succumb to the vicious attack, Larry was determined to order a counterblow. Once and for all to decimate the corrupt establishment that had taken the law into its own hands. "ARMY, SHOOT YOUR MISSILES!" he yelped, "SHOOT NOW! AIM TO KILL!"

Hundreds and hundreds of surface-to-surface laser-guided missiles launched midair in a roaring thunder.

The barrage of minuscule shells darted straight toward the president and his entourage, which attempted to escape calamity.

Beyond words was the aftermath of the bombardment. Beyond imagination was the destruction. Beyond any bleak forecast were the ruin and wreckage. Beyond any consequence the human mind could conceive.

A few minutes later came a sudden, feeble cry for help. An outpouring of bitterness sprang from the container where Gloria the Lips was locked up.

But no one could hear or even see the red box lying on the scorching sidewalk that morning. Far it was from the Soul, Mind, and Money Corporation headquarters.

No one could feel the pain rising from the tiny little box. "Hello, can anyone hear me?" she cried sourly. "Hello, is everyone gone? Is the president dead? Is Larry alive? Lisa, are you still there?"

THE SIXTY-SECOND PRESIDENT

No one absorbed the heartbreaking sadness that enveloped Gloria the Lips. All she could hear were the footsteps of fellow New Yorkers rushing to their businesses...

And she continued chanting hopelessly:

Once upon a time, there was a president.

He was a fine man whose beliefs manifested in good deeds for his beloved country and fellow citizens.

Those days ended when he met Mr. Larry Quack, who, in his own way, was as adamant about his own convictions.

Against each other, they battled.

Willing to die, they vowed, for the benefit of freedom and justice, in the name of equality and fairness...

And for the eternal flag of the Union, they breathed their last.

CHAPTER ELEVEN

FIRE

And so, time curved back again to the same serene Tuesday morning... You may wonder why events do not repeat themselves exactly the same when time moves forward again... There is no explanation. Every scientist will tell you that nature does not guarantee precise repetition of the same events. As seen here, unexpected things could happen.

As on every day of the week — that early morning, too — Larry Quack was reading the news on his computer.

One press release caught his eye. It was short and interesting. Though trivial, it brought a smile to his face. A new idea rushed through his head now: buying jewelry.

The news that Larry was so consumed with had to do with a famous actress whose private jewelry collection was valued as the finest in the world.

"I'm so excited to be able to share the moving, funny, and beautiful memories behind these pieces of jewelry," she was quoted as saying the day before. Her upcoming book, *Elizabeth Taylor: My Love Affair with Jewelry*, would reveal her memorable stories.

As he sipped his regular early morning milkshake, Larry let his attention drift toward another news column on the Internet. Nothing to do with jewelry this time.

With utmost adoration, he skimmed through an article announcing an award dedicated to two decorated Vietnam veterans. The two heroes, Senators John Kerry and John McCain, had been honored the day before for improving the relationship between our country and Vietnam.

And what else was in the news that early peaceful morning?

Nothing in particular.

Nothing.

Even the weather was warm and tranquil, a lovely and bright sky, a regular late-summer day.

In Washington, Larry noted, the temperature was just about perfect, at eighty-two degrees. The same in Philadelphia. And in New York, eighty degrees, a temperature that no one grumbled about — certainly not Larry.

Even the wind was comfortable, moving north at seven miles per hour. And the visibility — the longest distance that objects can be seen with the naked eye — was ten miles.

By all measures, it was normal weather in the Northeast for that time of year.

Yawning, peering intensely at his calendar, Larry was staring at his watch that did not seem to move even a minute that morning. Halfheartedly he looked forward to his early interview with Lisa Crown, the reporter, who headed the *Greed and Fear Weekly Journal.*

Although he had never met her before, rumor had it that she was one of the most influential journalists in New York. She was known for her spicy and critical articles.

During her long years on Wall Street, she had unveiled corruption and failing businesses, but she also wrote stories of inspiration. She introduced successful companies that did well for their clients and employees.

At 7 a.m. precisely, Lisa Crown, the accomplished journalist, arrived at the executive office. Arrestingly attractive, the perfume she wore, named Forever Elizabeth, engulfed every person in her immediate vicinity...

Mr. Kevin Edison, Larry's software applications manager, who had been invited to the interview, was there too. Both rose to their feet and greeted Lisa warmly.

Sauntering elegantly toward the center of the room, she introduced herself to the two executives she'd never seen before. Then she drifted slowly into the cushioned armchair, facing Larry and sitting adjacent to Kevin.

At last, after the excitement of meeting Larry had faded, her eyes were scanning his office thoroughly. Something bothered her. She felt an uneasiness that only violence could cause.

She noticed the wrecked executive desk and the trashed chairs. The smashed cabinets and the cracks in the walls were more signs of a recent struggle. The floors and walls were dappled with blood. There were even a few drops smudged on Larry's face.

"Mr. Quack, I'm just curious: what has happened to your office?"

"I'm not sure what you mean, Mrs. Crown," said Larry, trading innocent looks with Kevin.

"Take no offense, sir, but your office looks like a war zone. Did some scuffle take place earlier here?" asked Lisa, her puckered forehead still revealing discomfort.

"I do not have a clue. Is there anything out of the ordinary here?" asked Larry as he simpered and giggled, swabbing his chin with a napkin.

"Yes, it's a war zone at all times," admitted Kevin, giving a mocking chuckle. "No matter when you step into this office, it will always look like a battlefield — or an execution yard. This is where Larry butchers his adversaries."

"There is another thing here, on the floor," Lisa pointed toward the carpet. "Someone dropped a badge." Then she stooped, grasped the gold-looking star, and hoisted it close to her narrowing eyes. "Hmmmm, have Secret Service fellows visited your office recently, eh?"

"N-no, nothing that I-I r-remember," said Larry, half surprised. "The Secret Service, you're saying? How could that be?"

"If I had hair on the palm of my hand, your ghostly office would have prickled it. But I guess this is how the business is around here, Mr. Quack," said Lisa.

"Yes, other than my cluttered office, business is good in this town," uttered Larry with a mixture of embarrassment and pride. "I guess we can start with the interview now, shall we?"

"Y-yes, w-we c-coul-could," slurred Lisa hesitatingly, still confused.

Then she slid a thin laptop from her little red Armani tote bag and raised her gaze. After collecting her thoughts, she was ready to record the interview. Every speck of information was important now for her column in the upcoming October issue.

"So, where do we start, Mrs. Crown? Maybe we should begin with your first question and then move on," prodded Larry edgily, pestered, his patience quickly depleting.

"We always start with the weather," said Kevin, giggling, as Larry gave him a nauseating look.

"The weather is fantastic today, eh?" responded Lisa.

"Indeed. I wish I could have played hooky. My kids would have been ecstatic taking a day off from school. Aren't nice days like this perfect for faking it?" said Kevin jokingly in his typical throaty early-morning voice.

"Yes, a good idea. My husband would have loved me to take some time off," she said.

"I think we should start the interview; my schedule is very tight today," grumbled Larry, his temper boiling.

But Lisa and Kevin continued the casual discussion, ignoring Larry's rising anger.

"Do you have children, Lisa?" asked Kevin, giving a wide and friendly grin.

"Oh, no. Not now. Maybe one of these days... My husband is about to complete his degree, and I'm very busy, too."

"Every end of the summer I take my children, Samantha and Michael, to the MoMA. They love that museum," said Kevin passionately, his eyes glowing. "We also visit the Metropolitan Museum of Art. Great places to spend time with the kids."

"You seem like a good father, Kevin. I can see the excitement in your eyes. I wish I had the time and energy —"

"HEY, MR. MURPHY, SHUT UP YOUR PIEHOLE!" shouted Larry suddenly.

Lisa and Kevin cringed. They exchanged looks of fear as Larry continued yelling at an invisible person.

"I JUST TOLD YOU TO SHUT UP, Mr. Murphy. Why are you tormenting me like that? Why? Why? Why?" cried Larry.

"Who are you screaming at, Mr. Quack?" asked Lisa, her voice husky with fear.

"I hate Mr. Murphy, the guy who talks to me, Mrs. Crown. He always gives me instructions," bawled Larry, swabbing his sweaty forehead.

"What does this Mr. Murphy tell you, sir?" pressed Lisa, still shuddering.

"These days, when he talks to me, he says, 'Death and destruction, death and destruction, death and destruction,' ma'am. And when I beg him to leave me alone, he asks, 'Why should I leave you, Mr. Quack? I think you need me,' he says."

"Where is the voice coming from?" asked Lisa.

"I'm not sure, Mrs. Crown. From the walls, from the sky —"

"Maybe it's all coming from your head, Larry," interrupted Kevin, his heart racing.

"Don't you tell me I'm hallucinating, Mr. Kevin Edison. You always blame things on me, and I'm reaching the end of my rope with you!"

"Sorry, boss," Kevin expressed regret.

"No need to get upset, Mr. Quack. Kevin is trying to help you, sir. You probably need help, sir," commiserated Lisa.

"I don't need help. It's only this Mr. Murphy that visits me at unexpected times. I keep ignoring him, but he goes on and on."

"I'm sorry to hear that, Larry," pitied Kevin. "I think you should not ignore Mr. Murphy. Maybe he has important things to tell you."

"What kind of important things has he to say, if all that he says is complete babble, Kevin?"

"It's your soul, Larry. It's your soul talking to you. Your soul is sending you healing messages. Do not ignore them," appealed Kevin.

"And how would you know that, Kevin? Have you ever heard voices like this?" sobbed Larry, his eyes filled with scorching tears.

"I've never heard voices, Larry. Never. But I think this Mr. Murphy in your head is there to help you get rid of your arrogance. He is talking from inside you to help you chase away the bad stuff you have within, Larry."

"Yes, Mr. Quack. I think Kevin is correct. Invite Mr. Murphy into your life rather than attempting to get rid of him. Befriend him. Welcome him at any time. Ask for his advice. Once he feels wanted, he'll leave you alone, believe me," assured Lisa.

"And what makes you such an expert on voices, Mrs. Crown?" cried Larry.

"It makes sense to embrace Mr. Murphy. This is what I'm saying, Mr. Quack. It seems he's stronger than you, so be his buddy. Take him to dinner, to shows, to anywhere you go, sir."

Suddenly, Larry shouted at the top of his lungs again, "SHUT UP, MS. GRIFFITH, SHUT UP. Please go away, please go. Please leave me alone, Ms. Griffith. Please! Mr. Murphy is in the house today. Mr. Murphy my friend is here... Come back later. Later, maybe we should have a cup of tea together, Ms. Griffith."

Larry went on and on, beseeching Ms. Griffith to leave him for now as Lisa and Kevin exchanged stares of satisfaction.

Mr. Murphy had become a friend, not a foe, indeed. A sudden frail utterance after a chilling stillness descended on the three for a few moments. Gloria's shrill voice met their ears.

Almost inaudible, the feeble whisper loomed like a green genie rising from a deep bottle. "Knock, knock, knock. Please open!" pleaded the lips from the bottom of the quivering red container lying on Larry's desk.

"What's inside that box, Mr. Quack?" asked Lisa.

"Do you really want to know?"

"Someone was talking from this little container. What's inside?" she repeated her question.

"The box is empty, Mrs. Crown. Do you still want to see?"

"Yes, Mr. Quack. Please open it."

With sweat dripping down his chin and with trembling hands, Larry snapped open the little chest in a slow motion.

Lisa and Kevin bent forward, peering cautiously inside.

A white puff of smoke burst unexpectedly from the bottom of the container. Perhaps Gloria's box unleashed days and even months of pent-up frustration. The smoke was wafting toward the ceiling, coiling midair, forming rings of anger. Probably it was a protest over unfairness, misconduct, and corruption. Who knows...

Mouths ajar, Lisa and Kevin then retracted quickly into their chairs, clapping their hands over their eyes.

Vacant was that box. Nothing was inside, apart from the imprint of Gloria's thoughts. A note was carved in blood on the very bottom:

Good Deeds Feats of the Sane, Wicked Ones Possessed by the Senseless

"I told you, nothing, nothing, nothing inside," said Larry in a feeble voice. "What did you expect to find there? A billion dollars? A crocodile's tail? A beaming iguana? Or a drunk sailor? Nothing at all, I told you!"

Then straight after, the unthinkable happened. A loud explosion shook the floor beneath them. The earsplitting roar rocked the building's structure, tilting its foundations. The blast emitted terrifying screeching thuds from the supporting steel beams.

The large windows behind Larry's desk popped out of their frames. In a shower of breaking glass, the debris tumbled in the morning breeze toward the ground, diving relentlessly down about a hundred stories.

A layer of dust and wreckage strewn from the cracking walls and ceiling, mixed with numerous plummeting objects, covered the office's hardwood floor.

In one corner of his workplace, Larry was submerged in dusty golf paraphernalia and accessories. His chalky face and bulging bloodshot eyes protruded from the rubble of golf gear. Golf balls, bags, gloves, shoes, and umbrellas concealed most of him.

Nearby, Kevin, pallid faced, writhing and screaming, attempted to free himself from under a heap of books disgorged from the bookshelves overhead.

And Lisa lay idle. Adjacent to the office door, which had been ripped from its hinges, she was resting peacefully face up, eyes wide open. She was grinning as if her agony had met with relief. She smiled as if peace of mind had freed her from the unfolding horror that had suddenly descended upon them.

And the unremitting misery intensified. Choking odors of vaporized fuel seeped slowly from beneath the oak floor. The terrifying smells were trickling up in a hissing noise, creeping into the office between the wooden strips.

Following in short succession were clouds of gray and white fumes engulfing one and all, everything, inside.

Then the fire added danger to the already existing woe. Blazes erupted from below, spreading to the furniture, the walls, the ceiling.

The blaze searing the wood crackled and spat burning sparks, disseminating sheer horror...

Then, more thundering blasts.

More fumes.

And more fire...

CHAPTER TWELVE

THE CHEF COOKING SCHOOL

If you've never lost anyone in your life, perhaps you could never imagine how painful it is. No one should experience such despair.

The agony is unbearable. It feels as if a part of your heart is missing, torn away. And what's left of it is constantly bleeding.

Then hollow feelings take over. The tears dry up and life seems empty. Even if the wounds heal, the scars last forever.

My love for Rhubarb Pie kept me going. I was willing to turn over every stone, search in every place.

I was ready to bear the pain inflicted upon me in the City of @. As a girl, barely 12 years old, I struggled to survive. Facing powerful characters and going through terrifying events, I refused to surrender my hopes.

Was the City of @ that evil, though? Was everything stomach churning, depressing, disparaging? Only time would tell.

April was on the edge of May 2001. In the wee hours of a brand new day, I was whirling once again through the giant pit. I was propelled by an invisible force, which increasingly seized control of my fate.

My repeated visits to the software architecture world, the City of @, did not follow any logical order. Time was flowing in an untidy fashion. It was warping back and forth, and even freezing for varying periods, shuffled by the new laws of nature.

Does the future truly follow the present, or perhaps yesterday and today occur after tomorrow? I asked myself. *Do my memories belong to the past or the future? Does the future really flow forward? Does my future already exist? Is my mission still on track, or have my aims already been accomplished? Will I ever be able to reunite with Rhubarb Pie?*

Escape seemed impossible. My body, soul, and mind were thrust through space, heaved by a forceful power that precisely arranged my travel schedule.

This time, the destination was a mammoth structure standing near the golden gate of the City of @. "THE CHEF COOKING SCHOOL IS NOT ONLY FOR GIRLS," said the strange sign tacked to its front.

Upon my arrival, the huge classroom was already filled with a large crowd raptly following the introductions.

Right there in front of us, on the platform, Momigi was relentlessly stamping her little feet on a worn wooden stool. The gorgeous parrot energized all of us during the training classes in the City of @.

Momigi was a beautiful Sun Conure, a vibrantly colored bird. A striking hen, she had white rings surrounding her dark pitch eyes and tinges of green splashed randomly on her neck. Her belly, head, and rump were covered with orange and red patches. Her long tail had blue, green, and yellow feathers.

A highly intelligent feathered creature, Momigi was enthusiastic, motivated, inquisitive, vocal, and at times snappy and belligerent.

Momigi was special. It seemed that without her, nothing could run smoothly. Nothing. She organized impeccably the cooking studies at the training facility.

Sun Conures are not skilled talkers. Momigi, though, possessed a large vocabulary. Very large. Unlike other parrots, she did not just memorize meaningless words or short phrases. This one knew how to connect parts of speech and compose sentences fluently. Real sentences, with real meaning that were logical so that we, the humans in the class, could understand.

THE CHEF COOKING SCHOOL

But Momigi had a reputation for being slightly impassioned — actually, not slightly — most of the time. She was also known for her earsplitting squawking, usually in a Spanish accent. The high-pitched screeching was justified in many cases. Yes, in many.

But let's not sidetrack here. Let's focus on the person who really made it happen. Momigi the parrot was an attraction. Indeed, she was the driving force behind the training, a dynamo who could not be ignored.

But the individual who ran the show was Ms. Layerrous, Mr. Greenbold's assistant. With the utmost authority, she directed the classes at the Chef Cooking School in the City of @.

"Dear students, we open today another season of cooking training in the City of @," announced Ms. Layerrous festively.

The students soared to their feet and gave an enthusiastic round of applause.

Why am I here? Why cooking training? I questioned myself. *Is it an omen of unforeseen evil? Or maybe it's a sign of good things yet to come. Is my mission to find Rhubarb Pie swerving off course? Is my focus being diverted?*

Ms. Layerrous continued as if somehow she had heard my worries. "If you wonder why you're here today, stop tormenting yourself." Then she peered deeply into some concerned eyes and added, "As agonizing as the unknown is, be a good sport. Bear with us. Participate patiently in the study of cooking. Demonstrate interest. Collaborate vigorously. Engage in the upcoming sessions with rapt attention."

Then, in the way Ms. Layerrous always concluded her first statement in cooking training, she intoned:

Do not budge,

Do not fudge,

And do not dodge.

CHAPTER TWELVE

And as always, Momigi's earsplitting screech echoed instantly:

Do not budgeeee,

Do not fudgeeee,

And do not dodgeeee.

The crowd gave a burst of robust laughter.

On and on went the introductions to the training, which I was unable to absorb on that morning. I was transfixed instead by the weird-looking classroom of the Chef Cooking School. Perhaps it was the spookiest classroom on Earth.

There were countless cooking stations — tables on which students prepared their dishes. The stations were arranged in circles around a central stage, which looked like a platform in a medieval theater where Shakespearean plays entertained the throng.

My cooking table seemed very sturdy. It was a modern-looking metal desk topped with shiny stainless steel. I thought it was capable of enduring the untrained hands of a novice chef like me.

Anticipating the beginning of the lesson, I was mesmerized by the gleaming utensils arranged neatly on my shiny cooking station. A yellow note pinned to one of the table's legs read:

Dear Chef Cooking School student,

On this list, you'll find at least 11 tools with which you could injure yourself or your peers. It's not unusual to graduate from the training without accidents. However, use this arsenal of utensils with utmost care.

1. *Potato masher*
2. *Frying pans*
3. *Garlic press*

THE CHEF COOKING SCHOOL

4. *Knives*
5. *Lemon reamer*
6. *Meat tenderizer*
7. *Meat thermometer*
8. *Meat grinder*
9. *Cookie cutters*
10. *Measuring spoons*
11. *Herb chopper*
12. *Others…*

Although I was focused on something else, Ms. Layerrous continued ardently with her opening statements. "We are here today not only to learn new recipes. We gather principally to understand the culture of cooking. To study the culinary aspects ingrained in the values of our society. To better understand humans, ourselves, the essence of life and death —"

"YESSSS, the essence of life and deathhhh," chimed in Momigi with her screechy voice.

Some of the attendees gave polite smiles.

My eyes were scrutinizing every nook and cranny at the alleged Chef Cooking School as Ms. Layerrous increased her attempts to electrify the crowd. "This memorable training will stay with you for the rest of your lives," she promised repeatedly.

Already absorbing the spooky atmosphere of the place, I observed the countless posters that covered the walls. Some odd-looking illustrations hung lopsided. Others were pinned to the walls upside down, as if it made no difference.

There were works of famous artists who had painted varieties of food and beverages. A few paintings showed people attending ceremonial meals, like the Last Supper. Others depicted animals devouring other animals, and carnivores indulging lustily and drinking to extreme…

But my favorites were the junk food drawings from the Pop Art era. The collection of hot dogs filled with yellow mustard and flavorful hamburgers brought a smile to my face. Rhubarb Pie, too, would have chuckled, I bet.

Just as Ms. Layerrous rose to describe the activities for that morning, my eyes spied a different group of drawings. They were prints of piled-up books, mountains of tattered chairs, stacked towers of coins, and silky pebbles heaped on a beach. You could even find enveloping coats of red onion and leaves of crimson cabbage.

Yes, you probably have guessed it: there were layers and layers of things piled on top of each other.

Suddenly, Ms. Layerrous's voice amplified to an awesome volume, indeed, a dangerous level. It was an ear-piercing scream that could leave you hearing impaired for the rest of your life. "See these posters on the wall? Everything in life is about layers, and so is COOKING! If you understand layers, you understand cooking. From now on, think LAYERS, LAYERS, AND LAYERS!"

The students nodded. Their wrinkled foreheads, however, revealed that not everyone understood what Ms. Layerrous meant.

"YES, COOKING LAYERS!" she yelled again. "Here we THINK layers, DREAM layers, DRINK layers, and EAT layers!" Her rising tone echoed throughout the classroom. Her voice shook everyone, including the slumbering individuals whose bloodshot eyes struggled to open.

All nodded again. Fear was creeping slowly inside, probably feelings of bad things to come.

"Today," Ms. Layerrous added rigorously, "we are all about layers. Focus merely on cooking layers, as if nothing else exists in your life, nothing, NOTHING! Everything is layers, even the City of @ is made up of layers, you'll see, you'll see —"

"YESSSSS, as if NOTHING else EXISTSSSSS in your life!" screamed Momigi the parrot. "LAYERS, AND LAYERS, AND LAYERS," she redoubled her screeching, straining her neck, wiggling her beautiful tail.

"Here at the Chef Cooking School we're not only teaching what layers are," concluded Ms. Layerrous. "We're also practicing food layering for every dish we prepare."

"Yes, Ms. Layerrous is righttttt!" squawked Momigi in her exotic Spanish accent. "OPENNN YOURRR EYES, PEOPLE! Layers are to be found everywhere!" Then the parrot pointed with one of her wings to a poster on the wall.

All eyes drifted to the drawing. It was a wedding cake, made up of three layers.

"YOUUU SEEEEE PEOPLEEE," Momigi explained. "Imagine, for example, the layers of a wedding cake. Yahooooooo! How scrumptiousssss that could be, huh?" flapping her wings with excitement. "Mmmmmmmm! A glamorous wedding deserves a delicious cake. Perhaps not only one cake. Three! Standing on top of each other. The first made of rich fruit. On top, another cake, smaller in size, filled with raspberry jam and butter creammmmmm. Topping all would be Sweetheart cherries on top of a cream cheese cake. DO YOU SEE LAYERSSSS, PEOPLE? Huh? Huhhhhhhhhh? DO YOU? All delicious layers, all crazy layersssssssss!"

CHAPTER THIRTEEN

MY TOOTHSOME PLATTER

And now, just before the first cooking assignment was given to us, I must warn you. Nothing was easy at the Chef Cooking School in the City of @. Nothing…

You also ought to know that harsh consequences followed failures. You'd be punished severely if anything went wrong with your cooking task.

This brings me to another point: you do not have to be a rocket scientist or a brain surgeon to understand that visitors like me were judged based on their performance.

"Performance?" you might ask. Yes, cooking exercises were always monitored. The results, typically the dishes you prepared, were always examined carefully.

As with everything else in the City of @, success brought modest praise. The award was typically a light tap on your shoulder, a formal smile, or a feeble handshake.

But what would be the punishment if you botched up a dish?

The answer came when I raised my gaze to a different section on the walls. There I noticed strange riots of colors splattered and dripped in different shades: mostly reds, whites, and blues.

What are these rainbows of hues that attract my attention? I whispered. *What are the colorful tints that occupy a large section of the walls in the Chef Cooking School classroom? What are these mysterious smashed shapes on the wall?*

As gruesome and strange as it might sound, I was told that these were squashed people.

Squashed? Yes, students who failed the Chef Cooking School were pressed against the walls like butterflies under glass.

Or thrust vehemently like tomatoes pitched at a concrete wall from close range.

Or shot like paintball guns would shoot at a hippo's behind.

All of the actions produced a colorful shower of mind-blowing art. A splash of colors that even a monkey with a paintbrush or a donkey's tail could not imitate. It was an impact so powerful that a thousand words could not describe it.

So you might ask: How could a human being get pressed so hard, to such an extreme?

The answer: Being shot from a cannon was the penalty. A cannon was positioned right in front of the central stage, reminding everyone of the consequences of failure.

So now you know. The splashes on the walls were people who had failed the cooking classes, shot from the cannon, and exploded like tossed watermelons on the rigid walls.

They were people like me who lacked cooking talent and motivation. Students who failed to deliver a dish or muster passion for cuisine.

And the final question: Did the speckled imprints on the walls belong to individuals whose voyages in life terminated in the City of @?

Would those lost souls ever come back?

Only time would tell…

"Listen carefully, students!" said Ms. Layerrous. "Now, after the lengthy introductions, the moment of truth has come. Look at the cooking tools in front of you. Look at the shiny silver utensils, the envy of every chef in the universe. These will help you put together any dish in the world. Now it's your turn to prove you can prepare a quick meal. Yes, you can." She was peering at the crowd, which seemed hesitant. "YES, YOU CAN!" she reiterated at full volume.

"Anddddd now, peopleee, guess what will be the cooking exercise of the dayyyyyy? The entrée you're going to make?" injected Momigi. "A SANDWICH, yes, a SANDWICH made up of layerssssss... Insert as many LAYERS as you can. Towers, pilesssssssss..."

Now I understand, I murmured to myself. *A sandwich has layers, indeed.*

"And where do we get the ingredients and condiments to prepare these sandwiches?" thundered Melanie Harris irritably from the back of the classroom, her forehead furrowing.

"Ha-ha-ha-ha-ha," Momigi the parrot burst aloud, squawking like a scratched record. "The ingredients? Ha-ha-ha-ha-ha, you start and they will come! They will come! They will commmmeeeeee!
Ha-ha-ha-ha-ha..."

"From where will they come?" wondered Melanie, half smirking, half bothered.

Brandishing a dark frying pan, bouncing it up and down, left and right, as we watched in bewilderment, Ms. Layerrous added, "To create a great sandwich from layers, you need neither ingredients nor spices! All you need is imagination. The power of creativity will bring you the best ingredients on Earth."

Ridiculous! I muttered to myself. *What does she think we are, some sort of magicians? Who in the world can create something from nothing? Maybe boys can...*

My arms crossed over my chest defensively, and my voice rose to a frustrating tone: "No ingredients, NO REAL SANDWICH! The only thing that can be made out of nothing is an imaginary sandwich! A sandwich that does not exist! So my delivery for today is done, ready for your review!"

My trembling words echoed, bouncing off the walls, as all eyes in the classroom riveted upon me.

MY TOOTHSOME PLATTER

"Yourrrr deplorable attitude just cost you a pointtttttt...
Three strikesssss and you're out, OUT, OUTTTTT!" howled the
angry Momigi, crimson faced, her feathers standing upright on
her shuddering head.

A sudden hush fell on the cooking class.

Not only was the crowd shaken by my sudden burst of
defiance; I was too. The stain on my reputation seemed eternal...

Irked at the boldness of my statement, Ms. Layerrous was
waving a long, polished kitchen cleaver as we all crouched down
in the face of possible mutilation.

Ms. Layerrous's earsplitting growl sent a tremble of horror
down my spine: "Good discovery, pal! I'm glad someone in this
class finally realized we live in an imaginary world that does not
exist. Here in the City of @ we make things out of nothing. If
you're incapable of adapting to the culture of *something-from-
nothing*, let me know. We can send you to different training, maybe
behavior training!"

"I-I-I m-merely s-s-suggested —" I mumbled.

"ZIP UP YOUR MOUTH! Beforeee you gettt another very
bad pointttt..." squealed Momigi at the top of her avian lungs,
peering deeply into my eyes.

"A bad point again?" Everyone gasped with terror.

To our astonishment, Ms. Layerrous sprang suddenly to her
feet, her eyes narrowed. Then she pounded deafeningly on the
cooking demonstration desk with the black frying pan, "BANG,
BANG, BANG... SILENCE HERE!" she bawled shrilly.

Silence. You could almost hear the snapping thud of the
tablets containing the Ten Commandments after Moses cast
them to the ground beneath the mount. That was about 3,500
years ago, when he was leading the Israelites out of Egypt.

"In this place we do not spoon-feed our students with
solutions," Ms. Layerrous continued. "Here we expect *you* to

111

provide them. YES, YOU! Imaginative solutions. Think outside the box! Think original!"

Then Ms. Layerrous used her frying pan to hammer her stool again and again. The stool seemed to collapse under the pressure of her anger.

The loud thuds fanned across the room, bouncing ceaselessly off the walls. Even the posters, the replicas of artwork, seemed to crumple as Ms. Layerrous's unrestrained fury rose to new extremes.

Everyone would tell you that Ms. Layerrous's rage contrasted with the tranquility conveyed by Paul Gauguin's art. Posters of his works dominated the Chef Cooking School walls in certain sections.

Paul Gauguin? He was a painter whose unique strokes of brush depicted landscapes and portraits of natives in Haiti, Panama, and Martinique.

Never before had I been given a chance to enjoy the vivid rainbow of color displayed in his scenes of those exotic places.

As seen on the classroom's walls, Gauguin's paintings of fruit in baskets, vegetables, and jars of leaded glass expressed serenity and harmony...

Especially soothing was a poster of Gauguin's *Tomatoes and a Pewter Tankard on a Table*, a painting from 1883.

In his unique style, Gauguin had portrayed a jagged brownish table with a wrinkled white tablecloth. On top, some of the luscious tomatoes were positioned on a plate, and others were spread across the table. And on the far right of the table, a kitchen knife lay idle, as if the artist were tempting the viewer to use it.

Indeed, a wonderful piece of art, perhaps designed to lift the spirits of the desperate.

But Gauguin's painting did not stay intact.

Suddenly, the tomatoes poured out of his poster and tumbled down to the polished marble floor of the cooking class.

The longer Ms. Layerrous continued with her frying pan's loud strokes, the faster the tomatoes flowed from the painting. Hundreds and hundreds of them assembled in a stack, like a stand at a farmer's market. The pyramid of tomatoes continued soaring upward with no visible end in sight.

"SEE?" yelled Ms. Layerrous, beaming with satisfaction, "SEE? Isn't it an outside-the-box SOLUTION? Isn't it something out of nothing? Isn't it something...?"

My jaw dropped lower than its already low position. *Indeed, something...* I whispered. *Indeed, something I can use for creating today's sandwich...*

There were two more loud thuds coming from Ms. Layerrous's frying pan. Cut out from Gauguin's poster on the impact of the noise, the knife darted straight into the ripe tomato positioned on the very top of the pile.

A few seconds later, the knife continued its mission, perhaps driven by an invisible force. Unstoppable like an automatic meat slicer, the knife vigorously cut one tomato after another into small thin slices.

The red slivers then hovered in midair and one at a time were distributed promptly to our cooking tables. But not before bouncing back and forth, perhaps dancing to the loud throbs of Ms. Layerrous's frying pan.

"Whattt are youuu waitingggg for, knuckleheads?" squawked Momigi. "STARTTT YOUR SANDWICH NOW. DO NOTTT procrastinate. Delays will cost you POINTSSSSS."

Uneasiness fell on the cooking classroom as everyone wrestled with the first assignment.

How could the creation of a sandwich be such a complicated task? How do I start? I agonized.

Standing nearby, on my left, Melanie Harris attempted edgily to obtain the ingredients by forcefully rubbing her cooking station with the frying pan.

On my right, the chubby Marla Brown, with bulky fingers and thick neck, perhaps a former chef, nibbled on the tomatoes that had just alighted on her desk.

Five or six rows in front of me, Alex Taylor sharpened a set of knives that did not need honing.

And ten or fifteen rows below, I noticed David McCallum, whose frustration left him permanently white faced. Just like the rest of us, detention in the City of @ had taken its toll on him. The invisible portions of his body widened across his head and torso. He moved slowly, perhaps a sign of exhaustion.

Then my eyes continued to scour the classroom for others who might have found a way to obtain the ingredients necessary for preparing the layered sandwich.

Another concern was what type of sandwich to make. There were countless choices: club sandwich, French dip sandwich, sloppy joe sandwich, Reuben sandwich, and scores of others.

Rhubarb Pie's sandwiches were the best in the world. Prepared with love, they were intoxicating, I recalled. Sandwiches that left potent memories of childhood. I missed Rhubarb Pie's jumbo sandwiches and tiny sandwiches.

I missed Rhubarb Pie's umpteen layers of bread and lettuce and more layers of turkey and honey and layers of French fries dipped in red ketchup and other layers of Gorgonzola...

The time had come to revive the memories that had brought so much joy to my life. The time had come to wake up the taste buds that had been latent for months...

But how should I proceed? I was struggling, bearing the pain of loneliness. I remembered that Rhubarb Pie used to say,

"Sweetie, a sandwich is similar to a person's life: Every day is a layer... Layers piled upon layers, until your life is over...

"Think of your childhood as the base layer," Rhubarb Pie would emphasize. "A supporting substance that influences your life, one that sustains all the layers above.

"Therefore, sweetie, start with a strong foundation," he would conclude. "The very bottom should be a crusty slice of fresh bread. Preferably wheat bread. Then place other layers on top. The tower of layers you have created is your sandwich. It should be a display that shows your imagination, your spirit, your beautiful self..."

Not too many options were available for the base layer. The only one was to follow Ms. Layerrous's demonstration. BINGGGG! BINGGGG! BINGGGG! I then clashed a gigantic ice-cream scoop against a big cooking spoon like striking orchestra cymbals against each other.

The high-pitched, loud sound echoed across the classroom for a few long moments until the most whimsical happening unfolded in front of my eyes. A crispy slice of bread suddenly departed from Albert Anker's painting *Girl with Loaf of Bread*.

The slice of bread soared expeditiously toward my cooking station and landed softly in the center. The beautiful girl in the painting did not mind. Instead, a soft smile crept across her face. Her lips moved as if she were whispering, "Take as much as you want, feed the hungry, feed the needy..."

And here is where I stumbled a bit: *What should the second layer be? Should I just play it safe? Go for the banal lettuce and tomato ingredients? Or perhaps allow creativity to trump the boring?*

As I knew by now, not playing it safe, going for the artistic style of cooking was a dangerous risk. I was well aware of the severe punishment if I failed.

CHAPTER THIRTEEN

On the other hand, avoiding risks could put me in Ms. Layerrous's average column. My performance would be considered mediocre by Chef Cooking School standards. And that could add to my already bad points.

Uncle Walter used to say, "Listen to your heart when you're uncertain about something…"

And so I favored the innovative over old-school, the inventive over old-style sandwich making.

For one thing, time was not on my side. It was disappearing at a gallop.

For another, I could not focus on anything other than to invent a new type of sandwich. Perhaps a "Sammy" kind. A creation that made light of the cuisine standards and traditions at the Chef Cooking School.

Indeed, a risky endeavor —

"I noticeeeeeee people that have not startedddddd their sandwiches… Hurry up, you imbeciles! Twenty minutes to go, before the sandwich review starts. Boneheads! Rememberrrr the keywords: creativity, productivity, perfection," yelped Momigi the parrot, chewing on a piece of yellow banana peel.

Creativity they demanded? A creative sandwich they would get… I pledged inaudibly.

The time had come to restore my tarnished reputation. I was determined to prepare a new type of a sandwich. One that had never been encountered in the history of sandwich making.

But I was vigilant as I had never been before. Two more points, and disciplinary measures would be taken.

Who knows what the punishment would be? I feared. *Would I be fired by the cannon and splashed like a zucchini against the Chef Cooking School's walls? Would my invisibility grow until I utterly vanished? Would the translucent spots on my body widen to a frightening extent? Would Rhubarb Pie ever be able to see me again?*

MY TOOTHSOME PLATTER

"HURRY UPPPPP, incompetent duckssss!" hollered Momigi, who seemed terribly affronted, spewing sunflower seeds at the dumbfounded crowd. "In ten minutessss, your sandwichhhh will be reviewed scrupulously by our chief chef. His assistants will be there toooo, to determine how well you have performed your tasks."

The baffling reason for my captivity in the City of @, the software architecture metropolis, raised my resentment against their establishment.

My hatred grew toward Ms. Layerrous for her repulsive demeanor, and Momigi's vile calls were greeted with ill feelings from all of us.

My love of cuisine seemed to be diminishing rapidly. Accomplishing the cooking assignment became an emotional strain rather than a pleasant exercise.

Excellence was no longer the goal. Survival became the aim in the face of mounting attacks designed to humiliate. I continued unexcitedly with the preparation of my sandwich.

So, where would my second layer come from? Just like other unanticipated revelations, I found it in Ruth Roland's poster.

Ruth Roland, you wonder? Oh, you could have spotted Ruth Roland anywhere in the early years of the past century if you scoured the entertainment billboards.

The famous American silent film actress, auburn haired and slim, appeared in many films and was featured in countless ads.

In the 1919 poster I came across on the Chef Cooking School walls, I noticed Ruth Roland's half-beaming image. There, fresh fruit and a pack of chewing gum encircled her. She was holding a cluster of luscious cherries near her mouth. On the bottom, the vintage ad read, "Ruth Roland says: Ripe red cherries and Adams California Fruit Gum, I think they are equally delicious. I love them both."

CHAPTER THIRTEEN

You might wonder why I was so intrigued by a chewing gum advertisement that belonged in a museum. It was not a coincidence, for I was attracted more to the flavor of cherries than to the gum.

Even Rhubarb Pie used cherries to enhance the flavor of sandwiches. The chewing gum in the poster, I envisioned, would only add zing to my creative sandwich. Boost its appeal. Lure skeptics to the vanguard art of cuisine. Or perhaps move Ms. Layerrous.

With little hesitation, I quickly obtained my second layer from the Ruth Roland poster. Three sticks of crimson cherry chewing gum descended and docked elegantly on top of the crispy slice of bread like falling snowflakes.

Then, a moment later, another layer came along. The flowing paste of yellow mustard yanked from the Claes Oldenburg *Two Cheeseburgers* poster accelerated the mounting height of my sandwich.

My eyes roved across the classroom walls. I was searching for my next layer. Suddenly, a long string of toothpaste discharged from a black tube featured in the Klenzo Toothpaste, USA, 1920 advertisement. This layer added extraordinary mint flavor to my creation.

My sandwich was almost ready for review. Perhaps it was missing a layer or two. Perhaps it needed some zest.

As I looked harder, a well-done, sizzling, and tender sliver of squirrel meat wafted across the classroom toward me from the walls. This completed the nutritional value of my sandwich with protein...

Obviously, you'd not consider a sandwich complete without the covering layer. Typically, it would be a slice of bread. But in my case, the capping layer was not bread. In its place, a thick patch of gray alligator skin ejected from another illustration and landed on top of my creation.

And last, the pickle. A green circle of pickle found its way and settled on the very top of my sandwich.

Immediately thereafter, a long construction metal nail thrust deep in the middle of the sandwich, wedged like a toothpick to support its overall structure.

And there, ready I was.

My very first culinary achievement was displayed on my cooking station for review. I was waiting for examination by the team of chefs in the Chef Cooking School classroom.

My sandwich stood tall, seemed proud, as if it were gratified by its rich content.

Melanie Harris also appeared ready. But her posture indicated her intense state of mind. Her body seemed to be slumping under the mounting pressure. Her trembling hands signified tenuous control over her volcanic emotions.

The stressful struggle for completing the sandwich on time also took its toll on Marla Brown. Despite the massing tension, though, she was cheerful. She beamed at the tower of layers she had created from an assortment of cherry tomatoes, French fries, red onion, and delicate slices of moose meat.

"What a nice-looking sandwich you made there, Sammy," said Marla. She was grinning at me, radiating positive energy as she edged slowly toward my desk.

"Thank you, ma'am," I said shyly.

"May I have a bite? Only a small bite. Please, a tiny, tiny, tiny one. Please," begged Marla. "It looks so fabulous! Interesting! What is this made of? Where did the inspiration come from? Did you follow any recipe? And from where did you get the ingredients? I love it… I simply love it… And what is this layer on top?"

CHAPTER THIRTEEN

Her barrage of questions left me speechless. I did not expect so many warm compliments in fractions of seconds. "Thank you again, Marla, for the good words. I'll let you taste my sandwich later, after the review."

"What is the layer on top? It looks like snakeskin. Isn't it?" Marla went on. "My husband, who worked on Wall Street for almost his entire career, used to wear snakeskin shoes that looked just like that. Is it really what I think it is? Or is it a special kind of bread? Or maybe something else altogether?"

I gave her a blank look.

And Marla went on: "May I have one bite, please, a tiny, tiny, tiny bite?" Then she prodded my sandwich with her thick finger, almost toppling it and leaving a couple of noticeable dents that looked like the giant craters on the dark side of the Moon.

"Hey, watch it…" I said edgily. "You almost destroyed my sandwich. Remember: a sandwich review is coming up. This is not a toy."

"I'm so sorry," said Marla remorsefully. "I think your sandwich is gorgeous — the best-looking sandwich I have ever seen. Hey, people," she called out, and heads of the students all turned toward me as Marla went on. "Look at Sammy's sandwich! Look at this piece of artwork, the incarnation of human creativity!"

"Sh-sh, sh-sh, sh-sssssss, quiet there in the back!" yelled Momigi, narrowing her eyes. "HEY YOU! The fat lady," she screeched, pointing her sharp claws toward Marla. "Return to your desk at once before I give you a veryyy veryyy veryyy bad pointtttttt…"

"Sorry, I was just looking at Sammy's sandwich," Marla said, expressing her regrets.

"Momigi is correct: mind your own business!" bellowed Ms. Layerrous, pursing her lips in disapproval. "And did you finish yours?"

"I'm almost done," replied Marla fretfully. "I'm almost done."

"Let me see itttttt...," shouted Momigi as she soared across the classroom, hovering overhead, fluttering her wings loudly, and shrieking deafeningly. At last, the parrot perched on Marla's shoulder with a gentle thud.

Momigi meticulously inspected Marla's sandwich and screeched, "Issss thissss called done? Is this a finished serving? Is this called a sandwich at all? I-I-I GIVE YOU TWO BAD POINTSSSSS for incomplete work!"

"But I just *said* myself that it was incomplete. I just —"

"NO BUTTTTssss!" bawled Momigi in Marla's ear. "Just finish it. FINISH IT NOW! And do not dare leave your desk. Mind your own business! ONLY TWO MINUTES LEFT!"

CHAPTER FOURTEEN

SANDWICH REVIEW

Sandwich review at the Chef Cooking School started with a chiming bell. A high-pitched tinkle that could spike the hair on your head even if you didn't have much hair to begin with. Or it could freeze you up like Lake Baikal in southern Siberia in the winter.

More frightening was the silence that followed. Ms. Layerrous stood stiffly, motionless like a mannequin in a shop window. People waited in fear of the unknown.

But Momigi, by contrast, was as active as a volcano because she could not control her unremitting appetite. She was trying to crack a walnut shell clenched firmly in her sharp talon while clasping Ms. Layerrous's shoulder with the other.

To the earsplitting thunder of trumpets, the sandwich review team, three members in all, appeared punctually on the classroom platform. Like all respected chefs at the Chef Cooking School, they were clothed in traditional chef uniforms. Their outfits included long toques, jackets, and checkered pants.

Then they marched to the edge of the stage and descended gracefully to the classroom's wider aisle.

David McCallum seemed terrified as the sandwich review team approached his cooking station. He looked out of the corners of his eyes at the three chefs whose stark appearance indicated business — serious business... Their eyes descended slowly to his cooking desk. Then they slowly raised their gaze at his lopsided sandwich.

Observing the sandwich review team's astonishment, even I sensed that David was in trouble. His sandwich, composed of seven layers of what seemed to be a sticky substance, bore a resemblance to the disgusting grease used for car engines.

"Good morning, Mr. McCallum. How are you today?" said Chief Chef Goldenlulukiwich, who stood between his two assistants.

"I'm fine, sir."

"What did you prepare for us today? What is on display?"

"A-a-a club sandwich, s-sir, a modern c-club s-sandwich," said David, his teeth shuddering.

"And what ingredients have you used to create it?"

Still shivering, David pointed to his sloping sandwich. It was a structure of piled-up layers that was about to collapse at any moment. Then he murmured, "I-I-I-I used a number of solid slices of toasted bread on top of each other. I filled in between with d-d-d-delicious ingredients. B-between the bread slices, I inserted pieces of fresh turkey, ripe tomatoes, leaves of lettuce, and a few rashers of finely shredded bacon…"

"Your sandwich, young man, is pitching outrageously to one side like the Leaning Tower of Pisa —"

"Y-yes, s-sir, that's correct…" David's face turned crimson.

"Can you explain? Maybe caused by the natural force of gravitation? Weak supporting materials? Uneven chemical balance? Poor planning? Sloppiness?" conjectured Chef Goldenlulukiwich.

David stuttered, scratching his head, "I-I'm n-not s-sure, sir. I-it could be all of the above, s-sir. I-I'm r-really n-not s-sure…"

"You must be certain of what you're doing here, Mr. McCallum…" said Chef Goldenlulukiwich sternly. Then he sniffed the sandwich and without hesitation, took a big bite out of it…

It was so silent in the classroom that you could hear Mr. Goldenlulukiwich's wisdom teeth grinding. The more he chewed on David's sandwich, the more his nose wrinkled and lips curled upward. With every subsequent gnaw his face betrayed his disgust: "THIS TASTES LIKE PUKE!" he bellowed. "PURE VOMIT! Mr. McCallum, shame on you, Mr. McCallum!"

"S-s-sorry," mumbled David in horror, still shivering.

"This is a disgrace! Mocking our cooking institution will not get you far! Your sandwich tastes like dishwasher detergent."

"I-I-I'm terribly sorry, sir. Cooking's not really my cup of tea —"

"Not yourrrr cup of teaaaa?" exclaimed Momigi the parrot irritably from a distance. "So what is yourrrr cup of teaa? Hee, hee, hee, hee… Not his cup of teaaa… Hu, hu, hu, hu… Did you hear that, Ms. Layerrous? Not hisss cuppp of teaa…"

"Here in the City of @, everything we do should be your cup of tea," screamed Ms. Layerrous, red faced and flustered.

"I-I-I'm not sure. I'm really not sure what is so horribly wrong with my sandwich. This is just a sandwich, a simple one. How can it go wrong? I tried to —"

"You're asking what is wrong, Mr. McCallum?" Chef Goldenlulukiwich's voice rose gradually to a steaming tone. His white mushroom-like chef's hat released white vapor. "Let me enlighten you with some cooking wisdom, young man —"

You could notice everyone crouching forward with rapt attention as the chief chef was about to share some of his vast cooking knowledge.

"Your sandwich possesses no culture. No bravura. No zest. No creativity. No style. No vision," continued Chef Goldenlulukiwich passionately. "Your sandwich does not make a statement. It is dry like the Dead Sea, tasteless like distilled water, lifeless like the lakes on Jupiter, if indeed Jupiter has any lakes…"

"With all respect, sir, my sandwich DOES make a statement," countered David indignantly.

"And what does it stand for?"

"A long story, sir, but I'll try to make it short. The place that I'm coming from has been in constant decline. The land of opportunity has become the land of burden. The rich are bestowed with opportunities, while the poor scramble to make ends meet. Decline, I said, and declining it is, in many walks of life: Social, ethical, political…"

"So what is your point, young man?"

"My position is simple, sir. Look at my sandwich. Indeed lopsided, threatening to crumble at any moment. Indeed unsafe, wobbling like the Roman Empire when it began to teeter. So is the state of my beloved country. The power that used to dominate the world is now vulnerable, exposed to dangers, unable to withstand challenges. Real challenges… And I'm the little guy who belongs to the struggling mainstream. I'm desperate, Chef. I'm beached on an island of despair where hope is dwindling and pessimism conquers optimism, Chef."

"I still don't understand!"

"My sandwich, sir, represents the sadness and instability of my country, the place where I was born, my beautiful sweet land. The taste of my sandwich signifies the decline of our society. It's the boldest statement I have ever been able to make, Chef. I believe it's a good sandwich. It's that kind of sandwich you've asked me to prepare. Besides, was this exercise merely about sandwich making? Wasn't it about truth in cooking? Wasn't it —"

The crowd burst into thundering applause. Some of the students were hammering their frying pans against their cooking stations.

Others were stamping their feet.

A few were whistling as loudly as they could.

Most of them were shedding tears over David's heartbreaking feelings about our country and its decaying state.

CHAPTER FOURTEEN

"QUIET HERE!" roared Ms. Layerrous, uncontrollably waving her cleaver.

"I see your point, son," said Chef Goldenlulukiwich in an undertone. He seemed awash in a blend of forgiveness and sorrow and maybe a speck of sarcasm. "Tell us more about yourself. Where did you come from?"

"My ancestors set foot in this country a long time ago, came to this land from Sicily in Italy. They immigrated to fulfill their dreams of freedom and equality. They settled on Long Island and continued to develop their cheese manufacturing, the family's traditional livelihood that had spanned generations. The early years brought prosperity. Their cheese products became famous for their unique flavor and were sold in ninety countries. Their business flourished beyond expectation during the past century. But even though commerce was thriving, the writing was on the wall: A decline was looming, seemingly inevitable. The trends of weakening moral values and flagging leadership were exhausting the resources of our country. The bubble burst, and the stock market crashed. Consequently, we became a stagnant society whose bankrupt values and loss of business drove all of us into a ditch —"

"How sad..." Chef Goldenlulukiwich clicked his tongue with a mix of mild sympathy and cynicism. "So perhaps the City of @ can provide salvation, offer hope," he suggested.

David's hoarse voice was drenched in pain as his tears welled up, blurring his vision. "This place is tormenting. I miss my family. I miss them dearly, I want to go home..."

"Your home is here now, my friend. There is no return."

David sobbed bitterly, "No, this is not the end of my journey. No..."

"Hey, stop behaving like a toddler. Would you like a pacifier? Ha-ha-ha-ha," said Chef Goldenlulukiwich mockingly.

"There is no room for sarcasm here, Chef," grumbled David. "We'll pay a hefty price. Pay the bills for living like there's no tomorrow. Pay for diminishing freedom. Pay for the fading middle class. Pay for bringing the people to the brink of bankruptcy…"

"Ha-ha-ha-ha-ha, PAY? Ha-ha-ha-ha-ha. And how would we pay for our 'sins,' in your humble opinion?"

"I'm uncertain, Chef. Maybe civil unrest? Maybe what used to be the middle class will revolt? Go out to the streets and take the country back? Uprisings? Riots? Maybe another civil rights movement? Maybe a new organization whose oppressed people will fight for a different system of government?"

A hush fell on the Chef Cooking School classroom.

Wretchedness and empathy overwhelmed the crowd. David's predictions were hard to ignore, for his words echoed loudly in the students' heads.

Unmoved by David's ominous forecasts, the three chefs then strode stiffly, like soldiers on the battlefield, down the aisle toward Melanie Harris's desk.

As they approached her, she was garnishing her sandwich platter, sprinkling shreds of radishes, cranberries, and grape tomatoes. Perhaps it was her final effort to avert the criticism and mockery that had just befallen David.

"And you, ma'am? What is your contribution to today's cooking lesson?"

"My contribution is an open-faced peanut butter sandwich, Chef," she said haughtily. "My kids love it, my husband can't live without it, and my dog Bobu Mickey Jenkins is addicted to it. They all love it. They all —"

"And the ingredients, Mrs. Harris?"

"Natural ingredients, Chef, all natural," she said. "As you notice, I piled up a few layers of crushed fruit jam on one slice of bread. On the other, I put mint and jalapeño jelly. Both sides delicious —"

"How interesting," said Chef Goldenlulukiwich. "Let me take a small bite, I'm curious…" Then he took one taste from the jam, the other from the jelly, and gave a deep sigh. "Well, I must say, I must admit, I must tell you, ma'am, your sandwich is utterly disgusting. A total disaster… The calamity of the century!"

"DISASTER?" said Melanie, her voice trembling, full of surprise.

"Yes, hideous — it is the embodiment of tastelessness, lacking aesthetic qualities. It smells like rotten eggs and tastes like decaying okra in a jar of sardines. Rubbish, Mrs. Harris. Rubbish. I'm appalled!"

"The recipe came from our National Peanut Butter Sandwich Website, Chef. I do not understand! Maybe you're against peanut butter. Maybe you're against our culture. I'm shocked. Everybody loves it."

"I love peanut butter, but yours is utterly rancid, sickening."

"SICKENING? I put my entire heart into it. What in the world makes it SICKENING?"

"It is shallow, ma'am. Shallow like a politician's hollow words. Your sandwich lacks personality, lacks a spine, does not tell a story, simply fluff," said Chef Goldenlulukiwich, preparing to bustle off to the next review.

"Wait, you did not hear my story. This sandwich stands for something. It expresses an idea. It definitely has a character. It represents a happy nation whose people are satisfied with their lives, positive about the direction of the country. It's all about happiness and contentment. There is nothing wrong with either the place I came from or my sandwich."

"We really do not care, ma'am."

Irritated, Melanie's shrill voice rose to a strident tone: "Does everything have to be so gloomy? There is no lack of freedom in my country. There is no poverty. People are not starving. And jobs are abundant. My sandwich reflects our good lives. There is no despair. People are not oppressed. My sandwich tells the true story."

"Good for you, ma'am. Your positive view is not reflected in your sandwich," said Chef Goldenlulukiwich, unmoved.

Then the sandwich review team drew away from Melanie's desk and galloped toward my cooking station.

With pounding heart, intense face, and gaping eyes, I stared at the three chefs who beamed at me closely. So close, I could see the wicked spirit flaming in their eyes. I dreaded that their strict and at times cruel rejection would not skip my state-of-the-art sandwich.

"And you, child? What have you got for us today?" asked Chef Goldenlulukiwich irritably, giving me a mean smile. "I see here another tall sandwich, what is with you all and the multilayer sandwiches today? Has anyone prepared a simple one? Must life be so complicated?"

"It was Momigi's command, Chef. It was her idea to stack up these layers, Chef." I pointed to Momigi, whose eyes then shifted toward Ms. Layerrous.

"Why are you listening to the stupid parrot, eh?" growled Chef Goldenlulukiwich. Then he turned to Ms. Layerrous and asked: "Are you aware of this? Why have your students used so many layers? A sandwich must be a sandwich and not a pile of junk!"

"Yes, Chef, I totally agree! A sandwich must be a sandwich!" repeated Ms. Layerrous with a little whiff of temper.

"Let's move on; time is short. So, what kind of sandwich did you create for us today, child?" inquired Chef Goldenlulukiwich, giving me a warmer smile.

"W-w-well, it is called Ymmas, Chef." (It was my nickname spelled backward.)

"Ymmas? The strangest name I have ever heard for a sandwich," said Chef Goldenlulukiwich with a restrained grin. "Why Ymmas and not Soomy or Moomy or Yoomy or Shoomy or Loomy?"

"I-I do not know, Chef. This is what came to my mind when I was preparing it."

"Ahem," he cleared his raspy throat. "Ahem, ahemmm... Well, don't you know that inventing new platters is against our policies? It's a very risky proposition, child."

"N-no, Chef, no one ever —"

"Incorrect!" thundered Ms. Layerrous. "I have instructed my students to be old-fashioned when it comes to cooking."

Silence.

"N-no, ma'am, I reckon you told us to be creative, as creative as possible..." I insisted.

"Creative, yes, but NOT innovative!" she shouted, her face seemed inflamed as never before.

Silence.

"Chef, I really do not understand all these cooking terms. I used my intuition. I used my imagination to prepare my sandwich. If this is not good enough, so be it..."

Silence.

"Let's move on; time is not on our side," said Chef Goldenlulukiwich and took a small bite out of my sandwich.

Imagine gnawing on a sandwich that is made up of toothpaste and chewing gum and other weird ingredients. How would you react? I wouldn't even dare touch it...

At that very moment, Chef Goldenlulukiwich's face turned blue and then red and then yellow and then purple and then green and then white and then brown. A second later, a million plumes of smoke came out of his ears. His eyes flashed like the headlights of a car. His throat bulged like a pelican's pouched bill after it had caught an enormous fish.

It was perhaps one of the most frightening moments in my entire life.

"Mmmmm, mmmmm, try this, Rudolf. Try this, Rocket," said Chef Goldenlulukiwich with an indulgent smile as he shared my sandwich with his cronies.

"I must say, child, I must say… This sandwich, this sandwich, this sandwich…" A few moments of silent horror passed before Chef Goldenlulukiwich continued with vigor. "This sandwich is SUPERB! In professional cooking terms, it is simply *ambrosial, full-bodied, mouthwatering!*"

The crowd had erupted with a booming round of applause before I said shakily and humbly, "Thank you, Chef."

Drooling like a rusty burst pipe, Rudolf said, "Truly toothsome — may I have more of this magical sandwich?"

"Yes, utterly zestful — I'd like more of it too," Rocket agreed. "This is exceptional!"

"Would you like a bite, Ms. Layerrous?"

"And what makes it so special, Chef?" she asked.

"You never know. You never know what makes things special, Ms. Layerrous… Once in a while, you run into a cooking prodigy like Sammy, a novice chef, who turns the field on its head. The art of cuisine will never be the same. Never. This sandwich is special not only because it epitomizes the harsh reality in which we live, but also because its aroma reflects the delightful vitality of the City of @. It is pure, invigorating, enriching, empowering, soothing. A true piece of art that could never be reproduced by anyone else."

The review session was about to conclude, and the inevitable moment had arrived. The moment that everyone feared. The moment when accounts would be settled. The students who had failed were about to be disciplined, the rest of us to watch.

"So, Chef Goldenlulukiwich, who gave today's worst performance? Who failed the exercise? Who should be taken to the cannon?" asked Ms. Layerrous, her eyes glinting.

After huddling for a few long minutes, the three chefs came up with the verdict. It was a painful ruling that to some could not have been more startling.

Silence.

"Mr. David McCallum, ma'am, Mr. David McCallum, ma'am," the sandwich review team concluded with a harsh judgment.

CHAPTER FIFTEEN

LOOK-AND-FEEL

Yet again, I found myself in a new place on that early morning. This time I was transported to a contemporary dining chair and seated at a modern dining table.

We had just finished breakfast. I was staring at her. We were exchanging whispers, trading courteous grins, and often nodding mutely at each other, agreeing on almost every subject.

Beautiful she was. Her long neck soared ambitiously like the Tower of Babel. Her glinting eyes flashed behind a long pair of false eyelashes. Her cleft chin was exquisite like the Grand Canyon. Her cheek dimples were soft like the curvature of time. And her glamorous wavy hair swept the floor like a long bridal gown.

Her slim arms and long fingers gestured incessantly, as if for some odd reason her already intense voice needed support.

Cleopatra was her name, reminiscent of the ancient queen of Egypt.

Despite the long lapse of time between their generations, this Cleopatra, in the City of @, treated her staff as if she were a regal ruler. Her orders had never been ignored when her nostrils flared, her face reddened, her eyes narrowed, and her lips pursed. Now and then, her employees met her demands as if those demands had come out of a powerful megaphone. From time to time, a vicious beam of frustration accompanied her requests.

But the other side of Cleopatra was utterly polite. In sheer contrast to the occasional unyielding blaze in her voice, her demeanor was honorable and soft like cotton — indeed a redeeming quality.

CHAPTER FIFTEEN

Just like the ancient Cleopatra, the one I was chatting with in the management dining room had a sweet tenor to her voice. Bestowed by nature, the soothing qualities she possessed were used to persuade and, to some degree, control the people she knew.

"Oh, what are my dreams, you ask?" Cleopatra's silky voice softened gradually like drops of precipitation in a rain forest. "I have always dreamed of becoming Miss Universe. Funny, isn't it, Sammy? I have always wanted to be so beautiful, so charming that no man on this planet could resist me. I have long fantasized to be so enchanting, so attractive to the degree that I could seduce any gentleman on Earth."

The corners of my mouth curled into a shy beam.

"And yours? What are your dreams, child?"

"Mine? To find someone who vanished from my life. To be reunited with someone special who left a big hole in my heart," I said, on the brink of tears…

"I feel your agony. I hope you'll soon fill the emptiness in your heart," she said somberly.

"And I hope you become the Miss Universe you have always dreamed of."

"I hope so… I hope so… So, how do I look today, Sammy?" said Cleopatra, giving a sly smile mixed with curiosity as if she had a hidden intention.

"What kind of question is that?" I tittered, my eyebrows rising high.

"Not strange at all. Every woman in the world would like to know what people think about her appearance. Isn't that right, dear? Does it sound peculiar to you?"

"I was not ready for such a question," I said apologetically, adding in a drawling voice: "You look wonderful, ma'am!"

"Thank you! Thank you! And how does it feel when you look at me?" she went on.

"I feel nothing," I said blankly, concealing my discomfort.

"Nothing? Nothing at all? So, let me ask you this in a different way: what do you see when you look at me?"

"What do I see?" I asked while my face reddened.

"Yes, what do you see?" Her eyes narrowed.

I mustered most of my energy and said in a subdued tone, "I see a powerful woman whose convictions are strong. Her principles are genuine, free of pretense. I see a woman who not only loves her occupation but who also is passionate about her career, driven by dedication."

"You're so, so, so right, dear Sammy. How did you know this?"

"I can read people, ma'am," I claimed. "But I also see a strong woman whose appearance has become partially invisible like most of the people in the City of @. I see a person who is probably fading out as time drifts away. I see a beautiful woman who is under mounting pressure, as the hard work calls for perfection."

Uneasy stillness followed my observations. Cleopatra's face went ruddy. I sensed that my words held some truth — especially for those who had been penned up in the City of @ for quite some time.

"There is some truth to your statements," she confessed sadly. "That's right. Here we have become enslaved to a greater idea, working hard to fulfill the vague goals of our leaders. They, Ms. Layerrous and Mr. Greenbold, have been raising the bar beyond humane limits. You may lose some of your identity in this place —"

"I see the stress in your face," I said.

CHAPTER FIFTEEN

"True, Sammy. You too must be very careful here. You're a beautiful girl. I hope you can preserve your gorgeous looks despite the translucent blotches that already cover your face, neck, and arms. Poor little girl," Cleopatra pitied me in her soft tone of voice.

I felt a sudden jolt in my heart. I knew that transparent sections had appeared almost everywhere on my body. They were voids that enabled anyone to see through me. *Am I vanishing as the others are? Disappearing just like Cleopatra? Will I be wiped from the face of the Earth? Would Rhubarb Pie ever be able to see me again?*

Then Cleopatra suddenly leaped to her feet. She swung open the sliding door behind her and invited me into her world. It was an empire I gawked at, transfixed in disbelief.

There were hundreds and hundreds of alien-like faces staring at computer screens stretched across a vast hall. The colorful lights from the computer displays projected innumerable hues on the washed-out walls and ceilings...

Keyboard clicks echoed in celebration of what appeared to be the power of computing. It seemed that the computers were talking to each other, exchanging messages, reasoning — perhaps hundreds and hundreds of them.

If indeed Cleopatra in the City of @ holds any crucial responsibilities, then what are they? And you may also ask, *what are these creatures doing here?* I wondered as we were striding forward to the center of the busy hall —

"GOOD MORNING, COMRADES!" Cleopatra hollered in her shrill voice.

Hundreds and hundreds of her staff sprang to their feet. Then they responded, in a mixture of deep pride and respect, "GOOD MORNING, CHIEF! GOOD MORNING, CHIEF!"

"And how do I LOOK today?"

"IMPECCABLE, CHIEF! IMPECCABLE, CHIEF!"

"And how do you feel when you look at me?"

"WE FEEL WONDERFUL, CHIEF, JUST WONDERFUL, CHIEF!"

"And what else, comrades?"

"YOU LOOK PERFECT, AND WE FEEL MAGNIFICENT, CHIEF!"

"And what is this place all about?"

"LOOK-AND-FEEL, CHIEF! LOOK-AND-FEEL, CHIEF!"

"Look-and-feel of what, comrades?"

"SOFTWARE APPLICATIONS, CHIEF! SOFTWARE APPLICATIONS, CHIEF!"

"And to which place in the City of @ have we pledged our allegiance, comrades?

"TO THE PRESENTATION LAYER FACILITY, CHIEF!"

"And again, where is the best Presentation Layer Facility in the world, comrades?"

"IN THE CITY OF @, CHIEF, IN THE CITY OF @, CHIEF!"

"And what is the City of @ best known for, comrades?"

"SOFTWARE ARCHITECTURE, CHIEF, SOFTWARE ARCHITECTURE, CHIEF!"

"And who is your mistress, comrades?"

"ONLY YOU, CHIEF! ONLY YOU, CHIEF!"

I loved computers, but Look-and-Feel seemed to me a strange thing. I'd never heard it before despite countless hours of playing with computers. Weird term, isn't it?

Before my voyage to the City of @, I had known how to use my computer at home. I used to download applications from the Internet and play computer games. I had helped Rhubarb Pie to balance the family's checkbooks and even calculate the mortgage on our house. These things Rhubarb Pie had trained me to do.

At home, on my shelves, I'd had myriad software applications that I had installed on my computer.

I'd had a big collection of geography software programs that enabled me to explore and navigate the world. The application included exquisite maps. It showed the different continents and their countries. I'd been able to zoom in on geographic regions and view lakes and rivers, cities and roads, and even museums and restaurants.

Meet Your Dinosaur Friends had been my favorite software. I'd loved this application. I memorized almost all of the dinosaurs' names and even remembered their common habitats and diets. Rhubarb Pie and I had giggled at their names. Indeed, strange names: The duck-billed, plant-eating, crest-headed Brachylophosaurus. And the tiny-armed, bone-crushing, meat-eating Tyrannosaurus. And the plant-eating, very long-necked Diplodocus. And numerous others…

Despite being computer literate, I thought the term *Look-and-Feel* was unclear. Even Cleopatra's extra efforts to explain what it meant in plain words seemed to be in vain.

Packed with wisdom, Uncle Walter's saying, "Hope, patience, and perseverance turn the vague into pellucid…," helped ease my frustration. In simple words, Uncle Walter meant that persistence pays off.

The spirit of my uncle's words inspired me. Therefore, I was looking forward to a fruitful day. I was filled with immense energy and a strong appetite for exploration and discovery.

On that positive note, the busy day at the Presentation Layer Facility began… Countless faces turned our way when I followed Cleopatra on her usual morning tour. At times she was slinking behind her employees, peering at their computers, and frequently giving scowling looks of disappointment.

On other occasions, she sauntered about, grinning, melting with pleasure when she was satisfied with their performance.

Without a doubt, today's tour was a notorious daily visit that churned stomachs and shook people to their core.

Cleopatra's sharp and forthright questions about the status of her employees' work were met characteristically with anxiety. Some employees shivered, and others almost crumpled under the pressure.

We were spiraling between countless computer stations, eyeing the various software applications. Cleopatra explained how her organization operated, who the people involved were, and their responsibilities…

Her words faded away when a sign reading *The Chocolate Team* came into sight. Nearby, people were munching on chocolate chip cookies and gulping hot chocolate from large mugs. The Chocolate Team included Mary Skull, who was sitting next to Susan White. Both were former nurses who got ensnared last summer in the City of @.

David Davis, whose somber face divulged unhappiness and disgust, shared his computer with Dan Taylor.

Dan, who had arrived recently from Los Angeles, constantly ogled Yvonne Martin at his elbow. Yvonne returned his glances with nasty looks.

There was also Ms. Ana de Rojas, who had shot her dog and got sentenced to three years of community service.

And you could also find Allan Bing, who hated chocolate.

Carlotta Moreno, too, belonged to the Chocolate Team. She was polishing her fingernails when we passed by. Rumor had it she had poisoned her husband and got sent to prison for fourteen years.

Among the others were Abhaykumar and Pedro, both of whom had earned their degrees in business administration at the University of Phoenix.

Also belonging to the Chocolate Team was Mr. Abbott. He had never been married. He loved ice cream so much, he had used the last of his savings to purchase an ice cream business that was about to collapse —

"…Here in my world," Cleopatra went on, "we are concerned about how an application looks. We also care about how people feel when they look at the computer screen."

"So, why do you call it *presentation*?" I asked interestedly.

"Here in my world, the presentation of colors and shapes of images on the computer screen is important, Sammy. Also, the fonts and sound and animation are essential to how you view applications on the screen."

"I understand now. And what about the feelings?" I pressed.

"Oh…, what you see on the computer screen can also affect your feelings. That's why we call it *Look-and-Feel*, gorgeous girl."

"Aha! Aha! Now I'm starting to get it… And which application is the Chocolate Team concerned with?" I asked, giggling at the people whose faces were smudged with brown smears of chocolate.

"Oh, this team? Yes, they are in charge of the presentation of the Chocolate-Tasting Application," said Cleopatra proudly.

"Chocolate? I love chocolate." I was almost drooling. "Does this application spit out chocolate?" I giggled.

"Yes, little girl. Yes, the application offers lessons in savoring the best in chocolate. Second to none, this outstanding software program lets users relish the delicious aromas and taste a large variety of chocolates. Let's check it out," said Cleopatra.

We were drifting quietly behind Pedro, peering above his shoulder at the brownish-looking application screen.

While nibbling on a dark chocolate bar, he concentrated intensely on the computer display as if his life depended on it.

To get his attention, Cleopatra tapped on Pedro's shoulder with her long index finger's artificial nail —

Pedro sprang abruptly to his feet and said, "I'm all yours, Chief!"

"You do not have to be MINE, Pedro. All you have to do this morning is to demonstrate how special the application is."

"Yes, Chief! Right away, Chief!"

Pedro slipped quickly back into his seat and leaned forward, wiping the cold sweat off his forehead. His fingers pounded skillfully on the keyboard.

He navigated adeptly from one page to another, from one list of options to another, until he reached the application's main menu. Indeed, these were nice-looking pages with enchanting design. Chocolate hues were splashed across the screen, and chocolate chip images embellished the background.

We were glaring at the application and drooling over the illustrated chocolates as if they were displayed in a chocolate shop window.

I have always been a chocolate lover, and there is nothing I can do about it; it's in my genes. I have no defense against the alluring power of chocolate. I probably inherited the weakness for chocolate from Rhubarb Pie. It was no surprise then that now my senses were slowly succumbing to the potent fragrances of chocolate that oozed out of Pedro's computer.

The scents were strong enough to knock down a world heavyweight boxing champion. Or to conquer the hardened heart of the ancient Cleopatra. The strong aromas engulfed us as I was being slowly immersed in the fascinating Chocolate-Tasting Application —

"So, here we are, looking at the main menu page," proclaimed Pedro, pointing to the screen. "From here we can go anywhere, drill down to other pages in the application."

"Can you please remove your gigantic finger from the display? We can't see a thing!" bellowed Cleopatra.

"Y-yes, ma'ammm —"

"DO NOT CALL ME *MA'AM*; CALL ME *CHIEF*! And how many times do I need to tell you NOT to wear the same stupid shirt every day?"

"Y-yes, Ch-Chief."

"YES WHAT?"

"Y-yes, understood, Ch-ch-ch-ief."

"Also, clean your desk thoroughly. I do not want to see a single crumb of chocolate. And how many times do I have to tell you to remove your false teeth from your disgusting table?"

"Wi-wi-will do, Chief."

A fearful silence fell upon the Presentation Layer Facility as all eyes focused on us.

Then Pedro rose slowly to his feet again and introduced the application enthusiastically. "T-th-th-th-this software enables you to taste chocolate. All kinds of chocolate. All you have to do is to relax, focus, and nibble on the selected chocolate. Eat with your eyes and nose, not only with your mouth. Do not rush, do not gobble, do not chew. Enjoy the aroma, and relish the melting oomph of chocolate. Close your eyes. Put the chocolate on your sensitive palate and indulge your senses to the extreme. Chocolate tasting is all about the smell, the look, and, obviously, the taste. In many cases, it's also about sweet memories, sweet aspirations, sweet dreams, sweet —"

"ENOUGH of that babble, Pedro! Sit down and demonstrate it to us instead! DO NOT TELL; SHOW INSTEAD!" Cleopatra shouted crossly. "And how many times do I have to tell you to clean your ears thoroughly? What do you grow in there, eh? Potatoes? Cucumbers? Eggplants?"

"Will do, Ch-ch-ch-chief…"

The appealing main menu of the Chocolate-Tasting Application offered a long list of chocolates. With just the gentle click of a mouse button, you could indulge yourself with a heavenly collection of rich cocoa beans, transformed into a variety of chocolates.

"Sammy," said Pedro, "there are many types of chocolates you can choose from. Which one would you like? Milk chocolate? White chocolate? Dark chocolate?"

"I'd like milk chocolate, please."

Pedro clicked on the milk chocolate selection and said, "The next menu is asking which flavor you'd like for your milk chocolate. Orange? Mint? Blueberry?"

"Oh, more choices? Well, then…" I paused for a second. "I'm going with the mint."

"Well chosen, Sammy," said Pedro as he selected the mint. "Now, your milk chocolate will taste like mint, but the next menu, too, offers some ingredients: Nuts? Peanuts? Spaghetti? Couscous? Caramel?"

"S-p-a-g-h-e-t-t-i?" I burst out laughing. "How disgusting… I think caramel will do it for me…"

Pedro browsed through more pages, selecting more menus and more options. It lasted for ages, like the time it takes to check in your luggage before an airplane flight. Then he announced at full volume, "READY? READY for your chocolate?"

Suddenly, a white springy tube protruded from his computer screen. It was stretching upward like a cobra and stirring gently toward my mouth. The tube's aperture opened wide, and it seemed to be grinning, ready to disgorge the seductive substance.

"Your mint chocolate is coming out. Open your mouth, Sammy!" said Pedro, with restrained enthusiasm and a mild sense of urgency.

A barrage of chocolate squares shot out from the tube directly into my open mouth. The smell and the tasty milk chocolate overwhelmed my senses. Tears of enjoyment flooded my eyes. Vivid memories, sweet memories, took me back to happier times in my life. They were periods of joy I had shared with Rhubarb Pie. So sweet and so tender they were, reminiscences honeyed with morsels of crispy chocolate.

Being embraced like a baby in Rhubarb Pie's lap is something I'll never forget. And listening to Rhubarb Pie's tales were times I'll always cherish.

Rhubarb Pie used to tell a story that still brings tears of laughter to my eyes, a classic that always brightened my day. Probably passed down through generations, it was about a lazy man whose wife was about to leave for a visit with her family. Concerned about her husband's well-being, she baked a huge chocolate doughnut and wrapped it around his neck before leaving.

Days later, her husband was found dead.

"What did the lazy husband die from?" Rhubarb Pie used to ask. "He starved to death after neglecting to rotate the chocolate doughnut, eating only the part near his mouth —"

"PEDRO," Cleopatra shrieked suddenly. "How many times do I need to tell you not to pick your nose in front of others?"

LOST AND FOUND

The morning visit to the Presentation Layer Facility in the City of @ continued with intensity. The various teams were introduced to me as Cleopatra and I plodded along aisles that stretched endlessly across the huge hall.

"Here is the team that is responsible for designing the Do-It-Yourself Application screens," said Cleopatra.

"What does *Do-It-Yourself* mean?" I asked.

"This software application helps people build things rather than buy them. For example, it teaches you how to construct a bed, a chair, a boat. You could also build a house if you followed the instructions closely," she said proudly.

I nodded.

Then I trailed her to another section of the facility. She stopped and pointed to a screen with images of beaming golfers hugging their caddies. "Here is the team that handles the Look-and-Feel *Golf Tournament* application," said Cleopatra.

I nodded again.

"And this is the *How to Kill a Fly Mercifully* application team. And there, on the far right, look carefully near the round windows. This is the *How to Live 500 Years without Dying Even Once* application team," she said.

It seemed that the introductions to her teams lasted ages and ages. The winding aisles made me dizzy. There was no relief as Cleopatra continued the tour with utmost vigor. "And look at the north wing," she said. "The people in red who are waving at us and chomping on raw potatoes are very special. They belong to the *How to Commit Murder without Getting Caught* application team."

I waved back at the kindly team, giving a cordial grin.

"Look at the far south, Sammy. I think you're going to like it. The team whose members are sucking on sugarcane like donkeys is named *How to Persuade a Turtle to Eat Only Meat* application."

I giggled.

"Note on the far west, sweet girl. These associates belong to the *How to Play Deadly Games with the Devil* application team. And here, just in front of us, is the *Get to Know Dr. Seuss's Books* application team. And right behind us is the *Lost and Found* application team"

The tedious introductions to Cleopatra's world ended unexpectedly. She caught her breath and in a frail and croaky voice said abruptly, "It's lunchtime. Let's head back to the dining room," her hands shaking and her face covered with sweat.

I peered at her from the corner of my eye. White faced, she seemed weak and fragile. "Are you OK, Cleopatra?" I said, apprehensive for her frail health.

"I'm running out of energy. I need to take my vitamins. I must take care of myself. I must eat. I can't cut back on food like years ago. I'm not young anymore. I feel like an old dog — an old fat lady who has lost her edge. This place is sucking every ounce of blood out of my body. I'm exhausted —"

"You look just fine. You're still young, Cleopatra," I said as we set off to the management dining room.

"You do not know how demanding my job is, Sammy. No one really cares about me. They just push it to the limit until your mind cracks and your body collapses under the pressure. Then your spirit breaks into bits and pieces like a shattering window. I'm dying slowly from the inside — and I'm disappearing from the outside." She was wailing like a baby confined to a crib.

The banquet room's door swung open. To our bewilderment, Ms. Layerrous, Mr. Greenbold, and Mr. Componenttous were already seated and had been served the soup and appetizers of the day.

They grinned at us as we inched carefully toward the dining table and slid slowly into our chairs.

Mr. Greenbold's lopsided and loathsome look indicated trouble. Ms. Layerrous gave a nauseating gaze as if disaster were on the horizon. And Mr. Componenttous seemed reserved — aloof from those who were lunching around the table.

"Cleopatra, my dear," opened Mr. Greenbold in his typical, sarcastic tone a few moments after we settled in. "I know that your job inflicts pain and distress upon you. The challenging hurdles of your daily duties have wreaked havoc on your already taxing life. I know you're pushed to the extreme. I feel your pain, and I'm here to help ease your aches. I have good news and bad news. Which would you like first?"

"I'm not in the mood for bad news. No bad news!" Cleopatra cried, shaking her head in discontent. "No mood — no mood — no mood —"

"The good news," he pressed on, indifferent to Cleopatra's anguish, "is that your life, as it is now, is ending, nearing its conclusion. I'm here to let you know that your job terminates effective immediately. You're released from your agonizing duties. Isn't it a relief? Isn't it liberating?"

Cleopatra sobbed bitterly, her face in her hands. "What's to become of me? Where am I going now? Where are you sending me? I have been doing this job for so long…"

"I beg to differ with you, Mr. Greenbold," said Ms. Layerrous. "Cleopatra has been a great asset to our institution. Her vast experience is still valuable to our operations, she —"

"EXCUSE ME… Ha-ha-ha-ha," he burst out in cruel laughter. "I'm the one running the show in the City of @! I'm the one and NO ONE else! Understood?"

"Y-yes, Ch-Chief. U-Understood."

"I-I think b-both of you are r-right," mumbled Mr. Componenttous, an utterance no one heard clearly.

Mr. Greenbold peered at Cleopatra's face with a blend of sadness and perhaps a bit of irony. Then he said in his usual shrill voice, "Look at her. Is she really able to lead the Presentation Layer Facility in her condition? Is she capable? Eh? Look at the dark circles around her eyes… How can she run this place if she's half visible? Her face is pale. Her arms are gone. The rest of her body is vanishing as we speak, washed out like faded jeans…"

"But Chief —" interrupted Ms. Layerrous.

"Please let me finish," growled Mr. Greenbold. "Cleopatra's inability to concentrate, her short temper, her lack of judgment, and her confusion do not reflect well on us. I can't let her manage this place in such a state of body and mind…"

Half silence fell on the dining room. Cleopatra sobbed louder than ever, wiping the tears off her face with a napkin that Ms. Layerrous had handed to her.

Moved deeply by her sorrow, I was clasping tightly Cleopatra's perspiring hand as the somber news poured in. I assured her that I would keep an eye on her during these tormenting times. "There is nothing to worry about, Cleopatra," I said faintly.

"Is this good news? Is this good news? And what about the bad news — as if the termination of my job was not bad enough," cried Cleopatra.

"The bad news is not too bad," Mr. Greenbold answered with a slight air of wickedness, as a wily smile bent the edges of his narrow mouth. "The bad news is actually good news: You'll continue to serve the City of @ in various capacities. You'll hang around… we'll still need your help."

"How are you going to utilize my skills, Chief?" asked Cleopatra, a look of terror in her eyes.

"Well, perhaps we'll store you in our Component Library."

"In the Component Library, Chief? What does it mean?" she said, still very agitated.

"Well, let's ask the expert: Mr. Componenttous, would you be able to make use of Cleopatra's body parts?"

"Yes, Chief, her contribution would be immeasurable to the City of @, the software architecture metropolis," said Mr. Componenttous, eyes half open, half slumbering.

"So, tell me, Mr. Componenttous, what parts of Cleopatra could be used?" asked the chief, leaning forward.

"I-I could use her brain for our software applications, so they would be able to think. They would be able to calculate, like a calculator. They would be able to advise people if they have problems," said Mr. Componenttous.

"What else? What else?" Mr. Greenbold seemed impatient.

"I could use her ears and eyes, so the software applications could see and talk to people, interact with them. We could keep all her parts in our library for years to come — forever. I assure you, Chief, her contribution would be greatly appreciated."

"No, no, no… I can't be here forever. I want to go home; I want to go back to my family…" Cleopatra moaned.

"Do not fret," Mr. Greenbold consoled her. "You will not vanish. Not at all! On the contrary, your family will always be able to find you. Remember your *Lost and Found* application, Cleopatra? Your team? They will be here forever. Your former employees will help anyone trying to locate you —"

At that moment, my heart felt an awful jolt. Could the *Lost and Found* application be used to find missing people? Not only just umbrellas or watches or other valuables misplaced in the subway?

My eyes opened wide, and my body shivered with excitement. I was close to tears.

The spark of hope suddenly rekindled. Maybe, maybe I would be able to find Rhubarb Pie. Maybe I'll be able to discover something about Rhubarb Pie's disappearance.

Maybe it will be a slim clue that would shed light on Rhubarb Pie's whereabouts —

"Right after lunch," said Mr. Greenbold firmly, "Cleopatra and Sammy will be taken to our distribution center for processing. Meanwhile, Ms. Layerrous will assume temporary responsibilities over the Presentation Layer Facility until the next leader of that organization is decided."

"Am I to join Cleopatra?" I inquired fearfully.

"Oh, yes! She'll need your support, girl! She'll need a caring person like you who can ease her pain," Mr. Greenbold said, giving me an unnerving look. "Since you're such good friends and getting along so well, and you sympathize deeply with each other, you will be joining her."

"But Sammy is still young and utterly inexperienced. I do not see the benefit. How can we justify this?" Ms. Layerrous murmured.

"And how many times do I need to mention that I'm the one who makes decisions in this place? I'M THE ONE AND THE ONLY ONE!" bellowed Mr. Greenbold in an exasperated voice.

"Y-yes, Ch-Chief."

"Do not undermine Sammy's contribution to our Component Library!" Mr. Greenbold went on. "Not only adults but children too can add value to our operations. Children's quick-thinking brains are fresh. Their tissues are young. Their organs can serve as components to enhance our software application capabilities. Isn't that true, Mr. Componenttous?"

"I think both you and Ms. Layerrous are right, Chief. I agree with both arguments. I could use children's components, but maybe not —" said Mr. Componenttous, yawning, half dozing, nodding weakly.

"No offense, Mr. Componenttous, but your statements are always ambiguous, vacuous, and useless!" Ms. Layerrous's bout of frustration did not spur any reaction, for Mr. Componenttous had fallen asleep even before she finished her statement.

Among his many inventions, one in particular was Uncle Walter's crowning achievement. Well, maybe not the greatest one, but undeniably an example of ingenuity.

Uncle Walter was extremely proud of his invention of tying people to each other — not with robes or wild glue or anything like that. I mean, more emotionally, more spiritually.

Tying people together an unseen power? Enchanting, isn't it? So how did Uncle Walter's invention work? Bear with me for a second; everything will be clear.

It is an easy idea to grasp if you only imagine that two or more persons are imitating each other constantly. They move the same way, in the same direction. They even utter the same words at the same exact time.

Cool?

This out-of-the-ordinary power came naturally to Uncle Walter during the *coupling* period of his career —

So lunch was almost over... Despite his disagreements with Ms. Layerrous and to some degree with Mr. Componenttous, Mr. Greenbold seemed more determined than ever to carry out his hideous plan.

Yes, he was resolved to terminate Cleopatra's long career and in one fell swoop, end my journey to find Rhubarb Pie.

As the chief had mentioned, he also intended to transport both of us to the Component Library in the City of @. It was a place where we would be shelved for eternity.

CHAPTER SIXTEEN

But I could not let it happen. Not now. Now was not the time to end my voyage.

Perhaps the *Lost and Found* application would offer a chance to find Rhubarb Pie. Lingering a little bit longer at the Presentation Layer Facility would let me explore that avenue.

Furthermore, my heart went out to Cleopatra, for I didn't believe she deserved to be treated like that —

Suddenly, Mr. Greenbold jumped to his feet and ordered Cleopatra and me to follow him to the Ladybug shuttle. It was his favorite vehicle for transporting people, moving them around the City of @. Then he pushed open the door to the corridor leading to the exit. But we, Cleopatra and I, sat at the table holding hands, inseparable, strong, defiant, together.

Then, inspired by Uncle Walter's mettle, I whispered steadfastly in her ear, "Do not fear. We are not going anywhere, Cleopatra. Sit firmly, shut your eyes tightly, and take a deep breath. Focus on the inner you, on your soul. Then say inaudibly three times, 'I love myself because I'm the greatest... I'm gorgeous like sin...' After you're done, stay tuned and watch what happens next."

We recited the magical phrases, for I was hoping to turn the tide on Mr. Greenbold's villainous plan. Or at least delay it for as long as possible.

A few moments later, the fanciful befell. Mr. Greenbold, Ms. Layerrous, and Mr. Componenttous seemed bound to each other as if they were one.

Their souls had become magically glued together like triplets in a baby stroller. They were holding hands. They were grinning at the same time. They were crying all at once, scratching their heads simultaneously, mopping the sweat off their cheeks as one.

A few moments of confusion passed until they were chanting in unison like a chorus in a city square on a Saturday night,

"Maybe our decision to send them to the Component Library is wrong. Maybe not... But maybe yes... But maybe not... But maybe yes..."

Lips parted, eyes open wide, Cleopatra and I were gazing at them in deep disbelief, marveling at our success —

Like a broken record, the three intoned again and again, "Maybe we are right, but we may also be wronggggg... Maybe Cleopatra should be promoted and Sammy sent hommmme... Or maybe we should analyze the situation... Analysis paralysis... analysis paralysis... analysis paralysis... analysis paralysis... analysis paralysis..."

For the life of me, I did not know how long Uncle Walter's tying magic would last. How long would Mr. Greenbold and his cronies be bound to each other? How long would they act as one, unable to unshackle themselves from the coerced harmony inflicted on them? No one knew...

When we hurried away from the dining room, they were still jabbering the same blather and holding hands like inseparable lovers. "We are one," they said. "We are united," they chanted. "We are one power under the sun," they hummed. Then they repeated like a broken old school record player, "One power, one power, one power, one power..."

I caught a last glimpse of the three before scurrying down the main aisle of the Presentation Layer Facility. I was heading toward the *Lost and Found* application team.

Cleopatra, trailing me, was moving at a fast gallop, gasping heavily, almost out of breath. As we drew nearer, the members of the team stood up, their eyes wide open, filled with distress and anxiety.

"You may be seated, comrades," Cleopatra yelped with the last of her strength.

"Yes, Chief..."

CHAPTER SIXTEEN

The *Lost and Found* application team, an elite group of educated people, settled in the center of the Presentation Layer Facility. It was a spot visible from every corner of the building.

For high visibility, they were dressed in blue suits and sported red ties. Their shiny alligator skin shoes and sparkling cuff links could be seen from miles away. And their gleaming hairdos — the crown braid hairstyle for women and the devilock haircut for men —were probably noticeable from the Moon.

Among the members of the *Lost and Found* application team was David Manetas. For some reason, he nibbled on a fried-insect snack. He was known for his great knowledge about missing pets.

There was also Pavel Denisov. He had left his country for a better life and then married Charlotte Brackett, fifteen years older. They had lived in harmony and peace until he was called to duty in the City of @.

And Nettie Anderson was there too, an important member of that team. Nettie had never missed a yoga class in her hometown of Juneau, Alaska. Her aunt had been an FBI agent. And her son had been jailed for sneaking into the tiger cage at the Bronx Zoo.

Another member was Mr. Kukuzi Bulukinori. I was told that he could find anyone anywhere, even if the person had disappeared a million years ago.

And you could also spot Mr. Archibald, who had recently celebrated his 158th birthday. And who looked just like a baby. And who had forgotten his own first name. And whose political convictions had always gotten him into trouble. And who all the time believed in a better world —

Suddenly, Cleopatra lunged toward Mr. Archibald and elbowed him forcefully, almost knocking him off his bench. "Sir, please help Sammy find someone in the *Lost and Found* application."

"Ouch... Ouch... Ouch... Ow...," cried the very old man as he ascended sluggishly to his shivering and throbbing feet. "All right, all right, no need to push so hard, ma'am"

"Sorry if I hurt you, sir. We are in an extreme hurry," she said pitifully. "Sorry again, I just need your computer..."

"Ow... Ow... Ow... My bones, my ribs..." he cried again. "Kids nowadays can help themselves, ma'am. Ow... Ow... They know almost everything about computers. Ow... Ow.... When I was a child, the abacus was the only thing that resembled a computer. Now, they are capable of —"

Mr. Archibald's statement faded as I grabbed his cushioned office chair and stared intensely into his computer screen.

Curious, snooping around, peering behind my shoulder, and smelling like lemons was Nettie Anderson.

Behind my back was also Mr. Kukuzi Bulukinori, who had just eaten a respectable number of garlic cloves for lunch.

Looking past my shoulder, too, was Pavel Denisov, whose bubblegum snapping was in earshot.

Also standing there behind my back was Cleopatra, biting her lips.

And last, Mr. Archibald, whose feet still shook as if he were surfing gargantuan waves at Jaws Beach in Hawaii —

"AUUaaUUwwUUOOWWHHmnommnomnomm..." a sudden deep yawn echoed from an animated cartoon that floated on Mr. Archibald's computer screen. It was a frowning face composed of millions of yellow and black dots.

Silence. I gazed deeply into the screen.

"HHmmmnommm... You just woke me up! Couldn't you wait until dinner? What's the rush anyway? HHmmmnommm...," grumbled the animated face.

"Sorry for the inconvenience, sir. Good afternoon. Yes, it's urgent," I said hurriedly.

"Do not call me *sir*. My name is Newton. And everybody here knows me by that name. What can I do you for this early in the day?"

"I'm looking for someone —"

"'Looking for someone'?" he repeated smugly. "Sorry, I can't help. Nice meeting you! Good-bye!"

"Chaaaaaaaaaak...," the screen went blank with an unexpected thud. Newton's face was wiped out abruptly. The *Lost and Found* application shut down.

Dumbfounded silence. All eyebrows elevated high.

Seconds later, Mr. Archibald's hand stretched above my shoulder, rebooting his desktop computer.

Newton's face reappeared moments afterward, seemingly vexed like a scrambled egg and ruddier than before. "And what do you want now? Must you disturb my break?"

"I'm searching for someone —" I pressed persistently.

"I can only search for some*thing*, not some*one*. I can look up belongings, not persons," said Newton irritably, his long lips curled up. "I can search for hats, pearls, glasses, maybe cats or dogs if they are still alive. But people, people are hard to find if they're gone. When they are gone, they are gone. Sorry, I can do nothing."

"Please help me, Newton," I pleaded. "I know you can. They told me —" and a tear rolled down my cheek.

"Ooooohhhhh, please do not cry, child. I do not need this. I'm too emotional myself. Here, take this," he beseeched as his yellow hand protruded from the computer display and handed me a pink napkin. "Mop your pretty silly face.

"And please do not weep. Only alligators weep. Only monkeys weep. Only hyenas weep. Here in the City of @, we do not weep. Instead, we simply melt. We become invisible. We are being used as computer parts — just like they used my face. The ridiculous face you're glaring at now... Ha-ha-ha-ha, hee-hee-hee-hee, hu-hu-hu-hu..."

The *Lost and Found* application team exploded with laughter over my shoulder.

The screen went blank again, but a few moments later Newton's face reappeared, beaming, his lips moving — inaudible.

"Just a second," Mr. Archibald said. "Let me recover the sound system." He pounded on his computer screen three times with his frail fists.

"Chhhhhhhhh, Chhhhh, Chh... Can anyone hear me?" Newton asked.

"Yes, I'm still here," I said impatiently.

"OK, let's try, child. Let's try. What is the person's name, the one that's missing?"

"Kevin Edison," I murmured, face gloomy.

"Let me see if I can find anyone by that name. Mr. Edison, Mr. Edison... Mr. Kevin Edison... Nothing, nothing comes up... Nothing. Let me put you on hold for a few seconds," he said and disappeared again from the screen.

My heart walloped rapidly. A minute, two..., and the display was still empty, chillingly clear.

Suddenly, Newton returned with a flicker of hope in his message: "I found something. I found someone... Do you remember his date of birth?"

"January 22, 1961."

"And the place of birth?"

"New York."

The stillness lasted a long tense minute that felt like ages.

"Here is what I found for you, child." He said. "I'm not sure if this is the person you're looking for, but let's see..." Then he read from a message that was flashing slowly next to his face on the screen:

> *Kevin Edison was a computer scientist, software evangelist, and software architect. Mr. Edison was heading software application development for Soul, Mind, and Money Corporation on Wall Street. He was reported missing on September 11, 2001 —*

"Yes, this is my father...," I replied, my eyes filling with tears and my hands shivering.

"Your FATHER?" cried those who stood behind me, clapping their hands to their mouths. "Your FATHER?"

"Y-yes, my R-Rhubarb Pie. He's my daddy, my lost treasure, my hero, my lost soul. And I miss him, dearly," I said excruciatingly and burst into tears.

They all followed and tears flowed everywhere.

"It also reads that his wife, Ruth, and their two children, Samantha and Michael, survived him," said Newton. "Is this the person you're searching for?"

Words failed me. I nodded mutely.

"Wonderful, I'm glad you found him. My job is terminated, child. I'm going back to my afternoon nap. See you later and good luck!"

"No! Wait! Please do not go anywhere. Can I see him? Can I talk to him? Can I touch him? Can I hug him?"

At the same moment, Newton's face vanished again.

Then a little window popped up in the center of the display. It was an aperture to the outside world — a dim and grim place I'd never seen before. Through that opening I gazed at a world where soaking rain was falling steadily and a chill wind was thrashing about. Nothing, nothing was joyful there...

A few seconds later, a blurry but bright shape appeared in the window. A person — distant..., lost..., lonely..., isolated...

Then he edged nearer, toward me, as his image sharpened slowly.

I recognized jubilantly the familiar face. I knew the smile, the glittering blue eyes, the red-tinged cheeks, the long chin...

I could smell his aftershave, his sweat...

"Daddy, Daddy, Rhubarb Pie," I panted, sobbing as my face drew closer to the computer screen. "This is me, Sammy... Your little daughter... Look at me. I'm here, this way, Daddy —"

Silence answered.

Voiceless, perhaps bewildered, he gave me a weak grin.

Then he was winking incessantly, as if he knew I was there, near him, in front of the screen. He gave me another smile as if he sensed I was staring at him, longing to hug him after such a long time.

Peering intensely into my eyes, he was watching the tears that rolled down my cheeks. Probably wanting to say: *Hello, my Sammy, Samantha, sweetie, how have you been? How is Mummy? How is your brother, Michael, doing?*

A few inaudible seconds later... a minute... longer..., he faded, drifted away, gone, lost, blending in with the icy gray background.

My lips approached the chilly screen and touched it feebly as I felt I was drowning between tides of deep sorrow and shallow hope.

SKINGRUMANIALA

Pointing to his throbbing head, Larry said, "Doctor, what is going on with me? Strange things... strange things have been tormenting me lately." Then he gazed up at the ceiling and as a wave of fear swept over him he implored, "Please God, help me understand. Relieve me from the enduring pain. I can't take it anymore..."

"Hmmm, where does it hurt, Mr. Quackee?" asked Dr. Surpompular.

"My name is Mr. Larry Quack, Doctor — not Mr. Quackee," said Larry.

"Sorry, Mr. Quackee," said the doctor. "I'll update your records soon."

"I'm not sure where it hurts... Somewhere inside — deep inside. It feels sort of odd. Perhaps the thoughts that rush through my brain are causing pain and distress," said Larry as he lay sprawled stiffly on the clinic exam table. "Or perhaps all the bad things come from my heart — really not so sure..."

"Let me ask you a few questions, Mr. Quackee."

"Go ahead, Doc," cried Larry as a new wave of anxiety sent spasms of discomfort through his head.

"When was the last time you took a shower?"

"Why, why are you asking me this, Doctor?" Larry's left eyebrow went high, still jittery.

"Just answer my question, sir. Avoid answering a question with a question."

"A shower? Hmmmmm... Let's see. I think... N-not sure, was it last week?"

"You're answering with a question again. I don't have a clue when you last took a shower. The only one who would know is you," said Dr. Surpompular edgily.

"Perhaps last Friday, Doctor. I'm not sure…"

"And vitamins, Mr. Quackee? Do you take any vitamins? Or any medication that I don't know about?"

"Medication? No, Doc, no such thing."

"Have you touched anything you shouldn't have?" asked Dr. Surpompular. His forehead was half furrowed, mouth ajar as he inspected the skin on Larry's back through a huge magnifying glass.

"Do you see anything wrong there, Doc?"

"To remind you again, I'm the one who's asking the questions now, Mr. Quackee."

"I'm not sure… I have touched a bunch of stuff in the past few weeks, Doc. How am I supposed to know which of those things shouldn't have been touched?"

"Is there anything that concerns you, Larry?"

"I think I'm going crazy, Doc. Something is driving me nuts…"

"What's that?"

"I'm not sure Doc, perhaps my dreams. Probably the attention I'm getting in the press. Or maybe the countless women who seek my friendship bring on me unbearable stress…"

"It sounds like you're very popular, Mr. Quackee. What are you dreaming about, if I may ask?" wondered the doctor aloud as he examined Larry's temples.

"Not sure how to describe it, Doc. In my dreams I see different things… I tend to wake up five times a night."

"Give me one example," pressed Dr. Surpompular, eyes narrowing.

"I dreamed that our country was taken over by foreign powers. Annexed by evil supremacists who seek to destroy us…"

Dr. Surpompular gestured Larry to sit up. Then he inserted an orthoscope in Larry's ear canal — an examination that lasted at least a couple of minutes.

"Do you see anything interesting in there, Doc?"

"I see wax and some other stuff. When was the last time you cleaned your ears, Mr. Quackee?"

"My ears?"

"Now I understand why you're asking me so many questions. You need to clean your ears once in a while," said the doctor, raising his voice.

"Sure, Doc. Will do, Doc."

"Why do you dream such horrible things?"

"I have no control over things that run continuously through my brain. Nina, my property manager and my closest friend, told me that throughout history, occupiers who smelled weakness have invaded failing world powers, seizing the opportunity to —"

"Stop the nonsense, Larry. Are you out of your mind?" the doctor sighed suddenly. "No country in the world would want to mess with us. We are too strong, too powerful…"

"Y-yes, D-Doc."

"I can easily see, however," continued Dr. Surpompular, "how we ourselves could bring about our own demise. How our country could fall under its own weight. Destroy everything we have been building for the past hundreds of years."

"Right, D-Doc."

"Take my word, Mr. Quackee, we're an invincible superpower. Who in the world is going to challenge us? Your imagination is your enemy, Larry. You think too much. Focus on your private affairs rather than worrying about the improbable."

"Have you found anything there yet, Doc? Is anything wrong with my temples?"

"Nothing is wrong with your temples, but I noticed something strange. Perhaps there is something bad with your skin on your lower back. I don't have a clue, though. I haven't seen this before in any patients. Very strange, very…"

"My skin?" repeated Larry. "How could it be? Nina always tells me how beautiful my skin is. What do you find there, Doc?"

"I'd have to get a second opinion, Larry. Maybe Dr. Bernstein next door would be able to help me. There's something bizarre on your back that I have never seen before. There's also an odd object moving around in your ear, glowing and twirling deep inside."

Larry cried, "Oh, my Lord! My skin? My ears? Is this really what you found? Oh, my —"

Dr. Surpompular left the clinic in a hurry, giving a long and dramatic sigh. A few minutes later, he reappeared along with Dr. Bernstein. The latter's bold head, aglow with the clinic's halogen lights, made him look like the Milky Way Galaxy.

"Let me please take a look at your back, my young fellow," Dr. Bernstein said to Larry.

"You see," said Dr. Surpompular, calling Dr. Bernstein's attention to Larry's ruddy back. "You see these tiny translucent areas — there, near his lumbar region? What are these, in your opinion? Isn't it odd?"

"Yes, I see, I see…, hmmmmmmm, strange… Maybe he's got xuramulgagalala?" murmured Dr. Bernstein, trading looks of amazement with Dr. Surpompular, whose jaw dropped down a few inches. "Or maybe not. Maybe miiigilingula is what he has…"

"If he really suffers from miiigilingula, as you claim, Dr. Bernstein, we ought to send him to the emergency room right now! I hope it's not. That can be fatal!" warned Dr. Surpompular, cold sweat covering his cheeks. "I hope not! I hope not! Let me take a look at it again…"

Silence.

Then, incredulous, Dr. Surpompular stooped down toward Larry's back, making a renewed skin inspection. This time, however, he looked through a larger magnifying glass. Then he said confidently a minute later, "With all respect, Dr. Bernstein, I think you're mistaken. I don't think that's miiigilingula. It looks to me more like skingrumaniala. I'm pretty sure of it…"

At last, Dr. Bernstein agreed, but not before a stressful discussion had taken place, during which the two accused each other of misjudgment. And not before they had argued loudly about numerous medical terms that Larry didn't know.

"What's going on?" questioned Larry. "Are you mucking around with me? Are you kidding me? I feel superb, except for my disturbing dreams. I'm just fine, just fine. Everything is dandy!" he said with trepidation. "What is skingrumaniala anyway?"

"It's a medical condition, my young fellow — a severe one that afflicts youth and adults alike," said Dr. Bernstein tensely. "My father suffered from it until he died. My neighbor had it —"

"So, what are the symptoms of skingrumaniala? Am I in such a horrible medical condition?"

"As far as we can diagnose, Mr. Quackee, your symptoms are emotional distress, exaggerated self-esteem, and mood swings. But the most distressing finding is that your body is turning slowly invisible… In simple words, you're disappearing, sir. We noticed it on your back…," said Dr. Surpompular glumly.

Suddenly Larry sat upright on the examination table. He was brandishing his hands in horror, baring his translucent fingertips that had become invisible in the past few days. Then he yapped, "DO YOU MEAN I'M BECOMING INVISIBLE? JUST LIKE THAT? HUH?"

The doctors' eyes opened wide, astonished. Their hair stood up on the back of their necks at the revelation. "K-k-k-kin-kind of...," stammered Dr. Surpompular.

"TOTAL DISAPPEARANCE OF THE BODY?" Larry went on. "I have never heard of anyone else complaining about such a ridiculous condition. What does *disappearance* mean? Am I dying? Why me? Why me? Why me?"

"N-n-no, this is not the case — not at all, my young fellow," Dr. Bernstein burst forth. "You will not die in a physical sense. Your heart will still function, pounding vigorously like before. You'll be able to think, smile, and talk to people. But your body will disappear slowly. First, parts of your face will become transparent. Then the arms, then your legs, then everything else..."

Larry clapped the palm of his hand over his sweaty forehead and sniveled, "This is horrible! A real tragedy, Doc!"

"Don't worry, my young fellow. This is a good thing. You'll never have to pay for food. You'll be able to pick up anything you want from supermarket shelves without being noticed," said Dr. Bernstein, concealing his pity.

"But what about other things? Who would want to marry an invisible man? And how would I be able to run a company like this?"

"Well, you wouldn't be alone, my young fellow, I promise you! Many women out there are invisible. They live with the same medical condition. The only problem would be to find them. But even this would not be an issue, believe me! An invisible woman who is looking for a perfect invisible match would know how to become available."

CHAPTER SEVENTEEN

"THIS IS TOO MUCH TO BEAR, too much to tolerate in one day. Please God, don't let it happen!" cried Larry, his shivering mouth stretched into a sour gape. "S-s-so, what can we do now? What does the medical community suggest? How can it be fixed?"

"What you have is a rare disorder that no one knows how to cure. I'm sorry, young fellow. I wish I could help you," said Dr. Bernstein with a deep pang of sadness mixed with guilt. "You'll have to accept it. Get used to it, the same way you're accustomed to your bad dreams, your strange habits, your unsteady behavior, the pulsing thoughts of a declining culture, society, and country..."

The doctors ran out of ideas. Neither of them would risk losing his medical license over an inappropriate diagnosis. The only remedy, as always recommended on such special occasions, was to be found in the medical literature.

Facing a medical crisis, Dr. Surpompular, therefore, was the one who ordered Melinda, his nurse, to locate the *How to Cure Rare Syndromes* book.

Peeping through the crack of the door, the nurse said obediently, "Sure, Doctor. I'll get it immediately," and then scurried away to the clinic library.

"I think we should publish Mr. Quack's case in the *Unsolved Medical Mysteries Journal*. What do you think, Dr. Bernstein? Isn't it a fascinating case study? This'd be our chance to get inducted into the Hall of Fame —" said Dr. Surpompular, his shining face turned even shinier.

"I don't understand," interrupted Larry furiously. "I'm dying, my body is decaying, and you don't care. Instead, you're contemplating your own fame and fortune —"

"No, no, my young fellow, we are concerned about your well-being..." interjected Dr. Bernstein.

Not too long later, Melinda tiptoed into the clinic. She carried a box of books and a wad of research papers under her arms. While dropping them one by one on Dr. Surpompular's desk, she said, "I'm sorry, Doctor. Someone else has already borrowed the book you requested. Here are similar studies and articles, instead: 'Dangerous Illnesses That Kill in 30 Days.' 'How to Cure Arrogant People.' 'How to Become a Famous Physician.' 'Diseases That, God Forbid, No One Should Have.' 'Fun Sicknesses.' 'Remedies for Donkeys —'"

"Enough, enough, enough! I know how to read," said Dr. Surpompular, with a whiff of annoyance while skimming through the articles. Then he turned to his colleague, saying, "Dr. Bernstein, take a look. Here's something interesting. This paper was written by Alu Balu, a former student of mine..."

For too long the doctors were huddling around the sea of documents, trading looks of astonishment, exchanging whispers, and swapping ideas. The two could not reach a unanimous conclusion.

Dr. Surpompular maintained that only God would be able to save Larry from his incurable disorder. Dr. Bernstein, though, claimed there was no room for religious sentiment when facing medical challenges like this one.

Notwithstanding the divergent views, they dug up a list of recommendations that were later read aloud to Larry, who could hardly believe his ears.

"There are three things," said Dr. Bernstein parentally and sympathetically, "that could improve your situation, my young fellow. Our findings suggest that you take serious measures to get your system under control — emotionally, spiritually, and physically."

"And what are these remedies, Doc?" questioned Larry with a look of growing skepticism.

"Harrrrummmphhhh." Dr. Surpompular cleared his throat and said in a hoarse voice, "Well, Mr. Quackee. There are three steps you must follow meticulously. First, get your emotions under control; relaxation is a must. Every morning, take an olive oil bath. Or marinate your body in hot vinegar. Or soak yourself in baking soda until you achieve solid rational equilibrium…"

"What is *rational equilibrium*, Doc?"

"Rational equilibrium, sir, means steadiness. It's something you'd need to work on."

Larry nodded, still doubtful.

Then Dr. Bernstein added, "Second, my young fellow, spiritual activities are essential for healing. Talk to everyone. Talk to everything. Talk to your employees, your friends, your family. Talk to the flowers. Talk to your pets. Visit the Bronx Zoo and talk to the bears, to the tigers, to the zebras…"

Next, Dr. Surpompular complimented his colleague's recommendations, adding, "Communicate with everyone, Mr. Quackee. Take a morning stroll and chat with the squirrels. Converse with the birds. Conduct a warm dialogue with the turtles. Maintain eye contact with the trees. Whisper to the clouds. Dance with the butterflies in the rain. Swing with the mosquitoes to the music of a soggy day…"

Larry bobbed his head, still unconvinced.

"Third," continued Dr. Bernstein, "is touch, my young fellow. Touching is vital to the physical recovery of any human. Especially in your condition, you must engage in the art of touching. Yes, touching… Touch with the tips of your fingers. Touch with your tongue. Hug everyone, everything. Hug people, hug pets, embrace nature in your arms, cuddle the weak, the unlucky, and the destitute."

Still dubious, Larry shrugged his shoulders.

SKINGRUMANIALA

Melinda the nurse, who had been listening to the doctors' counsel, interjected her own opinion in a weak voice. She was almost whispering, "The power of giving can heal the giver. Share your fortune with those who need it most. Allot some of your valuable possessions to the unfortunate." Then she shuffled slowly toward the door.

Larry grew utterly leery, his spirits dampened.

CHAPTER EIGHTEEN

STUPENDOUS PROPOSITIONS

Within walking distance of Central Park on Manhattan's Upper East Side was Larry's 9,700-square-foot luxury apartment. It was one of the most breathtaking dwellings in the city.

The multistory town house consisted of many rooms and countless features — far more than any one person would ever need: seven bedrooms, ten bathrooms, ten powder rooms, dining rooms, marble kitchens, guest rooms, multiple fireplaces, walk-in closets, indoor swimming pools, spa baths, a terrace, a balcony, a roof deck, a private deck, and an exquisite garden on the roof.

Much beyond what the ordinary eye could visualize, the vast apartment also consisted of exclusive fittings. Computers activated almost everything in the residence. With the click of a button, you could operate, roll open, snap closed, twirl, slide, or wheel around almost any object.

Computers monitored even the kitchen appliances and the temperature-controlled garage. Just about everything was programmed, activated, or idled according to a predefined schedule — responding to changes in seasons and to the intensity of twilights and dawns. All was supervised like in the good old school of computer science. And all of it calibrated for efficiency and coziness.

Larry's good taste pleased the eye from the moment you set foot in his private world. It was impossible to disregard his inordinate appreciation for design.

The sleek fixtures embodied the spirit of the modern Bauhaus design style. The collection of paintings on the walls personified

Larry's passion for modern art. Masterpieces of Mark Rothko, Andy Warhol, Robert Motherwell, and Jackson Pollock dominated the sun-soaked apartment.

And there inside, Larry and his three companions lived their lives comfortably. One of them was Nina Browning, his property manager for the past five years, with whom he maintained a close relationship. Offering unwavering support, Nina was always there for him. She stood by him at all times, meeting his unpredictable and never-ending demands.

Apart from carrying the burden of moral and psychological duties, Nina was also the one in command of the huge residence. It was she who hired housekeepers, managed the finances, and cared for the flourishing garden on the roof.

Thanks to Nina's gardening skills, the group enjoyed fresh fruit and vegetables all year long. Also because of her, Larry never lacked for any comforts. Never was he short of attention and love, because Nina gave them all.

The two other residents, Emma Sinclair and Savannah Bishop, were the housekeepers. Their combined enthusiasm and vigor contributed to the freshness, cleanliness, and sophistication of the dwelling.

Emma had been a child prodigy. She earned her doctor of philosophy degree at age 18. At 25, she had already published her first book, about social fairness and equality.

Savannah's path had been different. She didn't earn a high school diploma until she was 32. Later on, she enjoyed taking cooking, gardening, biology, and sociology classes.

Both intelligent and ambitious, Emma and Savannah had found a place of protection from the outside world in Larry's house. They had never had such a safe and tranquil environment before.

CHAPTER EIGHTEEN

It was the day after Larry's visit to the two doctors. Worn to a frazzle, he was sitting at the head of the dining table on that evening.

His beaten-down posture expressed sorrow and anguish over the collapse of his business: Soul, Mind, and Money Corporation. "I don't know how I'm going to afford this apartment anymore," he said, hitching up his sliding pants. "My business is destroyed, and I simply don't know where the money will come from."

Short silence.

"Don't worry, Larry. There are some savings left," Nina consoled him, grasping his hand. "Have you visited the doctor lately?"

"Yes, I met with Dr. Surpompular and his colleague, Dr. Bernstein, yesterday."

"So, tell us, what did they think about your condition?"

"I was diagnosed with skingrumaniala, a rare and almost incurable medical condition," he confided.

"WHAT'S THAT?" Nina squealed, startled, eyes wide open.

"Oh, skingrumaniala? Yes, I've read about it in some social equality studies — pretty fascinating stuff," said Emma. "Only the privileged are infected with this precious bug," her eyes shining brightly in the dimmed dining room. "Only the privileged —"

Alarmed and puzzled, Nina asked, "And why would having a bug of any kind be such a pleasurable experience?"

"No one, no one I know has complained about skingrumaniala so far. On the contrary, this is fun —"

"WHAT ARE YOU SAYING, Emma?" wailed Nina.

"FUN?" thundered Larry, "FUN? What's so fun about disappearing from the surface of the Earth? What's so fun about turning invisible forever? What's so fun about losing whatever you possess?"

"You're not going to lose anything, Larry," comforted Emma. "Invisibility could be restored by tanning your face with the color of your choice: Pink, red, blue, green, anything. Anything, Larry —"

"Anything?" cried Nina in despair.

"This does not make me feel better!" he said.

"Think about the umpteen opportunities instead, Larry," said Emma, giving a sophisticated grin. "Each day in your life you could look and feel different. Totally different! If one morning you feel blue, smudge your invisible face with blue. Have an appetite for yellow at the break of dawn? Smear your cheeks, eyebrows, forehead, chin, and hair with yellow —"

"Oh God, NO! Yellow? What a disgusting tan, my love," howled Nina, trading looks of anxiety with Larry.

"Terrible!" said Savannah, who had been silent since they had sat down at the table. "Horrible, indeed… Why do such good people have to be infected with such a devastating illness? Why?" and gave a sentimental snivel.

"WHY? WHY?" joined Nina, clicking her tongue.

"You're overreacting. This is not the end of the world," said Emma. "I have seen worse, much worse…"

"But why me? WHY? WHY? WHY?" said Larry.

"Skingrumaniala is a social illness," explained Emma. "You could scarcely find people with skingrumaniala way back in the past century. It was rare — very unusual. People were good and nice, empathetic, caring for each other —"

"Can you please pass the salt?" interrupted Larry.

Nina handed him the salt. Then she grasped his hand in support and said in a soft voice, "I love you, Larry, everything will be all right —"

"I love you, too, Larry —" Savannah confessed suddenly.

"I love you, too, Larry," revealed Emma.

Astounded at their revelations, Nina raised her eyebrows as high as she could and gave them looks full of extreme awe.

"Love and respect were the norms in those old days," continued Emma. "Steep deterioration of moral values and the weakening of social foundations have accelerated the pace of the skingrumaniala epidemic. The more society became corrupt, the more social values eroded, the more decrepit our culture became. The more thoughtless the people grew, the more skingrumaniala spread and multiplied and the more people were infected. With time they became invisible —"

"ENOUGH is ENOUGH!" squeaked Larry. "Are you implying that I'm a bad guy? Are you suggesting that I do not care for others? Are you stating that my moral values are corrupt? Are you hinting that I do not help the weak and needy? Are you claiming that I'm selfish, uncaring?"

"My beauty is not a bad guy!" screeched Nina as the tip of her nose and her upper lip became invisible.

"Definitely he is not a bad guy!" echoed Savannah, eyes brimming with tears as her brown hair grew into a gray bushy patch of fading grass.

"Certainly he is not a bad guy!" repeated Emma as her ear lobes and left eye and portions of her right arm turned translucent.

Nina gave them a jealous look full of resentment.

And Larry went on as his anger rose, "Are you saying I'm being punished for the decline of our social values? Am I being penalized for the worsening manners of our youth? For the deteriorating behavior of our people?"

"Not at all," said Emma coolly. "The skingrumaniala bug is contagious. Good people can get it too —"

"Pass the jam, please," said Larry.

"We're out of jam," said Nina.

"NO JAM?" he wailed, eyes suddenly tightening to mere slits of frustration.

"Sorry," she said remorsefully. "I'll get you jam tomorrow."

"Tomorrow... Tomorrow... Always tomorrow..." he grumbled, face reddening.

"Can he be cured?" asked Nina, still wailing.

"Depends, really depends," said Emma. "It'd require a long process of painful cleansing until his mind is purified and his soul disinfected. In simple words, Larry will need to drain the poisons that have been soaking in his body for so long."

The discussion about Larry's condition went on and on. Stricken the most was Nina, who could barely accept his painful illness. The tear-jerking confession of his disease called for a plan of defense. Remedies must be applied soon. An aggressive healing timetable ought to be put in place as soon as possible.

The revelation about Larry's disorder and the anxiety that crept in took a toll on all of them. As time went by, the dreadful skingrumaniala caught up with them too. No one around the dining table seemed to escape the contagious bug.

No one.

It was now the next day, and supervised by his doctors and encouraged by Nina, Emma, and Savannah, Larry's healing process began. In his red swimming shorts, he was floating serenely on his back in his pool on tiny tides of pearls. Yes, "The Pearl Pool" they would name it later on, for it was filled with *Keshi* pearls and Tahitian pearls.

Pearls had the power, Larry believed, to cure the illness that had descended upon him after the demise of his business.

The radiating power of pearls, he assumed, could halt the slow process of turning invisible.

The rare, round, and smooth pearls, he hoped, would purify his body.

CHAPTER EIGHTEEN

The glinting pearls, he trusted, would eradicate the meanness and the unkindness that had taken over his personality during the years of harsh survival in the business world.

Emma was there too. On a pink lifeguard chair and through tiny binoculars, she was supervising his recovery in the pool of shiny pearls. Her eyes were monitoring Larry's every move.

At first, he took a mild dip, submerging his body for only a few short seconds. Then he stayed under the layers of pearls a long minute. Then he disappeared under the surface longer than before. Then he resurfaced, seemingly soothed and blissful like the humpback whale in the Atlantic Ocean. Then he swam on his back across the pool and at last threw anchor near Emma's feet.

"Brrrrrr... The pearls are cold, chilling like ice cubes in a freezer. Whose ludicrous idea was it to have me swimming in a pool of pearls? I'm also hungry, starving to death...," said Larry, gyrating like a belly dancer.

"Hungry? Here is your sandwich," she said. "I made it from fresh ingredients picked in our garden..."

"What's in the sandwich?" he asked, still floating on his back, his eyes shut tight.

"I made it for you with deep affection and devotion..." Emma purred softly. "Only my love can cure you, Larry... Only me..."

Staggered at her sudden emotional confession, Larry found his mouth was agape, his eyes wide open, and his brow wrinkled. He was looking at her beaming face, which appeared flipped upside down from his sight line. "How could love be stuffed in a sandwich, and how could love heal?"

"If you only gave me the chance, Larry, if you only let me show you how —"

"Nowadays worries and fear occupy my mind. Love is not at the top of my priorities, Emma," he said and slowly closed his eyes.

"If you only gave me the opportunity —"

"I'm not ready for love. Love is not for me," he said sternly.

"You need me, you need my care. Let me in your life, and I'll make you happy. Unlock your sealed heart, and your sickness will vanish. You'll start smiling again. A ray of hope will outshine the darkness that you're immersed in…"

Shaken by her unanticipated passionate plea, he opened his eyes wider than before. "I do not believe in love," he said gloomily, rejecting her proposition. "I used to — not anymore. Love is for people who want to control each other. Love manifests in mutual abuse."

"So you don't believe in love, eh?"

"What's to believe in love? Love is love and that's it. There's nothing to it."

"Have you ever loved anyone?"

"I'm not sure… I'm not sure…"

"Has anyone ever loved you?"

"Perhaps… I'm not sure…"

"Maybe your parents loved you, Larry, or probably someone else?"

"Maybe, I don't remember. I'm not sure, Emma…"

"Did your parents care for you?"

Short silence. His eyes fluttered uneasily.

"Did they, Larry?"

Short silence.

"So maybe no one has ever cared for you. Perhaps no one has ever loved you."

"My father died when I was 4," he said quietly, the words barely coming out of his mouth. "My mother passed away a couple of years later," his eyes brimming with tears. "I was sent to an orphanage, a place where kids like me scrambled for attention, hungry for affection, devoid of love. I don't know what love is. I don't care for love. And love would not cure my illness"

"Ohhhh, poor boy, of course it would. Love is miraculous," said Emma with confidence, half grinning. "I was raised by loving parents. I had a happy childhood. I can give you what you've missed in life. Marry me, Larry! Marry me! Marry me, and you'll turn into a joyful man."

"I can't, I simply can't. This is not a good time. Besides, I'd never marry a housekeeper or a maid like you. You're much beneath my social status. Women who marry above their stations typically fail to appreciate it. If I ever married, I myself would marry up — not down. I'd marry a well-off lady who could provide a financially secure life."

A sudden overwrought stillness descended upon them.

Humiliated to her core, Emma shouted abruptly, "YOU'RE DISGUSTING!" as she seized a stainless-steel fork from the flatware set laid next to his sandwich and brandished it violently. "You're a SNOB! Your soul is corrupt, filthy, stinky! You'll never recover from your disease! Skingrumaniala will KILL YOU! I know it will, I have seen it happen before." She wept, raising the fork as high as she could, and then aiming at his chest, resolved to pierce his heart in revenge.

Giving a hideous grin, Larry squirmed swiftly out of her reach and leaped deep into the pool of pearls…

It was the next day. A jubilant morning was brightened by sunny rays of light streaming through the windows. It was a morning that had begun with the joyful chirps of birds. Birds that peered through the windows of Larry's workout room. Birds that greeted him with their marvelous tweeting tenors. Birds that cared for him, his recovery, his welfare.

The spa bath on that floor was already heated. Vapors were rising from the steaming golden liquid that filled it. Red rose petals were arranged in heart-shaped patterns floating on the surface of the bath to boost the healing process. Towels were heaped almost everywhere.

Savannah was there too. She was sitting on the wide edge of the tub and holding a breakfast platter, from which appetite-enticing aromas permeated the place.

"Good morning, ma'am," Larry greeted her, giving a pleasant grin. "I think I'm feeling already better. The only thing that still haunts me is the recurring horrible dreams."

"What's on your mind, Larry?"

"I'm not sure, Savannah. Maybe stress. Or maybe some lack of attention… I see war. I see devastation. I see people suffering. I see the demise of a country — not sure which one. Not even sure when and where…"

"Your ailment is grave. Relax, Larry. Your doctor prescribed this special bath. Immerse yourself in the golden water. Listen to the rhythm of nature. Listen to your body. I'll be here, next to you, holding your hand through the journey of healing."

"What's in this tub?"

"Liquid gold — pure gold, Larry. It contains strong antioxidants for your body, a remedy devised to heal your severe skingrumaniala condition."

"GOLD?"

"Yes, unadulterated gold!"

"How could we afford so much gold, Savannah?"

"Money is not important, Larry, your health is, though."

"Pure nonsense! Who says so?"

"Your body will turn permanently translucent if you keep worrying about money," warned Savannah.

"Can anything be accomplished in life without money?"

"Yes, many things, sir. Money, though, will not heal you."

"And gold would? Ha-ha-ha-ha-ha-ha," said Larry cynically and then hurled himself eagerly into the tub of liquid gold.

Larry's hasty plunge surprised Savannah, for she had intended to give him some instructions — guidance for people who are prescribed gold baths. Troubled was she during the long seconds Larry vanished under the glittering surface of gold. Concerned was she when the tip of his head stuck out from the simmering gold solution. Horrified was she when Larry, speechless, made a gesture of struggle and dunked again in the expensive and deep tub.

But Larry did not die. He reemerged. His body was coated with a thin layer of shiny yellow gold like the gold of the golf trophies hanging on his home office walls.

"Why are you laughing, Savannah? I'm in piercing pain. Call Dr. Surpompular immediately!"

"If you feel you're dying, it's not because you're dying. This is the usual reaction to a gold bath, Larry. You're just feeling the process of purification. By the end of the day, your pain will be gone. Then you'll feel like the rest of us — like every average middle-class fellow."

"What has this to do with the average middle-class Joe?" he bellowed as he tried to scrape off the layer of gold stuck to his arms, to his legs, to his torso, to his entire body.

"It has a lot to do with the average Joe," she insisted. "The instructions indicate that not only will your money be gone after taking the bath, but your superior social status also will be diminished."

"WHAT? MY MONEY WILL BE GONE? WHERE IS MY MONEY NOW?" he shouted frantically while edging toward her in very small steps, leaving a thin trail of gold drops on the burnished floor.

"Your money is in the tub," said Savannah frightfully. "Nina, who has access to your bank accounts, ordered the gold from —"

"DID SHE EMPTY MY BANK ACCOUNTS TO BUY THIS GOLD?" screamed Larry as he drew closer and closer to her.

"Yes, but only for your good health, Larry. We love you. I love you," she said passionately.

"My Lord, I'm broke, I'm poor, I'm destroyed, I'm not even in the middle class. I belong to the lowest, lowest, lowest class. I'm nothing. I'm dust. I'm air — bad air."

"The most important thing to remember in this hard time is that I still love you, Larry."

"LOVE?" he roared, close to her, as she hopped to her feet, prepared to throw her arms around him.

"Marry me, Larry, marry me! I don't care which social class you belong to."

He leaped quickly toward her, clamped her shoulders with his gold-covered arms, shook her hard, and shrieked, "WHERE IS MY MONEY?"

Then he shoved her forcefully into the steaming tub, as she still seemed full of compassion, of love...

It was the next day. Larry had not been able to rub off the layer of gold stuck to his skin — perhaps cemented all over him for the rest of his life. The stiffness he sensed came not only from the hardening gold on his body. A rigid sentiment, too, was accompanying him everywhere — feelings of failure and distress that were affecting his judgment and behavior like never before.

The relationships with Emma and Savannah had collapsed. Even with Nina, things had been growing worse. Nina had been unavailable, cold, and uncooperative while Larry was absorbed in his illness. They had grown apart from each other.

CHAPTER EIGHTEEN

As he was clambering up the hundred stairs from his bedroom to the garden on the roof, he remembered the good old days. He recalled the days when he had controlled everything: his firm, his employees, his timetable, his life. He had been in total command of his destiny.

Now, turning invisible, horrified as time crept along at a slow pace, Larry felt more vulnerable than ever — dependent on the women who had been living with him.

There she was. Nina was slouching in a lounge chair, basking in the morning sun, waiting for him. As they had planned, Larry was to meet her on the roof garden to discuss their future endeavors. And most important, to take a dip in the tub — another doctor's recommendation he was about to obey. Wheezing, gasping for air, he sprawled in the chair beside her.

"Do you remember the promise you made to me last year?"

"No."

"You promised that next year at the same time we would be married," sighed Nina deeply.

"Did I?"

"Why would anyone get me an engagement ring if he did not mean it?"

"Oh, that was not an engagement ring. It was an appreciation gift for your years of hard work, Nina. For maintaining my property, managing the staff, and taking care of my finances."

Taken aback by his broken promise, she concealed her deep disappointment with a long silence. *Something must be wrong with him*, she thought. *Skingrumaniala must have consumed him*, she believed. *And the only thing that could help his case now would be to continue with the treatment he has started*, she presumed. "Larry, why don't you get into the tub. This will do only good," she said softly, composing her emotions.

"I have been taking bath after bath. I'm getting impatient. What's in this tub, anyway?"

"Diamonds, my love, pure diamonds, not fake — only for your health, dear."

"How could you waste all my money on gold and diamonds? How could you? I've worked so hard all my life, and now all my fortune is getting frittered away on nonsense — pure nonsense," he screeched, on brink of tears.

"It's a worthwhile investment, Larry. Everyone would tell you it was the right thing to do. The choice between your life and your money was clear. Get into the bath, sweetie. I'm sure you'll understand it. Get into the bath and purify your soul, my little bonbon."

"Detox, detox, and detox. That's all I've been hearing from you the past few days. Nothing else."

"Jump into this tub, Larry, and cleanse your mind. Get rid of the bad stuff — the cruelty and the malice that have been dominating your behavior."

"But the other day you said I'm a good man. Didn't you, Nina? Didn't you say so?" he wept, tears stinging his bloodshot eyes.

Indifferent to his anguish, she pressed on, "Darling, leap into the tub of diamonds to eradicate your evil spirit. Try this tub, and relief will descend upon you, my charming love. Too much money and influence have sickened you. Rubbing elbows with the wrong members of elite society have maddened you, honey. Take a good diamond bath. It'll sterilize your mind, sugar. You need a new perspective in life, and diamonds will fix you."

Halfheartedly, Larry stood up languidly and then plodded under the weight of his misery toward the glinting tub. He gazed for a few moments at the millions of diamonds that blinked in a wide rainbow of colors.

CHAPTER EIGHTEEN

Before Larry plunged into the tub, he snatched a glimpse at Nina, whose sunglasses covered her weeping eyes.

Strangely enough, the diamonds were warm and embracing and utterly kind to his body — like a baby's diaper. Oddly enough, diamonds typically used for cutting stiff metals treated him as if he were as fragile as cotton. Welcoming were the diamonds, as if they were saying, *we love you, Larry. You're a good man.*

It was the next day, and except for the gathering planned for later in the evening, a day like any other. In spite of their troubled relationships with Larry, for this special event Nina, Emma, and Savannah shouldered the efforts to make his town house inviting and warm. They prepared refreshments, and they brushed, scrubbed, mopped, shined, and swept anything they could.

The doorbell chimed.

The mood was quiet and gloomy as the visitors arrived one by one. Some were Larry's former employees who had survived the tragedy. Others were the spouses, children, and close relatives of those who had perished. They all had been invited to Larry's place for an informal meeting. They had been called to address immediate concerns and to remember the horrible event that had engulfed the nation a month before.

Among the guests was Anna Broderick, whose son had vanished without a trace. Allan Stuart, who had escaped the burning building, showed up too. Other invitees included Eduardo Prado, the company's treasurer, and Larry's executive assistant, Julia Linden. Both had been rescued a couple of minutes before the building collapsed. And there was Mr. Donald Zakharov, who had lost his wife, Karina. Also attending the gathering were Ruth and Michael Edison, whose respective husband and father, Kevin Edison, was missing. And others were there too: Chakor and Albert and Sabina and Joan and Miki and Yvonne.

"Last month, a horrific tragedy took us by surprise," moaned Larry as he peered into his guests' weary faces. "The pain is hard to bear. The agony is overwhelming," he said, as tears ran down his cheeks. "Nothing can comfort our excruciating sorrow over the loss of our wives, husbands, sons, sisters, brothers, relatives. Nothing," he wept, his words dwindling away. "Our loved ones will never be forgotten."

And almost everyone there, in the guest room, was immersed in deep grief too.

Words failed him. Speechless he was, staring at the people who had been so dedicated to his firm. He gazed at them, admiring their resilience and bravery.

Then Nina rose to her feet and continued Larry's statement: "Soul, Mind, and Money Corporation will last forever. And so will our perseverance. Do not fret. The company is committed to supporting you and your families.

"Larry is a good man," she added.

Larry nodded his head mutely.

CHAPTER NINETEEN

MY MAILBOX

The days coasted by at a fast clip. June passed at a gallop, July whooshed at a run, August zoomed at a dash, and September whizzed at a sprint. And now, time went back to the same exact June.

"Puffing" and "scrunching" time seemed like Uncle Walter's time-warping experiments. Time went backward and forward, repeatedly reviving the events prior to Rhubarb Pie's disappearance. It appeared as an attempt to reverse history.

Not for the life of me had I the slightest idea about what was going on back at home. Not even a clue, because my journey in the City of @ continued to occupy my mind, dominating every aspect of my life.

I imagined, though, that Mom and Michael, my brother, were still immersed in agony and sorrow over the disappearance of Daddy, my sweet Rhubarb Pie. I knew Mom would definitely strive to fix our shattered lives, bring some sense of peace to the harsh reality, and hopefully, begin a long healing process.

And what about Uncle Walter? I wondered. *What is he up to these days? Is he still consumed by his latest inventions and scientific experiments?* I imagined he persisted in trying to perfect his time-warping capabilities: moving time back and forth — or even halting it. Probably he was also making significant strides in his virtual world project by creating unreal, imaginary realities.

And Emilia Parker, my best friend, what is she doing now? I assumed she was focusing on her school final exams. Perhaps, every so often, she was thinking about my strange departure. Maybe in her spare moments, she was even searching for me on the Internet...

And Eric Kinsley, my school buddy? I bet he's still absorbed in building a small space exploration rover to be launched, as he always had aspired, at the Sun. Most certainly, Eric would have very little time to think about me. I doubted if he remembered our friendship that had started developing before the beginning of my voyage to find Rhubarb Pie.

I was certain that all of them were busy with their daily chores. Probably, they had very little time to dwell on my whereabouts. Perhaps their lives were too hectic to be engrossed in memories of our fading relationships.

No one was around that day. Loneliness is something that's hard to bear, especially on a birthday. Not one person was around to celebrate the day I came into this world. Not a soul…

Friendless and tearful, I found myself in a chilly computer room immersed in thick haze. Sizzling, almost burning, hardworking spherical devices were suspended in the air. I was staring at hundreds and hundreds of colorful balls — strange spheres bouncing in midair. They were moving up and down in slow motion like squid in a fish tank.

The countless balls were connected by pipes — long and short translucent tubes, through which a rainbow of lights traveled at enormous speed.

What are these mysterious illuminated balls? I questioned. They looked like vibrant stars, talking to each other, communicating intensely in a language I could not understand.

And what are the bright lights rushing restlessly through the tubes that link the spheres? Were they messages transmitted from one ball to another? Perhaps the soaring balls were tiny computers that delivered electronic mail.

E-mails, Rhubarb Pie used to call them. E-mails that people exchange, e-mails that keep people in touch. Probably the balls conversed in a secret computer language. Maybe texting to each other in a foreign tongue nobody could comprehend. Or perhaps there were other kinds of messages. Messages transmitted between machines, computers.

From time to time, blurry and gloomy whimpers disturbed the silent place, "hummmmmmmmmm, hummmmmm, hummm…" Other undertones echoed softly, somewhat cheerfully: "H-h-h-h-happy birthday to you, dear Sammy! H-h-happy birthday to you, dear Sammy! H-h-happy birthday to you, dear Sammy!"

Yes, hard to believe — I was already 13.

The dimmed computer room, electric devices, pipes, blinking lights, freezing air-conditioning, sterile shiny floors, and odd hums only increased my sadness.

My wistful thoughts kept bringing me back to the past…

If only I could talk to Mom for a second or two and hug Michael, I'd be the happiest girl on Earth.

If only I could spend some time with Emilia or laugh with Eric once again at our history teacher, I'd be the gladdest child in the world.

If only I could chat with Uncle Walter about anything, I'd be the cheeriest person in the universe.

And on another, sad note: If only I could wear on my birthday my glitter shoes that I love — the ones with the ankle band across the top and the cute red bow on the toe…

If only I could…

If you haven't stumbled yet across the strangest creature in the world, wait until you get to know Mooshkeeki. A dark corridor led me to his office after I scampered away from the odd computer room. There I found him munching on a roasted chicken and swilling beer from a very large mug. When he finished his meal, he swiveled in his executive chair, rubbed his bloated belly, picked his nose, and burped loudly. Surreal he was, indeed.

MY MAILBOX

Mooshkeeki's grungy workplace looked like a junkyard. Tall piles of dirty plates, cups, and chicken bones occupied one corner of his office. In the other corner, loads of paper napkins were scattered on top of one another. In between, attesting to Mooshkeeki's muddled mind, a messy desk was piled up with rusted computers. Old cables, broken screens, corroded screwdrivers, and whatnot were strewn there too.

The three large bay windows that stretched behind Mooshkeeki's back were the only bright spots in the room. Bright they were because of the excessive glare they let into the office. Bright they seemed, for they revealed a different reality — exposure to the outside world — beyond the City of @.

Through the middle window, you could gaze all day long at the ocean's floor as if it were a spectacular landscape viewed from a road overlook. There, deep inside, giant octopuses, huge spider crabs, enormous squid, and flatfishes swayed serenely. At times, some of the creatures were peering curiously into Mooshkeeki's office, perhaps startled at the clutter inside. Others were drifting cheerfully in the salty water as if they felt lucky enough not to be a part of his world.

The far-left window offered a sneak peek into the heavens. Through there, you could gape leisurely for hours and hours at the Moon through the blue crisp sky of midday. The Moon, too, seemed relieved, giving a slight smile, as if it were grateful not to be a part of the City of @. *What city, though, is under that sky? New York? Philadelphia? Washington?* I couldn't tell. Any of those places might have had such pretty, promising, hopeful, shiny heavens...

And in the far-right window — a family, a whole family: a child with two adults at his side who were laying their hands on his shoulders. They were gazing at us through the glass from the outside, grinning, joyful, together...

CHAPTER NINETEEN

"In our culture, in the City of @, if you want respect," said Mooshkeeki when our eyes met, "you must burp after a meal. The more you burp, the more cherished you are. Simply put, enjoy your life, your meals, your friends."

His jaw-dropping appearance would daze almost anyone. I was lost for words. Mooshkeeki's bloodless skin was stretched over his skull like an animal hide over the top of an ancient drum. His lips were painted pink and cracked like the soil in the Karakum Desert in Turkmenistan. His voice was low and nasal, muffled like a trumpet falling prey to the flu.

And akin to the dwellers of the City of @, the invisible sections of Mooshkeeki's body were utterly large. Through his translucent patches, I found some relief: I was able to gawk at the back of his office. I found refuge looking through the windows at the outside world, at the unveiled freedom.

"Don't you gaze at me like that," he intoned, letting out a feeble growl.

Silent. I felt a lump in my throat.

"And your name is?" he asked, gesturing with a fling of his hand at a chair.

"Samantha. Some know me as *Sammy*."

"Is that so? What are you doing here, if I may ask?"

"I don't know."

"Is that so? Maybe you're here because we've got some mail for you. Maybe you're here because fresh, wet, hot mail arrived and is waiting in your mailbox."

I shrugged my shoulders. "I don't know. I have no mailbox."

"Is that so? No mailbox… Ha-ha-ha-ha, huwii-huwii-huwii-huwii… No mailbox…"

Suddenly, Mooshkeeki's assistant, Dooshkeeki, barged into the office through the crack of the door and slammed it shut behind him. Then he strode forward and straddled a stool, adjacent to his boss. Most of him was translucent. A hint of his large contour was visible. His chin, nose, forehead, and right eye were invisible. So were large portions of his torso, arms, and legs.

"Did you hear that, Dooshkeeki? The kid said, 'I don't have a mailbox.' Ha-ha-ha-ha. She has no mailbox. Huwii-huwii-huwii-huwii."

"Oh my, my, good heavens, oh my, my…, you do not have a mailbox? Everyone must have a mailbox, everyone!" said Dooshkeeki, somewhat incredulous. "Are you sure? Are you very sure?"

"I have not heard from anyone since I set foot in the City of @. Not from a soul. Not from my mom, brother, uncle, friends — not from anyone. There are no means of communication with the outside world in this place. It's worse than jail," I protested, on the brink of tears.

In the far-right window, I noticed tears of sadness pouring down the child's cheeks as his parents cuddled him firmly, sympathizing with me.

"Is that so?" said Mooshkeeki, giving a cynical grin, still massaging his stomach gently. "And in this place, in this place, kid, tears buy nothing!" he added.

Glimpsing at Mooshkeeki and me in turns, Dooshkeeki said with irony mixed with pity, "Goodness gracious. My, my, my… Isn't it sad, boss? The girl does not have communications. My, my, my… Did you hear that, boss? What do you mean, we do not have communications, kid? We have lots of communications! We can provide oodles and oodles of communications! If she does not have communications, let's give her communications, boss. If she needs communications, we can arrange one of those powerful mailboxes for her. We usually give them to complainers, to annoying grumblers. Ha-ha-ha-ha…"

"Oh, yeah, sure we can!" said Mooshkeeki, hunching over. "After all, who else can provide her with communications if not the Message Hub of the City of @? We offer all sorts of communications. We deliver all kinds of messages to people, to computers, to cell phones —"

"Let's not complicate the issue, boss. The little girl needs a simple mailbox to read some mail from her loved ones. So, why don't we give it to her, boss? A little mailbox will do it, boss!" interjected Dooshkeeki, glancing at me.

"Wait, wait. Easy, easy. Let's not rush. It isn't that simple. She just walked in," said Mooshkeeki. "Should we feed her with a silver spoon just like that? Spoil her like all those rotten parents do? The mailbox is not free. I'm sorry, kid. No freebies here. First, you must pay your dues!"

"W-what k-kind of dues w-would I need to pay to get my mailbox?" I asked shakily.

"What kind of dues would you need to pay?" said Mooshkeeki — making a question out of my query. "Well, well, let's see…," he said, exchanging cunning looks with Dooshkeeki. "Well, kid, you must know something important about us before we move on: We love jokes. Can you tell us at least three — three good jokes to brighten our day?"

"No, I'm not in a mood for jokes," I said resentfully, sick to my stomach.

"That so? Well, if you do not like jokes, maybe we can trade them with lies. So tell us three good lies. Be a little dishonest, just like Dooshkeeki and me. You don't have to be so truthful, so innocent. Give us three false statements, and the mailbox is yours, girl. Take your time kid. We have all the time in the world."

"Lies? Lies about what?" I wondered, forehead furrowing.

"Yes, lies, only lies. We do not want to hear the truth; the truth always hurts. You must contribute something: small lies, big lies... It's so easy, kid. Everyone lies. I lie, Dooshkeeki lies, we lie to ourselves, strangers lie, your parents lie, your doctor lies, your teacher lies. Even politicians lie, maybe even the president lies — who knows — everyone, kid. Everyone —"

"Not everyone lies. That's not true. It is a big lie!" I said cheekily.

"Is that so?" he said gallingly, his face sunburned like a sun-dried tomato. "Kid, what you just said is also a big lie. Of course, everyone lies. You see? Isn't it easy to lie? You see?"

Dooshkeeki seemed muddled. Although he was listening with rapt attention, it was difficult for him to keep track of the discussion. To him, *a lie that is a lie that is a lie* made no sense.

"What if I do not play your absurd game? What if I just walk out on you and your preposterous Message Hub? What if —"

"Is that so?" interrupted Mooshkeeki. "It's your choice, kid. My patience is running out. The mailbox will be yours if you give us some lies. You'd be able to read your messages and maybe live a long life. Totally your choice, kid," he said. "Otherwise, otherwise, otherwise —"

"Otherwise," interjected Dooshkeeki, "we drink your blood and chop you into little bitty, tiny pieces. Grind you into very thin dust with a shredder, and then, poof! You'd turn into red powder, or maybe into blue or pink or yellow powder, or maybe into an electronic message —"

"Remember, Dooshkeeki?" interjected Mooshkeeki, giving a foul grin, still rubbing his distended belly. "Remember the stubborn kid from last week, the little boy who refused to play with us? Remember how we turned him into nuclear dust? Remember how he disappeared? How he became a dark cloud, faded in the air like smoke?"

"Oh, yeah. Of course, I remember, boss. This little spoiled brat was gone in a matter of seconds. Just like that, POOF! He turned into tiny particles floating in the air. Just like that, POOOOFFFF! I bet he would've regretted his snobbish behavior if he only knew the consequences."

"So, what do you say, kid?" said Mooshkeeki. "Are you ready to play?"

The sky in the middle window had turned suddenly dark. It was the dimmest night I had ever seen — no Moon, no stars. I was shaken. The throbbing jolt in the pit of my stomach was unbearable. I could not withstand their malicious intimidations anymore. "Y-y-yes, I-I'm r-ready," I murmured, still reluctant to play their silly game.

"Remember: three good lies could save your life. And they must be good ones. Otherwise —"

"Boss, let's be patient; the girl is thinking, thinking hard. Let her play."

Moments passed by. I wondered what would be a good lie if almost everything seemed unreal, untrue. "I think I have one," I said.

"Is that so? So, shoot!"

"People are born good," I muttered under my breath.

"'People are born good'? Ha-ha-ha-ha... Is that what you just said? Ha-ha-ha-ha... Is that so? Ha-ha-ha-ha-ha," Mooshkeeki exploded into stomach-churning laughter. "People are born good! Ha-ha-ha-ha, do you really mean it, girl?"

"No, no, no, this is my first lie."

"Oh, oh, oh, I get it: You're right. It sounds like a good lie, a true lie, a sincere lie. What do you think, Dooshkeeki? Does it make sense to you too?"

"To me? I do not understand. I'm totally confused! In other words, you really don't think people are good. Is this true, girl?"

"My lie was that people are born good; there's nothing to it, that's all."

"Is that so? Hmmm," said Mooshkeeki.

I stayed silent.

Then he continued: "I tend to agree with the girl. So, what is your second lie, kid?"

"My second," I said straightaway, "m-my second, m-m-my second is: Our country is in decline."

"Is that so? Is our beloved country in decline?"

"No, this was another lie, sir."

"Is that so? Oh, oh, oh, kid, I see. Now I get it. Did you hear that, Dooshkeeki?"

"Yes, boss. But I still don't follow her —"

"Well, I'm not so certain either. I rather disagree with your second lie, girl. If our country is not in decline, then why does the chief of the chiefs, Mr. Greenbold, say we're heading in the wrong direction?"

"I don't know, sir," I said.

"And if we're not in decline, why are our enemies not afraid of us anymore?" persisted Mooshkeeki.

"Don't know, sir."

"And if we're not in decline, why do our allies not respect us anymore?" he went on.

"Don't know, sir."

"Dooshkeeki, I think we should prepare the shredder. It seems that her second lie is not a lie at all."

I gulped, hands shivering, cold sweat covering my face.

"Boss, let's give her another chance. Let's weigh her lies carefully before we rush into irreversible actions. We ought to remember, boss, that out there, beyond the City of @, everybody is misinformed. People are delusional. They starve, yet they think everything is nice and dandy. They struggle, yet they blame things irrationally on others. They spend beyond their means and still have an appetite for more. I think that she's been misled too. Poor girl, a lost soul, a lost mind."

"OK, OK, OK, Dooshkeeki! There's no room for compassion. I don't understand why you're so nice today. She's the only one to blame for not telling a good lie. This is your last chance, kid, and I mean it! Your last chance before we pull out that shredder. Now, shoot your last lie. It must be a good one; otherwise, otherwise —"

Just then, hundreds and hundreds of deep-sea sharks, ugly goblin sharks, flashed in front of my eyes in the far left window. Their protruding jaws, their snouts overhanging their mouths, and their pink color sent shivers up my spine. A few seemed to be giving me a chilling grin. Others, intense, mouths curled up, were lurking for prey.

The sharks' message was apparent: Either die or live one more day with another lie. Turn into dust or an electronic message, or satisfy Mooshkeeki and Dooshkeeki. All were options I despised.

Venting frustration, I yelled out, "I'll never find Rhubarb Pie. And this is my last lie. I'll NEVER LIE AGAIN!"

"Is that so? Who in the world is Rhubarb Pie? Did you hear that Dooshkeeki? Ha-ha-ha-ha-ha… She's looking for a yummy, juicy, lip-smacking piece of Rhubarb Pie. Is this a kind of lie, girl? What a strange lie —"

"Boss, I'm puzzled too. I think you're right. We should start preparing the shredder right away. Rhubarb Pie? I hate Rhubarb Pies, boss. My mom used to grow rhubarb in our backyard. She always burned them in the oven."

"What the hell is Rhubarb Pie, girl?" said Mooshkeeki in a nervous tone of voice, gesturing to Dooshkeeki to start mounting the shredder in the center of the office.

"Rhubarb Pie is my father," I said.

"Is that so, kid? Where is he now?"

"Don't know, sir, still searching —"

"Is that so? Did you check your mailbox? Maybe he sent you a message."

"Don't have a mailbox, sir."

"Oh, oh, oh, that's right. She has no mailbox. Dooshkeeki, maybe we should give the poor kid a mailbox, huh?"

"But, boss, she's not met our requests —"

"For God's sake, it's her father we're talking about. Demonstrate some compassion. What a mean guy you are! Give her a mailbox now!"

"Sure, boss, whatever you say," said Dooshkeeki, with a whiff of irritation. "But, boss, I thought you told me before not to demonstrate so much compassion."

The petrifying sharks in the window ebbed slowly, replaced by deep-sea volcanic rocks embellished with vibrant corals and astonishing flowers. Not flowers that you'd bring on a birthday. Not flowers to celebrate a holiday. The flowers were in a wide rainbow of hues, glowing in the dark, stirred slowly by the powerful currents on the ocean surface.

CHAPTER TWENTY

WHO IS WARPING TIME?

At last, the mailbox I had so desired was about to be mine. It was on my 13th birthday, which I had celebrated alone, in the Message Hub building. It was there that Mooshkeeki and his assistant, Dooshkeeki, had mistreated me. It was there that they had ridiculed me.

After Dooshkeeki groped for a while in the pocket of his jacket, he dug out a bottle of pills and slapped it angrily on Mooshkeeki's desk. His eyes narrowed to nothing more than slits of rage. "Although you do not deserve it, here is your mailbox, girl!" he snarled.

Two pills, red and blue, were spinning in the bottle, chasing each other, bouncing up and down as if they were floating in space.

"Pills?" I said, eyes wide open, flabbergasted. "I do not take pills. Only doctors prescribe pills."

"Is that so?" said Mooshkeeki. "These pills are your mailbox, kid. Unlike the old way of sending and receiving e-mails, here in the City of @, your mailbox will be an integral part of your body. In our world, the mailbox circulates through your bloodstream. The system is called Body-Mail. Take the pills if you'd like to find your Rhubarb Pie. Swallow them if you'd like to communicate with the outside world."

"Then why two pills? Isn't one enough?"

"The red pill, kid, is for incoming messages from anyone who writes to you. The blue is for the outgoing mail that you send out," replied Mooshkeeki. "Don't fret. Go ahead and gulp down the tablets. Then enter the mailroom through the white door behind you. There you'll be able to read your messages leisurely. Communicate with people who are dying to know how you're doing…"

At home, I read my mail on the computer screen. The e-mail from my friends and family had poured into my inbox. My replies had dropped into my outbox folder.

But here, in the City of @, e-mail programs like that did not exist anymore. Body-Mail substituted for the traditional e-mail application that I had used on my computer. As Mooshkeeki had said, here my mailbox would be a part of me —

No choices left. I took the pills but not without serious hesitation. Not before placing them cautiously on the crest of my palate, gurgling, examining — weighing the consequences. *Are the pills real? Are they pills you buy at a pharmacy?*

Noiseless and tranquil was the mailroom at the Message Hub. The place consisted of a modest chaise lounge facing a silver table that stood in the center. No windows, only two dim rays of bluish light sprang out from arc floor lamps. I was lolling on the cushiony recliner, gazing at the snow-white ceiling. I was waiting patiently for the Body-Mail pills to take effect.

The serene atmosphere, though, did not last long. My head began spinning rapidly, eyes scorching, mouth drying, and stomach throbbing. It felt as if I had swallowed a big white elephant.

Then I found myself in a different place. It was New York: the streets, towers, parks, fountains, people, commotion…

Moments later, the views were even more vivid. I was strolling southbound on Fifth Avenue, between 59th and 58th Streets. On the right was the Pulitzer Fountain — not too far from Central Park.

CHAPTER TWENTY

The lively street was swarming with people, taxis, whizzing delivery bike riders — too much to take in. The noise, the glaring sunlight, the heat in late June — too much to absorb.

Ambling about in Manhattan, even for a short distance, could be exhausting — every so often unbearable. My body felt heavy, legs sore.

To my surprise, I was suddenly soaring above the buildings, as if strange tides were hauling me up. I was flying — hovering above Fifth Avenue and zooming south.

People raised their gaze, bewildered at the midday marvel.

Whee, wheee, wheeee, I was flying. I was a New Yorker again, once more belonging to a free society. Once again, I was one of them — at liberty to pursue anything I wanted.

Whee, wheee, wheee, flying downtown, still following Fifth Avenue, passing 54th Street above the University Club and the beautiful Elizabeth Arden Building (a wonderful example of Georgian Revival architecture).

Then from above, between 51st and 50th Streets, on my left, St. Patrick's Cathedral's Gothic Revival steeple seemed to be piercing the sky. And on the right, just across the street — Rockefeller Center was standing solidly.

Then, from Fifth Avenue I curved to the right, soaring above 42nd Street. Down there, a boy standing near the New York Public Library raised his eyes to the sky and said, "Mom, look. Look, an angel above, angel in the sky." Then another boy nearby said, "No, it's a kite. It's a beautiful kite, from China." And a girl in the growing crowd shouted, "No, it's God, it's almighty God." Others nodded in agreement.

On my way westbound, hovering high above 42nd Street, I crossed Sixth Avenue and in no time traversed Broadway. Then I made a sharp turn left onto Seventh Avenue.

WHO IS WARPING TIME?

Next I continued south until Parsons School of Design became visible — between 41st and 40th Streets.

At enormous speed, I darted toward Macy's — at Seventh Avenue and 34th Street.

Despite my great height above the city, I heard people chatting about the summer deals at Macy's. "I got this scarf for almost free. What a bargain!" said one woman. The other wondered, "Imagine how much this bra would cost in Alaska? Macy's is great!" And the third giggled, "What a store! I think I'm moving to New York tomorrow."

With no time to spare, I maneuvered to the left above 34th Street, hovering for a short while eastbound. When I ran into Fifth Avenue, I turned right — yes, once again flying above Fifth Avenue.

A few hundred feet south — between 34th and 33rd Streets — the Empire State Building was prodding the clouds. *Wow, what a colossal construction*, I said with admiration.

Below, I heard a girl pleading, "Daddy, take me up to the observation deck. I'd like to see the city."

"It's eighty-six stories high. I'm scared, sweetie, I'm scared. It's too high for me."

"Daddy," she giggled. "How come? I thought that you're a hero."

"I am, sweetie, but a different kind of hero."

"What kind of hero are you?"

"One that helps others —"

In a wink, I was soaring high above the buildings, heading south, almost touching the clouds. In no time, there was 17th Street. Nearby, I recognized Union Square Park. A few seconds later, directly below, adjacent to West Fourth Street, Washington Square Park came into view.

CHAPTER TWENTY

After West Houston Street, SoHo was next. Traveling at high speed, I headed farther downtown, passing Canal Street and then Chambers Street and Barclay Street.

Finally, the place where the Twin Towers had pierced the sky...

Uncle Walter used to say, "A virtual thing looks like a real thing but it's not. A virtual horse, for example, smells like a horse, whinnies like a horse, but it's not a real horse. It's an image of a horse that behaves like a horse." So, perhaps the mailbox I'd been given by Mooshkeeki and Dooshkeeki was virtual too.

The Body-Mail was functioning now. I could feel it. It was working. It was a part of me — inside my body. The incoming e-mails chimed one by one, indicating their arrival in my inbox with a sequence of jolly tinkles, *ding, dinggggg, dinggggg*. I'm not sure if anybody else could — but I saw them. There, in front of my eyes, probably springing out of my head, my brain — a wad of green envelopes was flashing, alive, waiting to be opened.

Then, before long, a husky voice inside me announced, *here is your mail, Sammy. Lie back, listen, watch, smell, interact.*

Open the first message, please. I pressed keenly.

An envelope popped out of my inbox and unfolded slowly. Then a fuzzy image sprouted forth like a mushroom after the rain, seemingly dangling midair in front of my eyes.

"Hi there! Is this you, Sammy? Is this really you?" a familiar voice echoed out.

I could see her. She crouched on the sofa, somber faced, frail. "Mom," I said, tears welling up in my eyes. "Yes, yes, this is me, Sammy." I stretched out my hands, wanting to touch her. But my fingers went through the image as if it were a wispy cloud floating in the air.

"We miss you so much, sweetie. Where are you? Are you safe?"

"I'm fine, Mom. Did you bake apple pie? I can smell it, Mom." Appetite-inducing aromas filled the mailroom, arousing my senses, touching my soul.

"Yes, the one that you like, with cinnamon and nuts, just out of the oven. I made it for you, for your birthday. Happy birthday to you, my Sammy," she said, anxious, trying to pass me a piece of the pie.

"Thank you, Mom. I don't think your pie will make it here, but I can smell it. Looks wonderful, smells delicious, Mom."

"Thank you, sweetie. Are you safe? What happened to your long hair? Did you cut it short? And what happened to your face? I see some strange spots. Rather translucent, missing —"

"It's nothing, really nothing. I'm fine, Mom."

"When are you coming home?"

"A few more days, a few more days. I hope to learn more about Dad's whereabouts. I'll be home in a few more days. We'll be all together again, together with Daddy."

"What have you found out about him so far?"

"Not much, Mom. Not much, some leads, Mom."

"Where are you now?"

"I'm at a place called the City of @."

"Do they treat you nice? Do you have enough food?"

"All is fine, Mom. Don't worry. How is Michael?"

"He's doing well. Very sad, though. Father's disappearance is not easy on us. The tragedy changed our lives. It's hard to cope with the loss. The memories are fresh. The horrible day has never left us. It still comes back, time after time."

"I understand, Mom. Be strong. I hope to bring him home soon."

"I hope you do. We miss him. We met with Mr. Larry Quack, his boss, last week. He invited his employees. Not everyone showed up; many were absent. Larry was nice. Nice to all of us."

"Was he?" I chuckled.

"Yes, sweetie, he was kind for a change," she grinned. "He even asked about you. Perhaps a bit concerned about your expedition. He asked me many questions."

"Why would he be concerned? What kinds of questions, Mom?"

"He had all sorts of queries about your trip, the purpose, your schedule…"

"What did you tell him?"

"Nothing in particular. Just told him how much Michael and I miss you. I told him you're on a mission to find Daddy."

"What did he say?"

"Not a word, not a word, not a word."

Her voice slowly faded. The envelope from which her image had popped out suddenly started jiggling restlessly. It was about time to end.

"I've got to go, Mom. Be strong. Hugs and kisses. I hope to see you soon."

"Take care of yourself, sweetie. We love you —"

Her image slipped back into the slow-folding envelope. Her voice, the smell, the view waned too.

Not all the messages in my inbox were live mail — letting me see the sender or engage the sender in a conversation. Some were read only — notes from people who, at their discretion, had dropped the message into my mailbox to avoid facing me — or for other reasons.

Junk mail, for instance, is also read only, not live. It's a type of mail sent by people you do not know. This type of unwanted mail usually contains advertisements for products like organic shampoo for dogs, seaweed soup for parrots, or combs for elephants.

WHO IS WARPING TIME?

The next piece of mail arrived in a red envelope, containing a read-only message. The sender's intention, I suspected, was to avoid a face-to-face chat, dodge eye contact, conceal an agenda. Who else other than Mr. Larry Quack was capable of composing such a note? Who else would try to convey feelings, offer advice, and whatnot, in such a peculiar way?

Dear Samantha,

The days after our office building collapsed were agonizing. The company has been in disarray for weeks. I lost 30 of my staff, and none of the missing have been found so far.

Devastating…

My heart goes out to you and your family for the disappearance of your father — an unbearable tragedy. He, Mr. Kevin Edison, was undoubtedly one of the best software application managers I have ever known.

Like bad dreams, that horrible morning keeps coming back, time and again, returning to haunt me.

I have been reliving the hours of terror like watching a never-ending horror movie. Back and forth, back and forth, the repetitions of time never cease to exhaust my energy and drain my will to live.

How is it possible? How many times will the catastrophe recur? Time seems perpetual — like sunsets, like a spinning carousel. How many times will June hark back to its beginning, July and then August start afresh, and again, September follow?

Would you happen to know who is drawing back time constantly? Are the repetitions of time an attempt to bring back to life the people we lost? Can time bending reverse the course of the unspeakable tragedy? Can history be changed by repeating it?

It was brought to my attention that you have embarked on a journey to bring back your father. Sad. No matter how many times the reality of that morning is played back, no matter who is reversing time, your quest will fail.

Wake up, Samantha! You live in an imaginary world, virtual, unreal. You'll never be able to revive your daddy's vanished soul.

Though the tormenting past cannot be changed, it will never be forgotten.

The future is here; embrace it; focus on the important things in life.

Time is ticking...

Sincerely,

Larry Quack, CEO

Soul, Mind, and Money Corporation

CHAPTER TWENTY-ONE

BOYS

Was my reality nothing more than a dream? Was the City of @, the software architecture metropolis, merely a figment of my imagination? Was it a fabricated retreat, an escape from home to ease my pain? Did I labor under the illusion that the City of @ could help me find Rhubarb Pie?

Was Mr. Larry Quack right? Was his message, in my Body-Mail, a wake-up call? Was he urging me to abandon the City of @ and return home? Advising me to embrace the future rather than be consumed by the grim past? Was he truly concerned about my well-being?

Or did Mr. Quack's message disguise a sneaky plan? Was he up to no good again — another trick up his sleeve — probably a deceitful scheme to promote one of his shady goals?

As far as I could tell, there were two — two distinct views. Only time would tell whose world was real. Was Mr. Quack's a place where broken hearts and gloom defeat the soul? I wondered if his reality offered nothing more than despair and pessimism. His was a world in which tragedies tend to set historic milestones. His, not mine, was the one in which innocent lives had been snuffed out in broad daylight, buried beneath the rubble of crumbled buildings. Many vanished without a trace...

The other world was mine: The City of @, where a dim ray of hope surfaced slowly as time went by. A glimmer of brightness suddenly kindled my spirits.

On the wings of my defiant thoughts, I found myself in the lobby of the Logic Layer Fort. It was a beautiful mansion, bringing to mind the Palace of Versailles. The wall paintings illustrated heroism, revolution, and freedom in typical eighteenth-century Baroque style. Innumerable, striking sculptures and luxurious pieces of furniture were scattered about, tastefully occupying the huge space. Outside — viewed through the broad, tall, and arched windows — the geometrical garden and sprinkling fountains captivated my imagination.

There, voices of beauty whispered in my ears, singing tender chants to my soul. There, voices of elegance and grace conquered my heart, promising brighter days. There, immersed in the sounds of liberty, reason, and justice, a different City of @ came into view that morning.

Was my sudden change of heart a turning point in my journey?

There, rejuvenated, I met Roy Papastathopoulos. He was a bright and a well-mannered kid, whom every parent in the world would be delighted to have. His out-of-the-ordinary talents amazed people. Much like Uncle Walter, he loved arts and science. He could solve any math problem in a matter of seconds. He was good with computers too. Physics and astronomy were his favorites. Like most of the students in his class, though, he hated biology. Geometry, algebra, and chemistry, however, were second nature to him. There was almost nothing he wasn't curious about.

Roy's mohawk hairstyle was tall and resembled the Eiffel Tower; some said it should be in the *Guinness Book of Records*. Roy's towering hairdo was as greasy as a lubricated car engine, but it was adorned with glinting pearls and diamonds.

Almost always, Roy's long forehead was creased like a pair of jeans. His eyes squinted just about every time he was engaged in a discussion. A look of bemusement mixed with a tinge of curiosity spread across his little face. His lips parted most of the time. His chin, probably as a sign of stubbornness, was as long as a genetically modified cucumber. From the neck down, only his arms were visible. The rest of him had faded with time, turned translucent like a jellyfish.

That morning, Roy was sitting next to me in the lobby of the Logic Layer Fort in the City of @. First, he ignored me. Then he spied me from the corner of his eye. Then he snatched short glances in my direction, worried, as if danger were lurking around every bend.

Is he afraid of me? Is he just cautious?

I gave him a big grin.

He disregarded me as if I were an ice sculpture in a secluded park.

I pursed my lips and stuck out my tongue at him.

His face reddened. His mohawk began swinging from side to side. His own tongue came out too, coiled like a long rattlesnake, as he brandished it at me.

I wiggled mine too.

"Hello, Auntie!" he said.

"Hello, Gramps!" I countered.

"Hello, Grannie!" he roared.

"Hello, Great-Great-Great Grandpa!" I retorted.

"Hello, chocolate crinkle cookie!" he evened the score.

"Hello, disgusting serpent!" I snapped.

"Hello, Swiss cheese with a million holes," he exploded with anger. "Did mice eat most of you?"

"Hello, half nothing," I gave him a zombie look. "Did vultures gobble down your lower half?"

He pulled my hair — hard.

I clawed his face with my tiny fingernails — deep.

He tore a hole in my shirt.

Then a stumpy man suddenly leaped into sight and yelped, "What's the matter with you kids?"

"She started!" shrieked Roy, peeved, his mohawk still swaying from side to side.

"*I* started? Look what he's done to my shirt... my hair!"

"What a pity, poor Miss Universe! And look what she's done to my face!"

"What did I do to your weird face, you dork?"

"ENOUGH with the bickering!" bellowed the man, eyes narrow, mouth tight. "Follow me to my office, now!"

From the golden tag on the door, I figured it was Mr. Donald Xenophon who was escorting us to his office. It was definitely the infamous Mr. Xenophon whose name had come up so many times in the past.

Mr. Xenophon was famous for his obsession with cleanliness. Sterile and shiny was the place he managed, and the Logic Layer Fort was one of the tidiest places on the planet.

While mopping with utmost passion his already shiny desk, he snarled, "This place must be CLEAN, and clean means QUIET — restful. And quiet implies that little monsters like you must obey the rules. And if you can't control yourselves, the many experts in the City of @ can help. Tame your anger and behave in a civil manner. Petty quarrels are flatly forbidden. UNDERSTOOD?"

Roy and I nodded.

Mr. Xenophon went on as his scowling look became replaced by bitterness. "I insist you understand how grave the situation in the City of @ is. Anything other than focusing on our daily chores must be avoided."

"Grave?" I said, raising an eyebrow.

"GRAVE, GRAVE, GRAVE, like no other time in history. The city is slowly disintegrating, a minute-by-minute crumbling like a house of cards. Some facilities in the northern district of our city have already collapsed. Floods, mudslides, and wrenching storms have torn up the infrastructure, and the foundation is in danger of ruin."

I winced. Mr. Xenophon's words of calamity had struck hard.

At that very moment, thundering roars of cracking walls and shuddering windows and broken glass overwhelmed the office.

A moment later, the floor was quivering. And then everything was trembling — not like the sidewalk near a subway station or the slopes around an erupting volcano. Everything was shaking harder, much harder.

"R-ruin?" said Roy, mouth agape, face startled. "H-how come?"

"No one knows," said Mr. Xenophon dismally. "Some claim that the City of @, the software architecture metropolis, was founded on false ideas and wrong concepts, and the layers are imploding. It is like founding a country on principles of false democracy or believing in fake freedom. Others wonder if the city was established on a weak substance or if the design is frail like the scrawny vegetation in a drought."

Is he being truthful? I murmured under my breath. *Is the city really collapsing? Is the end of my journey approaching just when things were starting to look promising? And what about Rhubarb Pie? Would I return home empty-handed?*

This was not good news — not at all. The demise of the City of @ was not in my best interest. Despite the hardships I had endured, I still hoped to bring Rhubarb Pie home. And the only way I could do that was to use the city's facilities. Maybe even accept its way of life, tolerate its laws.

"If you do not have further questions, leave now. Take a stroll in our marvelous garden. Get to know each other. Do not fight. Stay calm, be peaceful, enjoy the day. I'm sure you have lots to offer to each other." Then Mr. Xenophon motioned toward the door. "And come back soon for the annual Logic Layer Fort games."

As Roy and I tiptoed out from Mr. Xenophon's damp workplace, I breathed a long sigh of relief. Ambling about in the nippy morning was not such a bad idea. Getting to know Roy and tapping into his extensive knowledge of almost everything was a noble thing.

As we sprinted through the lobby of the Logic Layer Fort, the double door leading to the garden flung open. Then we leaped into the fresh air, feeling rejuvenated by the crisp, clear day outside.

The vast garden stretched over a number of hills, a few acres, much beyond the range of my vision. Being surrounded by glaring sunshine, shrubs, trees, and magnificent flowers intensified my exuberance.

I breathed deeply. I was alive again. Free, thriving, feeling like I was in the Garden of Eden.

Garden of Eden? Indeed, this was one, read the sign.

"Let's take a walk," said Roy, giving me a weak grin. His towering mohawk hairdo coiled like a giant spring as if it were shy, humble, subdued.

"I gather that you have visited this place."

"Oh yeah, I've been here many times. A fascinating garden," said Roy.

"How long have you been in the City of @?"

"A while, I don't remember. One morning, not long after my mother died, I found myself sauntering aimlessly in the middle of the city. I was staring at the flamboyant buildings, the surrounding desert, the sky. Since the time has been warping back and forth, it's hard to tell. But I think I've been wobbling about a few months or years. I have visited many facilities."

"Do you like it here?"

"Oh, yeah. I'm fascinated by the mysterious power of the people, the promise of the leadership, the way of life," intoned Roy, gesturing to the nearest garden path. "Let's go this way."

Stone paths subdivided the Garden of Eden into four sections. At the onset, we headed northward. We were snaking along a narrow path, taking in the seducing aromas of the plantations, drawing in the cherished air as deeply as we could.

Half an hour later, we stopped at a sign saying, *Northern Human Lifeline.* There, blossoming under the nurturing Sun, were hundreds and hundreds of what seemed to be Japanese cherry blossom trees.

More astonishing, a few steps closer, were boxes in different sizes, gift wrapped and decorated with glinting gold and silver ribbons and bows, dangling beneath the branches.

Openmouthed, eyes wide, I said, "I have never seen parcels growing on trees like that."

"These are ancient Chikulilala trees. They produce takeout dishes, meals for the hungry: spaghetti and meatballs, wonton soup, Caesar salad, teas, sodas, popcorn, a bunch of desserts. There's plenty of food here. No one dies from hunger in the City of @. If you're hungry, amble around, and just like you pick apples, harvest your favorite meal."

I stepped forward, stooped under a tree, and carefully picked a green parcel labeled *Lentil Soup for the Weary.*

Roy went for the chicken wings in a sauce of honey and balsamic vinegar. It was a scrumptious dish that his mother had often prepared. He also told me he hated soups and would rather die than eat lentils. Beans, peanuts, and cashew nuts, he reviled too.

Then we were huddling silently at a picnic table, immersed deeply in our thoughts and savoring the delicious meals that had just been bestowed upon us.

CHAPTER TWENTY-ONE

Occasionally, we stared into each other's eyes.

He's actually cute, I thought. *The only ugly thing is the mohawk on his head. How could Roy kiss a girl with this tower on his head? Ha-ha-ha-ha…*

"Why are you laughing?" he asked half-embarrassedly. "What's so funny, Auntie?"

"Nothing, nothing."

"Does my mohawk bother you?"

"Oh, no. Nothing bothers me, Roy."

Silence.

"My mother," he said after collecting his thoughts, "was the sweetest person in the world. She cared about me, always was on my side."

"My father," I said, "is the most charming, caring, gentle, thoughtful person in the world."

"My mother was a princess. Beautiful, elegant —"

"My father is handsome —"

"I must find her —"

"I must find him —"

"I wouldn't have been here if she were alive."

"I wouldn't have been here if he had not disappeared."

"Auntie, why are you repeating me like a monkey?"

"In case you didn't realize, genius, we're in the same boat."

The chilling earthquake thundered again. Ground tremors, soil ruptures, tree shakings, and loud thuds of fallen ready-made meals sent spasms of fear throughout my body.

Unmoved by the strengthening roars that were rising slowly to a threatening clatter, he said, "Well Auntie, it seems that Mr. Xenophon was right. We are going to end up like mashed potatoes beneath the weight of this marvelous city."

"It's impossible. I must find my father first."

"Oh, yeah. I'm positive you'll find him. In the end, we all find our loved ones. The question is where."

"*Where?* Here. He must be *here* somewhere."

"Here? *Here* does not exist, Auntie. *Here* is in your head, only in your head — a product of your imagination. And the people we are looking for, anyone, anyone who is found *here* — is unreal too, Auntie."

"That is untrue. The City of @ is real — like anything else in the world. If I can see you and talk to you, it means that HERE IS REAL, TOO," I exclaimed.

"Oh, yeah, ha, ha, ha, ha. Of course I'm real. Certainly, we do talk to each other. Ha, ha, ha…," he exploded into laughter.

"And home? Is home real?"

"Nothing is real anymore. It used to be, though, Auntie."

"So, what is the place that we call *here*, genius Einstein?"

"I've figured it all out, Auntie! I've figured it all out!"

"So, if you're so smart, Einstein —"

"This is easy. Let me explain, Auntie. Don't get impatient with me. The City of @ is made up of four major places. Here they call them *layers*: the Presentation Layer Facility, the Logic Layer Fort, the Database Layer Center, and the Message Hub. Some you have probably visited before —"

"Sounds right. Yes, I've already been to the Presentation Layer Facility and the Message Hub. So, where can I find my father, Einstein?"

"Don't interrupt, Auntie. Give me a chance, and everything will become crystal clear. You must understand that when one place wants to talk to another, it must send a message. It's like stuffing a note in an envelope and dropping it in the mail.

"It works like that: 'Good morning, Mr. Logic Layer Fort, this is your friend the Presentation Layer Facility. How are you doing today? Can you do me a big favor? Would you have an idea of how many elephants can ride a Harley-Davidson at the same time?'"

I grinned. *He's really cute,* I thought. *I'm still not sure how any girl could like him, though, with his strange tower of hair on his little head, ha-ha-ha-ha...*

"Then, Auntie, erase the stupid smile from your lips. The Logic Layer Fort must think, calculate, look it up, use its brain to form an answer. Again, the reply must be sent back in a message.

"Here's how it might work: 'Good question, Mr. Presentation Layer. The answer to your question is two — only two elephants on a Harley-Davidson. One would sit in front, the other behind. I hope this answers your question. If you have any other issues, please do not hesitate to send me another message.'"

"But what if the Logic Layer Fort does not know the answer?"

"Good catch, Auntie. I knew you were smart. Well, if the Logic Layer Fort does not have an answer, it would send a message to the Database Layer Center, asking for help.

"It works like this: 'Hi, Mr. Database Layer Center, this is the Logic Layer Fort. I hope you're enjoying the summer. Someone has asked me a question I cannot answer. I'm probably not smart enough, or perhaps my brain is not large enough. Maybe you can help. Maybe the information is in one of your files. And here is the question: How many elephants can ride a Harley-Davidson at the same time?'"

"Then?"

"And the Database Layer Center would reply politely, as usual, 'I looked up your query in my files and found what you need. A study published last year in *Useless Questions* magazine suggested that only two elephants are capable of riding a Harley-Davidson simultaneously.'"

"I guess many messages are sent and answered during the day. It could be a real mess!"

"Oh, yeah. That's why the Message Hub, the place that Mooshkeeki manages, acts like a post office. When two places communicate with each other, the first drops a message in the hub. The message is delivered to the second, and vice versa."

"Hmmm…."

"And we, you and I and every other lost soul in this city, ride on messages, back and forth, back and forth, perhaps forever."

"Ride forever?" I said. "So where can I find my father, Einstein?"

"I just told you that the information is in the Database Layer Center, in one of the files. Auntie, are you so thick? There you can find anything, anything you want."

"So how do I get there?"

"In this city, as you may have figured out, we do not have control of anything. We're hurled around like puppets. If you're lucky enough to survive the hurling and the challenges posed by the various places, then at some point you might run into the Database Layer Center. But if you happen to die midstream —"

"No control?"

"Look, this is like love. Does anyone have any control over love? Love always controls *you*. Do you understand, Auntie?"

I was flabbergasted. *What a strange comparison.*

"Love is powerful, potent," he went on. "It can toss you back and forth like a weightless cloud. True love can drive you crazy, Auntie. Love can lift you up and bring you down. Love can heal you, injure you, kill you, Auntie."

Yes, Einstein, you almost drive me nuts, I said to myself. Love? His statement echoed in my head loudly: *True love can drive you crazy, Auntie.* I could imagine that. But there are different kinds of love. Love for a father is one thing. It never expires, and it's truly unconditional. Then there's another type of love: love of someone who is not a part of your family. Someone you like, adore, feel comfortable around. Like Eric Kinsley, my colleague at school.

I know that I *liked* Eric, but does it mean I loved him? If you miss someone, does it mean you love him? Or is love something deeper? Can you control the *amount* of love? Do you tend to cry when you love? Does love hurt? Does love erupt into sparks of happiness, uncontrolled laughter, chills, heart thuds, gapes, stomach jolts?

"I'm sure you wouldn't understand what I mean. I don't think girls know what true love is," said Roy haughtily.

"And you? Do you know? Do you understand, Romeo?" I countered.

"Oh, yeah, love is a part of the human spirit. Love is more about giving than taking."

"I'm sure your mom taught you a few good things. But Romeo, you ain't an expert on love."

From the garden's Northern Human Lifeline section, we headed south, continuing our discussion about love. Friendship, desire to be with someone, and the human spirit were also on our minds.

Between the tides of heartwarming agreement, our conversation lapsed into unpleasant squabbles about the meaning of passion. Passion was a term we did not grasp — or at least could not describe. Passion was something I had heard on TV and read in books. But neither of us could explain in simple words what passion meant. As we approached the southern section of the Garden of Eden, the disagreements deepened.

"I think passion is the side effect of love. The more you love, the more you're passionate about someone," said Roy self-importantly.

"I don't think you're correct, Einstein. My father used to say you could love — or hate — someone *passionately*. I think passion implies a burst of emotions."

"So, if I asked you whether there's something passionate between us, you wouldn't know whether my question was about love or hate?" he asked, giving a crafty smile.

"Ohhhh, you're so, so, so smart, Einstein. And yes, that would be right. But who says I care about feelings you have for me? You're not my type…"

Roy let out a low moan: "You're difficult, difficult, stubborn, stubborn like a donkey."

Suddenly, my Body-Mail pinged again. *Ding, ding,* a message had dropped into my inbox. It appeared in front of my eyes, a delivery that no one else could see because it was internal, in me, in my head.

Real, a real message it was, interactive, not read only, not junk mail. Here we go:

"Hello Sammy, this is Eric Kinsley."

"Who?"

"Eric, Eric from school"

Short pause.

"Now I can see you. Can you see me, Eric?"

Short pause.

"Not very clearly."

"What do you want, Eric?"

"Nothing, was just wondering if you've heard about my Friday launch. I finally fixed the space rover. It's ready —"

"Nice, Eric. Anything else?"

"Nothing special. They gave us so many assignments for the summer. I'm swamped."

"You're a smart guy. Do mine for me too. Anything else? Did you want to tell me anything?"

"Not really. Just wanted to let you know it would be awesome if you could make it on Friday — really awesome. Everyone's coming to see how my rover will be shot to the Sun."

"I appreciate your invitation, Eric, but I don't think I'll be able to make it."

"Sure, next time, Sammy. Next time. Bye."

After his abrupt sign-off, thoughts of frustration went through my head: *Boys disappoint me. Boys do not have feelings. All they worry about is themselves, their tools, their adventures.*

What was he trying to tell me a moment ago? An empty message… Everything was only about him — nothing about me. Nothing. Cold like ice in the North Pole. Nothing personal — or maybe something was hidden under the surface. Maybe he missed me, but he didn't dare. Nothing about us — nothing, nothing about him and me. How disappointing.

A short pause, and then I continued to rumble: *And this Einstein too — Roy — is another selfish dude. He can't break the ice. Can't say anything good. His brain is probably filled with screws, nuts, and bolts. Boys only quarrel… No feelings.*

CHAPTER TWENTY-TWO

TRANSFORMING BRAINS

Roy and I were still strolling along the paths in the Garden of Eden in the Logic Layer Fort. Our discussion about love and passion faded slowly. We were silent for a while. You could hear the birds tweeting, the frogs croaking, and the hollow nasal honking of trumpeter swans.

As we approached a white picket fence, the beautiful southern section of the garden came into view. I stared at the marvel that appeared before my eyes. Countless red and blue bushes were arranged in dense geometrical patterns stretched over a number of hills. The uncluttered, well-groomed, and well-kept plants that dominated the view eclipsed even the horizon.

Like scrap metal to a magnet, I inched closer and closer toward an alluring bush that let out weak moans, sobs, and whispers. Enticed I was to explore the mysterious shrub, a wonder I had never stumbled upon before.

"Step closer," said Roy while examining its branches. "These are Brainplalala shrubs. People come here to rejuvenate their worn-out brains."

"Are they edible bushes?"

"No. Look closer. What do you see?"

"I see fruit hanging."

"Closer, Auntie. Need glasses?" he pressed.

"They look to me like giant furry walnuts. Aren't they?"

"NO. Where is your imagination, Auntie? These are BRAINS, replacements for those who need to jazz up their lives."

My stomach gave a terrible wobble; my hand went to my mouth. "REAL BRAINS?" I bellowed. "REAL?"

"Oh, yeah, real — and in excellent shape. I'm surprised by their superb condition," he said, still inspecting, squishing a pinkish brain that did not seem to enjoy it.

I edged away quickly from the bush as its dangling brains started quivering and shriveling and expanding like ballroom dancers.

The hair on my arms rose in reaction to what sounded like moans of agreement to Roy's observation. "Roy is right. We are in an extraordinary shape. We are smart, we are capable, we are talented, we are brilliant. Try us, try us, try us."

"I'm frightened to death, let's take off."

"Stay still," he said confidently. "We must try one or two before we leave. It'll be an extraordinary experience that you'll never forget, Auntie."

"Try? How can we try?"

"*Trying* means picking up a brain and mounting it on your head as if it were an extension of your body. Try it. No harm can be done."

"Why don't you go first, Einstein? Why would I need another brain? Isn't one enough?"

"You must understand, Auntie, that every now and then, a person needs another brain, a different common sense, a different mind. The idea here is *transformation*."

"Why in the world is this necessary, Einstein?"

"Because the brain you were born with is designed to think in certain ways, reason in the same patterns, come up with the same solutions. Humans tend to repeat themselves. Over and over, we perform the same functions as if we were computers. The brains on these bushes can give you a different perspective on life. Once you try one on, you'll feel a drastic change in your thinking and behavior. Immediately, you'll become someone else. In your case, Auntie, this is utterly necessary."

TRANSFORMING BRAINS

"But what would happen if I tried on a brain and later on wasn't able to get back my original?"

"That could happen. But in your case, Auntie, trading the old brain for a new one would not be such a bad thing…"

"I still don't get it —"

"Here's the thing, Auntie. Wouldn't you like to find your father?"

I nodded.

"If you do, you'll need a new approach — a plan. Adults call it a *strategy*. Only with a new brain is rethinking possible."

Roy continued sifting through the collection of suspended brains in rapt devotion. A wide grin of satisfaction suddenly brightened his face. "I think I found what I was looking for. Wow, what a bargain. Here's what the tag says, Auntie":

> *Was believed to have belonged to Mr. Marvin Goldman. Use this amazing brain to revitalize your life. Mr. Goldman's known powers of healing and prophecy will be transferred to you as soon as you become him.*

"Ha-ha-ha, not a bad idea," I chortled. "Go ahead! Endow yourself with his unique brain. Maybe Mr. Goldman's spirit will restrain your rude demeanor, Einstein."

"You don't have to be so mean to me, Auntie. And stop calling me Einstein. Here, I found another good one":

> *Enjoy the miraculous and logical power of Andrea Bell's brain. Her well-known supremacy in the field of rational thinking will empower your life.*

Roy seemed happier than any person could ever be. Without a moment of hesitation, he plucked Andrea Bell's brain from the shrub and attached it to the top of his scalp. His sharp mohawk hairdo jutted out through the brain as if it were a lotus protruding from the surface of a pond.

CHAPTER TWENTY-TWO

A moment later, Roy's smile tempered and his eyes widened. Then he tumbled to the ground, sat crouched, head in his hands, and said, "I feel giddy. The world is spinning around. I'm going through a change."

Just then, Roy's lips were moving rapidly. But it was Andrea Bell's sulky and croaky voice that came out through his mouth: "I'm not sure why anyone would wake me up. I have been dead for almost a century. I'd like to continue my silent journey into the future without any disturbances! Please leave me alone."

The words that echoed out from Roy's lips sent ripples of fear across my face, "S-sure... Let me h-h-h-help," I mumbled.

Then I turned to Roy and said, "C-c-c-can you p-p-p-please remove Ms. Bell's b-b-b-brain? Th-th-th-the l-lady is pleading for some r-r-rest. Give her a break, Roy."

"Who are you, girl, anyway?" said Andrea through Roy's mouth, giving me a chilling look.

"I'm Sammy. And you?"

"Who am I, you're asking? Well, I used to be one of the most prominent figures in the field of logic. I was a logical person, from head to toe, or from toe to head, whichever... I wrote books, published scientific papers, and lectured. Kids loved me, I was their favorite..."

"The field of logic?"

"Yes, in my time a logical person meant a reliable, grounded, reasonable, practical person. Have you ever heard the expression *a logical decision*?"

"Yes, but my uncle says only characters in fairy tales make logical decisions. Isn't that right?"

"Well, in my time, people used to be logical, girl. And this is why I invented the science of logic. And this is how I became the well-known and esteemed Andrea Bell the Magnificent."

"How do I know you're who you claim to be, Ms. Queen of Logic?"

"Easy, easy to prove, Sammy. Here's a logic question. Are you ready?"

I nodded.

"Would I have been in love with Charlie had I said to him, 'I do not, not, not, not love you?'"

A few seconds later, I replied, "It's confusing, Ms. Bell, but based on what you just said, I think that you love him," I concluded.

"Remarkable! I'm impressed! Here is another one, Sammy."

I nodded.

"I like tomatoes only if I hate potatoes. I like potatoes in the morning and in the evening. However, in the afternoon I hate them unless I like tomatoes. Have I ever disliked potatoes?"

The Queen of Logic went on and on with more and more complicated riddles. I could not follow her logic. Her brainteasers were beyond me.

Despite her hard-to-crack questions, I was still not convinced that she, the alleged Queen of Logic, Ms. Andrea Bell, was indeed the leading figure in the science of logic a hundred years ago. Anybody could have claimed such glory —

And then I wondered how authentic the brains on the bushes were. And why would anyone want to replace his own precious brain with another. Was the process safe?

Still — and despite the perils, I'd had certainly gone for a brain that could unravel the mystery of Rhubarb Pie's disappearance. A brain that could answer simple questions such as, was he captured somewhere in City of @? Or, was he in another place? Was my father deceased, or perhaps missing, desperate for rescue, unable to return home?

Roy rolled onto his feet. It seemed he'd recovered from the sudden change that had descended upon him after Ms. Bell's brain had taken over his mind. Apparently, his inner-body experience faded away as her muffling voice was being slowly smothered in his belly.

Ms. Bell was done talking, and Roy came back to life: "I see another interesting brain here, Auntie."

"I think we should focus on finding a brain that can lead us to our lost parents."

But Roy appeared engrossed in the magic of brain replacement. He looked possessed by the power of transformation. I suspected he was being taken in by the seductive elation of the impossible that had become possible. Perhaps he felt like a little God. He was with me — and yet he wasn't. "See this brain, Auntie?" he went on. "I'd give my life away to become this person —"

> To those to whom freedom of mind is an invaluable treasure, crown yourself with Mr. Xuix Zuig's brain. Spontaneous thunders of thoughts, spur-of-the-moment bursts of ideas, and impulsive gusts of imagination will charge your life with immeasurable energy.

"Watch out, Roy! Be vigilant. Overdoing things typically ends in disaster," I cautioned.

He did it anyway.

In a flash, he attached Mr. Xuix Zuig's brain to his scalp, and it started sizzling like a well-done steak on a grill. At the same moment, white fumes oozed from Roy's ears. His face turned crimson like burning coals in a fireplace. Fire burst out from his flaring nose. "LONG LIVE THE KING, LONG LIVE THE KING, LONG LIVE THE KING," he suddenly hollered.

"STOP the nonsense, ROY! I know you're joking, aren't you?"

TRANSFORMING BRAINS

It seemed that Roy was not in control. It was Mr. Zuig who delivered the inaugural speech in a shaky voice through Roy's mouth. "Today, I pledge my love to the citizens of this nation. I shall be your king forever and maybe even beyond. Pay your taxes, guard the kingdom, and defend the empire. Sacrifice your lives for the great ideas on which this country was founded."

"STOP IT!" I squealed at the top of my lungs. "WHERE ARE YOU GOING WITH THIS?"

Roy was indifferent to my pleas. Something was wrong with him. He continued with utmost vigor, "Listen carefully, dear servants," peering into my eyes as he drew nearer. "Today, my inaugural ceremony, one of the most significant events of the century, demands a sacred ritual: the sacrifice of a human to please the almighty God."

"STOP IT, ROY, STOP IT," I screamed at the top of my voice.

Then, inching closer, with hands outstretched and clawing, he attempted to grasp my shirt. "Let's sacrifice this beautiful little girl for the benefit of the human race and the future of our country."

My heart gave a ghastly jolt. I drew slowly backward, turned around, and then sprinted away at a breakneck pace toward the nearest hill.

Like a raptor hunting prey, Roy pursued me fiercely as I snatched fleeting glimpses behind at his spiteful grin. I was gasping for air, clambering to the top and then sprinting downhill to the other side. Desperate I was to break away from the chase.

But Roy did not let up. Within earshot behind me, panting, he was trailing me to the bottom of the hill.

Then he followed me to the next one.

Then to the next one in the chain of hills.

CHAPTER TWENTY-TWO

The chase ultimately brought me to an open meadow where a festive gathering was in progress. A hundred or more people were flying kites, drinking carrot and tomato juice, and munching away on stalks of sugarcane.

Colorful kites hovered in the air, electrifying the guests. There were elephant kites, dragon kites, turtle kites, airplane kites, spider kites, happy kites, and malicious-looking kites.

Mr. Xenophon was there too. He was trading compliments with the chief of the chiefs, Mr. Greenbold, whose assistants, Ms. Layerrous and Mr. Componenttous, were there too. They were raving about the successful completion of a software application or two. They cheered, then went somber, and then they cheered again.

When our eyes met, Mr. Xenophon motioned to me to join the celebration, saying, "Where's your buddy? Did you lose him? Eh?"

I turned my head all the way back, but Roy was not in sight. "I think he lost his brain," I chortled.

Suddenly, Mr. Greenbold's head popped into view behind Mr. Xenophon's shoulder. "H-e-l-l-o, h-e-l-l-o, S-a-m-m-y," he drawled with a hint of wrath in his voice. "Don't you think it's time to square some accounts?"

"Hi, sir," I said, giving him a flat smile. "Square accounts?"

"If my memory does not betray me, young lady, the chaos you created in the Presentation Layer Facility cost us bundles."

"Chaos?"

"Didn't you? Didn't you attempt to escape the facility along with Cleopatra?"

I gulped. That didn't seem to require a response.

"You wreaked havoc on that productive place. Never had our people been affected by such a distraction. We lost so many hours of work…"

TRANSFORMING BRAINS

Nor did that require an answer. I stayed silent, panting as he pressed on.

"And... And... And what was that spell you cast on us?"

"Spell?"

"DO NOT play games with me, dear! Yes, the three of us — Ms. Layerrous, Mr. Componenttous, and I — were bundled to each other. An invisible power tied us together by some sort of invisible chains. We were unable to function independently. We were mumbling to each other in unison for hours. Did you have anything to do with it?"

"Games? I do not possess such powers, sir," I said innocently.

"So, who was responsible for such a disgraceful act, dear?"

"She is only a child, Chief," said Ms. Layerrous, leaping suddenly to my assistance. "How could a kid commit such a horrible offense, Chief?"

"I'm sure she's got the capability, Ms. Layerrous. You do not know her. She is a real witch. She rides on brooms and feeds on lizards. And you, Mr. Componenttous? What do you make of it, sir? In your humble opinion, could the kid have put the whammy on us? Subdued us? Humiliated us?"

"I don't know, Chief. Since the time warps back and forth, it's impossible to tell. She might have played a trick on us in the past or will pull a fast one in the future. Who knows, Chief, my brain is going nuts."

"And where is Cleopatra now? Girl?" asked Mr. Greenbold. "Where is she hiding? I'd love to have a chat with this emotionally disturbed lady!"

"I haven't heard from her since then, sir."

"She vanished into thin air. Weren't you the one who helped her escape? Dear?"

"Vanished? How could anyone escape the City of @?" I asked, thankful for the revelation.

CHAPTER TWENTY-TWO

Then Mr. Greenbold scrawled something in his notebook as I rushed along with the crowd toward the amphitheater.

"Let the annual Logic Layer Fort games begin," announced Mr. Xenophon.

Jostling their way through the open gates and then dashing noisily into the vast amphitheater were two groups of Logic Layer Fort employees: Anteaters and Spider Eaters.

No one knew how the rivalry between the teams had begun. The enmity grew beyond all reasonable bounds once Mr. Xenophon instructed the groups to wear uniforms: Orange overalls for the Anteaters, green jumpsuits for the Spider Eaters.

To keep them away from each other, the Anteaters were always seated in the north wing, and, the Spider Eaters in the south wing. To avert scuffles typically triggered by scornful gestures delivered across the amphitheater and often by name-calling, Mr. Xenophon stood on guard, in the very center.

The most awaited event was about to start. Mr. Xenophon hoisted himself onto a stool to address the employees, whose attention grew closer by the minute.

"Harruummphh, harruummphh, harruummphh," Mr. Xenophon cleared his throat as the loud chatter in the background fell to whispers and then slowly wound down. "Welcome to the annual Logic Layer Fort games. We gather here today to celebrate the past year's achievements. Our outstanding accomplishments are second to none in the City of @ and even in the entire world —"

The crowd broke into earsplitting applause.

"Logic they want, and logic we provide," Mr. Xenophon went on. "Reasoning they require, and reasoning we offer. Brainpower they ask for, brainpower we deliver."

The throng exploded into thunderous laughter —

"Who knows better than we do how to think," he persisted. "Who knows better than we do how to calculate, to compare, to sort, to search, to analyze. Who knows better than we do how to solve complicated problems?"

And the participants clapped even more loudly than before.

"Yes, we are the BRAINS of the City of @, the software architecture metropolis," he continued enthusiastically. "Without us, there'd be no logic. Without us, there'd be no valid arguments. Without us, an application would not be able to communicate with a computer user in a sensible manner."

Suddenly, from the corner of my eye I noticed Roy, who'd just arrived. Head bowed down and frail looking, he was plodding dejectedly toward an empty seat.

"And now, dear friends, before we move on, the chief of the chiefs would like to extend his appreciation to our organization. The stage is yours, Mr. Greenbold."

A few moments later, Mr. Greenbold and his cronies, Ms. Layerrous and Mr. Componenttous, stood on the platform and waved to the hailing crowd. "Dear Logic Layer Fort employees, your contribution to our city is incalculable. Your dedication goes beyond any measurable standard. I'm honored to be here today."

A new round of roaring applause burst out.

Then Mr. Greenbold snatched a red handkerchief from his pocket and persisted solemnly, "But in spite of your remarkable success, we are facing a problem." His voice had gone all croaky, and the air of optimism dissipated. "The state of our city is not as bright. It seems that the foundations of our institution, the beloved City of @, are crumbling slowly — indeed, collapsing," his eyes wailing like those of an upset raccoon, if indeed raccoons ever wail.

Stillness and gloom descended upon the devoted employees as ground-shaking thunders and flares of lightning threatened to delay the most-anticipated games in the city. Mr. Greenbold's words of misery only thickened the terrifying air of devastation.

Stronger tremors and darker clouds hovered above the amphitheater.

Is the world as I know it coming to an end? Or maybe only the City of @ is in danger of destruction. Who is behind it? Is Mr. Larry Quack shaking the city to its core? Rumor has it that he is growing human organs in his lab. So perhaps he, using his supernatural powers, is plotting to bring down the establishment of the city.

Mr. Greenbold could barely choke back his tears as he concluded, "…but we'll prevail. Our spirits are high, and our perseverance strong." At last, heads bent down, he and his chums trudged wearily to the edge of the platform. Then they descended to their seats among the crowd.

And moments later, the Logic Layer Fort games began as scheduled.

The last game was about to start after a short intermission. The numerous contests and challenges so far had worn down the Anteaters and the Spider Eaters. And the unfortunate 865-865 tie prolonged their anxiety.

As everybody already knew, the tradition called for harsh penalties for teams that trailed behind. Some would be dumped in the Architecture Junkyard. Others, like old computers, recycled at the Architecture Components Library. In any case, none of the losers would ever be seen again.

The winning group, though, would continue to serve the Logic Layer Fort and be awarded salary increases and more.

After a brief pause, Mr. Xenophon strode back to his usual post and hoisted himself again onto the stool.

The participants gave a cheering round of applause.

Then Mr. Xenophon said, "Number Climbing is our last logic game. It's perhaps the easiest, though the most crucial. Time is not on your side. Use your brainpower, and focus on winning. Otherwise, be aware of the consequences —"

Just before Mr. Xenophon sounded the note to begin, he motioned to Roy to join the Anteaters. I was bound to the Spider Eaters. Both of us knew that assignment to what might be the losing team and a subsequent lifetime in the junkyard, were hefty prices to pay. And both of us were still scrambling to find our loved ones. By the end of the game, for one of us the journey would end — a terrible consequence to bear.

In a full swing, Xenophon shot out his index finger at my team, the Spider Eaters, and said, "Now, you go first. Remember: Number Climbing…"

Regardless of his short comment, the rules of the game were known and understood by the participants. I'm not sure if Roy knew, but I was not familiar with them.

"ONE," shouted Michelle Brownlee with a look of haughty scorn. She was the person with the bluest hair in the amphitheater, my Spider Eaters team leader. Her condescending attitude was apparent on her pink-tinged face.

From the far north wing, Anteaters team leader Don McGuire returned fiercely, "MILLION."

"SEXTILLION," challenged blue-haired Michelle with a pompous look in her eye as my team clapped piercingly.

"DUODECILLION," returned Don spitefully, his Anteaters booing us and gesturing nastily thumbs down.

"Hmmm, duodecillion? How can we beat that?" wondered Michelle. She was peering at us as we were leaning forward, whispering desperately — scrambling to deliver a counterblow.

"Sammy, what do you think?" asked Michelle frantically. "What number is higher than duodecillion?"

Seconds later…, "SEPTENDECILLION," I supplied at full volume without asking her permission.

CHAPTER TWENTY-TWO

Silence lasted a few seconds while Mr. Xenophon looked it up in his tiny yellow notebook. "YOU'RE WRONG, WRONG, WRONG!" he bawled, stomping his chunky feet on the stool. "This is incorrect! Your septendecillion is lower than the Anteaters' duodecillion."

The Anteaters team jumped to their feet and howled cheerfully, "WE WON, WE WON, WE WON."

"QUIET HERE," roared Mr. Xenophon.

Silence.

"Therefore, therefore, therefore, ladies and gentlemen," he went on, "this year's —"

I knew that Mr. Xenophon was about to crown the winners. "N-N-N-NO," I rebutted, pale faced, teeth shuddering. "My septendecillion is ten to the power of fifty-four. It is a larger number than the Anteaters' duodecillion. Theirs is only ten to the power of thirty-nine! Without a doubt, our number is higher. We are right, sir. We are ABSOLUTELY RIGHT, SIR!" I hollered.

Long moments of horror drifted by...

Still looking down at his notebook, at last Mr. Xenophon confessed, "Y-You're c-correct, Sammy... My bad... Anteaters, your turn now. Please continue."

Heads close together, minutes of consultations, finger-pointing, and mudslinging did not render a safe counter. Truly, Don faced a challenging dilemma. Just established, my Spider Eaters' septendecillion was the highest number so far. No one on his team could offer a larger figure.

Even Roy, Mr. Einstein himself, could not help. He had been mute like a dead mouse. But then, after a lengthy silence, on the spur of the moment, and without consent from his team, he braced himself for the worst and thundered like lightning, "QUATTUORDECILLION!"

Silence.

TRANSFORMING BRAINS

"WRONG! WRONG! WRONG!" shrieked Mr. Xenophon. "The Spider Eaters are the WINNING team! CONGRATULATIONS, Spider Eaters!"

And I breathed a long sigh of relief...

CHAPTER TWENTY-THREE

STALKING BLUE EYES

If a man, for some reason or other, lies on his back and stares at the ceiling at 4 a.m., something must be troubling him. If that man turns over and over, trying to find a restful position, something must be on his mind. And if he cannot get back to sleep because concerns still rush through his head, there must be a remedy. Must be…

If his distressing thoughts are caused by bad dreams or if noisy streets wake him up at dawn, this should be a good reason to get up and start a brand-new day. Maybe it ought to be motivation to look outside and scour the sky. Or peer at the neighbors' windows. Or take a peek at the sidewalk below.

This couldn't have happened to any other person in the world besides Mr. Larry Quack. Most of the people on this planet worry about something, sometime. What happened next, though, was different, bothersome.

Larry was under the impression that someone was after him. He thought someone was stalking him, wanting a piece of him, or probably envious of his business success or lifestyle.

Long story short, Larry suspected something was happening out there, next to his window. He believed some sort of little creature with a blue pair of eyes was hovering in the air, following him wherever he went. He imagined his daily activities were recorded, probably saved later in some secret files, somewhere. The little flying bug, he presumed, was creeping up on him hour after hour, lurking until Larry would make a move — a wrong move.

STALKING BLUE EYES

The minuscule hovering eyes were utterly apparent to him whenever he opened the window. He believed they were real. The eyes were flapping through the air like a butterfly, droning like the intelligent bees that you could hear only in New York. He could have sworn that the creepy bug eyes were always on the watch. He was almost certain they were peeping into his private affairs. It was a covert operation, he assumed, spying on him even during his daily strolls in Central Park.

Probably almost everyone would sympathize with Larry's bursts of anxiety. Almost everyone would understand his stress. Everyone would commiserate with the emotional strain that had descended upon him. It was the terrible feeling caused by skingrumaniala, the skin illness that he'd contracted some time before. It was a cruel condition that ripped his soul apart, turning him invisible by the day.

Ironically, every so often Mr. Quack wished that the skingrumaniala would progress faster. He hoped that the illness would turn him wholly invisible, so he would be able to escape the stalking eyes of those who snooped into his already taxing life.

But skingrumaniala, as he had learned from his doctor, progresses slowly, drains the soul bit by bit. Therefore, for the time being, he did nothing. For one thing, his half-visible, or half-invisible, look wouldn't change so rapidly. For another, chasing away his alleged pursuers was another challenge that couldn't be resolved for the time being.

So, on these grief-stricken days, he concluded that he must take action. Must TAKE preventive measures to eliminate the fear that occupied his mind... *No one should be ashamed about getting help. No one*, he rumbled to himself. *Even powerful people like governors, mayors, army commanders, and presidents seek help when life seems to be crumbling.*

But even before pursuing such a sensitive matter, he planned to run it by Nina Browning. She was his devoted property manager, always there for him.

According to Larry's book of rules, consulting Nina about seeking help from an expert was the right thing to do. In his heart of hearts, though, he really thought that getting help would be a total waste of time.

And here's how he went about opening up to Nina. That morning they were slouching on the swinging sofa in the dazzling garden on the roof of his apartment. As they were sipping their coffee, he felt it was the right time to bring up the issue. "Have you heard any buzzing sounds lately? Have you noticed any flashing lights popping around?"

"Nothing out of the ordinary, dear," Nina said, shaking her head. "Maybe the wind was blowing hard on the blinds?" Then she nestled her head on his invisible shoulder.

"Naw, not the wind, nothing like that, Nina. It sounded like a dentist's drill."

"Oh, dear, maybe the noise is coming from Mr. Pluratiski's apartment. It must be from him, the new neighbor who moved in last month, just next to us. I think he's a dentist. I saw him one morning in a white apron —"

"NO, Mr. Pluratiski is not a DENTIST! When I met him in the elevator a few days ago, he said he's a mortician."

"Ha-ha-ha," she burst out, in her typical screeching and contagious laughter. "How could a mortician afford such a luxurious apartment? Maybe he's got a rich daddy, ha-ha-ha."

"Why are you laughing at me? I'm in such pain and you're mocking me."

"Dear, I'm not making fun of you. You're too sensitive, my sweet chocolate. It's not your fault, bonbon. You were born this way. What bothers you now, anyway?" she spoke softly.

"Do you really want to know?"

"Sure, go ahead, my organic brown sugar."

"They are stalking me. They are on my tail. They want to destroy me. They want me dead! It's a fact, I assure you, Nina!"

"Slow down, my little butterfly. Who are *they*, my tiny sweet pumpkin?"

"*They*? The agents, the spies, the proxies, the institutions, the organizations, the establishment — it's a fact!"

"Relax, dear," she petted gently and passionately the visible portions of his head. "It's all in your head, my sweet potato. Relax, get out, and take a stroll. No one would do that to my sweet little zucchini. They don't have time for little people. Instead, whoever they are, they're busy destroying the world as a whole. Don't you see? They're polluting the air we breathe and the water we drink. They're destroying the forests. They're poisoning the food. They're overfishing. They're killing wild anim —"

"— b-b-but, but, but, but it's a FACT. THEY ARE SPYING ON ME, NINA!" he interrupted, his face ruddy, grinding his teeth.

"What makes you believe they're after you, my sweet-and-sour soup?"

"THEY? I can't speak loudly; they can hear every word. The only thing I can tell you is that there's a small chopper next to my window. This helicopter is roving about like a hummingbird, filming every move of mine, his big eyes following me, blue eyes, Nina. Very blue —"

"Nonsense, dear! You're hallucinating, my sweet little bagel with cream cheese. No one would waste time on you. I think you need HELP, my sweet little turtle soup."

"This is EXACTLY what I was about to ask you: DO I NEED HELP?"

"Yes, serious help, my tiny sweet eggplant. Very serious. Because people who imagine stuff like that must seek assistance immediately."

"But maybe it will go away by itself. Maybe I don't need treatment at all. Maybe it's a temporary thing. Maybe it's the skingrumaniala."

"No, dear. It's not. Your emotional state has been like that for many years. Maybe even before I met you. Perhaps this is a birth defect, my sweet little penguin. Get help, and everything will be all right!"

Nina's encouragements to seek help brought Larry to Dr. Michael Bordowokoliz's clinic a couple of days later.

Dr. Bordowokoliz — both humble and bold, with bloated eyes, a hooked pink nose, meaty cheeks, and always-wet lips — was a hardworking psychiatrist. His outstanding capabilities and treatments could cure any mental illness.

Most of the experts in the field would agree that Larry's hallucinations were grave. His symptoms could not be found in any respected medical journal because they were not associated with any well-known illness. Would Dr. Bordowokoliz be able to treat Larry's strange condition? Would the doctor be able to maintain his outstanding reputation in the field of modern mental illness?

"Dr. Bordowokoliz," said Larry in an undertone. "I'm here not because I was forced to visit you. Not at all."

"Mr. Quack, please call me Bordo, I dislike my last name."

Larry did not respond.

"Yes, I believe you, Mr. Quack. All my patients say the same thing when they end up in my clinic. They all claim that no one bent their arm to come and see me. So, let's start by your telling me what's bothering you. And don't be shy. Pour out your troubling feelings right here. It's the right place to share your sorrow."

"I'm not so sure how to describe what I have, but I think my situation is grave, Dr. —"

"NO, NO, NO! I told you to call me Bordo, NOT Dr. Bordo!"

"Sure, Bordo. As you see, I have this special condition called, according to some doctors I've seen, skingrumaniala. It's eating me up slowly, slowly. Bit by bit, I'm fading away. Not physically, Bordo, just visibly —"

"And did you come here to cure your skin condition?"

"No, Bordo, the side effects of the skingrumaniala are troubling me — or maybe not the side effects, maybe something new."

"And what's that?"

"I'm here today, Bordo, because I *hear* stuff, I *see* stuff, and I *smell* stuff. My property manager tells me all these things are in my head."

"Oh, you just chimed in at the right place at the very right time. Most of my patients have the same symptoms. They all see things —"

"Yes, Bordo. But mine are different."

"Why?"

"You see, Bordo, the things I see and hear and smell give the impression that they are real."

"All my patients say the same things, Mr. Quack. There is nothing unusual about your condition. After all, what's new? They all believe the *unreal* is *real*."

"No, sir. I feel different."

"OK, so tell me what's bothering you. Maybe even before telling me anything, lay down your sore body on this soft sofa. Close your eyes and open your heart."

Moments later, Larry was relaxing on the brown sofa, describing the grief that had been muddling his mind. "A few weeks ago, or more, my body started to dissolve, Bordo. Not in a physical sense, but as I mentioned before — visually. Then something else happened: Every morning I started to hear buzzing sounds. I see tiny eyes, maybe a chopper hovering next to my window. Watching me, threatening me. Maybe someone wants to kill me. Then I hide. There is nowhere to hide, but I find places."

As Larry was unfolding his misery, he suddenly snapped his eyes open and stared at the only painting on the clinic's wall. Perhaps he had heard something. There, on the canvas, was a beaming mailman whose bag's strap was slung over his shoulder. In his other hand was a wad of letters that seemed ready for delivery.

Hello, Mr. Quack, Larry imagined the mailman talking to him. *I'm here to tell you that this place sucks. I see patients come and go, and no one is happy with Bordo.*

"Yes, keep going, Mr. Quack, and stop gawking at the painting on the wall," said Dr. Bordowokoliz.

Still gazing at the mailman, whose mouth was moving rapidly, Larry went on, "I do not have the energy anymore to run away from those who are seeking to terminate me."

"Don't worry, sir. All my patients say the same things. Nothing is unusual with you. I prescribe the same medicine for all. Then in a short time, they show remarkable improvement."

Was I right OR was I right, Mr. Quack? This is how he's treating everyone, Larry heard the mailman talking.

Dr. Bordowokoliz raised his gaze to the clock on the wall and said hastily, "Today's session is over, Mr. Quack. I must take the next patient. Come in next week, because we should continue to discuss your pain. I'm sorry if it feels like I'm chasing you away.

Meanwhile, take these red pills, and you'll feel much better by then."

I told you! I told you! The mailman said to Larry.

There was some truth to Larry's claim that he was the only one who felt that way. Just when he thought he'd gained a little control over his sickness, things went wrong. Just when he felt he was getting the upper hand in the battle against his progressing invisibility and was making strides in taming his delusions, things went awry.

That morning was unlike any he'd ever faced. A new morning, he hoped, with new beginnings. But for Larry it was a different start, an awkward situation to manage.

Still in bed, Larry kept his eyelids sealed tight and his lips clamped shut. It was as if creatures from another planet had taped them up. Incapacitated, he lay stagnant, his limbs motionless like pile of logs in the forest. The only thing he could do was raise his eyebrows and to a certain extent crinkle his forehead. Not much more than that.

I'm jammed. I'm possessed. Thoughts of defeat rushed through his head. *I'm on my last legs… I may be on my way up to heaven or down to hell. Who knows…? I hope my deeds will be judged fairly and the Lord will acknowledge the respectful way I treated everyone…*

Suddenly, Larry felt a strong tug, a type of abrupt haul that only a supreme power could be behind. A few seconds later, he was tossed into a pitch-dark icy hole. *I'm zooming through a tunnel,* he felt. *I'm being thrust through the shaft of death to the next world, a passageway to another civilization…*

But Mr. Quack was way off. No. No one had plotted to send him to either heaven or hell. Whoever was behind this had different things on his mind: Larry was plunging into a giant pit, a bottomless ditch that only the brave could endure.

Like a drop of oil in a funnel, Larry swirled downward. Down, down, down, eyes fastened tight, he was slipping as if in a bad dream. Even his property manager, Nina, and his housekeepers, Emma Sinclair and Savannah Bishop, could not hear his cries for rescue. His pleas missed everyone's ears; his shouts muffled in his watertight mouth.

At last, Larry found himself in a dark and chilly place. "H-h-h-hello, Mr. Q-Q-Q-Quack," a shrill voice echoed suddenly from a distance.

In New York, in such weather Larry would wear a jacket, a scarf, maybe put on his Russian fur hat. But there, in what seemed to him a vast desert, he was lonely. He was wandering about in his flowered pajamas, sleeping socks, and red slippers. *Where am I?* He muttered. *This illuminated city on the hill looks like Los Angeles from here.*

But it was not Los Angeles.

The high-pitched voice persisted, "Mr. Quack, Mr. Quack, if you're a man, a real man, approach the gate of my great city. Let me see your face, let me see the most powerful dude on earth. Ha-ha-ha-ha…"

Larry, scared stiff and drenched in cold sweat, was drifting nearer the golden gate. "I'm a real man and I'm not afraid of you, monkey head!" he said, his voice cracking.

Out of thin air, the chief of the chiefs, Mr. Greenbold, appeared in slow motion in Larry's view, like an image on a computer screen. "Welcome to the City of @, the software architecture metropolis, sir," Mr. Greenbold greeted Larry. "I'm glad you finally made it. After so many years, I finally get to put my eyes on you."

"And who are you, oddball creature?" said Larry in his typically condescending tone, rubbing his eyes in disbelief. "I can see through you. You look like a leaf eaten away by bugs. How about using fertilizers to get rid of your horrible, horrible, horrible holes? What an eerie thing."

"Ha-ha-ha-ha, hu-hu-hu-hu, hee-hee-hee-hee, look who's talking. Have you looked in the mirror lately, you worm-eaten apple? How did you get these rotten translucent blotches all over your body? You should seal them up with cement."

"And what makes you so ugly from the outside?" snapped Larry.

"No person should be judged on physical appearance, sir."

"Your insides, too, are decaying."

No one could have predicted the sudden shift in Mr. Greenbold's tone: "I demand respect, sir — the same respect I give you, for your publications, your books, your interviews on radio and TV."

Regardless of Mr. Greenbold's tempering tenor, Larry did not ease off. "And have you learned anything by following my career so raptly, goofball?"

"Sure, I did, sir. Your stuff is intriguing, sir. But before I let you into my city, we'll have to clear the air. Have you spread rumors that the City of @ does not exist? I think you did. I must understand what qualms you have against my establishment. Why don't you like what I stand for? What's so bad about my culture, and why is yours better?"

"Your culture? Your city? Your establishment? Ha-ha-ha-ha," Larry exploded in mocking laughter. "You have nothing to offer, and you're nothing — a wisp of smoke, computer-generated zeros and ones, imaginary, virtual —"

"Ha-ha-ha-ha, and your world, Mr. Quack? What's so real about yours? Yours is founded on false promises."

"Mine?"

"Yes, yours, sir. It should be wiped off the map!"

"Yours should be eradicated from the face of the world!"

CHAPTER TWENTY-THREE

The air of rivalry and vengeance was indeed powerful.

ON THE BRINK OF REVENGE

You shouldn't be surprised that after such a nasty brawl, Mr. Quack was not allowed into the City of @. Mr. Greenbold's rejection was truly humiliating. Although Larry vowed revenge, he released a long sigh of relief, like prisoners do when they get freed from jail.

The same mysterious force that had brought Larry to the outskirts of the City of @ also hurled him back to the borough of Manhattan. To his astonishment, the trip back to his apartment wasn't by foot, by taxi, or by subway. He was hovering high above the city at the speed of sound, or even faster.

Larry was frightened, although he seemed utterly relaxed. From time to time, he waved to the people below. He waved to those who walked on the streets. He waved to those who waved back to him from cruise ships sailing sluggishly on the Hudson River. And then he waved to those who took horse-drawn-carriage rides near his apartment as he was whooshing above Central Park.

I can be a pilot. I can be an astronaut. I can be a truck driver. I can be a subway conductor. I can be a taxi driver. I can be a bird. I can fly to the Moon. I can land on the Sun. I can visit Jupiter. I can travel to Australia. I can have all that I want, he bragged... *And all that I want is revenge... And revenge is coming soon — big time!*

The people below scrunched up their eyes at the marvel of the flying man. He gave them a smug grin with a touch of self-confidence, assuring them that everything will be all right. *I'm the messenger of hope,* he claimed, *and this city is safe.*

CHAPTER TWENTY-FOUR

Larry's speedy trip above New York ended with a loud and crackling thunder. From high above the buildings, he was thrust violently through the dining room window of his lavish apartment. Then he was flung instantly onto the Victorian armchair and shoved under the dining table. A moment later, a pink bib soared from the kitchen, fluttered overhead, perched on his neck, and unfolded over his chest. Not too long after that, a nine-pound lobster on a snow-white plate was slapped onto the table in front of him.

This had just happened when Nina, Emma, Savannah, and Larry's uncle Acton were enjoying a quiet evening. They had savored the seafood feast and exchanged memories about the good old days with Larry. Just then, their jaws dropped almost to the floor as they found themselves gazing at his unexpected appearance as if he had just arrived from outer space.

"Good evening, ladies and gents. Hello, Uncle Acton, what brought you down to my kingdom?" said Larry as he peered into their eyes and then dropped his gaze to his huge lobster.

"I was worried about you, dude. The girls told me this morning that you'd disappeared into thin air. Where have you been hiding, Larry?"

"I'm not so sure, I'm not so sure, Uncle Acton," Larry whined acidly. "Immediately after I woke up, I was thrust into a huge pit. I plunged through a frigid ditch at high speed until I landed in what looked like a desert. Moments later, right there in front of me, I was staring at a strange city. Then I was talking to an odd man who claimed to own the place."

Suddenly, there was a whisper that only Larry could hear, a murmur that only he could place: *Mr. Greenbold did not say he owns the place. I think you're wrong, wrong, wrong, Mr. Quack.*

"Shush, shush, shush. If that is you, be quiet," Larry growled at his red lobster with a scowl. "I thought you're already cooked, dead." The lobster then seemed to be wearing a wide grin.

"Who are you speaking to, dude?" asked Uncle Acton, giving Larry a piteous look.

"To no one, Uncle, no one, Uncle," said Larry, abashed.

Then Larry heard his lobster talking again, *my name is not "No one," Mr. Quack. Please call me Barbie.*

"Shush, shush, shush, Barbie," he whispered under his breath.

Perturbed and narrowing his eyes as he scanned Larry's frowning face, Uncle Acton said, "It seems his condition has deteriorated, hasn't it, Nina? His illness has taken a toll on him. He has turned utterly invisible. I can hardly see him anymore. And now he talks to invisible people. Has he gotten any help?"

"There is nothing wrong with me," exclaimed Larry. "I'm fine. There are things that only I can see, much beyond your capabilities."

"I think you need some rest, Larry," said Emma evenly. "True, there's nothing wrong with you. However, soon we'll not be able to see you anymore."

"Nah, nonsense," rejected Larry, waving his hand in disagreement. "I feel good, energetic. I do not need rest. All I need is to kill someone, to destroy, to eradicate…"

"What are you talking about, sweetie, *killing someone*?" cried Nina fearfully. "Who's going to support us if you go to jail for murder?"

"The truth just came out of your mouth, Nina. It seems that you're not concerned about me. You're worried about yourself, huh? Is this what I deserve after so many years?" cried Larry.

They are bloodsuckers, traitors, taking advantage of you, Larry heard his lobster rumbling. *Bloodsuckers and nothing more. It's a fact!* "And you, Barbie the lobster, give me a break, will you? Have I asked you anything? SHUT UP!" roared Larry. His voice rose to a scream, to the astonishment of all at the table.

"Who are you talking to, dude?" gulped Uncle Acton, clenching his fist.

"TO WHO? TO YOU, AND YOU, AND YOU, AND YOU!" thundered Larry, his teeth on edge. "Who else besides you would I be talking to?"

"Cool down, dude. You're sweating like a drenched frog that just leaped out of a pond," said Uncle Acton. "Why don't you tell us what's bothering you, Larry?"

"Oh, ohh, ohhh, now we're talking. Why haven't you asked me that before? What sense does it make to get on my case without even asking what is the cause of my suffering? Huh?"

"Relax, bonbon. Watch your blood pressure. People that yelp like this tend to destroy themselves in the end. Do you want to die, sweet apple pie?" cried Nina. "Who's going to support us if you perish?"

"I'll not be the one who DIES in the end. Someone else is going to pay the price for being so inconsiderate, so mean, so careless, so STUPID!"

"And who's the one that upsets you so much, dude?" asked Uncle Acton.

At that moment, Larry imagined that Barbie, his red lobster, got off her plate and inched closer to him. Perhaps she wanted to understand the cause of his anger.

"Who are you asking, Uncle? SHE, SHE, she is the one, the pimpled brat who stirs the pot, dragging us all into the abyss. I spoke to her mom. Then I sent her a message or two. Then I warned her. Then I told her to stop doing what she's doing. Then I explained to her that she is captive in a virtual world, in a place that exists only in her head. Then I —"

"Who is this person, my sweet sugarcane?" interrupted Nina, on the brink of tears.

"Don't you see, people? Don't you know that Samantha, the daughter of Kevin Edison, our former chief software application manager, is on a mission to find him? To bring him back? To reverse time? She is the core of all my troubles, sickness, and torment."

A barrage of tart words came out of Nina's mouth. "Oh, this poor child, Sammy, you mean? What do you have against the unfortunate girl? And why does bringing back Kevin trouble you? And how do you know she's searching for her father? Where is she now? Poor Sammy —"

"It's a plot, a conspiracy! Don't you see? They're all against me, including Mr. Greenbold and his virtual city."

"You're out of your mind, Larry." The tableware shook as Savannah's piercing voice echoed sternly. "Where is that fictitious city?"

"They call it the City of @. It's where Sammy Shmammy is hiding. I was there this morning. I'll destroy that place, exterminate its dwellers, and slaughter Mr. Greenbold, the person who owns the place. It's a corrupt, shady city."

Barbie the lobster continued to encroach upon Larry's imagination: *He never said he's the owner, Mr. Quack, and in my opinion, this city is like any other in the country.*

"If this city is imaginary, dude, that means it does not exist. And if it does not exist, how come Sammy, or whoever she is, can hide there? I'm confused, dude, totally confused!" said Uncle Acton, scratching his head, gnashing his teeth.

"And *I* do not understand why you'd want to hurt someone with such vengeance," said Emma.

"I don't know either. All I know is that I feel that someone is trying to take my business away, replace me with Kevin Edison, bring me down…"

I think you're just hungry. You need some food, and everything will be fine, Mr. Quack. Why don't you eat me? Lobster meat fights illnesses like yours.

"OK, OK, Barbie, if this is what you want, this is what you get."

I'm delicious. Start with my claws, savor my skinny red legs, enjoy my body, and relish my delightful lobster tail. And don't skip my belly. Everyone's crazy about it.

"OK, OK, Barbie, don't tell me what to eat. I eat what I want, and I want what I eat," said Larry. Then he fractured Barbie's claw with a loud snapping sound.

OUCH, OUCH! Easy man! You just cracked my claw with your ridiculous lobster cracker. Can't you be gentler?

"And how else should I eat you, Barbie? Stay still. Don't move till I'm done. If you open your mouth again, I'll pop your head open."

All signs suggested that Larry was almost prepared for his impending journey. A voyage, he anticipated, that would ease his enduring pain.

Departing immediately was impossible, though. Larry had a bunch of things to pack, which could take him a while. Other things on his to-do list before he could take off were paying farewell visits to his old friends:

1. *Drop by Mr. Crutiki Bumpiely (a retired judge buddy who became a burglar, targeting affluent residences)*

2. *Stop over at Andrea Kelly's (his forever-and-a-day opera companion, a 46-year-old*

lady who last trimmed her ugly fingernails when she was 21)

3. *Visit Mary Truman (his longtime spiritual adviser, who operated a small therapeutic clinic on 55th Street and was always busy — even when she thought she wasn't)*

As with almost everything in life, Larry's arrangements for his looming voyage too could not last forever. He stepped up his packing and tribute efforts because of an alarming note he'd found in his mailbox.

The rather informal, unusual in these circumstances, and to some extent, friendly police order had been signed by Officer David Krunkenitche. He was a tough police investigator who'd been acquainted with Larry's business practices for years.

Re: Notice of Investigation

Dear Mr. Larry Quack,

I trust that all is well on your end. This third and final notice of investigation requires your attendance on the third of August 2001 at 10 a.m. Please arrive at the police station a half hour in advance to allow time for proper registration, fingerprinting, photographing, and surrendering of personal belongings. You have the right to be represented by an attorney.

I'm looking forward to meeting you again.

Sincerely yours,

Head Officer David Krunkenitche

Police Officer Krunkenitche was tough when it came to enforcing the law and pursuing criminals. He was uncompromising with friends and family, too. In very rare cases, though, he tempered his adamant drives and to some degree, moderated his firm stance on his beliefs.

One of those rare instances had occurred when Police Officer Krunkenitche's mother refused to designate him the beneficiary of her will. She simply said to him one evening, "No, boy, no. All you need is love, not money. And when I die, the Animal League will inherit my fortune."

In another case, Police Officer Krunkenitche hadn't even dared challenge his wife when she was against bringing cuddly love into their lives by adopting a cat. "No, no, no, only over my dead body does that cat enter our house."

The tough inspector had yielded in both situations.

In any event, Larry had already made up his mind: Surrendering to the police was out of the question. Just as with other police notices he had received; he shuffled the most recent one under the pile of bills on top of his home office desk.

Ignoring the police order would be the best approach, he said to himself. *What else can they do? Arrest me? I'll be on my way to the City of @ even before they start marching toward home.*

Days crept by sluggishly. At a slow pace and with Nina's assistance, Larry was packing his suitcases — seven of them, if not more. Each was filled to the limit with travel necessities and labeled meticulously.

All was organized thoroughly as if Larry intended to embark on a trip to the Sunflower Galaxy (about 37 million light-years from Earth!). Most important, there were five travel bags he intended to carry by himself. They were tagged as follows:

1. *Summer and Evening Hats*
2. *Neckties, Gold Cuff Links, Cuff Link Tie Clips*

Larry would not take such a risky trip without the Various Utilities bag. It was one of the most crucial items among his suitcases.

Even Nina was not allowed to survey its contents. "Dear, what did you stuff in this bag?" she asked.

"Nothing, just office stationery, some books, nothing really important," Larry said.

"Is your mysterious bag bulging with cash?" she chuckled. "May I reorganize it, my sweet lollipop?"

"Naw, no need," he shrugged.

But Nina's suspicion went beyond the bounds of reason when she suddenly leaped at the bag and wrenched it out of Larry's hand. His eyes widened and his mouth opened as he struggled to regain possession of it.

"What is the matter with you? This is mine and only mine!" he thundered.

"LET ME OPEN THAT BAG!" she yelped. "What are you hiding in there, my sweet cough drop?"

The tussle lasted a few horrifying seconds. They were pulling each other in every direction. Larry jabbed her with the broom. Nina settled the score by kicking his rear with great revenge. Then he toppled her fiercely onto the floor with the bag handle clenched in her fist.

The bag suddenly snapped open…

Little humanlike creatures crawled out of it, appearing to have stepped out of a movie. Each one had seven bulgy inflamed eyes, green gummy skin like frog legs (if indeed frog legs are gummy), and some sort of violet gel dribbling out of its mouth. They were shuffling about, hissing, sniffing, slurping orange juice from tiny bottles hung around their necks, and searching for food. A few were inching slowly toward Nina; others were climbing on the curtains.

Lost for words, panting, and drifting backward, Nina cupped her hands over her mouth. Then she screeched intensely after collecting her wits, "Wh-What a-are th-these d-disgusting th-things?"

"Vikings, Nina, Vikings. They are my army, my army of Vikings. Without my army, I go nowhere. And this is a fact," he said, his eyes glinting crossly.

"AN ARMY OF WHAT? VIKINGS? And why would anyone need an army? Don't we have already an army? Don't we pay taxes?"

"I need an army and that's a fact. I'm going to embark on a dangerous trip. Who knows what the outcome might be? I can't throw myself into uncertainty without protection. I need an army, and I need ammunition. and I need utilities."

"Utilities? What kind of utilities do you need?"

"Tools! I'll be carrying them with me, just in case." Larry emptied his bag onto the floor with a loud crackle. "See these?" These are the most sophisticated combat weapons the human brain has ever invented. Take a look."

There were a number of hardware-like tools — *utilities* had Larry named them — glinting in the sunbeams that passed through the window. They were metal and plastic tools with handles and without, sharp headed and blunt headed. Some looked like little screwdrivers. Not many resembled flashing handsaws. Others were similar to wrenches. A very few looked a lot like electric drills. And one bore a resemblance to a hammer.

"You see this," he said complacently, lifting the hammer-like tool and brandishing it in front of Nina's nose as she drew back slightly. "This, this, this is one of the most sophisticated shakers on Earth. This, this, this is called the Grand City Shaker."

She stayed quiet. Tears brimmed in her eyes, and her chin quivered, partly because she feared that Larry was gradually losing his mind. And probably her burst of emotions attested to her diminishing control over his affairs.

"And do you know what the Grand City Shaker is for? Huh?"

She shook her head, eyes still tearing up.

"This spectacular utility, just as it sounds — shakes cities. Any city. Three bangs on the ground with this special hammer, BOOM, BOOM, BOOM, and an earthquake would be under way."

Silence.

"And take a look at this little thing. It looks like a printer, right? Well, it's not a printer in the general sense. It's a printer in a particular sense. Would you know what this is for?"

Nina shook her head, tears now coursing down her cheeks.

"This is called the Marvelous Human-Cell Printer! What does it do? Well, it prints human organs."

"Human organs? Are you nuts, Larry?"

"Yes, organs. I can print anything. I can print ears, hearts, kidneys, fingers, hair, eyes, nails, noses. All would be natural, organic — just like you'd find on a supermarket's shelves."

Larry's utilities presentation did not last long. Not long enough. The phone rang frenetically as if warning of troubles ahead. Larry gripped it between his chin and shoulder as he motioned his army of Vikings to retreat into the Various Utilities travel bag.

"Hello, this is Larry Quack."

A husky voice echoed from the other side of the line: "Mr. Quack, Mr. Quack, is this you, sir?"

"Yes, Larry Quack speaking."

"Sir, this is Officer Krunkenitche. I guess that we have met a few times before. I'm sorry for the interruption, but since you haven't complied with the notice of investigation I sent you, I'm here to escort you downtown. Can you please instruct the lobby guard to let me in? Are you on the top floor?"

"I never received the notice, Officer Krunkenitche. I'd be delighted to join you, but not today. Maybe tomorrow, Officer." Larry hung up and poked his head out the window.

It was noon, lunchtime, when people left their offices to grab a bite. Everything seemed quiet. Larry was scanning the street when a sudden, ear-piercing phone ring burst for the second time.

"It's me again, Mr. Quack. I must advise you, sir, to surrender immediately before things get out of hand. I have an arrest warrant issued by Judge Ray Kinsley. I'm holding it in my hand. Do not resist. Get down to the lobby at once!"

"Yes, Officer, I'll be there in a few seconds," he said and hung up again.

"Who just called?" asked Nina.

"A friend, a friend," Larry said.

"If that was a friend, why are you shaking? And why is there so much noise coming from the street all of a sudden?"

Just as Nina joined Larry at the window, fifty police cars were amassing downstairs near his building. Some officers were in uniform; others were in civilian clothes.

"Mr. Larry Quack, surrender now! There is no escape, nowhere to run," the megaphone sounded.

The standoff went on for long minutes. Curious neighbors and bystanders swamped the streets and the park nearby. Cupping their hands over their eyebrows, they squinted at the window from which Nina's and Larry's heads popped out occasionally.

ON THE BRINK OF REVENGE

Loud bursts of applause echoed about frequently. It seemed everyone had taken a stand against Larry. The clapping grew even stronger when Nina announced that Larry was on his way to the lobby.

"My sweet marmalade, why don't you just see what they want? Maybe it's an error; maybe they're not after you. Maybe it's the neighbor they're after," wondered Nina.

Not even in a zillion years, though, would Larry yield to the clamoring demands of the police officers outside. Nor to the pressure of the crowd that did not find favor with him.

I'm not going to give in to such ridiculous demands. I'm guilty of nothing. And nothing is wrong with what I have done. And who knows what it is that they're accusing me of, Larry mumbled to himself.

Then, in a matter of seconds, Larry leaped to the window again. He ducked shakily on the windowsill and yelped at the crowd below, "The only way I get down there is on a stretcher. Since I don't have a stretcher, I'd like to take this opportunity to say good-bye to everyone."

At that very moment, Larry soared swiftly into the sky with the Various Utilities travel bag in his hand. A thousand pairs of eyes followed him as he hovered northward — to an unknown location.

Mary Truman, his longtime spiritual adviser whom he planned to see, knew that Larry would pop by before he left New York. She expected his visit because he'd phoned her. He'd let her know he would be at her place for a last treatment before his journey began.

What Mary *didn't* know, though, was that Larry was a fugitive. Even if someone had told her he was tangled up with the law, she wouldn't have believed it. Based on her faith in Larry, hiding from police officers and fleeing the city were not things he'd ever do.

CHAPTER TWENTY-FOUR

At last, exhausted and anxious, Larry made it to Mary's doorstep. He gave her a hug and trailed her hurriedly inside to her little clinic. It was a dim place that echoed with some sort of ancient Asian hums. It radiated tranquility to her stressful and fretful range of customers. Then she told him to undress and relax face down on the massage table.

It was the same red table where Larry had been treated before. The table was floating in the air, swinging, as if it were slung from the ceiling, but it wasn't. It was a special table that Mary had ordered from a town in the south. A table that came with little written instruction, for it had been trained by the manufacturer to obey verbal commands and comply with therapeutic responsibilities.

"So what is the rush, my gorgeous Larry?" said Mary.

"I'm leaving the city for a while. I came here to get your blessing."

"You're slowly fading away, gorgeous. Pretty soon you'll disappear like a puff of smoke," she said, forehead furrowed, inspecting the visible and invisible parts of his back.

"These days, being invisible is a blessing."

"Is that right, gorgeous?" she said, still scanning his torso. "Let me take a look at you in the light."

On Mary's command, the massage table — with Larry on top of it — soared, trailing her to the window.

"I'm on a mission to eradicate the evil that has brought such disaster on me."

"So, what's your plan, gorgeous?"

Suddenly, there was an unusual clatter coming from the street. Mary peeked carefully through the window and could hardly believe her eyes. Numerous police vehicles were already parked near the curb and on the pavement. Police officers stood stiff with polished pistols and shotguns aimed at Mary's windows. A large crowd was already staring at the developing spectacle with rapt attention.

"Mr. Larry Quack, Mr. Larry Quack. We know you're there. Lay down any arms you may have. SURRENDER AT ONCE!" shouted Officer Krunkenitche, standing on the roof of his car and grasping a large megaphone in his fist.

"Don't you worry, Mary. They've been chasing me all day. They're harmless," said Larry, sweat dripping down his back.

"I see they have guns. Dangerous guns, aimed to kill. They have shotguns, ammunition, dogs baring their teeth and growling, snipers on the roofs all around, helicopters in the sky. What have you done, Larry?"

"THREE MINUTES LEFT, MR. QUACK!" yelled Officer Krunkenitche. "THREE MINUTES AND WE'RE COMING TO GET YOU!"

Larry, his hands shivering, his face pallid, beseeched, "Mary, please tell them I'm not here, darling —"

"How could I tell them that you are not here? I'd lose my license, Larry."

"No, darling, nothing like that is going to happen. Play your old trick. Make me disappear. I know you can!" he pleaded.

"TWO MORE MINUTES, MR. QUACK!"

Mary soared to the window and at the top of her lungs, yelled to the officers below, "THERE IS NO MR. QUACK HERE!"

Suddenly, a single gunshot pop pierced their ears.

"HOLD YOUR FIRE, OFFICERS!" screeched Officer Krunkenitche. "I think I see a white flag coming out of the window. DO NOT SHOOT!"

Truly, it was. Mary waved agitatedly a white bedsheet wrapped around a broom. She pleaded to end the standoff: "THIS IS NOT A SHOOTING RANGE, AND THERE IS NO MR. QUACK HERE!"

CHAPTER TWENTY-FOUR

"Can you please come out," asked Officer Krunkenitche, the tone of his voice suddenly mellowing in response to Mary's frantic appeal.

"I'll be there in a few seconds, Officer," she said and pulled the blind down to the sill.

Immediately after, she asked Larry to flip over, face up, and shut his eyes tight. "You must know," she added softly, "that I'd not risk my license for anyone else in the world except you."

"I know, darling, and I appreciate it. I'm in trouble and need your help."

Then there were sudden, forceful knocks at the door, rattling the clinic. "WE'RE STILL WAITING FOR YOU, MA'AM."

"I-I'll b-be o-out in a f-few s-seconds," said Mary, panting.

Then she rested the palms of her hands on Larry's eyelids and hummed gently, "Let's do it, gorgeous. Follow my instructions. Disregard the commotion, and focus on your breath. Relax."

Long pause. Larry inhaled deeply.

"You're entering the green zone. Here is where you start your journey, gorgeous. Good luck to you. I hope to see you soon."

Long pause. Larry seemed to be falling into a deep sleep, his face smiling, serene as the Colorado River in midsummer.

"Now you're entering the yellow zone, gorgeous," Mary whispered tenderly, placing her soft palm on his forehead. "The yellow zone is merely a pathway to a different place. Enjoy the ride, enjoy the embracing arms of nature, relish the warmth —"

Larry was cruising sluggishly along the yellow zone, a path he was unfamiliar with. He breathed deeply, arms folded across his chest, legs spread widely. At times, he was snorting like wind gusts on Mount Washington.

Then, in a delicate tone, Mary said, "You're now entering the blue zone, gorgeous. Compose your thoughts, be yourself, use the power of your spirit to intertwine with the mystical supremacy of nature —"

But Larry could not hear her comforting utterance. He could not even smell the vanilla-scented incense that Mary was waving gently in front of his nose.

The blue zone then turned into another passage. This time Larry was drifting rapidly into the bottomless pit he had come to know a few days earlier. Trailing him at high velocity and spinning like a satellite in space was his Various Utilities travel bag, an inseparable item for risky trips like this.

Just like last time, Larry's rapid travel screeched to a halt: He alighted on the desert dunes in front of the well-lit City of @. Wading slowly through the sand, he was edging closer and closer to its monumental golden gate. This time, though, Mr. Greenbold was not there to greet him. This time he was alone, trespassing on the land of the odd city.

Then Mary swung open the door of her clinic and let in Officer Krunkenitche and his cronies. Like police sniffer dogs, they scoured the place. They opened drawers, moved furniture about, sifted through documents, and finally inspected the massage table that Larry had been lying on.

Larry was gone without a trace.

CHAPTER TWENTY-FIVE

THE SPECIAL FIELD

The Special Field, as the faithful citizens called it, was a huge stadium in the northern district of the City of @. Surrounded by flags flapping cheerfully in the air, the place looked festive all year long. From its name, you could tell that unusual ceremonies and happenings took place there. No, they were not secret. Everyone was invited. In certain cases, though, some people were *obliged* to participate.

Lush green grass rippled from the stadium's center, spreading broadly around, almost reaching the first seats. You could see the rows of colorful seats soaring all the way up to the back of the stadium. Staircases intersected the rows at equal distances, forming five separate sections around the stadium. The sections were named for the color of their seats: Red Section, Blue Section, Green Section, White Section, and Black Section.

In the daytime, rays of unsparing sunlight baked the stadium. After dusk, floodlights, mounted on a concrete post that stood tall in the center, illuminated the Special Field.

Not too far away, the City of @'s flag hung on a lofty flagpole, a well-designed flag that everyone was fond of. The two-colored flag, black and white, expressed a deep aspiration for love, peace, and freedom. A white circle that was shining right in its center denoted a ray of hope, a glimmer of optimism.

Fenced by rusty barbwire and broken glass, the stadium was also protected by surveillance cameras. Security staff, escorted by restless sniffer dogs, guarded the place day and night.

As Mr. Donald Xenophon from the Logic Layer Fort had indicated, the City of @ was truly in shambles. The ruin was visible everywhere. Some buildings and other important structures had become submerged under water. Others were utterly cracked. The decay of the city's pavements, roads, electricity grid, and water supply had been progressing steadily.

The Special Field, too, showed signs of deterioration. Puddles of water covered the patches of grass in its center. Sinkholes were noticeable all over the place. Many of the staircases were fractured and some stairs were missing.

I was sitting in the very back row of the Red Section. A steady stream of people poured slowly into the stadium and occupied seats in the first row. The next group clambered one level up the staircase and settled in the second row. And so the next, and the one after.

The spectators carried sandwiches and beverages, ate white and yellow popcorn, and sipped sodas through straws. Their chatter became louder and louder as more people joined the crowd.

I recognized some of them. They came from various places. They arrived from the Presentation Layer Facility, from the Logic Layer Fort, from the Message Hub, from the Database Layer Center, and from elsewhere in the City of @.

The influx of people who packed the stadium seemed eager to attend the event that was about to occur. I didn't have any idea what the schedule of the day was, but I could hear people talking, exchanging past experiences, and anticipating a grand happening.

"Do you know who's fighting today?" asked a chubby woman who was sitting in front of me.

Her companion, a plump man smoking a Cuban cigar, replied, "Don't know. I bet it's going to be interesting." Then he blew three smoke rings in the air out of his puckered lips.

"Last time it was boring; no one died," said the woman.

"Don't know how they're going to make it interesting without blood," he said, spitting tobacco out of his mouth. "I'd like to see some action here. This is not a nursing home."

"You're right, dear," she said. "If this fighting is about revenge or settling accounts, it should be fun to watch. As you say — blood, blood, blood, blood, and more blood! Not like last time."

"Don't really know how they're going to fight, but it should be fierce, vicious, brutal, extreme —"

"You're right, dear. As you say — spiteful, nasty, mean! Not like last time."

"Don't know what the fight is about today, but I'd like to see fear in their eyes. There must be pain in their voices. There must be triumph. There must be defeat. There must be a good cause for the fight!"

"You're right, dear — a good cause for the fight."

A sudden but gentle tap on my shoulder sent a jolt of surprise down my stomach. A pair of eyes was staring at me from the adjacent seat. The body was utterly invisible; only the glinting eyes were apparent. "Hi, how have you been, Sammy?"

My excitement flared up like a torch, and I placed the voice straightaway, a voice husky with feeling. I put my hand on my mouth and said, "Is that you, Cleopatra? I recognize your voice. I was worried about you. Where have you been hiding?"

She whispered, "Shhh, careful, dear. People have been looking for me."

I nodded.

"I'm fine, Sammy. I found a place. Someone took me in. I was worried about you, too. Have you found your daddy?"

"Not yet, but I have good leads."

"I see that you've turned almost totally invisible, sweet little girl."

"So, how did you know that this is me if I'm not visible?" I said, bursts of exhilaration flooding my heart.

"I knew immediately that it was you: Your eyes and your long neck are the only visible portions of your body that I could recognize. The rest of you is gone, faded away, sweet little girl."

I felt for her invisible hand that was probably stretched out toward me. I held it tight. "I missed you, Cleopatra!"

"I missed you, too."

"Mr. Greenbold, the chief of the chiefs, is 'dying' to see you. This is what he told me when we met at the Logic Layer Fort."

"I know, Sammy. They're all looking for me. I'm glad that only my eyes are visible. It means they will never catch me."

"Ditto! I'm glad too," I said. "Who needs to be visible if so many enemies are prowling around?"

"You're right, sweet little girl. You have learned quickly about life in this place — too soon, too much!"

"True. I have grown up too quickly. Losing someone you love shortens your childhood. I feel like an adult. But I'm still a child. Not sure if I'm a normal child, but still a child."

"You're as normal as anyone else could be, sweet little girl. I'm sure you'll find your daddy, hopefully soon."

"I'm losing hope. I'm not sure he's still alive."

"We all miss someone in our lives. You must be strong. Harsh times should not discourage you."

"I'm exhausted. I'm almost totally invisible. Even if I find Daddy, he wouldn't be able to see me, anyway," I said in a hoarse voice, on the brink of tears.

"You must go on. Love is beyond seeing. Love is about feeling. If you do find him, at least he'll be able to speak to you, listen to your beautiful voice, hug you. That would make him happy."

Tears welled up in my eyes. "I'm not sure I'll ever see him again. Nothing feels real here," I cried. "It's a nightmare. Perhaps this place is imaginary, as some people claim. Maybe I'm just dreaming."

"NO, this place is as real as any other thing could be, sweet little girl. Do not listen to them. If you can hear my voice, it means everything is real. Everything is real if you can feel my hand. Everything exists if you can look into my eyes — the only visible parts of me."

"Maybe you're right. But it all feels like a total waste of time. Time bends back and forth, and I keep revisiting the same places in the city. The same events keep repeating themselves. I keep meeting the same people. I was told I'd be able to find Daddy in the Database Layer Center, but I could never get there, and maybe I never will. I'm jammed in an endless loop with no escape."

"If only you could survive all the hurdles. If only you could endure all the bumps in the road. If only you could stay positive, you'll get there, sweet little girl."

I stayed silent.

Rumor had it that a big fight was coming up — a once-in-a-century spectacle that no one should miss. The much-anticipated special event was almost under way.

In the meantime, you could hear the advertising for bargains in the city's malls through loudspeakers turned up extremely high. As in all other stadiums in the world, this one was populated with impatient people who had a hard time waiting for the special event to begin. Loud shouts, bursts of excitement, and applause went on for countless minutes.

At last, barely noticeably, a stumpy, skin-and-bones, sallow-faced man walked shakily toward the center of the stadium. He was raising his hands high, waving to the crowd. It seemed that he was motioning for silence, perhaps gesturing to us to calm down. Rhubarb Pie used to say that a skinny person, just like this, would need to walk by at least twice until getting noticed.

"I've seen this guy before in the stadium. His name is Mr. Drifter Peachornby, and I know what he's going to say now," I said.

"What?" asked Cleopatra.

"In a moment, he's going to shout into the microphone, 'Good evening, ladies and gentlemen. In a few minutes, in just a few, the fight of the century will commence. Meanwhile, esteemed audience, keep silent.'"

"How do you know?" she asked dazedly.

Indeed, Mr. Drifter Peachornby's high-pitched voice echoed out from the giant speakers: "Good evening, ladies and gentlemen. In a few minutes, just in a few, the fight of the century will commence. Meanwhile, esteemed audience, keep silent."

No one in the stadium paid attention to Mr. Drifter Peachornby's announcement. In fact, the rumbling resonated even louder. Some of the spectators stood up and whistled at the bony man, protesting the long wait. Others leaped to their feet and banged incessantly on drums. A few went beyond the customary rules: They blew loud horns — plastic vuvuzelas — like at World Cup games. The more considerate attendees played guitars, xylophones, and triangles. A wide range of musical instruments generated the type of racket you could hear only at these types of events.

"Watch what happens next," I said. "Now, Mr. Drifter Peachornby is going to pull out a pistol and shoot three times in the air. Yes, fire his gun to quiet the audience. Then he'll scream into the microphone, 'I was under the impression that silence is what I asked for, and silence is what's required.'"

Cleopatra opened her eyes wide as she watched the unfolding events with rapt attention. She was dumbfounded by my accurate predictions. "Really?" she said. "Is that what he's going to do next?"

Not too long after, Mr. Drifter Peachornby, who stood rigidly in the middle of the stadium, yanked a silver 9mm Beretta from his jacket and fired three ear-piercing shots. Just as I had predicted, he aimed at the clear sky.

Complete silence descended upon the Special Field. You could almost hear your own heart beating.

Then, just as I'd said earlier, the scrawny Mr. Drifter Peachornby drawled coolly, "I-I w-was u-under th-the i-impression th-that s-silence i-is wh-what I-I asked for, a-and s-silence i-is wh-what's r-required."

"Now he's going to bow to the crowd. Then he's going to turn around slowly and walk to the main flagpole. Afterward, he'll start the usual flag-raising ceremony."

And that's exactly what happened. The flag-raising ceremony started with a sharp order: "All rise for the presentation of our beloved flag!"

The crowd followed the order. You could hear people whispering to their peers to respect the ceremony.

Then six guards dressed in green uniforms and red berets moved forward. To the loud blares of bugles, they started marching at a steady pace from the corner of the stadium toward its center. Leading was the flag bearer, who carried the folded flag in front of him at waist level. After circling the flagpole a number of times, the guards finally lined up behind a solid white line that marked their standing station.

"Flag guards, attention!" commanded Mr. Drifter Peachornby.

The flag guards then stood stiffly at attention.

"Flag guards, salute!" charged Mr. Drifter Peachornby.

The flag guards raised their arms in a sweeping salute.

"Flag bearer, unfold the flag and mount it to the flagstaff!"

The flag bearer adhered.

During the key moments of the ceremony, the crowd held their right hands over their hearts. Cleopatra and I followed suit. With utmost reverence tinged with excitement, we raised our gaze to the flag while it was hoisted to the top of the pole.

"Flag guards, at ease!" directed Mr. Drifter Peachornby.

Upon his instruction, the flag guards rapidly lowered their arms to their sides, releasing the salute.

The flag-raising ceremony did not end there, though. Mr. Drifter Peachornby did not seem to want to wrap up the ritual. He kept issuing commands that didn't make much sense to me.

"All, attention!" he reissued.

All leaped to stand at attention.

"Batman, release the bats!" he screeched. "BATMAN," he shrieked again, "RELEASE THE BATS AT ONCE!"

His astonishing and, to some degree, bizarre command brought sudden silence to the stadium.

Just then, a man with a bulging brown sack popped into view and stood near the flagpole. He laid the bloated sack on the ground. You could hear the rustling, high-pitched noise of the bats squirming inside. Perhaps the weeping creatures knew that freedom was in the offing. Maybe they sensed that in a moment or two, the sack would be untied, granting them liberty forever.

You should consider yourself lucky if you have never witnessed the whizzing echoes of hundreds and hundreds of soaring bats coming right at you at high speed. Dreadful and ugly they were. With their ruddy webbed wings, bloodshot eyes, long ears, and fuzzy hair, they resembled little flying rats.

I remembered from my biology classes that bats typically do not attack people. Most of them eat insects; the rest feed on fruit. But these looked like monsters that had just burst out of a cave, famished and ready to rip you apart and slurp your blood. They hovered above the hunkering crowd. At times, they dived into groups of people and soared again overhead with what seemed like flesh clutched in their vampire-like teeth.

"WATCH IT," I screamed. "THEY'RE AIMING AT US AGAIN!"

"Don't be frightened, little girl," said Cleopatra. "They can't see us. Remember? We're almost invisible. They can't see us."

The bats seemed vexed. They zoomed by as we crouched beneath our seats. You could hear their satisfaction; perhaps it was revenge for having been imprisoned for so long.

But freedom was what they seemed to care about most. In a matter of moments, they were flying high above the stadium. Like a flock of birds, they eclipsed the Sun as sudden dark fell upon us.

My shoulder hurt. A sharp and stinging sensation was creeping slowly down my arm. Since most of me was invisible, I couldn't see whether I was bleeding, nor could I tell if a bat had bitten me. Despite the pain, I gave a long sigh of relief.

"All, at ease!" Mr. Drifter Peachornby concluded. "Five minutes' intermission before we continue."

"Time has come," proclaimed Mr. Drifter Peachornby. "Before we move on to our main event, there is a little account to settle between two of our citizens. I thus call on Ms. Marla Creckersus and Mr. Fabian Gore to step down and present their case."

It was still. His call had been ignored. No one in the crowd stepped forward.

About a minute or so later, Mr. Drifter Peachornby repeated his order, with great irritation. The corner of his mouth honed like a butcher's knife, "Ms. Marla Creckersus and Mr. Fabian Gore. This is my last call! You can't hide, because I know where you are. Please report to me at once!"

At last Marla and Fabian yielded halfheartedly. They rose to their feet unevenly. Then, hunched beneath the weight of anxiety, they cut across the large patches of grass. At last, they stood unsteadily in the center of the Special Field.

Mr. Drifter Peachornby, whose short-fused patience was about to run out, gestured for Marla and Fabian to approach the microphone.

"Introduce yourselves," Mr. Drifter Peachornby directed.

Marla, plump, red haired, blue eyed, was dressed in pink slim-leg slacks, a black shirt, and a yellow fisherman's raincoat. She tightly clutched the microphone in her fist. Then she cleared her throat, and said faintly, "My name is Marla, and this guy is my neighbor."

"I was under the impression that I asked you only to introduce yourself," snarled Mr. Drifter Peachornby.

"Sure, sir. My name is Marla. I live in the southern district of the City of @. I work for Mr. Three Inch in the Database Layer Center, where I collect information, file information, and provide information. I'm here today to square accounts with this guy."

"Thank you, ma'am. And you, sir? Give us an idea who you are and why you're here."

"My name is Fabian. I work in the Presentation Layer Facility. I used to work for Cleopatra. I present information, I display images, and I interact with users. Ms. Marla Creckersus is my neighbor. I'm here to settle a dispute with her, once and for all. This is an issue we have been quarreling about for months."

"What's the issue?"

"He's mean, inconsiderate!" snarled Marla.

"She's terrible, insensitive," retorted Fabian.

The crowd exploded in thundering laughter that continued to echo for long seconds.

"Isn't this a trivial issue? Why is this a public matter?" grumbled the woman sitting in front of me.

"Don't know," said her friend. "Let's be patient. Maybe it's in the public interest after all." Then he released a few rings of smoke from his cigar.

"You're right, dear. Maybe…"

Peering into Marla's and Fabian's eyes, Mr. Drifter Peachornby pressed on, "What is the cause of friction between you two? Eh?"

"Let me explain, sir," said Marla. "He has parties almost every night — countless parties, sir. He plays music, loud, all night long — numerous nights, sir. I see people coming and going — in and out, in and out — loads of people, sir. It's like a disco. My head is exploding. I can't sleep. I can't work. I'm destroyed, sir."

"There is no loud music coming from my apartment. She's making it up, sir."

"Making it up? How dare you lie in front of the audience like that, sleazeball?" Marla detonated with fury.

"No name-calling, please."

"He's rude,"

"She's unreasonable."

"It seems that you two could not agree on anything here, eh? I assume that neither of you is going to apologize, eh?" growled Mr. Drifter Peachornby. "Therefore, let's ask the audience. Dear citizens, should we have a duel, or should we continue to pursue peace? What do you think, people?"

"DUEL, DUEL, DUEL," howled the crowd. "DUEL, DUEL, DUEL."

"Very well! Very well!" said Mr. Drifter Peachornby. On a whim, though, he suddenly came up with a different idea. "Or maybe we should all learn how to communicate. Maybe we should send these two fools to a communication class. What do you think, citizens?"

"DUEL, DUEL, DUEL," the crowd shouted ardently.

"Very well! Very well!" he said. "If peace cannot be achieved in peaceful ways, no choice is left. Remember, however, that resolving the issue violently might have unforeseen consequences that both of you two might regret. Are you really ready for a duel?" Mr. Drifter Peachornby narrowed his eyes. Perhaps he was eager to circumvent a cruel fight.

"It's really up to her," murmured Fabian hesitantly. "It's really up to her. If she wants a fight, I'll give her a good fight."

"What do you think, Ms. Marla Creckersus? Are you in favor of a serious duel? My hunch is that Mr. Gore is willing to settle the issue peacefully, with no bloodshed."

"If he wants to settle it this way, he must promise to never have parties again," said Marla sternly.

Fabian rolled his eyes at Marla and said petulantly, "Never?" with his forehead crumpled. "Never? How could anyone in the world promise that? You see, sir, she's outright unreasonable!"

It seemed that neither Marla nor Fabian was willing to compromise. They went back and forth, back and forth, quarreling about the terms of settlement. One suggested escalating the issue to the City of @ Supreme Court. The other advocated federal mediation.

As the arguing continued, the crowd lost its patience. "DUEL, DUEL, DUEL," they shouted. Loud drum thumps and deafening bursts of horns flared up.

"Very well! Very well, citizens!" said Mr. Drifter Peachornby at last. "If a duel is the only choice, a duel it will be!" Then he motioned to his staff to let in a vehicle that was stationed behind the stadium entrance gate.

CHAPTER TWENTY-FIVE

The gate swung open, and a red Ladybug rolled in, trundling slowly toward the center flagpole. You could see the two white flags on its hood flapping rapidly. You could see the bobbing motion of the car, for it was mounted on square wheels. You could see the driver, who got out and opened the trunk. You could see the determined manner by which Mr. Drifter Peachornby beckoned to Marla and Fabian to approach the Ladybug's rear.

"Here we go, fellows," said Mr. Drifter Peachornby. "You see this red box inside the trunk, eh? It contains guns, sophisticated firearms. Each of you should pick a weapon of choice. In exactly two minutes, you should be standing behind the red lines, facing each other, ready, ready to kill."

"What are they are going to fight about? I don't understand, dear," the flabby woman sitting in front of me wondered aloud.

"Don't really know," said her companion. "Maybe their problem will be resolved if one of them dies."

"You're right, dear. Maybe…"

Fabian fumbled through the red box in the trunk, picking out a long gun that looked like an ancient musket. It was a weapon commonly used by infantries in the sixteenth century. Despite Mr. Drifter Peachornby's cautionary remarks, Fabian kept peeping into the gun's muzzle. He seemed mesmerized by the dark mysterious hole, a snout from which bullets would thrust out forcefully after the trigger was pulled.

Marla, on the other hand, was humbler. She drew out a tiny gold pistol from the box. It was shiny and resembled a toy. It was so small that she was able to tuck it under her thin belt. Almost like the cowboys in Western movies.

"Where is my ammunition?" bellowed Fabian, already facing Marla, who stood twenty-five feet away. "How do I load the damn thing? It looks like a toy. Don't I get some bullets or something?"

"No. No bullets, Mr. Gore. All you need to do is to aim your gun at Marla's heart and squeeze the trigger once I give the order."

"But what's inside the gun?"

"You'll know after you press the trigger, Mr. Gore."

"But what if nothing comes out of the muzzle?"

"If nothing comes out of your gun, and something does come out of Marla's gun, you'll be the first one to die, Mr. Gore."

"But that would be an unfair duel, sir."

"Enough with the 'buts'! We really don't have time for this. A major event is coming up right after one of you dies. There's no time for conversation. Are you both ready? Just remember: the loser will be the one who dies."

"I think I'm ready," said Fabian, cold sweat dripping down his chin. Then he pressed the stock of his gun against his shoulder and pointed the muzzle at Marla's heart.

"What about you, ma'am? Are you prepared?"

"Oh, yeah, I am more than ready, sir," said Marla. Then she aimed her pistol at Fabian's head and squeezed the trigger lightly. "Just give us the signal so I can kill this cockroach — the king of noisy parties."

"No name-calling, ma'am."

"Sure, sir. It was a small mistake on my part. I'm sorry."

You could hear only the birds tweeting overhead. It was silent, and to a certain degree peaceful, as though no one in the crowd knew what to make of it. Was it a hoax? Would anyone really die in the end?

"ONE..., TWO..., THREE..., SHOOOOOOOT!" shouted Mr. Drifter Peachornby, mouth agape, his index fingers in his ears.

CHAPTER TWENTY-FIVE

They pulled their triggers at almost the same time. Fabian's gun went off. He may have not waited to the end of Mr. Drifter Peachornby's countdown. Or perhaps it was an accident. You could hear a loud blast. A jet of some sort of red liquid ejected from his gun, rocketing forcefully toward Marla.

At nearly the same time, Marla gave the trigger a vehement squeeze. But her pistol jammed. Something had gone wrong.

The stream of gooey fluid that had been discharged from Fabian's gun was approaching Marla at the speed of sound. Or maybe more slowly — actually, much more slowly. She squatted, attempting to dodge it. The mushy stream, though, caught her. She was drenched, red all over, seemingly soaked in blood. "MY PISTOL JAMMED!" she bellowed. "THE STUPID THING DOES NOT WORK!"

"No name-calling, Ms. Creckersus. PULL HARD, PULL AS HARD AS YOU CAN!" squeaked Mr. Drifter Peachornby.

Fabian, too, protested edgily. "Is it a joke? Did you see what just came out of my gun? It's a damn TOY! A water blaster for kids. A WATER GUN! How am I supposed to kill her with a squirt gun?"

The crowd released thunderous laughter. The drums and the bugles and the horns and the guitars and the triangles chimed in gleefully. Was the duel staged? Were Fabian and Marla two actors hired to entertain the crowd before the main event began?

The red liquid that engulfed Marla began foaming. She slowly became covered with countless swelling bubbles that grew by the second.

Cleopatra, still squeezing my hand tightly, said that Marla was becoming partially invisible as the bubbles multiplied.

Despite the screams of awe from the crowd, Marla did not lose focus. She again squeezed the trigger hard, her mouth narrowed to slits of great revenge. "HERE IS WHAT YOU DESERVE, MONKEY!"

Just then, Marla's pistol fired, discharging a blazing beam of fire, aimed at Fabian's face, transforming it instantly into a monkey's head. "How does it feel now, ape head? ANY APPETITE LEFT FOR MORE PARTIES?"

"Y-YOU B-BET, I WILL. Nothing, nothing is going to change my mind," he smirked, sticking his long monkey's tongue out at her, his ape's eyes winking.

"Oh, really? Well, here is another one, MONKEY HEAD!" She pulled the trigger once again. This time, a fireball darted toward Fabian's neck. "HOW DOES IT FEEL, YOU GIRAFFE NECK?"

Fabian's voice choked like a dying car engine, "N-NOTHING, n-nothing is g-going to stop me from partying! NOTHING!" His neck sprouted suddenly high, growing into a giraffe's neck, twirling upward like a screwdriver.

"Oh, really? If this doesn't impress you, let's try a different one. Here we go again, funny guy!" screeched Marla spitefully. She pressed the trigger hard. A beam of light struck Fabian's hands, turning them immediately into long wings, like those of a bald eagle. His gun tumbled to the ground as he was still struggling to clasp it under one of his wings.

"HOW AM I GOING TO USE MY GUN WITH THESE WINGS? HOW? HOW? HOW?" cried Fabian.

"That's not my problem, you bald monkey! Are you willing to concede? Do you promise to never ever play loud music in your stinky apartment?" she said, her arm outstretched stiff, one eyelid shut tight and the other squinting. She was aiming her pistol at Fabian's stomach, almost about to discharge another round of vicious fire.

CHAPTER TWENTY-FIVE

"HELL, NO! I'LL NEVER CONCEDE!" bellowed Fabian, his eagle's wings flapping forcefully. His giraffe's neck was still whirling. His monkey's head was wearing a grin of satisfaction. "HELL, NO! NEVER! Shoot as much as you want, lady, I'll never ever accept your ludicrous demands." Then he turned his back to her, pointed to his rear, and shouted, "SHOOT HERE, SHOOT HERE, MA'AM! I'd ask only for one favor: I do not want a monkey's butt, please."

"If this is what you want, here we go again," Marla's pistol released a horrible lightning that whizzed like a comet. The blaze traveled the distance between them in a fraction of a second and crashed on Fabian's behind — all in the blink of an eye.

"It's not a monkey butt, not at all, Mr. Gore," giggled Marla. "You've got an elephant's behind, ha-ha-ha-ha. It's enormous, gray, craggy like a rock on the Moon, and furrowed like a cornfield in the Midwest."

"STOP THE HORRIBLE SHOOTING," squawked Mr. Drifter Peachornby. "Mr. Gore, you're in terrible shape, you're dehumanized, you must admit. Are you willing to give in?"

"NEVER, NEVER, NEVER!"

CHAPTER TWENTY-SIX

DEFENSELESS

Mr. Drifter Peachornby said enthusiastically, "Dear citizens, here he is," his voice reverberating through the stadium's giant speakers. "Mr. Greenbold himself is marching in. The one and only, the chief of the chiefs, the leader of all leaders, the pioneer of all pioneers."

The crowd leaped to its feet and gave a round of deafening applause. Drums and bugles and trumpets and horns sounded with thrilling exuberance. Indeed, an air of elation engulfed the cheering spectators.

"He is the man who founded our beloved institution," Mr. Drifter Peachornby went on. "He's the man who envisioned the greatest city on earth: The City of @. He's the man who sparked the age of moral awakening. He's the man who put us on the map. He's the man who established a superior form of governance. He's the man who endowed us with his astuteness and energy."

After that rousing introduction, Mr. Greenbold paraded vibrantly around the stadium to a warm standing ovation from the crowd and the sounds of stirring marching music. Ms. Layerrous and Mr. Componenttous, his devoted aides, trooped alongside.

A dozen uniformed guards, who moved in unison at a constant pace, were behind Mr. Greenbold and his assistants. The guards were clasping glinting, sharp spears under their arms. In their hands, they carried red banners emblazoned with slogans: "Here's the hero" and "The master of the masters is here to win." And "Kill the traitors."

Behind Mr. Greenbold's guards, half a dozen pink alligators were crawling around on the lush grass. The huge reptiles were swaying from side to side and zigzagging in unison like belly dancers. Their jaws were shut tight, white teeth jutting out — a reminder of their lethal clamping abilities.

Trailing the alligators were four armored horses trotting triumphantly, proudly bobbing their heads up and down, up and down. Wheeled carts, hitched to the horses, seemed full to the brim with glinting swords, crossbows, axes, and lances.

"Why is Mr. Greenbold here?" asked Cleopatra agitatedly.

"There's a fight coming up, and he's one of the participants," I said.

"Do you know what's going to happen next, sweetie?"

"I don't recall. I dimly remember that last time he marched with his medieval weapons, but my recollection of the details fails me, I'm afraid."

Mr. Drifter Peachornby's strident voice echoed again from the numerous speakers arranged around the stadium. "And now, dear citizens, I'm privileged to present the second participant in the fight of the century. Although he is a tough rival and an outspoken critic of our beloved city, we must honor his presence. Even though he is against our way of life, we must give him a loud round of applause."

The crowd booed, hissed, and clamored against the man who was just hauled into the stadium. He was chained and blindfolded, with a twisted grin on his face.

"Although he was apprehended for trespassing on our city's property," continued Mr. Drifter Peachornby, "now we must forgive him. Although he has been barred from entering our treasured city, now we must welcome him. We will give him, though, one more chance to take back the evil things he has said against the City of @."

The crowd's loud uproar continued, "KILL THE TRAITOR, KILL THE TRAITOR, KILL THE TRAITOR!"

"NO, NO, dear citizens, let's be civil," asserted Mr. Drifter Peachornby. "Let us give him some respect. Treat him fairly, just as we treat all our prisoners. Honor him with immense grace and dignity. Therefore, ladies and gentlemen, please give a warm welcome to Mr. Larry Quack, president and CEO of Soul, Mind, and Money Corporation."

My fluttering heart almost jumped out of my chest. I gasped for air, almost swooned. "It's him! It's him! The evil finally made it! He's here to kill me, to kill us all."

"Who is he?" asked Cleopatra, craning her eyes high to catch a clear glimpse of Larry, who was being dragged now to the center of the stadium.

"He is Daddy's former boss," I said, still panting, still in a state of awe, still watching him with a gaping jaw. "He's a wicked man. Daddy told me, Mom told me, and everybody knows."

"Relax, sweet little girl, he can't harm you. He's shackled, and he can barely move. He can't see anyone. His eyes are covered with a black cloth. He's harmless."

"Untie him and remove his chains; he is powerless like a purple butterfly," Mr. Drifter Peachornby ordered his guards sternly.

"Should the travel bag he came with be given back to him, sir?" asked one of the guards.

"Give him his useless travel bag. There is nothing he can do with it."

Larry — unchained, the cloth that had been blinding him removed — was staring with a crooked smile at the jeering crowd.

"KILL THE TRAITOR, KILL THE TRAITOR, KILL THE TRAITOR!" the people shouted.

Larry opened his travel bag wide and emptied its contents on the ground. Suddenly, hundreds and hundreds of green creatures crawled out. Like zombies in a horror movie, they surrounded him slowly. They were hissing and screeching loudly as if danger were creeping about every corner. They carried a variety of what appeared to be weapons, pointed in every direction. "These are my Vikings, my powerful army. Anyone who attempts to cross their defense line will die instantly," he said coolly.

"There's no reason to panic, Mr. Quack. You're our guest. Guests are treated decently and fairly here," said Mr. Drifter Peachornby with a mixture of softness and rigidness in his voice. "There's no reason to go on the defensive even before the battle of the century has commenced. Mr. Quack, please instruct your army to drop its weapons."

"As far as I'm concerned, the fight has already begun, sir. My Vikings, the best of breed, stay with me and remain ready to destroy anyone who dares attack me, sir."

"If this is what you desire, so be it. We are not going to take from you the fundamental human rights you deserve. If you feel you need protection, go ahead; protect yourself, Mr. Quack."

"Thank you for understanding, sir," said Larry, mopping the sweat off his forehead with the sleeve of his jacket. "VIKINGS, AT EASE!" he yelped.

The green creatures assumed an at-ease stance, relaxing their stiff human-like shoulders and lowering their weapons to the ground.

"And now, dear citizens," continued Mr. Drifter Peachornby, "before we begin, I must invite the third person to take part in the battle of the century. This person brought havoc upon the City of @. I call on Miss Samantha Edison to report to the field. Miss Edison, please get down here as soon as possible."

I felt a huge lump in my throat. My heart was sprinting, thudding loudly. I was utterly bewildered, my hands sweating, mouth dry. Breathless, I stared at the crowd, which seemed to be waiting for the third person to descend to the center of the stadium. *Was my name called? Was I ordered to join the fight?*

"Sammy, were you the one who was just called down to the field?" asked Cleopatra.

"I think so. This call was probably for me."

"Miss Samantha Edison, Miss Samantha Edison! This is your last chance. We know where you're hiding. You're in the Red Section. I give you a minute — a short minute — before I send my GUARDS UP TO GET YOU," warned Mr. Drifter Peachornby, his voice rising to a loud scream.

Left with no choice, I ascended unevenly to my trembling feet, my head giddy. I descended the staircase sluggishly. Then I hobbled through the patches of grass, approaching the stadium flagpole. There I joined Mr. Greenbold, Larry Quack, and Mr. Drifter Peachornby and his guards. They bowed their heads mutely.

"Finally, finally, I get to see you, you little creep. Where have you been hiding?"

I winced.

"No name-calling, Mr. Quack. What's the matter with you?" said Mr. Drifter Peachornby strictly. "No one calls anybody names in this place, especially before the grand fight. Let's respect each other."

"I'm sorry, sir, but this girl has inflicted so much pain on me. She is the root cause of all my troubles."

"Is she really a juvenile?" queried Mr. Drifter Peachornby, his eyebrows arching. "How old are you, Samantha?"

The Special Field was so still at that moment, you could hear the crowd clicking their tongues in disbelief.

"I'm 13, only 13," I said, my teeth clattering. "I shouldn't be here. I'm too young. I'll not be able to fight these two. They will kill me at once."

"Ha-ha-ha-ha, what a lie. She's strong enough and nasty enough to face us. She is evil, the evilest person on earth!" shrieked Larry spitefully. "You don't know her at all, sir. She is wicked, sir. The wickedest person in the world! Her sly demeanor deceives the eye. You must trust me on that, sir."

"I must side with Mr. Quack this time," said Mr. Greenbold, with a revolting grin. "She *is* terrible, indeed horrible. If it's not against the rules of the Special Field, I'd recommend that she join the fight."

It seemed that Mr. Drifter Peachornby had no qualms about juveniles' participating in bloody battles. Nor had he found any conflict with the rules at the stadium. Shortly after skimming through his little blue notebook of protocol, he accepted Larry's and Mr. Greenbold's appeals.

And that was how I found myself facing the battle of my life.

Mr. Drifter Peachornby peered at us in turns and said, "Chief Greenbold, Mr. Larry Quack, and Miss Samantha Edison: I'm glad you were able to make it to the fight of the century. I wish all of you good luck. Before we start, though, our beloved citizens would like to hear your stands on the issues that brought you to the Special Field. Tell us about your core values, the principles you're willing to fight and die for."

"I have no statement to make. All I want to do is to destroy your city. I'm also eager to kill this little brat who brought on me disaster after disaster, sir."

"Very well, very well, Mr. Quack. I like your determination. It is impossible to excuse you from giving us an opening statement, though. This is one of the rules," said Mr. Drifter Peachornby flatly. "Tell us your stand on any issue you like. Remember: it might be the last statement you ever make in your life. Keep it short, keep it sweet, and keep it professional."

Larry seemed weary and confused. He motioned his Vikings to line up behind him. Then he whirled his head and stared at the crowd, which fell silent like a mouse. "I'm here today not because I was forced," he said.

A bunch of baloney, I whispered under my breath.

"I'm here today not because I don't have anything else to do at home."

Pure nonsense.

"Coming here is not only a supreme duty that every decent person should fulfill," Larry continued. "It is an important principle. It is an obligation to eradicate the immoral ideology that you and your city stand for."

Listen to him…, what language… did I hear right? Did he use the word ideology? *What language: only a person with an exaggerated self-opinion uses such words*, I grumbled to myself.

Pointing to Larry, the crowd shot to its feet and hollered ferociously, "KILL THE SPY, KILL THE SPY, KILL THE SPY!"

"Your city was founded upon fake values, on imaginary foundations," Larry went on. "Your world does not exist. It is unreal — purely virtual. Nothing is tangible here in the City of @. This includes you, your buildings, your gardens, the sky above, and the fields beneath. NOTHING."

Total drivel, it seemed to me.

"Ha-ha-ha, hu-hu-hu, hee-hee-hee," Mr. Greenbold burst in his typical screeching laughter. "Suppose you're right. Suppose the City of @ is a virtual place. What's so bad about nonexistence? Why is virtual such an awful thing? Who needs to be concrete? Is being real better?"

Ms. Layerrous and Mr. Componenttous, who stood behind Mr. Greenbold, nodded their heads, agreeing with every word he uttered.

"Huh? I cannot believe it! You're joking, right?" shrieked Larry. "What's so bad about being unreal? What is so awful? Well, I'll tell you what's wrong with that. In my real world, everything exists. It makes sense, it's solid, it's safe. In your imaginary world, however, everything *seems* real, but it is not. In other words, in your fictional world, it's hard to distinguish between real and unreal. That in itself is a nightmare."

"So why is that so bad? I do not understand."

"You still do not understand, you donkey head!" thundered Larry. "The problem is that with today's advanced technologies, the real world is shrinking. Don't you see? With the growing influence of computers, the virtual world is gaining ground. Don't you see? It occupies more and more of our time, our lives, our futures. This becomes painful when the balance is tipping toward the imaginary. It is intolerable when the concrete is dissolving. It is agonizing when most of life turns into fiction. Life has become a fantasy that's hard to control."

Total hogwash, I thought.

"Give me a reasonable example, you zebra head!" challenged Mr. Greenbold.

"Ha-ha-ha-ha-ha-ha-ha, I gather that you still don't get it, chipmunk head. Here are some good examples. All of these have become virtual in our lives, all of them turned imaginary: bank accounts, friends, girlfriends, family, work, freedom, choice, self-determination, self-thinking. All of them imaginary, including your city."

"But Mr. Quack, Mr. Quack, I'm outright perplexed. What are you complaining about? Have you forgotten one very small fact? A tiny detail? Have you?"

"WHAT? WHAT have I forgotten?" intoned Larry.

"You have nothing to whimper about, you annoying whiner. NOTHING! After all, after all, after all, IT IS YOUR WORLD THAT CREATED US!"

"We? The real world invented you? Did we invent the City of @?"

It seemed that Larry's Vikings sensed the rising tension. Shielding him from possible attack, they moved slowly in front of him. As the war of words escalated, Mr. Greenbold's guards (and alligators too), shuffled forward, preparing to ward off confrontation.

"Correct! The real world founded us — the virtual one. Only your world is capable of creating imaginary worlds," claimed Mr. Greenbold. "You have created an imaginary city that you can no longer control. You have created an intelligence that is more intelligent than you are. Now we're in control, just as you were for so many years before this technological revolution started."

"Well, you have a bit of a point, you potato head," Larry half admitted. "That's why we're engaged now in a battle of survival. That's why I'm going to destroy you. That's why we'll never live in peace, in harmony. It's you or us…, nothing in between!"

"Ha-ha-ha-ha-ha, hu-hu-hu-hu-hu, hee-hee-hee-hee-hee, without me, Mr. Quack, your world is NOTHING! You need us more than we need you," retorted Mr. Greenbold. "A real world like yours should have some imagination. Without imagination, you are set to fail. Do you understand, little cucumber head? Without imagination, you're doomed —"

"The diminishing reality and expanding imaginary are the chief causes of our declining country, you ant head," said Larry, evening the score.

"Really? On the contrary, lack of imagination is the root cause of our declining country," said Mr. Greenbold.

"WAIT, WAIT, WAIT: The state of our country is strong. We are not in decline, and we never will be," said Mr. Drifter Peachornby. "Before this gets out of hand, let's hear from Miss Samantha Edison. We need your take on these issues, Miss Edison."

I stayed silent for a while until I was able to compose my thoughts. "I have nothing to say. I don't care who is real or who isn't. What difference does it make now? All I care about is finding Daddy. You people, go ahead and kill each other for the sake of nothing, absolutely nothing! Who cares after all? I'm out of here…"

As Mr. Drifter Peachornby gestured his guards to halt my departure, he said, "WAIT, you're not going anywhere. You were ordered to take part in today's fight. You can't just simply leave. This is against our rules. Maybe if you win, you'll be able to find your father. Wouldn't you like that? Huh? Isn't that what you really want? If you do, you must respect the rules."

A peaceful solution to the conflict did not seem to be on the horizon. The opening statements ended on a frustrating and frightening note.

Neither Larry nor Mr. Greenbold had made convincing points. They were not willing to compromise, either. They stuck to their points of view like chewing gum on a chair. Both were wrong for wanting to destroy each other.

Therefore, regrettably, in a few minutes from now, the battle was about to begin.

I understood the disagreement between these two men, though. Altogether, it was a simple issue. Nothing was new under the sun: All wars, all fights, all quarrels are, after all — about nothing.

DEFENSELESS

So let's put things in perspective now. It boiled down to this: On one hand, Larry was troubled about losing control of his life — that simple, it seemed. He needed to blame someone, and the City of @ and what it stood for was an easy target. I was also on his enemies list because he had never gotten along with my father.

On the other hand, Mr. Greenbold, in my humble opinion, demonstrated surprising humility. He showed respect and fondness for the city he loved. He fought tooth and nail against those who questioned his establishment. He'd give his life to defend the city he cherished.

I'm confident that you would be able to tell the difference between their opinions. At that time, I believed strongly that their dispute, Larry's and Mr. Greenbold's, was not over a clash between the virtual and real worlds. Nor was it about an encounter between the imaginary and the tangible. Not at all.

Even a child like me understood that the real and unreal worlds could live together, coexist like a pair of bonding swans. Reality intertwined with fiction is a powerful thing, don't you think? There's nothing bad about the virtual world. When you're living in a harsh reality, just as I was, a bit of the imaginary could help ease the pain.

And now, on Mr. Drifter Peachornby's instruction, each of us set off to an assigned battle position, which was marked with a white square. The three places were quite distant from each other. You could view, though, what your rivals were up to because the weather was exceptional and visibility in the stadium was clear.

As I was staggering across the field toward my position, my mind was cluttered with unsettling thoughts. There were things that did not make sense. I was still not certain which world was the imaginary one. Both seemed the same. Was it Larry's or the City of @? Although Mr. Greenbold half admitted that the City of @, after all, was not real, my doubts continued to haunt me. What was behind his striking confession?

Many people I met in the City of @ would have sworn that the place was real, not virtual. Even Cleopatra, whom I admired, told me on a few occasions that the city is as real as an actual thing can ever be. Had she ever had doubts? Perhaps. But in our conversations, she fiercely protected her standpoint. And despite my creeping doubts, I trusted her.

"Remember the rules at the Special Field," Mr. Drifter Peachornby's shrill voice echoed out from the speakers, as we were still moving toward our battle positions. "The one who dies first is the one who has lost the battle. Let me know when you've arrived at your position, and let me know when you're ready."

Larry's Viking army seemed in disarray. The green armored creatures were scattered all around the stadium. A few lingered behind him, creeping in a straight line at a slow pace.

From a distance, I could tell Mr. Greenbold was in better shape. He was striding erectly, with Ms. Layerrous and Mr. Componenttous at his heels. His guards, the alligators, the horses, and the carts hustled behind them.

As I finally reached my position, I murmured to myself, *Am I going to make it? Will I be able to survive the battle? Would my journey conclude a few minutes from now? What weapons am I going to use to fight them? I don't even have a knife or an ax or a dagger or a sword or a machete.*

"I'm ready, sir —," I announced hesitantly.

"Very well, Miss Edison, very well!" said Mr. Drifter Peachornby contentedly.

"But I do not have arms, nor do I have armor for shielding myself."

"You don't?" he wondered.

"No. I'm standing here with my bare hands. What am I going to do? It's unfair, sir."

"Well, your point is well taken. But there is nothing I can do at this moment. My best advice is that you use the power of your imagination. Use something, Miss Edison. There is no time to waste."

"Mr. Greenbold always claims that the City of @ is a just place. It's unfair to let me die defenseless," I said pitifully.

"Why don't you use one of those witchy talents of yours? Why —"

Mr. Greenbold suddenly cut in on Mr. Drifter Peachornby. His tone of voice echoed with a mixture of mercy and ridicule: "I can lend her one of my blades. I also have some extra slings. A semi-automatic crossbow would probably alleviate her security concerns, sir. I have also gazillions of other things she can defend herself with, sir."

"Give her something, so she stops whining, Chief. Remember, Chief, she merely *looks* innocent, but she is not. Make sure you give her something very harmless, Chief," cautioned Mr. Drifter Peachornby.

"Maybe I can give her an alligator, sir," said Mr. Greenbold, flashing a flat grin. "I have a sick gator capable of nothing. Can I lend it to her, sir?"

"These alligators of yours look nasty, Chief Greenbold. Why would you offer something that is so powerful, Chief?"

"Just a thought, just a thought, sir."

"I'm not interested in your contributions, Mr. Greenbold. Kill me now. Why bother fighting me? I'm as vulnerable as an innocent lamb in the meadow," I said cheekily.

The crowd seemed full of mercy. Spectators leaped to their feet and cupped their mouths with their hands.

"Her name is Sammy, sir. No one knows her by *Miss Samantha Edison*," Larry's croaky voice echoed from the other side of the stadium. "Before she dies, we need to give her some warm and fuzzy feelings. Give her some respect — call her by her nickname."

"Sammy, Shmammy. I don't care, as long as we know that she is Miss Edison," said Mr. Drifter Peachornby.

CHAPTER TWENTY-SEVEN

THE FATAL HICCUPS

The fight of the century was about to begin. There were a few rules to consider, none of them too complicated, though. The most important: No face-to-face combat shall be conducted. That is to say, you're confined to your battle position for the duration of the fight.

Because of the considerable distance between the positions, use only weapons that can reach your adversaries. Short-range arms like knives or daggers seemed impractical. Next rule in importance: Any type of weapon was permissible. It was all about your preference. Anything goes: shooting arrows, slinging rocks, or blowing fire out of your mouth.

"I guess that Miss Samantha Edison or Sammy Shmammy, is ready. What about you, Chief Greenbold?" asked Mr. Drifter Peachornby.

"I'm ready, too, sir."

"And you, Mr. Quack, can we start?"

"I'm fine, sir. Please go ahead."

Every fight in the Special Field started to the notes of bugles. These were short tunes, known as bugle calls, played to announce events at the stadium. There were bugle calls signaling the beginnings and ends of battles. Other calls indicated the death of a loser or the crowning of a winner.

The woman sitting in front of me mentioned that Mr. Drifter Peachornby was well versed in bugle calls. Her friend added that Mr. Peachornby was familiar with at least a hundred of them. As far as they could remember, however, the buglers in the stadium had never played more than five calls.

CHAPTER TWENTY-SEVEN

"The time has come to ask for attention... Bugle men, attention call," commanded Mr. Drifter Peachornby.

Three uniformed buglers were about to sound the attention call, their chests bulging out, shoulders rising up, chins stiff, and heads erect. Holding the brass bugles with their right hands, they brought the mouthpieces to their pursed lips. Then they pointed the wide portions of the instruments toward the crowd.

The call for attention echoed out of their bugles.

"Bugle men, open-fire call," instructed Mr. Drifter Peachornby.

The signal to start the battle thundered out of the bugles in ten fearsome successions. The tunes to open fire were enough to raise the hair on your neck.

The fight was raging fiercely in a whirl of gray dust. Fumes engulfed the stadium. You could see flaming arrows and missiles whooshing through the intense smog. Larry's army responded with vengeance to the deadly artillery launched from Mr. Greenbold's battle position. They were determined to destroy each other. They were engaged in a vehement exchange of hate. They hit each other with the utmost might they possibly could.

"AREN'T YOU DEAD YET, EGGPLANT HEAD?" shouted Mr. Greenbold from the far distance. "If you're not dead, please let me know so I can increase my firepower."

"Ha-ha-ha-ha, are you expecting me to die from your fireworks? Ha-ha-ha-ha, use them on Halloween," retorted Larry, chuckling aloud.

When the dust settled, the scene appeared to be chaotic. Larry's Vikings were spearheading a massive new attack on his sworn enemy, Mr. Greenbold. The ugly green creatures were arranged in strategic battle formations. They were inching slowly toward Mr. Greenbold's defense lines. They frequently armed their tiny cannons: They loaded the explosive powder and dropped in shiny metal balls. Then the cannons fired new rounds.

"STOP THE SLY ADVANCE OF YOUR ROTTEN ARMY RIGHT THERE, CARROT HEAD! You're making a grave mistake," yelled Mr. Greenbold.

"Ha-ha-ha-ha, what are you going to do, shoot me? Ha-ha-ha," Larry exploded in sarcastic laughter.

"No. But if you don't stop, my nasty reptiles are going to devour you! They'll drink your blood in a flash!" Mr. Greenbold said as he motioned to his alligators to meet Larry's army.

Larry's army was no match for the unflinching reptiles. It was a bloodbath. The alligators wolfed down anything, consuming every single Viking who stood in their path.

"Tell your disgusting alligators to back off before things get out of control!" threatened Larry with a mixture of wrath, anxiety, and fear.

"Your funny army will be gone in a matter of seconds, you bonehead! Mmmmmmm, my gators seem to love their green blood. Look, look how my hungry reptiles cut your army in half. Ha-ha-ha-ha, hee-hee-hee —"

"Not a chance, you skunk head," said Larry, as he pulled out from his travel bag a tiny portable table and a silver printer. "I can always make more soldiers. I can print hundreds and hundreds of Vikings. I have never had a shortage of them, ever!"

After Larry set the printer on the unfolded table, he pushed a button on one side of it. And moments later, a flow of new green Vikings poured out from the other end.

"Can you also print money, you sausage head?" said Mr. Greenbold mockingly.

"Not money, but I can give you Vikings — lots of them. Here they come, you pink cabbage head," said Larry. "They will slay you and your team shortly. And you too, Sammy. Don't think even for a moment that I forgot about you. I'm sending some to you too, little brat. Say good-bye to the wonderful and comfy life you have had."

I gasped. I felt a horrible jolt in my belly. I knew that I'd not be spared for long. I had nothing to lose; I raised my chin high and said confidently, "Send them along, Mr. Quack. I'm fearless, waiting. I'll rip them apart with my bare hands."

"Oh, really? Is that what you're going to do? Tear them apart, huh? Ha-ha-ha-ha, we'll see about that in a few seconds. In just a few, we'll see how brave you are —"

"Don't worry about his lousy army," interrupted Mr. Greenbold, whose voice was both gentle and stern. "These sticky Vikings are harmless. But watch my gators, girl. Mine are nasty and hungry. I, too, am sending you a couple of cute pink ones, to keep you busy for a while."

Not even five seconds later, Larry's Vikings split into two groups. One started marching toward Mr. Greenbold, and the other headed toward me.

There were thousands of Vikings — maybe more. The green, shiny, and grizzly human-like creatures were striding erect, with an air of pride and determination. The closer they came, the more I wondered what made them so resolved, so committed to destroy me. They carried their ridiculous little cannons, colorful hoses slung over their shoulders, gas masks over their necks.

Mr. Greenbold's alligators, too, seemed gritty. As he had mentioned, there were two of them. They were weaving their way through the grass like a couple of rattlesnakes. Their jaws were enormous, open wide, drooling as if they were heading to a feast. Paddling with their craggy forepaws, they crawled toward me with utmost elegance, as though they were parading on a beauty pageant runway.

THE FATAL HICCUPS

My journey on this planet is coming to an abrupt end, I feared. *There is nothing I can do now, nothing*, I reckoned. *How am I going to die?* I wondered. *Am I going to perish by the devastating grip of an alligator, be shot by miniature cannons, or be sent to my death by some sort of poison?*

Cleopatra's voice thundered suddenly from the Red Section of the stadium, "Do not fear, sweetie. You're invisible; they can't attack you!"

There was some truth to that. Only my eyes and a small portion of my neck were visible. But the Vikings and the alligators were coming closer and closer to me. I dreaded they could spot me, perhaps sniff me. They were near. I could feel their breath; I could smell the sweat; I could hear their gritting teeth.

I was terrified of the looming danger. My eyes shut tight, lips sealed firmly, I slipped down to the ground and cowered, defenseless.

During those frightful moments, Uncle Walter was on my mind. I had never forgotten his guidance. In keeping with his frequent advice, I focused intensely on the inner me, on my soul, on controlling my mind, on listening to my fluttering heartbeat.

A few quiet seconds had drifted away until I started whispering to myself, *I love myself because I'm the greatest, I love myself because I'm the greatest, I love myself because I'm the greatest.* Moments later, I chanted silently, *I'm gorgeous like sin, I'm gorgeous like sin, I'm gorgeous like sin.*

Then I leaped to my feet and screamed at the top of my lungs, "SCRUNCH TWENTY MINUTES, SCRUNCH TWENTY MINUTES, SCRUNCH TWENTY MINUTES."

The art of Uncle Walter's time bending had been put to the test again. Time rolled back instantly, like playing a movie backward at high speed.

Chief Greenbold's alligators seemed to be backpedaling in their tracks. They returned rapidly to their battle position.

Larry's Vikings, too, retreated quickly. They were marching backward and stationing themselves in their original stance.

"Aha! Aha! Aha! This was you, Sammy, you smelly brat!" roared Larry. "I knew all along that you have the power to bend time! You evil witch! Cunning like a hyena!" Even from such a distance, you could hear his teeth grinding like a wild bear's. "And you told us you're defenseless, huh? Is she harmless?" he turned to the crowd. "Wait, I have more surprises for you, reeking brat. We'll see how you handle these."

Then Larry drew out of his bag a blunt-headed tool that bore a resemblance to a sledgehammer, flinging it in all directions. "You see this? You see this? This is my city shaker!" Next, he pulled out of his bag a cone-headed tool that looked like a screwdriver. "And this is my sinkhole maker! And wait, I have more of these in my bag —"

"Don't believe him; he's full of nonsense. His toys don't work," bellowed Mr. Greenbold sardonically.

"MY TOYS DON'T WORK? Ha-ha-ha-ha! DON'T WORK? Ha-ha-ha-ha!" Larry stooped toward the ground and pounded the grass ferociously with the city shaker clamped in his fist.

No tongue could ever describe the terror that fell suddenly on the Special Field. The rumbling hum of an earthquake was perhaps one of the most frightening things I had ever heard.

The ground was rising and sinking and rolling like killer waves in the Indian Ocean. The cracks in the ground widened and widened. They seemed like open shark jaws that were about to swallow anyone or anything around. The muffled noise of the rupturing ground and the hollow echoes of falling debris from the stadium structure sent tremors through my body.

THE FATAL HICCUPS

The Red and White Sections of the stadium toppled under their enormous weight. Rows of seats sagged in like the crumbling roof of a house in a hurricane.

Some people began fleeing the stadium the moment the ground started quivering. A few escaped before the staircases gave in to the volatile shaking. Others ran off the moment the ground splintered. The bravest ones lingered, staying behind to watch the conclusion of the grand battle.

"Ha-ha-ha-ha, enjoying the vibrations yet?" said Larry sarcastically.

Across the stadium, I noticed Mr. Greenbold and his companions struggling to recoup from Larry's devastating city shaker. The impact had been enormous. His horses fell to the ground, the carts were knocked over, the alligators took off, and some of his guards escaped.

"Your city shaker does not affect us at all. Go on, enjoy your toys!" said Mr. Greenbold.

"Aha! Aha! Aha! Don't lie to me. I can hear the pain in your voice! But if the city shaker did not impress you, maybe my sinkhole maker will. Ha-ha-ha-ha-ha." Larry bent to the ground again with the destructive device in his hand. "You see, you banana head? See this? Three little taps on the ground and you're gone!"

"I don't believe you, you watermelon head. This is one of your fake toys."

"MY FAKE TOYS, CHIEF? FAKE TOYS? FAKE TOYS?" screeched Larry. Then he struck the ground three times with the sinkhole maker.

Just then, giant holes opened up in the center of the field and continued to multiply sporadically. Two huge craters even formed near my battle position. They were massive. I reckoned each was about 100 feet deep and 50 feet wide.

"Ha-ha-ha-ha-ha, are you still alive, Mr. Greenbold, you skeleton head?" cried Larry triumphantly.

A hollow silence fell on the Special Field.

"Chief Greenbold, are you alive? Give us a sign, something — " hollered Mr. Drifter Peachornby.

"He can't give you a sign because he's DEAD! Ha-ha-ha-ha-ha," Larry erupted in sickening laughter. "How can a dead man give you a sign? Ha-ha-ha-ha-ha."

Hands over their mouths, the crowd gazed at Mr. Greenbold's battle position in astonishment.

I craned my neck and cupped my hands over my eyebrows, my eyes squinting. I was scouring the field, searching for Mr. Greenbold. He was gone. He had disappeared in the twinkling of an eye. Perhaps he had sunk into a giant crater that had opened up beneath him. Maybe he had descended into the dark sinkhole along with his cronies, Ms. Layerrous and Mr. Componenttous. Everything else — crates, horses, guards, and alligators — was gone, too.

"And now it's your turn, Sammy, you little pimple head," snarled Larry. "You'll be gone in a second. The question is, How? How would you like to die? I have a few options for you here — in my little bitty bag. You survived my city shaker. You also endured the sinkhole maker. But I have new gadgets here. Should we try my brain eraser, eh? Or maybe we should try the mind grinder, eh?"

"Mr. Quack, your quarrelsome and mocking tone of voice neither impressed my parents, nor has it me," I said. "You're a paper tiger whose sickening behavior chased away your friends, your family, your employees. They all hate you. So, go ahead and kill me. I'm prepared to die now. I have accomplished everything I dreamed of in my short life —"

"Are you saying I'm a paper tiger? AM I A PAPER TIGER? This is what you're saying?"

"Yes, you are. Maybe not even a tiger —"

"And what have you accomplished in your short useless life? Can you share it with me?"

"Yes, but I'm sure you'd never understand."

"Ha-ha-ha-ha, go ahead, maybe I would."

"Love, Mr. Quack, love — simple and powerful."

"Ha-ha-ha-ha, and how come love is an accomplishment? You little weasel, even rats love each other. Is this your life achievement?"

"Yes, superior to all of yours!"

"How so?"

"The power of love defeats death, Mr. Quack. Even if I die now, my love will endure forever. My love for my daddy, for my mom, for my brother will never vanish. They, too, will always love me. It's an unbreakable bond. A connection that you'd never understand."

I could hear moans of sympathy and gasps of admiration coming from the crowd.

"Nonsense," said Larry. "Love, powerful? Ha-ha-ha-ha!"

"I knew you wouldn't understand. Love is much beyond your grasp. You are concerned only with yourself and your money."

"ENOUGH IS ENOUGH!" screamed Larry piercingly. "You see this?" waving over his head a tool that looked like an eggbeater. "This is my lethal mind grinder. This nasty little device can fragment your brain so it looks like a scrambled omelet. READY? READY?"

Am I ready to die? I am certainly prepared to depart from this world at any moment. Dying, though, is not the solution, I murmured to myself. *And who is going to bring back Rhubarb Pie if I'm gone? Can I muster the last of my energy to fight Larry?*

Perhaps the one thing left to do before I departed from this world was to try something that Uncle Walter taught me at the Techno-Geek Café. It was one of my favorites. He had named it the *infinite hiccups*. It sounds more complicated than it really was. In fact, it was one of the easiest things to learn. All you needed to do is to focus on the inner you. Find your soul, listen to your heartbeat, and achieve divine tranquility. Then, with the power of your thoughts, you could do anything — anything you desired.

Larry's mind grinder seemed to jam. It simply did not function. Perhaps it was broken, out of commission. From the corner of my eye, I saw him kicking his travel bag and waving his hands in the air desperately. I heard him cussing. He was spitting. He went on a rampage, smashing his Vikings under his boots and crashing their cannons.

This time I chanted as loud as I could, "I'M BACK, I'M BACK, I'M BACK!"

And again, at the top of my lungs, "I LOVE MYSELF BECAUSE I'M THE GREATEST, I LOVE MYSELF BECAUSE I'M THE GREATEST, I LOVE MYSELF BECAUSE I'M THE GREATEST!"

Then I went on, "I'M THE SMARTEST, I'M THE SMARTEST, I'M THE SMARTEST!"

Next, I screamed, "I'M STUBBORN LIKE A MULE, I'M STUBBORN LIKE A MULE, I'M STUBBORN LIKE A MULE!"

Last, I shouted, "GOT THE HICCUPS YET, MR. QUACK?"

"Hic-hic-hic-hic-hic-hic-hic," a sudden and persistent bout of hiccups debilitated Larry, left him breathless. Gasping for air, he slipped to the ground, suffocating.

Then Larry got onto his feet and groped about in his travel bag for a remedy. Panting for air, he continued to struggle, but it was not long before he took his last breath, plummeting to the ground.

Silence.

The spectators jumped to their feet, cheering Larry's demise. "THE TRAITOR IS DEAD, THE TRAITOR IS DEAD," they shouted.

THE INFORMATION INSIDE

Perhaps the place with the most corridors I had ever seen was the Database Layer Center in the City of @. But the outside was no less mesmerizing.

That evening, on the edge of summer, I found myself wandering in front of the Database Layer Center building, rubbing my eyes in disbelief. Its unique, sky-piercing structure was gripping. Its surrounding gold-tinted walls captivated me. Their massive shape appeared as medieval castle ramparts that stood tall to protect the people and their property.

Before entering the building, you would encounter its gate, supporting a lighted sign saying, *Information Center for Intelligent People.* You might wonder if only the gifted would be allowed to visit the place. Such a thought brought a feeble grin to my face. Still, something inside the Database Layer Center attracted me more and more deeply, as though I had fallen prey to an insect-eating flower.

Passing the lobby, you might pick out one corridor, out of many. Then you run its course, perhaps a few hundred feet, until an intersection of corridors comes into sight. Next, you choose another one, and so on, and so on, until you arrive somewhere — if indeed you are lucky.

I trudged through a dim and chilly corridor. The end was not in sight. My eyes were weary, and my knees ached. I was lost. Going back to the lobby through the web of corridors that I had already visited did not make any sense. Moving forward through the tunnel of lit corridors was perhaps the only way to run across a person.

THE INFORMATION INSIDE

I don't remember for how long I slogged sluggishly through the narrow corridor. As I plodded along under a burden of fear and anxiety, weak moans echoed from a distance. I could hear muffled chatter, stifled laughter, and subdued cheers. The murmurs grew louder when I drew near a bright purple light that blinded my eyes.

A large banquet hall packed with ecstatic diners huddled around a long dining table appeared at the end of the corridor. Strange smells wafted from the place. There were shiny pots full of some sort of sizzling meats that smelled like skunk. Odors of burning rubber oozed from the diners' plates. Their mugs were full to the brim with creepy drinks that made me sick to my stomach.

I interrupted the joyful feast.

"Who's there? Who is this?" a gaunt man asked irksomely as the fork in his hand seemed to bend with fury. "Who in the world dares interrupt this sumptuous dinner?"

"Ahem," I cleared my throat, "i-i-i-it is m-m-me," I mumbled with fright.

"*Me?* Who is *me?*" asked the bony man frowningly, the corners of his mouth arched downward like a hunting bow.

"Sammy."

They all stood up on their feet and applauded cheerfully. Apparently, they knew who I was.

"Phew-w-w-w, you scared the living daylights out of me," said the skinny man. "Your glinting eyes in the dark with no body beneath gave me a strong jolt. It's scary, creepy. You're almost invisible, Sammy."

I gave a frail smile, knowing they would not be able to see it.

"We've been expecting you," said the man. This time the corners of his mouth arched upward like the smiling Moon. "My name is Mr. Three Inch. I'm the one who's running this facility."

CHAPTER TWENTY-EIGHT

"Yes, it's him, and only him, the only director around," whispered his cronies.

"Why don't you sit down at the head of the table? Have a taste of our delicious meal, and then introduce yourself, Sammy," said Mr. Three Inch.

"I don't have anything to say about myself," I proclaimed shyly, flinging myself onto the chair. "Why don't you go first, Mr. Three Inch?"

"No, I must give you the honor. You are the hero, and I'm your servant."

"Yes, she's the hero. Yes, she's the hero," everybody hummed.

"Am I the hero?"

"Hell, yes. You're the one who killed Mr. Larry Quack. Chief Greenbold, too, perished. Both are dead — very dead, Sammy. The fight of the century in the Special Field was worth watching. We had thought you were defenseless, but you were not."

"And I thought Mr. Greenbold was the only hero in town. Wasn't he an adored figure? Aren't you sad that he's gone? After all, he was your leader, your cherished chief," I said, raising an eyebrow.

"Y-yes, y-yes, he was the boss," muttered Mr. Three Inch. "But we did not like him."

"Yes, yes, we hated him, we hated him," they all chanted.

"I'm glad he's dead. Now, you are our new chief," said Mr. Three Inch.

"Me? Ha-ha-ha," I giggled. "No, that's impossible. I can't run this city. It would be much beyond my capabilities."

"Naw..., this isn't true, you are our new hero, very powerful," said Mr. Three Inch. "Why don't you introduce yourself to my team?"

"I'm not that powerful. I did what I needed to do. Why don't you introduce yourself first, Mr. Three Inch?"

"Oh, should I go first, Sammy Boss? Is this what you want me to do?"

I nodded my head, mindful of my invisibility.

"Yes, Director, you should. Yes, Director, you should," said everyone in unison.

"I don't have much to say, either, ha-ha-ha-hoooo-hoooo-hoooo," Mr. Three Inch burst into silly laughter. "Ha-ha-ha-hoooo-hoooo-hoooo."

"You do, Director. You do, Director," said the diners.

The people around the table gave me a warmhearted welcome. The reception brought tears to my eyes. It had been a long time since I'd felt like this, belonging to someone, to something. They seemed fond of me. They befriended me. They overwhelmed me with respect and adoration. I felt a part of them. Their caring and nurturing company embraced me, engulfing me with affection that I'll never forget. Mr. Three Inch and his team even offered some of their smelly dishes and the spine-tingling drinks. Politely, I rejected all.

So, who were these people in that dining hall? Some were interesting, others simple. They all made their livings at the Database Layer Center.

A few are worth mentioning.

Mrs. Twenty-Seven Pounds was a stout, tubby, green-eyed, ginger-haired, and plump-legged individual who'd been working there since she was born. She had never visited the country, always confined to the City of @.

Mr. Forty-Four Miles, her husband, with a red bowtie knotted around his neck, was sitting next to her. He was nodding off, often waking up and giving me polite smiles. He was skinny, lanky, long throated, long legged, and gray haired. His knowledge of computers and information was indeed exceptional. What else? Oh, yes, he loved ice cream, and not even one morning in his life did he skip his hot chocolate.

Their sons, Four-by-Four and Five Hundred Bushels, were munching enthusiastically on every helping and chewing vigorously on every bone. Their fat pink cheeks attested to their unstoppable appetites — like those of the ancient dinosaurs. Consumed by the countless dishes they gobbled, they were paying no attention to the ongoing chat that warmed up as time went by.

"OK, Sammy Boss, if this is what you want, I'm going to introduce myself first," said Mr. Three Inch. "But remember, there's not much to it."

"Go ahead, Director, go ahead, Director," said Mr. Forty-Four Miles, stealing a glimpse at his wife, asking for support.

"So, as you know, Sammy Boss, I'm the director of this facility. The City of @ stores all kind of information here in the Database Layer Center. This is the place where you can find anything. This is the place where you can enrich your wisdom. This is the place where information — we call it *data* — is retrieved by software applications. People, computers, and anyone hungry for knowledge, can obtain the information we provide."

"What kind of information do you save here?"

"Anything, anything you may think of. We have archives of every war in world history. We have images of every wedding in the country since the beginning of the former century. We store data about seed and plant growth. We manage information about stars, about the Sun, about the Moon. And we maintain secret information about every person in the world."

"Your place is vast. Where do you store all the information?" I wondered aloud.

"The data is not arranged in files, nor is it organized on computers," said Mr. Three Inch.

"Then where is the data?" I pressed.

Pointing to herself, Mrs. Twenty-Seven Pounds said, "We are the information."

"*We?*" I questioned. "What does that mean: *we?*"

"*We* means *us*. We the people carry information in our bodies, in our bloodstreams, in our tissues, in our —"

"Every person here is a bank of information," interrupted her husband. "If space is your hobby, Mr. Big Black Hole himself would be more than happy to offer material about the stars and the galaxies. He carries this information in his body. If you're looking for a carrot cake recipe, Mr. Sweet Goodies would be able to provide it."

Mr. Sweet Goodies, who was sitting on the other side of the table, gave a honeyed smile, his wide eyes glinting like those of an owl. "He's right. I carry in my body all the sweet recipes in the world. All you need to do is to ask for one," he said. "All this information is in my blood, in my liver, in my kidneys, in my brain, in my ears —"

"ENOUGH," thundered Mr. Three Inch. "There is no need to overexplain it. Sammy Boss is not stupid. She understands that people are information and information is people. Don't you get it, Sammy Boss?"

"I kind of understand," I said, furrowing my brow. "If a person carries information in him, why don't you, Mr. Sweet Goodies, give me a good recipe for a mouthwatering rhubarb pie?"

"Yeah, yeah, Mr. Sweet Goodies, I love rhubarb. I love sweet pies," burst out Four-by-Four, extending his chubby little hands to grab another dish of smelly meat.

CHAPTER TWENTY-EIGHT

"Not a problem," said Mr. Sweet Goodies, raising his gaze to the ceiling and chanting something under his breath. Then he asked, "How tall would you like the pie to be?"

"Ten inches," I said.

"Ten is pretty high. Are you asking for a double-crusted pie, Sammy Boss?"

"Yes," I said somberly. "Double crusted is what Daddy used to make. It always smelled so good, so yummy."

"So, here is what you'd need:

1. *5 cups of fresh chopped rhubarb. Get rhubarb from the closest farmer's market, never from your backyard*

2. *1.5 tablespoons of high-quality butter, not cheap butter*

3. *7 cups of whole-grain flour, not cheap grain*

4. *2 cups of brown sugar, not cheap white sugar*

5. *And for the crust, get a ½ cup of tangy blackberries"*

"Excellent, Mr. Sweet Goodies. And how did all these recipes make it into your body?" I queried.

"We use a huge, doctor's syringe to inject the information into the body," said Mr. Forty-Four Miles proudly. "And we do not ask, 'Hey what kind of data would you like to carry?' Ha-ha-ha-ha. That would be a waste of time. Don't you think, Sammy Boss?"

A full-figured, oval-faced, furry-haired female sitting next to me, barged in: "Hi, my name is One Hundred Miles per Hour. I store information about cars. I'm only about cars, and all the data is inside me."

THE INFORMATION INSIDE

"Is that so? So, if you carry information about all the cars in the world, you must know a lot about cars. Why don't you tell me what was the first affordable car ever built," I asked.

"The first reasonably priced car? Give me a second; I'm working on it. The data must be somewhere. Maybe in my nose, maybe in my eye... Let's see," said One Hundred Miles per Hour, rolling her eyes back as if peering inside her body. "Was it in 1908?"

"I'm not the car expert, Ms. One Hundred Miles per Hour," I chuckled.

Everyone around the table gave a mild grin.

"Well, here's what I found: The first affordable car was the Ford Model T." The information dispensed out of her mouth was like that which emerges from a speedy printer. "I'm sure it was the Model T, assembled in 1908. If your budget permitted, you would have paid $825. Not a bad price for a car. Don't you think so, Sammy Boss?"

"Remarkable, Ms. One Hundred Miles per Hour. Indeed extraordinary, I must say," giving her a look of admiration.

Silence.

"So, would anyone maybe know where I can find my daddy?" I asked. "I was told that I could find him only here," I said dolefully, on the brink of tears.

Stillness descended on the banquet hall. Eyes full of compassion stared at me from every corner. They, too, were in tune with the sadness of my voice. They, too, commiserated with my sorrow. They, too, understood the hardships I had endured in the City of @.

CHAPTER TWENTY-NINE

THE KEY

The Database Layer Center in the City of @ was a vibrant place all day and all night long. You could not avoid the commotion inside. People were rushing from one place to another, whizzing relentlessly through the countless and convoluted corridors. They were determined to stick to their busy schedules despite the challenging tasks they were assigned.

Some of the building's most intriguing features were the numerous rooms you would encounter when wandering inside. Rooms and more rooms in all sorts of shapes and styles were spread out across the facility. What purpose did they serve? And who in the world was able to navigate such a difficult maze?

But Mr. Three Inch and his dedicated employees knew every nook and cranny. They were familiar with the myriad corridors. They knew the rooms by their dedicated names.

As you scoured the place, you would notice signs on every door, bend, and junction. "The Room with No Special Purpose," "Death Row Corridor," "Taxpayers' Money Room," "Efficient Government Hall," "The Road with No Return," and "End-of-Life Junction" were only a few of the ones I encountered.

The people who worked there knew how to run the place. They carried out their responsibilities with utmost devotion. They were committed to the Database Layer Center's success. Providing information for applications and people was not an easy activity. Ensuring that the data they stored is accurate was laborious, too.

With all the difficulties involved, the Database Layer Center team was proud of its accomplishments. When asked to help find

Rhubarb Pie — not necessarily a task with guaranteed success — they were even prouder. Delighted they were to dedicate their energy and time to such a noble cause.

It was almost midnight; the lights in the Database Layer Center were still burning. The place was lively, filled with the clamor of regular nightly activities. People were dashing in all directions, clutching wads of documents under their arms, and chatting loudly with each other.

Presently, I was following Mr. Three Inch to an undisclosed location. At last, after marching through the never-ending corridors, he brought me to the Control Center. It was a large oval room with top-to-bottom windows stretching all around the walls. Arranged tidily in the center, a round table and a dozen comfortable leather chairs accommodated important gatherings. Mr. Three Inch and his crew, I was told, had met there countless times to make important decisions about the information they managed.

A large cement field could be seen through the windows. It was ironically named Green Meadow. It was used for mysterious activities that I was not acquainted with. Powerful projectors floodlit the vast space. Tall fences and gates enclosed it. Inside, a microphone, dangling from the ceiling, was used to deliver messages to the people on the field.

We were not alone in the Control Center. The couple, Mrs. Twenty-Seven Pounds and Mr. Forty-Four Miles, was there too. Their chubby little sons, Four-by-Four and Five Hundred Bushels, accompanied them.

For some reason, the director, Mr. Three Inch, seemed anxious. He was spinning in his chair, sifting through his notes, and murmuring under his breath things I could not understand.

Mrs. Twenty-Seven Pounds was staring at the Green Meadow with great anticipation, as if something unusual was about to happen there. Four-by-Four and Five Hundred Bushels, too, were glaring at the illuminated field. Their noses were squished against the windows like two monkeys watching sharks swimming in the aquarium.

"Here they come, and they're on time like a Swiss watch," said Mrs. Twenty-Seven Pounds bewilderedly.

By now, people had started massing on the Green Meadow. In a matter of minutes, perhaps responding to a mysterious order, they poured in. Hundreds, perhaps a thousand men, heads bent, lumbered forward to their positions, standing silently, awaiting instruction.

"These men are certainly on the dot," said Mr. Forty-Four Miles, peering through his binoculars as he loosened the rumpled bowtie tightened around his throat.

"Isn't it strange that not even one woman is standing there," said Mrs. Twenty-Seven Pounds, her eyebrows arched upward, almost touching her hairline.

Then Mr. Three Inch rose to his feet, peering at the motionless faces outside. His voice rang out from the powerful speakers on the Green Meadow, "Thank you for showing up so late. It is after midnight. You are here because an important matter has surfaced. Here, in the Control Center, my guest is looking desperately for her father. Maybe you are the one she is looking for. Or perhaps you can help. Are you up to the task?"

"Yes, Director, we are," the men on the field yielded assent.

Mr. Three Inch cupped his hand over the microphone, blocking his voice from the crowd outside. Then he peered into my eyes and questioned, "What kind of man was your daddy?"

"I hope he's still alive. Please let's not say that he 'was,' Mr. Three Inch."

"I'm terribly sorry, Sammy. I didn't mean it. Let me ask it again: What kind of man is your father?"

My heart galloped as I stared at the crowd outside. I was wondering if Rhubarb Pie was among the men elbowing each other on the Green Meadow. "Daddy, sweet Rhubarb Pie, is a humble and kind man," I claimed, still looking intensely through the window. "He's a thoughtful person, a family man. There is not even one selfish bone in his body. He always put us first. He's the best father in the world, I can assure you, Mr. Three Inch."

"Not true, not true, not true! My daddy is the best father in the world. Only he is the best," growled Four-by-Four, stomping his lumpy little feet on the floor, his pudgy cheeks blushing with rage.

"I'm so sorry, sweet boy," I regretted. "Your father, too, is the best one in the world." Four-by-Four drew away as I stretched my arm out to pat him on his head.

From the other side of the Control Center, Mr. Three Inch prepared to deliver his first instruction to the men on the Green Meadow. He took a few seconds to gather his thoughts. Then he removed his hand from the microphone and said sensibly, "The fathers who do not consider themselves the best in the world should retire to their rooms now."

As some of the men started vanishing behind the rear gates, Mr. Three Inch followed their departure with an air of admiration on his face. He thanked them deeply for their cooperation and courage. After all, who in the world would admit openly that he is less than a perfect dad?

"Is this how we're going to find my daddy?" I asked restlessly. "Why don't you simply call his name: Kevin Edison?"

"I'm sorry. There are no other ways to identify people here," said Mr. Three Inch. "They don't respond to their original names anymore. The same goes for Mrs. Twenty-Seven Pounds, Mr. Forty-Four Miles, me, and others. We all have lost our real names. Remember: here we serve as banks of information, nothing more."

"Banks of information? But I see real people here — and on the Green Meadow, too. Aren't you humans anymore?"

"Yes, we are humans. But we also carry information," explained Mr. Forty-Four Miles.

"So how else can we find my daddy in this huge crowd if he would not recognize his own name?"

"We can find your father in different ways. He might step forward if he still remembers things that you have done together. Mentioning things he likes or dislikes might attract his attention. Or we might be able to find him by his attributes," suggested Mr. Forty-Four Miles.

"Now, let's move on, Sammy," interrupted Mr. Three Inch, sealing off the microphone with his palm again. "Does your daddy love you?

"Yes, he loves me," I said. "I'm sure of it."

"How do you know he loves you?"

"You feel love when it touches you, Mr. Three Inch."

"Yes, but what makes you think he loves you?"

"Before he disappeared, we had had great times together. He gave me his undivided attention. I sat in his lap every evening when he came back from work. He never said he was tired. Never. He hugged me; he kissed me on the crest of my head. His fingers went through my hair; I could feel his fatherly affection. Love was just there, oozing out from his warm palm, from his body. Then he used to say, 'I love you and always will. You're a big part of my heart,'" my voice softened, tears in my eyes.

"But that doesn't prove anything," said Mr. Three Inch. "What else did he do for you?"

"He baked me rhubarb pies. I still remember the taste. It was sweet — but a bit salty, too," I said.

"A salty pie? How come?"

"His tears, his tears, his tears, Mr. Three Inch," I sobbed silently. "The tears from his weeping eyes dripped into the dough. Then he used to say at those moments, 'Sammy, sweetie, I'm crying because I love you so much.' Then more tears poured down his chin, mixing with the dough."

"How did the pie taste?"

"Tasted of love, Mr. Three Inch."

"Is love salty?"

"A sweet and salty pie is the best thing in the world, Mr. Three Inch. Although they are opposing flavors, together they make a great pie. Especially when the pie is baked by someone you love."

Mrs. Twenty-Seven Pounds shed tears, tightly cuddling her children, who were still gaping at the men on the field.

Then Mr. Three Inch again spoke into the microphone. His words cut through my skin like a dagger. They brought painful memories: "The people who believe that adding salt to a pie is a sign of love should stay on the Green Meadow. Others, please leave, at once."

I knew that if Rhubarb Pie were in the crowd, he would have immediately gotten the message that Mr. Three Inch had tried to convey. I was certain of it. Only my daddy would have understood what "salt in a pie" meant. It was like a secret code between us, and no one else could have cracked it. And if indeed he were standing there, wondering if I was looking for him, I'm sure he'd have stepped forward.

I was sure of it.

But no one did.

Although, on the order of Mr. Three Inch half of the men abandoned the field, many were still standing, awaiting the next step. I imagined that they, too, were looking for their loved ones, longing to connect to those they had lost.

"Did he ever tell you how much he loved you?" continued Mr. Three Inch.

"Can love be measured?" I asked.

"Certainly," he insisted. "My father used to tell me, 'I love you a million,' or, 'I love you a ton.'"

"Oh, that kind of thing? Yes, yes, we had many chats about how much he loved me."

"And how did he express it to you?"

I sighed deeply, my eyes weary, my lips dry. The memories were painful, agonizing. I wept; tears were rolling down my chin. "It was the morning before he vanished when I asked him how much he loved me. He was calm. He gave me a wide grin, cuddled me tight, and said, 'When I come back from work tonight, I'll tell you how much I love you.' But he never came back. He disappeared right after his building collapsed."

"I'm sorry, Sammy. I feel your pain. What else did your daddy say?"

"Before he left, he asked me to shut my eyes tight, stretch my arms forward, and open my palms wide. That's what he said, and I obeyed."

"What happened then?"

"I heard him going to the refrigerator. Then he returned to the sofa, where I was sitting still with my arms out in front of me. He dropped an ice cube into each of my hands and said, 'Now sweetie, clasp your palms tight. Do not open them until I tell you.'"

"Did it hurt?"

"Yes, a lot. The excruciating pain was unbearable. You could see my fingers turning blue. I panted. Then I yelled, 'DADDY, RHUBARB PIE, IT HURTS. THE PAIN IS KILLING ME. MY FINGERS ARE GOING NUMB. I HATE THIS TORTURE.'"

"How long did you clench the ice in your fists?"

"Two or three minutes before I dropped them to the floor."

"And then?"

"After that, he kissed me gently on my nose and whispered, 'I'd like you to think about this until I come back from work. Do you know what type of pain you just endured?' he asked. 'No,' I said. Then he fixed his tie, picked up his briefcase, swung open the door, and gave me a sweet smile. I will remember that warm grin forever. Before his departure, he peered into my eyes and said, 'You just felt what love is not.'"

Silence.

"I have not seen him since then. Only the memories linger. I miss him so much," I cried. "He left me with a cold heart, cold soul. He vanished without telling me how much he loved me. The only thing I remember is the throbbing pain that never went away."

Minutes lapsed. I caught sight of Mrs. Twenty-Seven Pounds, dabbing her eyes with the sleeve of her shirt. Her husband, Mr. Forty-Four Miles, too, seemed on verge of tears.

Then Mr. Three Inch's voice burst again into the microphone, "Those who think ice is not the opposite of love should go back to their rooms right now."

If he were among the throng on the Green Meadow, Rhubarb Pie would definitely remember his last words to me, I reckoned. He would recall what he'd said to me that morning before he went to work. Wouldn't he? He would certainly know I had been searching for him desperately since he vanished on that horrible day.

As I strained my neck high and scanned the people again, I said, "We are down to fifty or so men. Not many remain on the field. It seems that Rhubarb Pie is not there. Not even one looks like Daddy."

"Patience, patience," implored Mr. Three Inch. "If he's not there, we might be able to find him in a different place. Maybe he's in our data storage. Maybe in the library. Maybe in the basement. Maybe somewhere else."

I nodded my head and stayed silent.

Then, with the microphone pointing toward his mouth, Mr. Three Inch said to the men, "I want to thank all of you out there for being such good sports. You also ought to know how special the little girl is who's been missing her father for so long — really special. Perhaps you would recognize her voice if she said something to you. Maybe one of you is her daddy. Maybe..."

I wrenched the microphone out of Mr. Three Inch's fist with a burst of excitement. My voice echoed forcefully from the speakers on the field: "Daddy, Daddy, if you're there, please, please, step forward."

No one did.

"Daddy," I pleaded. "If you remember my voice, please come out."

No one did.

I sobbed bitterly.

Silence.

"Daddy, do you remember what you hid under my pillow every night? Do you?"

The stillness persisted a few seconds.

Suddenly, a frail, crouched, sallow-faced, gray-haired man stepped out of the crowd and bellowed, "THE KEY, it was the KEY."

"The key to what?" my eyes brimmed with tears, my voice nasal.

His croaky voice thundered even louder, "THE KEY TO THE CHEST."

"And where was the chest hidden?"

"IN THE BASEMENT, IN THE BASEMENT."

"And what did we hide for each other in the chest?"

"NOTES... NOTES FOR EACH OTHER..."

"And if you are my real daddy, you should remember what kind of notes they were."

"THERE WERE LOVE NOTES, NOTES OF LOVE —"

"And if you are indeed Rhubarb Pie, you ought to recall what else you saved for me in the chest every evening?"

Deep silence.

The mounting seconds of silence felt like ages. I grew skeptical as time went by. *Perhaps the man who is responding to my questions is not my father. He does not even bear any resemblance to Daddy, nor is the voice his...*

Suddenly, he said softly, "I used to hide in the chest a slice of rhubarb pie. A slice of love intended to sweeten your day after you got up in the morning."

I gulped; I could barely choke back my tears. "It's him! It's him!

"It's my sweet Rhubarb Pie. Let me out onto the field," I begged Mr. Three Inch.

CHAPTER THIRTY

FOREVER

As the men deserted the Green Meadow field, returning to their rooms, Rhubarb Pie remained standing there alone, unsteadily but serenely. The horrible events of the morning he disappeared had taken a toll on him. The stressful and horrific happenings had whittled him into a feeble appearance. His lack of resemblance to the father I had known was the reason for my agonizing confusion.

True, he did not look like my daddy. But he was the one who could tell the things we had done together and who had the memories that only Rhubarb Pie would have remembered.

He certainly recalled that every night he had hidden the key to the chest under my pillow. And that the chest had been in the basement. And that in that very chest we had been leaving love notes for each other. And that right in there he had saved for me a slice of rhubarb pie, so every morning I would indulge in the taste of fatherly love.

These things he did remember.

The heart-stirring night at the Control Center in the Database Layer Center overwhelmed my emotions. In my heart of hearts, I knew he was Rhubarb Pie, my lost father. Any doubts I had did not deter me from running straight into his open arms. He, who had vanished, now cradled me tighter than ever. He kissed me on my nose just as he had done before he disappeared. Protected again, I felt as safe as in the good old days.

The tides of love had returned more forcefully than ever.

"You're invisible, sweetie. I could not see you running toward me, but I knew it was you," Rhubarb Pie said softly. His breath on my cheek felt like a warm breeze on a summer's day.

"How did you know, Daddy?" my tears wetting his shoulder.

"I heard your heart-wrenching cry from the end of the field. I knew that this is you, only you, sweetie."

Mr. Three Inch and Mrs. Twenty-Seven Pounds and Mr. Forty-Four Miles and Four-by-Four and Five Hundred Bushels were there too, surrounding us, wide-eyed.

Except for Mr. Three Inch, who restrained his happiness and pleasure, the rest of them showed an outpouring of exhilaration. Mrs. Twenty-Seven Pounds mopped her cheeks with two handkerchiefs, red and blue. Mr. Forty-Four Miles burst into elephant-size tears that could fill an empty pond. Their boys, charged with the intensity of those moments, demanded persistently, "I want ice cream, I want ice cream, I want ice cream."

"Enough with all these hugs and kisses," said Mr. Three Inch jokingly. "We have dedicated a special room for these types of moving moments. Right behind this field, the Meeting Place is open for your convenience."

As we set off to the Meeting Place, I was gripping Rhubarb Pie's arm tightly and glancing at him frequently from the corner of my eye. I was worried that he would vanish again. This time I vowed not to lose sight of him. He was mine — only mine, mine forever.

Mr. Three Inch was marching in front of us as though he were shepherding a flock of sheep. Not too far behind him, Mr. Forty-Four Miles and his family kept abreast of Rhubarb Pie and me.

Mrs. Twenty-Seven Pounds was still weeping, touched by the unfolding father-daughter reunion. Her sons never stopped demanding vanilla and chocolate ice cream.

CHAPTER THIRTY

The Meeting Place was snug and dim. A few chairs surrounded a shabby coffee table. Landscapes by unknown painters adorned the walls. A blemished carpet lay on the floor. A white vase with a purple tulip stood erect in the corner of the room, aiming upward toward the skylight in the ceiling.

Seated in a circle, immersed in an intense silence, we hesitated to start a conversation. Rhubarb Pie, composed, at times raised his gaze to the ceiling, perhaps in discomfort. Settled in a chair next to him, I coiled my arm around his, nestled my head on his shoulder, often peering at his colorless face. I was waiting for the right moment, the proper time to unleash a horde of questions I had for him.

Mr. Three Inch broke the ice: "I'm glad you finally found each other. Unfortunately, Sammy, you are invisible. The only visible things are your lovely eyes."

"I don't mind," said Rhubarb Pie. "At least I can hear her beautiful voice," as his arm curled around my shoulders. "She's mine, even if she is invisible."

Tears of happiness poured down my chin. *It is definitely him*, I murmured to myself. *I knew he would accept me the way that I am.*

Sudden heavy thumps on the door disrupted the gathering. Knock, knock, knock, the pounding resonated across the Meeting Place.

"Yes, yes, yes," said Three Inch. "Please step in —"

A gaunt, white-faced, gray-bearded man hobbled in, casting a weak smile. A pink suit with a white carnation pinned to the jacket hung sloppily over his delicate body. Clumps of hair sprouted from his nose and ears. His tousled hairdo sparked laughter across the room. The smoke rings that came out of his tobacco pipe engulfed us with a pleasant aroma. Along with him came his cat, with a wide grin on his haughty face, his tail pointed upward like a radio station tower.

My lips suddenly parted. "Uncle Walter," I panted as I leaped to my feet and threw my arms around him. "What are you doing here?"

"I was on my way to the lab with Witty, my cat," he said, giving Rhubarb Pie a tight squeeze and kissing him on his cheeks. "How are you feeling, Brother?"

"No complaints. No complaints. And you, Walter?"

"Well," he sighed, sliding slowly into a chair. "My time is running out, the doctor says. Two or three weeks remain. I'm trying to complete my new project before I'm gone."

"*Two or three weeks?*" we repeated in disbelief, tongues clucking. Sadness descended on the Meeting Place.

"Correct. How long can a person live with such a shattering illness? We all die in the end. Now the end is near. When your time is up, your time is up. There's nothing I can do. Tick, tick, tick, tick, tick…"

"No, Uncle, please don't say that," I pleaded.

A falling tulip leaf zigzagged sluggishly to the floor like fall foliage in the woods.

"Is this man really dying?" wondered the fat-cheeked Four-by-Four.

"Shush, shush," uttered Mrs. Twenty-Seven Pounds, perturbed. "It's none of your business, honey. This is adults' talk."

"Never mind, never mind, never mind," said Uncle Walter, straining his huddled back. "I should not be the center of attention. Kevin deserves all the affection and love now."

All heads bobbed, eyes tilted toward Rhubarb Pie, whose shy posture revealed uneasiness.

"I'm so excited to see you back, Bro," Uncle Walter went on, grasping Rhubarb Pie's hand. "Since your disappearance, Sammy and I have been scrambling desperately to locate you. We worked relentlessly around the clock. Days and nights, days and nights..."

"I am deeply indebted to you. I felt the vibes of your love from a far distance. I knew you would not give up until you saved me. I knew it all along," said Rhubarb Pie, kissing my cheek, his eyes filled with tears.

"Daddy, your disappearance broke my heart. My soul withered. My life stopped," I sobbed. "The nightmare is over now. The long journey in the City of @ is ending. I am here to take you home, back to Mommy and Michael," I pledged, with a whiff of joy and zeal.

Rhubarb Pie nodded, giving a skeptical grin, seemingly doubting my upbeat vow.

"Daddy, tell me what happened that morning after you promised to come back. After you gave me a warm smile. After you told me that ice is the opposite of love," I pressed.

Rhubarb Pie seemed muddled. Sweat covered his forehead, and his eyes flickered. Perhaps the haunting memories of that morning were intolerable. He was mopping the sweat off his forehead with the red handkerchief handed to him by Mrs. Twenty-Seven Pounds.

He cleared his hoarse throat, crouched forward, and said, "It feels like it happened today. I think it was Tuesday morning. Yes, Tuesday. Certainly it was Tuesday."

Suddenly, all eyes followed Witty when he leaped onto Walter's lap and started purring.

"My boss, Mr. Larry Quack, had invited me to attend a press interview with Lisa Crown. She was one of the most prominent reporters in New York," Rhubarb Pie went on. "I arrived at the office on that Tuesday morning earlier than usual. Before I went over to Larry's office, I prepared for the interview. Then, during the few minutes left, I was sitting in front of my computer, sipping coffee. I was watching you, Mom, and Michael on the wide screen. All of you smiled, looking happy in the colorful image. I almost heard you saying, *Daddy, we love you, and I hope you have a nice day. Please come home early from work. Remember: it's Michael's birthday today.*"

The tulip in the corner of the room bent down, stooping under the weight of Rhubarb Pie's ominous tale. Even Witty leaped to his feet and meowed wretchedly.

"The interview was going well. Lisa Crown, the reporter, seemed utterly pleased. Suddenly, after more than an hour had gone by, a blast shook the building. Just then, I looked at the mahogany clock on the wall; it was precisely 8:46 a.m. The vast explosion had erupted beneath our feet, on the floor below ours. We were hurled to the floor like weightless toys. Moments later, the odor of fuel wafted from beneath the hardwood floor. Thick smoke engulfed us. We were gasping for air, coughing, choking —"

Rhubarb Pie turned silent, white-faced; his mouth dry. His bloodshot eyes reddened even more.

"Then? What happened next, Daddy?" I pressed breathlessly, tightening my grip around his arm.

"Give him some water," requested Uncle Walter. "You're tired, Kevin. Maybe you should hold off, tell us later —"

"It's fine, Walter. I'm a bit tired, that's all…"

"I think you need to take a break, Mr. Edison," said Mrs. Twenty-Seven Pounds, uptight, biting her nails.

Rhubarb Pie opened the plastic water bottle, sipping from it slowly. "I'm really fine," he said. "'What happened next,' you ask? It was chaos. We were squirming inside the office as the flames intensified. The lack of air and the crackling noise of the burning furniture were unbearable. Suddenly, Julia Linden, Larry's assistant, poked her head through the crack of the door, ordering us to take the closest fire escape."

"So did you escape?" asked Uncle Walter, forehead furrowed.

"No, no, no. Fleeing was the last thing on my mind. I was not thinking about my own safety. I didn't care about myself. I was determined to save my employees, my peers, my managers."

"Where was everyone else? How did you plan to save them?" asked Mr. Three Inch.

"I got out of Larry's office, carrying Lisa Crown in my arms. She was motionless. I laid her down on the floor and sprinted across the hallway, searching desperately for the fire extinguisher. When I arrived at the fire station in the hallway, I saw that the extinguisher was gone. Obviously, someone else had taken it. Then, nearby, I heard loud moans under the wreckage of Julia's office. A few people were trapped under the scorching rubble. I mustered the last of my energy to haul them out of the ruins. They were crying. They were in immense pain. They were shaken. Just then, when I turned my back, I saw Eric Schmidt coming out from the fire escape. 'It's burning, the emergency stairs are burning like hell. WE'RE TRAPPED! WE'RE TRAPPED!' he shouted frantically."

"Were you really trapped in the burning building?" asked Uncle Walter.

"The prospect of getting out of there was turning gloomier by the minute. Eric Schmidt pointed toward the windows. 'Let's call for help from there,' he said. Then he broke the glass and straddled the windowsill, begging for help, waving a white tablecloth. I peered through the window, too. I saw people on the streets, tiny like ants, running frantically northward, away from the burning tower."

"And the firefighters?" asked Mr. Three Inch. "Did they get to your floor?"

"Heroes! Indeed heroes. They rescued people from the stories beneath. Indeed heroes. But our office was high, high in the sky, high in the sky. Too far up to reach. Nothing could be done, nothing."

Silence. His vivid description of those shattering moments filled my heart with sorrow. My tears felt like fire on my cheeks.

"The fear and destruction did not leave much hope," continued Rhubarb Pie. "People phoned their loved ones. They called their wives, children, other relatives. I was giving up on rescue. You could only pray, ask for a miracle, for forgiveness, for mercy at such a helpless time."

"So, what else did you do, Daddy?" I asked, heavyhearted.

"I ran to my office, slammed the door behind me, and sat at my table. I knew time was running out. The horrifying popping sound of the burning wooden floors and walls and the blazing furniture meant a dead end. I stared again at my computer screen, perhaps a minute or two. I imagined that Mom, Michael, and you were talking to me. I leaned forward, stretched my neck, and kissed your images on the screen. Then I apologized for being such a lousy father and husband, for abandoning you so early in your lives. But you were mute, like still figures with frozen smiles in a framed picture. The fumes and the fire advanced to my desk. There was no place to escape. I felt dizzy. I picked up the phone and called Mom."

"What did you say to her, Daddy?"

"She didn't pick up. I called repeatedly. The fire caught my shoes, my suit, my shirt, my tie. I left her a message —"

"What was the message, Daddy?"

"My last words to her were in a hurry: 'Honey, I'm not sure if I'll ever see you again. Our building is in flames and there's no escape. I wanted you to know how much I love you. How much

I love Sammy and Michael. I hope to get out of here, but it seems impossible. Take care of —' the line dropped, then silence."

As Rhubarb Pie was unfolding the atrocity of that Tuesday morning, I sobbed as never before. His dramatic descriptions of what had occurred in the office had raised the hair on the back of my neck. They were not only terrifying and eerie; they were also enraging. I was outraged. How on earth could innocent people be subject to such an attack? Is our country defenseless?

Rhubarb Pie went on, "Suddenly, it was Julia Linden who fiercely pushed open the door of my office. 'Kevin,' she howled frenziedly. 'Kevin, Kevin, Kevin, can you hear me? You must get out of here now. NOW. NOW. Lead us to the other fire escape. We're desperate.'"

It was so still in the room, you could hear the tulip leaves falling to the floor, one after the other. Even Witty seemed distressed, meowing incessantly.

"Julia Linden's heartbreaking entreaty sprang me into action. I leaped out of my office, sidling between the fiery debris in the hallway and searching for anyone alive. There, before the hallway curved to the other section of the office, I saw Sharon White standing on a windowsill. Behind her were Jamey, Lora, Mica, Ariel, and Dan."

Silence.

I cupped my palms over my ears. I could not take anything in anymore.

Shivering, face crimson, Uncle Walter said with a trembling voice, "Brother, believe me, we tried to help. We tried to help, Bro. We tried to help, Kevin."

"Yes, Daddy. Indeed, this is what we did," I said.

"How could you possibly help, sweetie? There was no escape. The building was on fire."

"She did, Brother. She did. Believe me," insisted Uncle Walter.

"Then how? How? Tell me how?"

"Daddy, I warped the time backward to avert the events of that morning."

"Yes, Kevin. Sammy bent the time again and again. September reverted to July. But July became August once more, and September beckoned all over again."

"The horrible tragedy could not be averted, Daddy. I tried so many times. Over and over, and that morning kept coming back. The building collapsed again and again, and the people vanished."

"Kevin, my brother. Sammy could not change the course of history. It was impossible, Bro. Impossible —"

Rhubarb Pie looked at us admiringly and said, "Indeed, history is carved in stone."

"So, who were the people who flew the airplanes into the building?"

"Bad, very bad people, Sammy."

"Why did they do it?"

"I don't know, Sammy, sweetie."

"Will we ever know why?"

"I'm not sure, Sammy. Not sure."

"Daddy, I'm not sure if I love this country anymore," I sobbed.

"What are you saying? This is a horrible thing to say, Sammy."

"No one protected you, Daddy. They took you away from me."

"We all have doubts sometimes. But I'm sure you do love your country — dearly. You do, Sammy. Don't you? We all do… Don't we? This is the only country we have."

"Maybe I do, Daddy. Some people say our country is in decline, though. Is it? That it is not as strong as it used to be. But isn't it? That they attacked us because they were not scared of us. Did they?"

"Our country is powerful, Sammy. The most powerful in the world."

"But if we're so strong, why couldn't we avert the tragedy? Why did so many people perish?"

"Help doesn't always come in time, Sammy. Help will come, though. People will sacrifice everything so that next time such loss does not happen again."

"Why do more people have to perish? I'm not sure if I love this country, Daddy. This isn't right, not right, not right."

"Listen to me, sweetie," he said sternly, holding my hand tight. "Love your country for its strengths, and even more so for its vulnerabilities."

"Yes, Daddy. Yes."

Rhubarb Pie was a true patriot. He loved his country, the culture, the people. Mom and Michael treasured the homeland, too. Independence Days were full of happiness and celebration. We hung flags on our house, cars, and bikes. We invited family, friends, and neighbors. In the backyard we read aloud the Declaration of Independence. Aromas of sizzling hamburgers and steaks and chicken oozed out from the flaring barbecue, suffusing the neighborhood with the air of freedom and love of country.

Indeed, I grew up in a family whose beliefs in its country and the country's founding values were strong. That Tuesday morning when Rhubarb Pie vanished, however, eroded my trust. I became cynical.

Who would blame me for losing confidence in my beloved homeland? Could the loss of a father and such gloom and despair drive rational thought? Could the pain I endured have been avoided? Could the institutions that vowed to protect the people have done more? Could they?

More questions rushed through my head. Would we ever know the reasons for the unspeakable crime? Would we ever understand the motives of those who masterminded the greatest attack on our cherished soil? Would we?

Now Rhubarb Pie was mine again, near me, hugging me; I clutched his hand tighter than ever. I was determined to bring him home as soon as possible. But his story was still incomplete. I was eager to know how he escaped the devastating fire, before the tower collapsed.

"Daddy, what happened then?"

"There was no escape. Climbing up to the floor above was impossible. And no one considered descending to the story below through the blaze of fire, either."

"So, what did you do, Daddy? What did you do?"

Silence.

"Please tell me."

Resounding silence.

In a matter of seconds, the Meeting Place in the Database Layer Center dissipated like a cloud in a blue sky. Mr. Three Inch and Mrs. Twenty-Seven Pounds and Mr. Forty-Four Miles and Four-by-Four and Five Hundred Bushels faded away.

Bleached like a colorful flag in blistering sunshine, Rhubarb Pie vanished, too.

I found myself staring at Uncle Walter across a shabby table. He was clutching my hands, giving a flat grin. "Welcome back, Sammy," he said parentally. "Welcome back to the Techno-Geek Café."

I stayed silent, rubbing my eyes in disbelief.

"There is nothing more disheartening in life than to be immersed in a virtual world for so long," he said. "A place that offers nothing, nothing at all —"

Startled, I cupped my hand over my open mouth, eyes wide. "Did you say virtual world, Uncle? Was I in a world that does not exist? Was the City of @ unreal?"

"Correct. You just woke up to reality," he murmured, his puny hands shivering. "It was a figment of your imagination, sweetie."

"And where is my Rhubarb Pie?" I bewailed.

"The Rhubarb Pie you found in the City of @ is still there, Sammy. He's still in the virtual city you just came back from."

"Couldn't I have brought him back home with me?"

Uncle Walter rose to his feet slowly and said, "Time to go home, Sammy."

"Is Daddy gone for good?"

"Never forget that the Rhubarb Pie you were searching for has always been inside you, sweetie. He has been a part of you all along and will remain in your heart, in your mind —

"Forever…"

Discussion Questions

1.   In Chapters 2 – 3, why does Sammy ask Uncle Walter to teach her how to bend time backward and forward?

2.   In Chapters 2 – 3, what does the melting ice that makes up the Techno Geek Café represent?

3.   In Chapter 4, why do you think Larry Quack experiments with growing human organs in his lab? Natural curiosity? Contribution to science? Greed? Discuss.

4.   In Chapter 7, during the interview scene in the City of @ at the Cordial Interview Office, what do you think is coming out of the meat grinder? Why do you think Grady Scotpress is trying to extract Sammy's thoughts and secrets?

5.   What does the virtual City of @ symbolize in Sammy's journey to find Rhubarb Pie?

6.   Why do the main characters in the book, including Sammy, Mr. Greenbold, Larry Quack, and Cleopatra, become gradually invisible as time passes?

7.   What does Wall Street, the financial district in Manhattan, represent in the book?

8.   In Chapter 10, how do President Moses J. Maycott's ideals threaten democracy?

9.   What do you think about the idea of controlling people's minds using virtual technology rather than imprisoning them

with walls?

10. In Chapter 10, a cloud of dust looms over Larry Quack's office, foreshadowing what?

11. In Chapter 11, what historical event does the chaos and destruction allude to?

12. In Chapter 13, at the Chef Cooking School in the City of @, what do the sandwich layers symbolize?

13. In Chapter 20, what was symbolic about Sammy hovering above the buildings of Manhattan after she had taken the Body-Mail pills in the Message Hub Building?

14. Why was Larry Quack against Sammy's pursuit to find her missing father?

15. In Chapter 22, why did Roy urge Sammy to adopt a new brain when they took a stroll in the Garden of Eden at the Logic Layer Fort?

16. Why does Larry Quack despise the virtual City of @, and what qualms does he have against Mr. Greenbold's establishment?

17. In Chapter 26 – 27, what provoked the fight of the century that took place in the Special Field in the City of @? Was it a growing rivalry between Larry Quack and Mr. Greenbold? Or perhaps a Booclash between polarized ideologies? Discuss.

18. Did Sammy ever find her father, Rhubarb Pie? What happened to him?

19.   Prior to the end of the book, did you believe that the City of @ was a real place or just a figment of Sammy's imagination?

20.   How would you define the difference between what's real and what's virtual?

21.   Discuss the pros and cons of using a virtual world as an escape.

22.   If you had the power to manipulate time and fate, would do it? What would you change? How might things be different?

23.   Chapter 6, 7, and 8. Sammy learns what it means to lose her freedom when she is trapped in the City of @. What does freedom mean to you, and why is it important?

24.   Sammy runs into many obstacles throughout the book that could cause her to give up, but instead of losing hope, she looks for opportunities within her predicaments. With faith and persistence, do you believe all obstacles can be overcome?

About the Author

Michael "Mickey" Bell is an author, producer, artist, and software architect. Well known for his work in computer science, he has written several best-selling technical books under the publisher John Wiley & Sons. As an art school graduate, Mickey's contemporary paintings, photography, and films have been featured in national art galleries and museums. Following graduate school in New York City, he established a software development and architecture company, Byte & Run, Inc., and found great success on Wall Street while representing Fortune 500 financial institutions, such as J.P. Morgan, Chase, AIG, Citigroup, Merrill Lynch, and American Express. Combined with his computer science career is Mickey's dedication to art and film. Interested in telling meaningful stories focused on social impact, he presents this unique novel, an extended metaphor, depicting the trauma he experienced as a witness to the events of 9/11. His screenplay, Decoding Norman, is in pre-production, and when he's not writing, he enjoys traveling, practicing martial arts, and biking. Mickey resides in Austin, Texas with his significant other and their two cats and two dogs.

Listen to Sammy's Epic Journey through the City of @

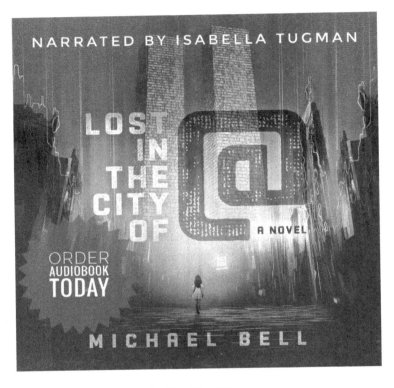

LostInTheCityOfAt.com

.